HIDDEN
Monster

AMANDA STRONG

CLEAN TEEN PUBLSHING

HIDDEN *Monster*

clean teen
PUBLISHING

ISBN: 978-1-940534-93-0
Cover Design by: Marya Heiman
Typography by: Courtney Nuckels
Editing by: Cynthia Shepp

For more information about our content disclosure, please utilize the QR code above with your smart phone or visit us at

www.cleanteenpublishing.com.

FOR MY SON, ELIAS.

Never stop believing in yourself!

CHAPTER
One

step, step, breathe, breathe, step, step, breathe, breathe. My shoes kept a steady rhythm with my burning lungs. I veered off my regular path, opting to hear the crunch of the leaves beneath my feet. The image of my mom's disapproving face was ignored as I leapt across a gurgling brook. *Breathe, breathe, crunch, crunch.*

If I wasn't mountain biking, I was running. I craved speed and freedom. I had to escape the oppressive perfection of living in the Campbell home. Thinking of my two older sisters, one model and the other a star volleyball player, my legs lunged, lengthening their stride. Not good at team sports and terrified by cameras, I knew my family felt my height was wasted on me.

Even Jeremy gives me a hard time.

A stitch pinched my side. *Breathe, breathe.* I knew I was going too fast, not pacing myself right. Something was urging me on, pushing me to scale the hill before me, and plunge deeper into the woods. I refocused on my rhythm, my inhales and exhales, and my body realigned itself, goose bumps shooting across my arms. *There it is.* I'd hit my second wind and I surged on, not caring where my feet led.

It's freedom! Complete and—

There was a rush of air, a whistling in my ear, and a sting to the back of my arm. Instantly, I tumbled to the ground, sliding into the damp morning dew. Cold dirt filled my nostrils as blackness enveloped me.

I heard my own labored breathing long before I realized I was somewhere in between awake and asleep. Forcing my eyes open, I gasped. My senses took everything in at once—the smell of wood shavings, the scratchy ropes on my wrists and ankles, and the pressure of the mattress beneath my body. I screamed, but the empty room with wooden floors and stacked logs for walls was empty. No one burst through the door in the corner.

Realizing it was useless and only making my throat raw, I fell silent. Panic flooded me. How did I get here? I pressed my thoughts to retrace my steps, but my mind felt sluggish. My last memory was running in the woods just before sunrise. I could still feel the burn from the autumn air hitting my lungs. Now the solitary window painted a yellow rectangle on the floor. The room felt stuffy. *It's probably late afternoon. But is it the same day?*

The minutes rolled slowly into hours, the silence suffocating. What had my therapist said to do when I was scared? *Breathe deeply and don't panic.* It was too late for that; all the years of therapy after my childhood accident were rendered useless. *I'm drowning all over again.* Only this time, it wasn't water filling my lungs but pure fear and terror pressing down on my chest. I gulped in dry air, my eyes burning with tears.

No one's coming to save me. A sob escaped me as the real horror of the situation washed over me. *I'm tied up. Someone knows I'm here.* What would happen when they came back? As the last rays of light were snuffed out by the shadows of the night, that someone came through the wooden door.

<hr/>

"Just tell me—what do you want?" I asked, knowing it was pointless. In the three weeks—or had it been longer?—of my imprisonment, I had yet to get an answer. He never spoke.

I blinked, trying to clear the blurry blob that occasionally floated across my right eye. Never having glasses before, I was annoyed by my hazy vision. I blinked again, my eyes refocusing on the figure pacing the room. What had started as a dull headache was now a hammer drumming at the back of my eye sockets. *I need water.* My stomach grumbled with nauseating hunger.

There was no escaping the noxious, pinstriped mattress, except for the periodic bathroom breaks, which weren't frequent enough.

My jaw quivered, and I clamped my mouth shut. *Don't start chattering now,* I commanded myself, knowing it usually ended with my whole body convulsing. October was merciless on my bare skin; my arms and legs were permanently smattered with goose bumps.

Stupid running shorts. I wished for the thousandth time I'd listened to my mom and worn a *sensible* sweat suit that day. The swish-swish of his warm ski parka and pants seemed to mock me, as he continued his route of six steps forward and then six steps back again.

First time in my life that I love my leg hair.

Too late, I realized it was quiet, the rhythmic swish-swish gone. In one impossible leap, he was next to me. I squeaked out in surprise. This wasn't the first time he'd come close, but usually he ambled over, producing a long needle from his pocket.

Silently, he pressed his face against mine, the black ski mask tickling my forehead and nose. I shied away, terrified by both his touch and the change in his behavior. My bindings made my attempt to move useless, so I squeezed my eyes shut. My chest heaved up and down as my heart galloped against my rib cage. *It's ok. He's got a needle. The pinch's coming still. It'll be over soon,* I consoled myself.

The ski mask lifted off my face. I tried to steady my pulse, inhaling slowly. Not daring to open my eyes, I waited, but there was still no pinch. The stillness stretched on, with only his heavy breathing letting me know he was near. Never talking, the mechanical sounds he produced reminded me of Darth Vader. I long since decided that he was actually a human and the protruding square under his mask was just a voice modulator. *He's still a monster.* His growling sounds sent chills through me.

Maybe he has food. I cracked my eyelids, peeking through feathered lashes. His body leaned over mine, elevated by knuckles planted in the mattress. Terror rippled through me. *Why isn't he drugging me? Why isn't he drugging me?* I welcomed my arm being stuck with a needle. It was my only escape from this nightmare.

With tall boots, gloves, and a long, knit mask, I hadn't known if my abductor was male or female at first. Now with the way he moved, stared at me, and shoved water bottles and bread into my mouth, I knew he, *it,* was a man.

The bed lowered as he sat down next to me, his weight pulling my body toward him. The bedsores on my backside smarted at the slight shift. Even with his face covered, I could feel him ogling me. One hand reached out, stroking my matted hair down, brushing errant strands from my face. I gritted my teeth, resisting the urge to bite his glove. He hadn't actually hit me before, but I didn't want to take my chances. *Maybe I should bite him. Maybe it'll end this misery.*

The breathing halted as the ski mask cocked to one side.

His voice slurred. "What do I want?" I bit my lip to keep from gasping. He'd never responded before. "It's obvious, isn't it? I want you to fall in love with me."

Holy freak! He's more insane than I thought! I swallowed, forcing my dry tongue to moisten my mouth. "I'll *never* love you!"

He chuckled, the sound like a horror movie. "Yes, you will. You see, I've always loved you, Samantha, or should I call you Sammy?"

He knows my name? Dark spots popped in my vision, and my body felt like it was floating several feet above my head. *Crap, I'm going to pass out!*

He touched my arm with his gloved hand.

"Don't!" I hissed, and he instantly recoiled. Dumbstruck, I stared at the ski mask. *Is he really listening to me?* I didn't want to faint or be drugged. Not if this was my one chance to talk to him. Pulse pounding in my ears, the adrenaline cleared my mind, giving me courage. "Please, I need water."

He cocked his head to the side, as if considering, and then produced a small water bottle from his pant pocket. A gloved hand tugged my hairs out as he elevated my head, but this time, he didn't shove the bottle against my lips. I drained it within seconds, not satiated, and wanting more.

I asked again, "What do you want? Why am I here?"

"I already told you. I want you to fall in love with me."

"Then let me go! Untie me," I begged as something wet tickled my lips. I licked the salty tear away.

He didn't say anything, just sat next to me breathing.

"Who are you?" I persisted. Again, silence. "How long are you going to keep me here?"

"That depends on how long it takes."

"For what?"

"For," he paused, "you to love me."

I resisted the hysterical laughter bubbling within me. *He's serious, completely psychotic, but serious.*

"How can I," I hesitated, "fall in love with someone I can't see? Why don't you take your mask off?"

"No!" he barked, jumping to his feet.

Relieved he was further away, I decided to push him. *This might be my only chance.*

"Can I know your name at least?"

"No."

"Ok, well, how do you know me then?"

"I've known you a long time."

I shuddered. "Do I know you *personally?*"

"Yes." The voice modifier made it sound like a growl.

My body began shaking. "What do you want?" I whispered.

"Why do you keep asking the same question over and over? You're smarter than this. That's why you're so unique, Sammy. You're not only beautiful, you're brilliant."

Okay, maybe he doesn't know me that well. I'm anything but brilliant. Stay calm. Keep him talking. "Why are you drugging me? Why can't we just talk then?"

His sigh sounded more like a roar. "You ask too many questions, Samantha. You need to sleep now."

"No!" But he grabbed my arm with one hand, while the other produced the all-too-familiar needle. "No," I begged. "I can sleep without it! I don't need it!"

"Yes, you do. I know what's best for you. Trust me; this is for your own good. And this one is a special blend; I made it myself. You'll sleep wonderful tonight."

I thrashed against the ropes, but it was no use. The tip of the needle burned my skin.

He paused and then glanced down at me, his ski mask moving with his mouth. "Wait, I want to tell you something first." I could no longer feel the point of the needle against my skin. "You *are* going to fall in love with me *Samantha*. It's only a matter of time. You'll be mine one day. One day you'll lie in my arms and kiss my lips." His gloved finger traced my lips.

I turned away and spat, "Never! I'll never love you!"

"That's where you're wrong. We're meant for each other, and no one can ever love you like I do. You were always *my special girl*."

My head snapped back to glare at him. *Special girl?* Only one person said that to me. A sinking sensation flooded my body as I gasped, "*Jeremy? Is that you?*"

The needle inserted, but I no longer cared about the pinch and the burn it caused. All I knew was the scrambled voice that said, "I guess you'll never know now, will you?"

I struggled to respond but the drug worked fast, seeping through my veins like ice-cold water hitting an empty stomach. My body welcomed it, drifting off into the black void it created.

CHAPTER
Two

I actually had a dream, even if it was running in an endless forest, Jeremy right on my heels. Stumbling on the uneven ground, I felt arms wrap around me from behind, crushing the air out of me.

I bolted upright screaming. *Wait. I'm sitting up?*

Still in my one-bedroom prison with daylight coming through the window, I stared at my rope-free arms and legs. Instinctively, I hugged my knees, wincing when my wrists bumped into each other. The ropes had left raw sores behind.

Got to move. I shoved my legs over the side of the bed, but discovered even touching my feet against the ground sent waves of nausea through me. Teeth gritted, I forced myself to stand. *I need to get out of here.* I staggered across the floor, terrified by how weak I was. Was it just not eating or all the drugs? Thinking of those needles, I grabbed the door handle, praying the masked man wasn't on the other side waiting. I exhaled in relief, seeing only trees and long grass.

So, it was a cabin. Once early fall set in, many summer cabins in Durango remained empty all winter. I set out as fast as my legs would allow—a wobbly gait at best. *Which way?* I felt disoriented and lost. Recognizing some of the mountains, I tried to gauge where I was in relation to the highway. Saying a quick prayer, I made up my mind and headed to what I hoped was north. The longer I walked, the stronger my legs became, but the more painfully my head throbbed. After what felt like an hour, I sat down on the ground, smashing my head between my hands. The pain was excruciating; I was afraid my skull might actually split open.

Have to keep moving. I pressed on. Five minutes later, I saw another cabin. I pounded on the door, but it too was vacant. So were the next four I found. Still, it comforted me cabins were appearing more frequently now. *I must be getting close to the main highway.* Wanting to find help, I began running but, within seconds, my body protested, lungs on fire. Gulping in deep breaths, I continued walking briskly.

Wishing I were better at interpreting the sun's position in the sky for time, I decided if it moved a few inches, it surely meant I'd been walking for hours. Exhausted and thirsty, I collapsed to the ground. *I need just a few minutes.* I curled into a ball, draping my arms across my eyes, trying to shield out the light and get some relief from the migraine. It felt like seconds later that I was back in those woods again—sprinting for my life.

I heard Jeremy yelling, "We found her! We found Samantha!"

Why's he saying that? There was a chorus of voices shouting now. My head panged in response. *Why are they so loud?* Dogs were barking. Someone touched my shoulder. I jerked away, trying to sit up. My body felt glued to the ground though. I glanced up to see brown eyes gazing down at me.

Where's the mask? And then my mind caught up to all the details. *I'm lying on the ground. He's wearing an EMT jacket.* I peered around at the people gathering closer. One of the dogs was trying to reach me, its tongue hanging out, as its owner pulled back on the leash.

"The tip was good; we found her! Call her parents," a voice yelled out from somewhere in the group. The man with brown eyes was leaning in. "Samantha, we're here to help you. Are you all right? Are you hurt anywhere? Can you understand me?"

Too many questions. I tried to slur out words. *Oh my gosh, I can't talk! What was in those stupid shots? Am I permanently brain damaged?* I shook my head and then nodded, hoping he understood.

"We're contacting your parents; they'll be here soon. Can I put this blanket around you?"

I realized then that I was shaking uncontrollably and nodded back at him. The man helped me sit up and cloaked me in a thick blanket. I reveled in its warmth.

He held up a water bottle. "Do you think you can drink?"

I nodded, and he gently lifted the bottle to my lips. I drank fast, too fast, and after a moment, I stopped. Turning to the side, I threw it all up. I tried to apologize, but the world was spinning. The man's face kept going in circles before me; I closed my eyes.

"We need to get you into the ambulance." I forced my lids open to see the man with brown eyes had said it. "Can I help you stand up?"

I nodded, and he pulled me up. It seemed effortless.

He pointed toward the gurney approaching. "We need to get you up on that. Do you think you can stand?"

I nodded, though I wasn't sure my legs would hold. Every part of me was shaking. The two EMTs helped me up; the narrow bed felt stiff and cold to my bare legs. Hands were pushing me back. Dizzy, I didn't resist. Then straps made their way across my stomach and sternum.

"No!" I croaked as my hands shot out, ripping the binding out of the EMT's hand.

The man with brown eyes said, "It's okay, just relax."

I struggled to sit up, but I ended up rolling off the side instead. Hands grabbed after me. *Not another bed, no more ropes!* There was a high-pitched screech, as the ground seemed to jump up at me. When my body smacked down, I registered it was my own manic screams I heard. The man with brown eyes was helping me up again.

"It's ok," he soothed. "You're going to be all right. No one's going to hurt you now." I wanted to believe him. "We won't tie you down, okay?"

I nodded and let the two EMTs help me up on to the gurney again.

"We need to start an IV," the brown-eyed man said, "You're pretty dehydrated. Can you hold still?" The other EMT touched my arm as the brown-eyed man said, "Just a little prick—"

Prick? I lost it, clawing the other EMT away. The brown-eyed man tried to calm me, but I panicked at the strong hands pulling me down on to the gurney. Both of my arms were pinned now. I felt the pinch in my arm and sobbed. *He's got me again!*

Brown eyes swam above me. "It's ok, Samantha. You're safe now."

CHAPTER
Three

"Samantha? Samantha, are you in the bathroom?" my mom's voice called from down the hall.

Staring at the long, blonde locks lying at the bottom of the bathroom sink, I set the kitchen scissors down. With a long sigh, I looked up at my reflection. *Better.* I tugged the oversized gray hoodie back on over my tank top, leaving the hood down, and opened the door.

My mom gasped from behind me. "What in the world did you do to your hair?"

Turning around, I stared at the tan carpet separating us. I stated the obvious, "Cut it."

"I can see that, but why on earth would you..." My mom's words trailed when I met her gaze. She forced a smile. "It looks good, Sammy, but can I take you to my hair dresser to even it out a bit?"

I shrugged. *Great, stupid therapist will want psychoanalyze why I don't want to be attractive all over again.* For the past four weeks since being found, my therapist had grilled me on why I'd only wear worn-out sweatpants and ratty T-shirts. *Why's she so dense? It's the only way to be safe.*

Riding in my mom's sedan, I fumbled with a fast food napkin I found in the glove compartment. My mom chatted the entire way to the hair appointment and I never responded, leaving her in a one-sided conversation. I knew she was pretending not to notice.

Wish I could pretend it all away. I sickened as the memory of Jeremy coming to the hospital popped into my head. It had been the day I was discovered in the woods, and I had screamed accusations at him. The police had ripped apart my now ex-boyfriend's life and found nothing; he had alibis for everything. We'd dated over a year.

That's over now. I'm sure he despises me. Being the biggest story on the six o'clock news, I wanted nothing more than to crawl under a rock for the past month. Some of my friends had come to see me, my best friend, Mack, being my most-frequent visitor. I knew he'd understand anything. He'd become my shadow years ago, not long after my near-drowning experience. He'd never question my fear of water, never balked at being left behind on lake trips; he'd always just hung out with me. Even with all our history, he did all the talking when he came to see me. I said little. *Poor guy.* I just wasn't the same.

"Whenever the therapist thinks it's a good idea, we can get you back to school. I'm sure you're dying to start your senior year, right?" my mom asked, interrupting my reverie.

I cringed. *Not really.* But I nodded back at her. If it were up to me, I'd never go back. Halls full of teenagers terrified me. *The monster could be anyone. I suppose the only comfort is that be Mack will be there... and Jen.*

"Here we are," she said, shutting off the car.

Once I was seated in the salon chair, the stylist eyed my hack job. "Mm," she hummed.

My mom grimaced. "You've seen worse, right?"

The stylist nodded immediately. "Oh, yes."

I wanted to roll my eyes at both of them. *As if a hacked haircut is the worst thing in the world.* Instead, I pointed at the hair chart on the station next to them.

"I want that one," I interrupted.

Both women stared at me.

"What?" my mom asked.

"I want to dye my hair *that* color." I purposely stared at the stylist, not my mom, as I pointed at the chestnut-brown sample.

The woman with auburn hair, caked makeup, and French-manicured nails, glanced at my mom for guidance. My mom's hazel eyes appeared puzzled. "You want to dye your hair, Sammy?"

"Yes."

"Honey, no one's going to recognize you with your hair short and brown——" my mom began.

"That's the point."

"Are you sure? I'm sure Brenda can do a really cute hairstyle for you."

Cute? I stiffened.

My mom must have seen it because she rushed on with, "Sure, hon. You can dye your hair."

Brenda tried to work her 'magic,' but when she pulled the towel off my head, revealing short, wet, black hair, I could see the pain in my mom's eyes. *It looks boyish. Perfect.*

The ride back home was quiet. Once my mom parked, I wordlessly made my way to my bedroom. I was too tired to keep up pretenses any longer. When sharp pains shot down my abdomen, I collapsed on my bed, curling into a tight ball. *Lousy stomach, always killing...*

I hadn't realized I'd fallen asleep until there was a tap on my door. "You awake?" my dad asked, his 6'3" frame filling the doorway.

I rubbed my eyes. Sitting up, I gave him a small smile. "I am now."

He entered and sat at the foot of the bed. After a moment, he glanced at me. "Mind if we talk a bit?"

"No." I let my eyes fall to my fingers clasped in my lap.

He sighed. "Samantha, I can't pretend to know what you're going through right now. When your mom and I got the call that they'd found you, well, we've thanked God every day for your safe return." His eyebrows gathered as he glanced over. "But watching you now, I can't help but feel maybe my baby girl's still lost somewhere, fighting to survive."

I swallowed. My dad's eyes welled up as he gazed back at me. I felt a shattering within my heart, and I gasped at the pain. Something wet dripped off my chin. Glancing down, I was surprised to see wet streaks on my arm.

"I'm sorry, Dad."

His arms were around me instantly. "Don't you ever say sorry; I'm the one who's sorry. It kills me I couldn't protect you from this. We just want to help you get through it all." Though I appreciated his words, I didn't think there was anything anyone could do to help me. *What's done is done.* My dad released me and sat back. "Maybe we need to start over. Move somewhere new?"

"No, I'll be fine. I don't want the whole family to uproot for me."

"Your sisters only live here on and off with school, I can put in for a transfer at work."

"Dad, you worked really hard to get promoted. Besides, Mom would never want to leave. She's involved in every kind of committee imaginable."

My dad shook his head. "I don't care about my promotion. And your mom can get involved somewhere else. You're more important than those things."

Never having had a son, I was the closest thing my dad had. While my older sisters coddled baby dolls, I snuck water snakes into the house. My dad and I had a bond that my mom and sisters didn't understand, but even still, the thought of moving panicked me.

"Please Dad, it's okay, really. I don't want to move."

He waited for me to say more, and it killed me I couldn't. This wasn't like me with him. *Guess closing my heart to fear means shutting everyone out, including Dad.*

"What more can we do?" He sounded defeated.

I hated to see him hurt on my account. *I'll be ok, as long as I'm never beautiful again. Why can't they understand that?*

"I don't know. I'm sorry I'm not the same anymore." The words sounded flatter than I intended.

He flinched and then gave me a halfhearted smile. "Time, we

just need more time to heal, that's all." His words seemed to be directed at himself more than me.

I mumbled, "Yeah, I just need time."

He paused, the hesitation obvious, and then asked, "Have you remembered anything new that might help us?" His jaw clenched. "I know you were sedated most of the time, but maybe he said something?"

My face heated at the memory of the nurse checking for DNA on every part of my body. It was a relief to know he'd done nothing to me while I'd been unconscious. There was one thing I hadn't told a soul. I couldn't repeat the monster's promise—that one day I'd fall in love with him. Even thinking the words paralyzed me with fear.

"It's all really hazy now," I answered, while thinking, *If only that were true*. With my therapist pushing me to talk about it in our weekly sessions, it was easier to say I was forgetting it all.

"Okay, well, I'll let you get back to resting then." He stood up, giving my foot a squeeze before leaving.

Lying back on my bed, I counted backwards from one hundred. It was something I'd done in the cabin. It lulled me to sleep, letting me escape my reality.

CHAPTER *Four*

I really like this. I let the silky, sky-blue material glide between my fingers. *Funny, I don't remember it. Wonder if Mom got it. Guess she's sick of my sweat suits.* I swayed to the right and left, the nightgown shimmering with my movement. Not one for dresses, I thought it strange that I didn't mind it hitting my ankles. Glancing down at the low-scooped neckline, I stepped forward, my feet landing in cool, damp grass.

What am I doing outside? A full moon lit up our backyard; the storage shed, the old swing set, and the remains of this year's garden all bathed in a cool, blue light. Instinctively, I wrapped my arms around myself. After the cabin, I thought I'd be permanently chilled to the bone. However, tonight I was comfortable, even warm.

A breeze lifted my hair, sending it flying into my face. Securing the strands with my fingers, I was shocked to discover the blonde locks stretched down to my waist.

It's never been this long. I glanced around again. *This must be just a dream. Well, if it is, I'm going to run.* I took off, my feet gliding through the grass. I slowed only to unlatch the back gate, and then I plunged into the dark woods. I felt no fear. This was a dream after all. I was glad the nightgown moved with me, not hindering my movements as it should. My lungs didn't burn, like they would've running this hard without warming up.

Confident it was definitely a dream, I pushed myself to go faster, my feet barely skimming the ground as I shot through the trees. Then in one leap, I wasn't on the ground at all. *Sweet! I'm flying!*

Something expanded on either side of me as I instinctively flexed and retracted muscles between my shoulder blades I wasn't aware I had. At first, it felt stiff, unyielding, like this was the first time they'd been used, but within a heartbeat, everything warmed up, the contractions smooth and effortless. My lungs felt twice their size as I breathed, the air entering chambers that felt starved for oxygen. I glanced over and gasped.

This is seriously the best dream ever! A pair of long, slender wings buzzed back at me, their furious movement turning them into a blur of silver against the black night. I soared as I trailed my hands along the tops of the trees, the orange, red, and yellow leaves dancing in my wake. When my cheeks and jaw muscles ached, I realized I was smiling ear to ear. I shot forward. *The monster's finally gone!*

The landscape below shrank as I pushed my wings harder. Then, wondering if this dream meant I should leave Durango, I stopped abruptly. Hovering, I gazed down at the scenery below me. Meandering through the farmland, the Animas River shimmered in the blue moonlight. Cows nestled together, trying to keep warm. Every detail felt so real, even the earthy smell of plowed fields in the breeze. Sighing, I decided to turn around and head back. When the night air pressed against me, feeling cold, urgency engulfed me. I shifted to the right, diving down several feet. Within minutes, I recognized the woods.

Oh good, I'm close. The panic to get home was intense. I glanced up to see the black night was paling. Watery yellow was breaking through in the east, rosy plumes blossoming in the sky—dawn was close. Back aching between my shoulder blades, I decided not push my wings any further and landed. My naked feet registered the shock of the frozen ground beneath me as I shuffled forward. With every step, my body grew heavier. *Crap... I'm not going to make it.* I felt myself tumbling down.

CHAPTER
Five

I stretched my legs out and then recoiled into a tight ball on my side again. "Brrr, where are my covers?"

The bright light was making the back of my eyelids pink, but I didn't want to wake up yet. *Just a few more minutes.* My hands reached for Grandma Johnson's quilt, but instead felt cold dampness. Confused, I tried to rouse myself completely, but found my body rebelling. Every muscle felt stiff and sore.

A snuffling sound in my ear caused me to bolt up, fatigue forgotten. A black nose filled my vision and a large, wet tongue ran up and down my face. I fell back as a dog jumped into my lap.

"Misty! Where'd you go, girl?" The voice was definitely male. I scanned the area, seeing only golden-brown grass and a thick forest of trees. The dog, Misty, whined and jumped off my lap, disappearing into the woods.

What's going on? I staggered to my feet, my joints popping. *Feels like I slept on a rock.* Misty burst through the underbrush and tried to jump into my lap again, almost knocking me over. I tried to push her down, not wanting another face bath.

"Oh jeez, I'm sorry! Misty, get over here, girl. What are you doing? Get off her!"

My head jerked up to see a man emerging from the thick woods. Wearing a baseball cap, a blue sweater, black gym shorts, and flip-flops, he seemed harmless enough. He held a leash in his hand—one the dog was obviously not attached to. Misty instantly flew from my arms and shimmied back to her master, her tail between her legs.

AMANDA STRONG

While the man leaned down and re-attached the leash, I tried to compose myself. Smoothing my hair back with my fingers, I was horrified to discover it was caked in dirt.

"Sorry about that. Misty's pretty friendly," the man said, straightening up. He was close enough now to see the face beneath the hat. He was younger than I'd thought. Nothing about his features was out of the ordinary. He had aqua blue eyes, a straight nose, and lips bent into a crooked smile. The over-all effect left me ogling.

When his eyebrows shot up, I gasped. *Please don't tell me I'm still in that nightgown!* Glancing down, I was relieved to see a white T-shirt and gray sweatpants. Knowing I was bra-less, I gratefully zipped up the matching jacket. Shifting my weight, I realized my feet felt numb. *Where the heck are my shoes?*

I caught him studying me. "Uh, no problem," I replied. "Well, I better get going." The guy's gaze darted to my feet and then back up. He arched one brow.

Yeah, I know I look crazy, I wanted to shout. Embarrassed by his wordless stare, I turned and strode away. He didn't hesitate to follow. *The nerve!*

"Hold up," he called after me. "You must be Samantha." That stopped me short. I spun and stared at him. His smile faltered, and he struck out a hand. "Hey, I'm Blake."

I didn't move, and his hand dropped. "My family moved in a few doors down, last week," he offered, like I should have known this. "My mom met your mom—"

I cringed. *Maybe I should pay better attention to Mom.* "Oh sorry, yeah I'm Samantha." He grinned. I hated that it both irritated and attracted me. "It's nice to meet you Blake, but I better get home." I wanted him to get the hint and *leave me alone.*

"I'll walk with you. Like I said, I live real close," he offered.

My stomach sickened but I nodded and picked up my pace, hoping he'd drop back or just go away. He kept up, as did Misty, who trotted happily between us. *Well, at least I'm not far from home. If he tries anything, I can scream and try to outrun him.* Although, peeking over, I realized I didn't feel as afraid as I thought I should.

"So, what were you doing out here? It's sort of cold for a walk without shoes."

Wish I knew! I tried to deflect him. "You're one to talk. Aren't you wearing flip-flops?"

He chuckled, his exhales producing little, white clouds. "Yeah, I guess you're right. Misty likes to get out early. I didn't realize how cold it gets here though."

I was about to ask where he'd moved from when it dawned on me that if he was awake, then maybe it was late enough for my family to be too. *Oh no...*

"What time is it?" I blurted.

"Uh, six, maybe six fifteen..."

I inhaled sharply.

He glanced over. "What's wrong?"

"Sorry, got to go!" I called, sprinting away, leaving him and Misty behind. I knew I looked nuts, running barefoot in the woods, leaves strewn through my hair, but I didn't care. I just prayed I'd be able to reenter our home and get in my bed before my parents discovered my absence.

At least it's Saturday. My sisters and parents weren't exactly early risers on the weekend. I slid the backdoor open and tiptoed through the kitchen. Taking the stairs two at a time, I was relieved to see the house was dark and quiet.

Once in my room, I shot a glance at my vanity mirror. *Ugh.* Black smudges under my eyes left them looking bruised, my sweat suit was covered in enough dirt to appear brown rather than gray, and my hair... for a moment, I remembered the feel of it slapping against my back as I ran. I ripped a brush through, pulling out the remaining leaves.

Stripping out of my clothes, I dug in my pajama drawer and found a cotton nightgown. Glad for the first time my mom insisted on me using makeup wipes, I tugged one out and scrubbed my face until my skin felt raw.

I crawled into bed and hoped my toes would thaw. *Why was I out there anyway?* I had a sinking suspicion I'd spent the night out there. *Great, I sleepwalk now, just what I need.* After a few minutes, my thoughts shifted to Blake. I hated to admit that I wished our walk had lasted a little longer.

Maybe it'd be good to hang out with friends again. *Blake doesn't know about my near-drowning accident, or about what happened in the cabin. He doesn't think I'm crazy like everyone else does.* I grinned and then groaned. *Darn. After this morning, he probably does.*

CHAPTER
Six

After helping around the house that morning, my mom informed me the sweatpants had to go, at least long enough for her to wash them. So for the first time in a month, I pulled my favorite jeans on. They slipped right off my hips, landing on the floor.

Tugging the ends of my hair with my fingers, I peered at my reflection in the mirror. *When did I get so pale?* Wearing only a T-shirt and underwear, I turned sideways, noticing how far my hipbones protruded now. Since coming back from the cabin, I had a hard time keeping food down. *Ironic, since the whole time I was there, I daydreamed about food.* I didn't want to worry my parents, but seeing how gaunt I was, I was sure they probably were anyway.

I'm sure my sisters have noticed. It was no secret they struggled with eating disorders, especially Jocelyn with modeling. Krista would rather eat and spend endless hours at the gym. I'd never thought of myself as fat, just more athletic. I didn't want to be skin and bones; I wanted to feel strong. It panicked me to see so little muscle definition in my thighs and arms.

Sighing, I dropped down to my knees in front of my dresser and dug out a pair of Jocelyn's hand-me-downs that had always been too tight for my liking. I slipped them on as the doorbell rang. I ignored it, figuring it was just another boy coming to see my sisters.

My mom's voice carried up the stairs. "Hello, you're Katherine's boy, right?"

Knowing my mom wouldn't know the names of my sisters'

suitors, let alone their moms, I peered out my bedroom door, curious.

"Yeah, I'm Blake."

Blake? My chest constricted with nerves. *What's he doing here?*

"My mom wanted me to invite your family to dinner tomorrow night," he said, answering my unspoken question.

"Oh, we'd love to! Why don't you come on in? I'm so glad you came by. I realized when I met your mom the other day that we neglected to exchange phone numbers." My mom's voice grew louder. They were coming into the living room now. Being the first room at the top of the stairs, I shrank back into my bedroom, not wanting Blake to see me when they passed the staircase.

"That's what she said. She wanted me to give you her number too," Blake said.

"Oh perfect. Let me write mine down to give to her, or better yet, I'll call her myself. Want to sit down for a minute? I've wanted you to meet my daughter. She's about your age. Actually, I think you're in between two of my girls."

My throat closed up. *Will he say he met me already? And that it was out in the woods? Oh gosh, months of therapy, here I come!*

"Yeah, my mom said she's a senior like me."

He's covering for me. I couldn't help but grin. *Wonder if I should go down?* I didn't have to wonder long. My mom's head popped into the doorway.

"Samantha? There's someone I'd like you to meet."

My stomach fluttered as I nodded. I descended the steps, tugging at the bottom of my T-shirt to smooth it down. Once I was in the room, Blake jumped off the couch. Still wearing the baseball cap, he was now in jeans and a zipped-up jacket. I wanted to say something to him about wearing more clothes now that he knew how cold Durango was. Instead, I tried to tuck my hair behind my ear, realizing too late it was too short for that, my fingers fumbling with nothing.

"Samantha, this is Blake. His family moved in where the Kelly's use to be. His family just invited us over to dinner."

One half of Blake's lips twitched into a smile. "Nice to meet you."

"You too." My face heated.

"Why don't I go give your mom a call?" my mom announced, grinning as she rushed from the room. I tried not to be annoyed by her excitement. She was only anxious for me to return to normal life.

Glancing back at Blake, I thought it was kind of funny that we shared a little secret, an inside joke. *Only problem is, I am the joke.*

Blake must've been thinking the same thing because as soon as my mom was out of earshot, he said quietly, "So, I take it you made it home *in time.*" His crooked smile grew.

"Yeah, about that, thanks." I wasn't sure what else to say.

"No worries." He paused. "I sort of get it. I mean, the part about not telling your parents. But I still can't figure out why you were out there. I'd say jogging, but you weren't wearing—"

"It's a... long story." *One I'm not sure I really understand myself.*

He glanced at me. "Ok, how about we just get to know each other first? Save long stories for another day?"

His smile was contagious. I grinned back at him and pointed at the couch. "Sure. Want to sit?"

He didn't answer but plopped down on the middle seat. I stared at him, his grin a bit too cocky for his own good now. I chose the loveseat instead.

"So where'd you move from?"

"Anaheim." He snatched a square throw pillow off the couch.

"I've been to San Diego once, when I was little." He looked like he was waiting for me to say more, so I added, "I don't remember much though, just the beach."

For a split second, his eyes widened, and then he was spinning the pillow between his hands. "San Diego's cool. How about you? Have you always lived here in Colorado?"

"Yep, born and raised."

"So why haven't I seen you at school?" he asked.

At the same time, I said, "Have any siblings?"

We urged each other on to go first, but I wouldn't give in. He shrugged and said, "Fine, you win. I have an older brother and a younger sister."

"How old?"

"My bro's twenty-seven, I think. He's a doctor, married, and has a kid."

I was surprised to see him pull out his wallet and show me a picture of a little, towheaded boy.

"He's cute," I said, noticing how Blake caressed the picture with his thumb before tucking it away.

"They're still back in California. Going to miss my little man." His voice grew soft. He cleared his throat. "Then there's me; I'm eighteen."

"You're already eighteen?"

"Turn nineteen in April." He caught my look of surprise. "My parents held me back. Don't ask me why—they thought I'd be the star football player or something. And then there's my sister, Anna. She's fourteen."

"I've always wanted a younger sister."

"No, you don't," he said, but he was grinning.

"So, are you?"

"Am I what?"

"The star football player?"

He snorted. "Hardly. I'm all right, I guess. Now it's my turn. Why haven't I seen you at school? It's not big. I sort of already know everyone there."

I could tell by his unenthused tone he wasn't impressed by the selection. I supposed I couldn't blame him, moving from California. It was a little different here. Still, it was all I'd ever known. I cleared my throat. "I'm not going right now."

"Why not? Don't tell me your homeschooled."

HIDDEN *Monster*

"What's wrong with homeschool?"

"Nothing, I would just rather you be at the high school with me, that's all. It's a little dull for my liking."

I eyed him. *Does that mean you find me interesting?* "No, I guess I should be homeschooling. My parents think it's best if I stay home for a bit. Work some stuff out."

"That's cool," he said. "But don't stay out too long, kay? I could use a friend."

"Oh, I'm sure you have plenty of friends. You just want someone around that's insane." *Way to put that out there.*

"Exactly, you got me." The way his eyes danced back at me, unhinged me. I was saved from coming up with a response when Krista burst through the front door. Cradling her cell between her chin and shoulder, she blurted, "Whatever, no way, girl!" Glancing at Blake and then at me, she added, "Got to go, call you later."

Wearing tiny running shorts, which showcased her long, shapely legs, Krista shed her light jacket, leaving her in a low-cut, sheer white tank top. *Krista does love making guys drool at the gym.* I glanced over at Blake; sure enough, his eyes were glued on my sister, his mouth gaping. *Maybe I should hand him a napkin.*

"Hey guys, what's up?" Her eyes were riveted on Blake.

Here comes Krista the flirt. "Blake, this is my *older* sister Krista."

She flinched. "Watch who you are calling old, Sammy!"

"Nice to meet you." Blake's tone was different. I couldn't tell if he was flirting or not.

Inwardly, I sighed. *Krista will have her fun teasing and flirting until she has Blake wrapped around her little finger, and then she'll dump him flat. That's her MO. And I can keep on being his friend. Safer.* Although, I thought as Blake and Krista bantered, *Blake just moved here. So maybe, I shouldn't be happy with my sister's new interest. After all, Blake's still in high school, and isn't that taboo since Krista's a freshman in college now?*

"We're actually only like six months apart," Krista teased.

Guess the high school thing doesn't bug Krista. After all, they are 'only six months apart'.

Blake glanced at me, as if remembering I was there still. "You guys must be close."

Ha, hardly. I stared at my sister. Didn't she have enough college boys? Did she have to still draw from the high school pool too?

Krista met my gaze, but she didn't seem to notice my glare. "Well, see you around, Blake. I have to get in the shower. That kick box instructor was brutal, and I'm such a mess." Krista's grin grew more pronounced. "You're cute. Have any *older* brothers?"

Oh, gag me, Krista. I tried to keep my eyes from rolling.

"Married."

"Darn!" She winked, her diamond nose stud twinkling under the light, and then jogged up the stairs.

I drilled holes in the back of Blake's head. "I can set you up."

He faced me and cocked his head to the side. "What?"

"I'm just warning you now, she's a tiger. Likes to chew them up and spit them out, if you know what I mean."

"Oh. So maybe you're not best friends, huh?"

"Sorry to burst your bubble, but no. Seriously though, I think she's into you, if you like her."

"Naw. Not my type."

"Whatever, I saw you checking her out!"

Blake wrinkled his nose. "Was it that obvious? Man, I'm losing my game." His tone remained playful, and I couldn't tell if he was serious or not.

"Krista's every boy's type. Don't even try."

He pointed his index finger at me. "You really don't know me that well. Besides, why are you giving your sister such a hard time? You're just as pre—"

"You're such a liar," I cut in, suddenly uncomfortable. "I know *that* about you now."

He chuckled. "Hey, I better take off. Gotta help my dad out today."

I was disappointed to see him leave. I hadn't smiled in a long time; it was nice. Wordlessly, I followed him to the front door. His hand rested on the doorknob, but he didn't turn it. Instead, he faced me, his aqua eyes suddenly close. I dropped my gaze, landing on the hair poking out from his baseball cap in curls. I stepped back, my face flushing.

He cocked his head to the side. "Your sister called you Sammy. Which do like better?"

"Whichever, I don't really care."

"Mm, I'll think about it." He squinted, as if he really did need to decide. Then half his face hitched up in a smile. "Will I be seeing you in the morning again? You know, you should at least wear some socks this time."

I wanted to slug his arm, but didn't think we knew each other *that* well yet. Instead, I said, "Kind of hoping it's not going to become a habit."

Blake grinned and left. I had barely shut the door behind him when my mom waltzed back in from the kitchen. "You and Blake really hit it off!"

"Mom, were you listening in this whole time?"

"No, I just heard the door shut and came in," my mom said, feigning innocent.

"Mom..."

"Ok, I heard bits and pieces. Oh, Samantha, I'm so glad you found a new friend! I think this is just what you need right now!" I wanted to argue she was wrong, but I couldn't. I had friends, Mack being one of them, but for whatever reason, I felt she might be right. *Maybe Blake is just what I need.*

CHAPTER
Seven

I didn't know why I even bothered. One glance at my sisters made it all seem pointless. With little effort, they looked stunning, and Krista, I noted, put in considerable effort. *Guess the tiger's on the prowl again. At least I'll smell good,* I thought, slathering lotion on my arms riding in the back of our SUV. According to Krista, four houses was way too far away to walk in high heels.

Katherine Knightley opened the door and I immediately knew where Blake's aqua eyes came from, although hers were framed with black lashes instead of dark blond. "Please, come on in." A girl stood behind her who was already taller than her mom was, but I guess that wasn't too hard since Katherine was several inches shorter than everyone in the room was. Blake's dad towered over his wife.

The girl's eyes darted to mine, and her pink lips split into a smile. "Are you Samantha?"

I nodded. "Yeah, Anna right?" Anna's eyes looked like they might pop out of her eye sockets.

She gasped. "I'm so excited to meet you! Blake's told me so much about you already. He said you're totally into mountain biking too. That's way cool! I just got a bike and—"

"Anna!" Katherine cut in. "Let the poor girl get in the door before you talk her ear off."

I glanced at Katherine. "I'm fine. I'd love to take you biking, Anna." My parents exchanged a quick glance, and I wondered why. *Isn't this what they wanted? And when did I tell Blake I mountain bike?*

Like he knew I was thinking about him, Blake entered the room.

I hated that my eyes were drawn to him. Not wearing a hat for the first time, I was shocked to see how thick and curly his sandy blond hair was. The curls hung loosely around his ears and neck, not long enough to look shaggy. *Just wavy enough to make me want to run my fingers through it,* I thought, irritated with myself.

Apparently, Krista felt the same way; she maneuvered next to him in a very obvious manner. I felt smug satisfaction that Blake took pains to walk around her to be next to me as we entered the dining room. Katherine had announced that dinner was ready.

"I was disappointed this morning," he muttered under his breath.

"I told you, it's not going to become a habit."

He glanced over at me as we sat down next to each other. I was relieved I could actually eat dinner. It was the first real meal I'd gotten down without feeling the need to find a toilet bowl immediately. My parents glanced at each other again, this time smiling. After eating, we milled around the living room. Krista had Blake cornered against a wall across the room, flirting shamelessly with him. It irked me to see him laugh and respond. When Krista's cell phone rang for the third annoying time, she excused herself from the room. I glanced at Blake, and his eyes met mine. I dropped my eyes to the floor, wishing I didn't care who Blake talked to. There was movement in my peripheral as he sat down next to me.

"Thanks a lot," Blake muttered.

I glanced over at him. "For what?"

"You left me with the tiger."

"Looked like you were enjoying it from where I'm sitting."

He grunted. "Hey, want to sit on the porch? I need to escape while I can."

I nodded, excited to have my new friend all to myself. Following him out the front door, I spied a swing with floral cushions. Again, Blake plopped down in the middle seat. *Does he think I'm going to snuggle with him?* He saw my hesitation and gave me a lopsided grin.

"Sorry, habit." He scooted over, making room for me.

I sat to the side, pulling my knees to my chest. He pushed off with his feet, and the swing rocked back and forth.

"So you don't like her attention?" I wanted to know the truth.

"Mm well, that's not *entirely* true. I mean, she *is* pretty good looking—" He stopped when I punched him in the arm. I didn't care how well we knew each other. He deserved it. "What?" he chuckled, shifting away from me. He stopped laughing and moved back, sitting closer than before. "No, I don't like feeling like a caged goat."

I wished I didn't like feeling the warmth radiating from his body. *It's just cold out here.*

"Are you going to be at school tomorrow?" he asked, giving me a side-glance.

"I don't think so."

"Darn. I have to endure another day of the girls calling me Mr. Knightley."

"Why do they do that?"

He shot me an incredulous look. "You're kidding, right?" I stared back at him, clueless. "Every girl has *that* movie memorized. I've spent my whole life having girlfriends think they're the first one to say I'm *their* Mr. Knightley."

"Who's that?"

"Really? You *really* don't know what I'm talking about?"

"No, should I?"

"Huh, every other girl does." For some reason, his words stung me, like I wasn't a normal girl by his standards. "Jane Austen, *Emma,* ring any bells?" he asked.

"No, I've never seen the movie."

"It's a book too."

"Well, I've never read it either." I tried to hide the hurt I was feeling. It was stupid to feel this way.

Blake gazed back at me and then to my surprise, whooped. "How refreshing to meet a girl who's not hell-bent on finding *her* version of what a guy should be."

I wasn't sure how to take his comment, but the way his eyes caressed my face made my insides twist. I broke eye contact. "For hating this Jane Austen so much, you seem to know a lot about her."

"It's not *her* I hate. It's watching those eight-hour movies!"

"Wow. No wonder I never saw it."

"Ha, I was exaggerating, but it feels like it. Complete torture. Amazing what a guy will endure to make out."

Blake talking about kissing filled my stomach with butterflies. "Sounds like Hollywood girls are hopeless romantics if you ask me." I wrapped my arms around my knees.

"Yeah, I guess they are. Are you getting cold?"

"No, I'm ok. You'll like the girls here, then. A lot of rich hippie-dippies."

Blake chuckled. "Your family doesn't really fit *that* mold."

I shrugged. I couldn't deny my family received attention because of our good looks. "My mom's sure proud that at least one of us followed in her footsteps."

"What—modeling? I'm surprised Krista doesn't do it."

I glared at him. "I know, it's shocking."

He glanced at me. "I mean, she loves... the attention."

At that, I grunted. "She could, but she loves to party too much. It drives my mom crazy."

"Why don't you model?" Blake pushed off the ground hard, the swing swooping.

"You're kidding, right?" Gazing at the front lawn, I felt his eyes on me. I cleared my throat. "I'm not exactly model material. And even if I were, I'd hate it. Much rather be out running or on a bike."

I glanced his way, and he grinned back at me. I flushed and rambled on. "My dad bought me a bike when I was twelve, and I've been hooked since. My mom thinks it makes me too tomboyish."

"No way. Then you're one smoking hot tomboy."

My pulse quickened. *What do I say to that?* I was saved by a yelping sound. I glanced around.

"Oh, that's just Misty. I have her out in the barn," Blake said, giving the swing another push. "She must've caught your scent again."

I gave him a funny look.

"I'm serious!" He threw his hands up. "Her sense of smell's real sensitive. That's what makes her a good bird dog."

"Bird dog?"

"Yeah, she lets us know where the birds are by sticking out her nose and front paw. Man, the other day she must've caught your scent because she pointed and took off on me."

"Are you saying I smell like a bird?"

He grinned and then leaned in close, his nose brushing against my cheek. When he inhaled, goose bumps shot across my neck.

"Are you sniffing me?" I mumbled, finding it hard to breathe.

"Yes," he murmured, taking his time, and then he sat back. "You definitely don't smell like a bird."

My heart hammered against my ribs. "Oh good. What a relief."

"You smell good. What perfume are you wearing?"

"Uh…" My mind went completely blank. I was still recovering from his face being close to mine. "Just lotion."

His intense gaze made me squirm.

"So you must like to hunt since you have a bird dog?" I blurted.

"Yeah, I do." His brows gathered, like something else was on his mind other than hunting. When he cleared his throat and asked, "Samantha, mind if I ask you something?" I knew I'd been right.

"Sure, what is it?"

"Your friend Jen's in my English class." His words made my stomach plummet. One thing with Jen was when she decided she liked a boy, nobody got in her way.

"She told me… that something happened to you. That you were kidnapped."

I wasn't sure why his statement caught me off guard. I'm sure lots of people had told him about my abduction since it was big news in a small town. I clasped my hands together, my fingers feeling cold and bony, and forced myself to make eye contact.

"Do you mind if I ask what happened? She was a little vague other than going on and on about it being weird and things didn't add up."

I had to force myself not to gasp. *Maybe everyone really does believe I made it up.* A reporter showed up on our door weeks ago asking if my dad thought I'd invented the wild tale since there was no real evidence to back my story. My dad had slammed the door in his face.

"Samantha, are you okay?"

I met his gaze, squaring my shoulders. He was bound to find out sooner or later. "Yeah, I'm fine and no, I don't mind you asking. I was just out running one morning." My memories took me there. I could feel the rhythm of my breathing again. "Next thing, I'm falling on the ground. I woke up tied to a bed. I was alone, at least for a while."

I swallowed hard. "Then he came."

Blake's eyes narrowed. "Who?"

"I don't know. He had a ski mask. He even changed his voice."

"Wait, he *spoke* to you? What did he say *exactly?*"

I bit my lip hard. *Should I tell him?* I cleared my throat. "Most of the time, he just injected me with some kind of drug that knocked me out. But the day before I got away, he said… it was for my own good."

"What? *What* was for your good?" The intensity on Blake's face made me pause. A lump took up residence in my throat.

He sat back. "I'm sorry. We don't have to talk about this anymore." His jaw muscle bulged as he closed his mouth.

"No, it's okay. I should've told you sooner. I guess I figured maybe you'd heard about it on the news or maybe I just couldn't tell you. Either way, I didn't want you to see me that way, to think of me… like that."

He glanced over, the muscles in his face relaxing. "What do you mean? Like what?"

"Well, you know. Everyone thinks I'm crazy. I'm sure Jen alluded to it too. No one believes me."

"Are you serious? Well, they're idiots, Sam." His voice softened as he said my name, and for a split second, I felt like he might scoop me up in his arms, but he didn't. "For the record, I believe you. And I only think you're half crazy." He gave me a lopsided grin.

"Gee, thanks." I sort of liked that he called me Sam.

He continued to gaze at me. "Hey, speaking of Jen."

Were we speaking of Jen? "Yes?" I asked when he didn't say anything else.

"Do you think you could rescue me?"

"From what?" *Great, let me guess.* I forced the words out. "Does she like you or something?"

He shrugged.

"Oh. You like her then? You want me to set you up?" I asked.

"No, and no thanks! Why are you always playing matchmaker for me, first your sister, now Jen?"

"I'm-I'm not," I stuttered. "I don't know what you want. You're so confusing and a total flirt. I can only imagine how bad you flirt at school!" When he chuckled, I thought, *So you have been flirting with Jen.* "Just tell me how to rescue you then." The image of him with Jen drove me bananas.

"I'll ask your mom first. Then you have to say yes, if they'll let you go."

"What are you talking about?"

"The Halloween Dance," he announced, like I should've known. "Jen wants me to go with her and dress us up like Emma and," his face contorted slightly, "Mr. Knightley."

Although I'd never seen *Emma*, even though Blake thought that made me some kind of weirdo, I did know Jen liked old-fashioned 18th-19th century stuff. I giggled. "Don't tell me, you have to wear tights or something." When he didn't say anything, I busted up. "Okay, no way I'm I bailing you out!"

"Laugh it up, chuckles. I'm not wearing tights, and I'm not going with Jen. You're going to be my date. I'll wear anything you want me to, if you say yes."

I stopped laughing. "Wait, you want to go with *me?*"

"I hate dances. At least if you're with me, you'll keep me amused, make it bearable."

"It's just a school dance? Why even go if you hate it so bad?" *Crap, I can't get between Jen and her prize!*

"You have a point. But it is Halloween and I may not like dancing, but I do like going out and doing *something.*"

"Well," I stalled, "you don't want to go with me. I'm the world's worst dancer. I—" I stopped talking because Blake had hopped off the swing.

"Oh whatever, you can't be that bad." His hand grabbed mine, pulling me up with one tug.

"What are you doing?" However, my question was pointless. As he twisted and turned me, it was obvious he was trying to do some kind of manic dance with me. I felt dizzy with my feet going two different directions. When he dipped me, I knew I was in trouble, my weight pulling me hopelessly to the ground. My body buffered both of our falls. I grunted, his weight leaving me gasping for air. He immediately lifted himself a little, elevating his weight with his knuckles on the wooden porch. I stared up at him, breathing hard.

"Are you okay? Did I hurt you?" His words tickled my face. I nodded, my eyes staring hard at his lips. They looked so much fuller while he was suspended above me.

He cocked an eyebrow at me. "You weren't kidding, were you? You *literally* have two left feet."

"Ha-ha, very funny." I pushed against his chest. "You're just as bad as me. Now get off. You weigh a ton!" He jumped up and held a hand out to me. "You're a lot heavier than you look," I muttered as he pulled me up easily.

"And you're too skinny. Please don't tell me you're anorexic."

I took a step back. "No, I'm not. Are you always so honest all the time?"

"Sorry, bad thing about me, I suppose. I wasn't trying to be mean but as I recall, you just called me an ox."

"I never called you an ox!"

"Well, you implied it, said I was fat."

"I didn't say you were fat either!"

"Yes, you did, said I weighed a ton." His eyes sparkled back at me.

Oh, he drives me crazy! "Well, you do, okay. Maybe you're all muscles. I don't know!"

"Want to see?" He began lifting his T-shirt up.

"No! You're terrible!" I yanked his shirt down, but it was too late. I caught sight of his hard abs. Once he was covered again, I added, "I can only imagine how relentless you are to poor Jen! You better man up and go with her. She endures you day after day in school."

Blake's expression turned impish. "But I don't want to go with *her*. You'd be so much more fun. Look at how you dance; that's hours of entertainment just waiting to happen."

I wasn't going to let him have the upper hand. I grinned. "Well, even if I wanted to go with you, and I'm *not* saying I do, I doubt my parents would let me." *Or Jen, for that matter.*

"Let's go see, shall we?"

"Blake, wait." He was already throwing the front door open, clearly not listening to me. It clanged shut behind him. I slumped in my seat. *Now what do I do? Even if my parents say yes, what do I say to Jen?* The last time I'd even smiled at a boy she was interested in, it wasn't pretty between us. *Why are girls so catty?* I hated it. *That's probably why my best friend has always been Mack.*

Thinking of Mack now, my heart panged painfully. I relished the ache; it meant I was finally feeling again. The detached numbness I'd wallowed in for the past month was ebbing. Being around Blake had lifted the fog for me; it made me want to feel the sunlight on my skin again.

Wrapped up in my own thoughts, I almost missed the crackling sound. My head snapped up. I scanned the yard, nothing but grass and oak trees. I found the stillness of dusk unsettling, the silence stretching on, too eerie. I hopped off the porch swing and pushed the door in. It swung too easily, and I collided with Blake.

"Hey," he said, grabbing my arms to steady me. "Where are you off too?"

"Um, to see what's going on." I was trembling, the ominous feeling still nagging at me.

Blake grinned. "So, what do you want to wear?"

CHAPTER
Eight

"**S**tupid therapist," I muttered darkly. During my torturous hour of therapy the day before, Dr. Brady told me I needed to tap into my subconscious mind so I could heal 'properly'. *How the heck do I do that?* She was convinced all the answers were locked away in my brain somehow. *Ridiculous.* If I were honest, I knew I was just looking for a scapegoat.

After leaving Blake's house, my parents asked me if I was ready to go back to school, now that Blake had asked me out. I wanted to clarify to them I hadn't told Blake yes, just a soft maybe. I wasn't sure how Jen would take it yet. I needed to see her first, assess how bad she'd fallen this time. Now sitting in my room, I couldn't shake the nausea threatening. It was still dark. I'd awakened long before my alarm had gone off. *What was I thinking? I'm so not ready for this.*

Stomach still churning angrily, I climbed into my mom's car an hour later. *No turning back now.* It was my first day as a senior. I tried to ignore the fact that the monster could be there, hiding in plain sight.

I wasn't prepared to have both Jen and Jeremy in the front foyer when I walked in. *So much for slipping in unnoticed.*

"Oh my gosh!" Jen rushed toward me. "Wow, Samantha, I hardly recognized you. Your hair is—" She left the *ugly* unsaid.

"Hi Jen." My gaze darted to Jeremy. The last time I'd seen him, I hadn't been in my right mind. I hadn't cared about throwing away our relationship. *But now?* How many times had I twirled that black hair between my fingers? I peered up into his dark blue eyes.

"You cut your hair. It's dark too, looks good." Jeremy smiled at me, his teeth white and straight.

I licked my lips. "Thanks." I assumed he'd ignore me, maybe even yell, but be nice?

Jen grabbed my arm. "It hasn't been the same without you." Put together like usual, her blonde, spiral curls bounced on her shoulders. Her words felt sincere. *And why wouldn't they be? These are my closest friends. Speaking of which, where's Mack?* I searched the passing students, hoping to see spiky hair. He'd been calling himself Mack from the old eighties rap, 'Daddy Mack will make you wanna jump, jump,' for so long, I sometimes forgot his real name was Warren. Even his teachers called him Mack. Part of me wondered why I hadn't at least called him to let him know I was coming back to school today. *I've been lost in my own world.*

Right on cue, Mack beelined for me, glasses askew, bright green eyes bulging, and a huge grin splitting his face.

"Sammy, Sammy, is that my beautiful friend returned?" He pulled me into a bear hug and being taller than he was, I easily caught Jeremy's eye roll. He always hated our 'thing' as he put it.

Afraid I'd have no air left, I squeaked out, "Hey, Mack!" *For such a small guy, he sure is strong.*

He released me. "About time you're back." His eyes were wide, studying my face. And then he grinned. "Ooh, I likie." His hand made its way to my hair.

I playfully swatted it away. "Yep, it's almost as crazy as yours now."

"Almost, baby, almost. So what's your schedule? Do I get the pleasure of your company in any classes?"

Jeremy shifted his weight. "Hey, see you around, Samantha."

"What? Oh, yeah. See you, Jeremy." I watched him sulk away.

Mack whispered something to Jen, and she giggled. Once Jeremy was gone, she slapped Mack's arm, saying, "Looks like

Jeremy's already annoyed with you."

"He's lame. Glad you cut those ties, Sammy," Mack said.

Jen shot a glance at me. "Wait, you did?"

Doesn't she know Jeremy ended it? "Well, Jeremy——" My words were drowned by the bell shrilling.

"Shoot, I'm late! I've got to go. Talk at lunch?" Jen scampered away, not waiting for a response.

"Oh Jen." Mack sighed dramatically. "You're so lovely." He'd had a crush on Jen for as long as I could remember. *So things are back to normal; Jeremy leaving in a huff over Mack, Mack pining over Jen, and Jen giggling, clueless about how Mack feels.*

That was the only comforting thing about my day. Three classes later, I felt another pair of eyes gawk at me. Part of me wanted to scream, *Yeah, I'm the weird girl now,* and the other wanted nothing more than to run and hide. Was it him? Was he watching me as I darted to and from class? Or worse, was he in one of my classes, biding his time? I shuddered. Someone touched my arm, and I jumped.

"Looks like I lucked out." I glanced up to see Blake sitting down next to me. "We have Government together."

"Goodie for me." I meant every word. "I haven't seen you at all today. What classes do you have?"

"Well, English for one. And Jen just told me I'm to give her my answer by lunch." He looked at me expectedly, but the bell rang and on cue, Mr. Giles stood up from his desk.

Stroking his scruffy, gray beard, he began, "Please open your books to page ninety-three. Let's talk congress. Matt, can you start reading the first paragraph?"

I found the right page, already dreading my turn to read, I usually stumbled on the words. My palms were sweating when I noticed movement in my peripheral. I glanced over. Blake sat with his book unopened, staring back at me. I raised an eyebrow at him. *What?* His hand hovered in the space between us, down low. I bit my cheek to keep from laughing. Was that a note in his hand? *What are we,* in third grade now? Still, I subtly retrieved it. *Gee whiz! Why'd you fold it ten times!*

Finally, I read:

Are you going with me or not? I'm not going with Jen.

I stared at the paper. Should I just write, *I can't because Jen likes you?* In the past, I always felt like I let my friends down when it came to things like this. I wrote two words and handed it back to him.

He opened it and rolled his eyes. Mr. Giles, oblivious to our little game, called on Blake. My stomach dropped for him. He hadn't been following along in his textbook, but he answered the question anyway. *Wish school came so easy for me.* Forty-five minutes later, class ended, and Blake's hand landed on my arm. I glanced up from stuffing my books into my bag.

"What am I to make of this?" He held out the paper.

"Just what it says, I can't."

"And why not?" We exited the classroom, entering the crowded locker hall. "And don't say someone else asked you first, because this is a girl's choice. Besides, I asked you before you even knew about it."

"It's complicated."

"Complicated? Dancing with Jen's going to be complicated!"

I smiled in spite of myself. At least I knew Blake wasn't interested in Jen. Too bad she hadn't picked up on that yet. "Blake, Jen's my friend, and I've learned long ago not to come between a friend and her—"

"I'm not her man, if that's what you're going to say," he cut in.

"So why don't you just tell her no then?" *Why make me be the bad guy here?*

"Okay, I will. And then you have to be my date."

"No, wait." I sighed. "That won't work. She likes you. That means she'll hate me either way."

"Are all girls this ridiculous?" I peeked over to see he was grinning. "Why's everything got to be so difficult?"

I glanced around, feeling the gawking eyes.

"You don't even know about difficult," I muttered.

Blake halted, and a student collided with him from behind. He ignored the cuss words thrown his way, pulling me to the side. Once against the lockers, I stared back at him. Concern filled his eyes, confusing me.

"I'm so sorry, Sam. Here I'm being coy with you—how are you holding up?"

"I, uh, I'm fine."

"Has today been," he hesitated, "weird?"

You win the weird prize, I wanted to say. *One minute, I'm ready to slug you, then the next, I want to kiss you madly in some dark corner.* "It's been good and bad." My stomach rumbled, and we both heard it.

My face flushed, and he grinned. "You hungry?" he asked.

"Starving." Lately, I couldn't get enough food in. Blake continued walking, and I followed. The cafeteria wasn't far.

"So what's been bad about today?" he asked.

I glanced over at him and sighed. "Well, for one, I'm not sure what to think of Jeremy."

He made a sour face back at me.

"What was that for?" I asked.

"You're talking about the Jeremy that sits with Jen at lunch, right?"

"Yeah?"

"And he was your boyfriend, right?"

"Yes."

"Oh, nothing. He's a total tool, that's all."

I made tsking sound. "He's not *that* bad."

Blake glanced at me and shrugged. Entering the lunchroom, we parted ways to get food and met up at Jen's table. I plopped down next to her, and Blake sat across from us. Seeing how Jen beamed back at him, I knew I did the right thing telling him no, as much as it pained me.

"So? Are you going to be in town or what, Blake?" Jen asked, her lips shining with pink gloss.

I caught eyes with Blake. *There's your excuse!* He ignored my accusing glare and instead made eye contact with Mack, who sat down next to us. I could have sworn something passed between them, and Blake shook his head ever so slightly. *Okay, that was weird.*

Blake cleared his throat. "No Jen, I'm not leaving. I can go with you."

This is the right thing to do, I reminded myself, trying to ignore the hollowness I felt.

"Shoot, Sammy." Mack sighed heavily. "I know you wanted to ask me and all, but I'm already taken."

"You are?" I was sort of surprised.

Mack opened his mouth, but Jeremy brushed against me as he filled the open seat on my right.

"I know its girl's choice, but if you don't have a date, Samantha, I'm free," Jeremy said.

CHAPTER Nine

I clicked my seatbelt in and stared ahead. I knew he was mad at me. When Blake asked if he could give me a ride home, I called my mom to let her know she didn't have to come get me. As the engine purred to life, Blake flipped the heater off. It was still on high from the morning. Now his car was warm from sitting in the sun all day. It felt good to me, but Blake turned the AC on low. I wasn't sure what kind of muscle car it was. The black leather interior was comfortable and soft. Even the floor mats were meticulously clean.

"Is this the Dukes of Hazard car?" I asked, breaking the silence.

"What? The Dukes' car was a '69 Dodge Charger."

"Oh, it's orange like it though."

He glanced over and grinned. He didn't seem mad.

"Sorry, about Jen and everything," I admitted.

"Don't be. You got your wish. I'll be forced to wear tights all night. But you do know you owe me, right?" He threw the car into reverse, his feet working the clutch, brake, and gas pedals.

"Owe you? As I recall, you weren't completely honest about this whole thing."

"I suppose you're right, but in my defense, it was all an innocent mistake. I started school and didn't know anyone. And then Jen's all over me. And she wasn't *bad* to look at."

I rolled my eyes. "And you flirted shamelessly."

"I was nice to her. If she mistook that as flirting, it's not my fault."

"Well, when you look like you do, being nice is flirting." *Oh gosh, did I say that out loud?*

45

Blake glanced over. "You think I'm good looking?"

"No! I mean, some girls might, okay, whatever, back to your story," I stuttered, sinking lower into my seat. *I can't believe I just fed his humongous ego!*

Blake chuckled softly. "So, back to my *story.* Jen asked me before I'd really gotten to know you. I wouldn't count meeting you in the woods as a great intro."

"Wonder why…"

He glanced over at me. "I didn't know about everything then. I thought you were high or something."

"*What?*"

"Well you *were* out in the woods barefoot. Looked like you just woke up. You have to admit that wasn't exactly *normal.*"

I felt myself bristle.

"Come now, don't get like that. You're the one who rejected me, remember?" he quipped. I opened my mouth and snapped it shut. When he put it like that, he was sort of right. "So, what are you going to tell the douche?"

"He's got a name, you know," I said. He waited, and I mumbled, "I guess my lame-o excuse of 'let me ask my parents' won't get me far, will it?"

"Nope. You tried and failed with me with that one."

I grimaced. He wasn't going to let me live this one down, was he? "Well, I'm just not going, that's all."

"Oh no, you aren't going to weenie out of this. You're going."

"But that means I'm *Jeremy's* date." Blake was quiet. I glanced over, and we locked eyes long enough for my pulse to quicken. Then he stared ahead at the road again. We were on our county road now. I'd be home soon.

I forced a smile. "It'll be fun. We'll be in a group this way."

"Yippee."

I rubbed my hands against the sides of my jeans and then

pointed at the couch. "Want to sit?" It hadn't taken Jeremy long to show up on my doorstep.

"Yeah, sure." Jeremy sat on one end of the sofa, and I sat on the other. Tucking one leg under myself, I turned to face him.

"I asked your mom if you could go and she said yes," he announced.

Dropping my eyes to the cushion between us, I picked at a loose thread I'd found. "Oh. Good."

"You don't have to if you don't want to. I know the last time we saw each other, it wasn't so great."

I glanced up. "About that, I'm really sorry for what happened. I know you were on the news and everything. I understand why you ended things with us."

Jeremy's gaze shifted to the floor. "I'm sorry. I didn't realize what you went through." He glanced up at me. "I never told anyone we broke up. They all think we're still together."

I gaped at him. "Wait, what?"

He rushed on. "I'd hoped, still hope, we can pick up where we left off."

I tore my gaze away from his blue eyes, not sure if I was mad or happy. I supposed I still had some feelings for Jeremy, if sweaty palms and a nervous stomach counted. It was strange to think only two months ago, we'd been on this very couch, making out when my parents were away. Yet, even as my face flushed at the memory, I didn't know if it was the same for me. I didn't feel the same anymore; I felt afraid.

I swallowed hard and glanced back at him. He was waiting for an answer. My heartbeat felt irregular. I cleared my throat, needing more time to decide.

"I can't promise anything yet. We might have to pretend we're starting over. I'm not sure if I can——" My words were cut off by him moving closer and his lips landing across mine.

He kissed me softly and for some reason, I didn't resist at first. He pulled me closer, his arms wrapping around my back. Memories flooded in. This was familiar to me—the feel of his mouth moving with mine, his hair tickling my skin, and his faint cologne filling me with longing. And then I was falling into a dark place. No, more like tumbling. I couldn't breathe. I couldn't move. *No, no, no! Not him!* My mind screamed at me. I pulled back abruptly.

He looked crushed. "Sorry, I thought maybe if you remembered how it felt, that maybe you'd want me again," he mumbled.

I did want him. At least, some parts of me wanted him. Other parts were repulsed, and all of me was confused. "Jeremy, it's not that. It's just that I'm not ready for anything yet." I hoped he'd understand and let me go. I was scared he might try kissing me again.

He did release me and stood up. "Ok, I won't push you then. I'm happy you're going with me to the dance."

I stared back at him. *I am?*

CHAPTER *Ten*

"**W**hy did I tell Jeremy *that?*" I groaned. The day of the dreaded dance had finally arrived and the costume Jeremy bought for me lay on my bed, still in its package. I glared at the model wearing it. *There's no way I can pull this off.* When Jeremy had asked me what I wanted to wear, 'fairy' had popped out of my mouth. Since my dream of flying, I was obsessed with them.

"Cool, you'll look hot in a short—" My glare had him stammering, "Or I mean, nice in a long dress. And I'll be what... an ogre? What goes with fairy?"

Nothing, I'd thought, but I offered, "I don't know, maybe a wizard."

Now on my bed was a costume way too skimpy for my liking. *Guess everyone wants to be Tinker Bell.* I sighed, yanked the gown from the bag, stripped, and slid it on. Glancing at myself in the mirror, I gasped. I could see my bra through the sheer material.

I stripped, found a white tank top to put under it, and redressed. *Not great, but better.* Thankfully, the bottom of the skirt had enough layers of tulle and silk not to be see-through. I never wanted to play dress up as a little girl. What made me think I'd want to do it now that I was seventeen? *Complete nightmare.*

I snatched the wings next. Once they were secure on my back, I grunted at my reflection. The costume bag read *Dragonfly Fairy*, but pink gauze stretched around a bent wire hanger hardly captured the strength in the efficacious wings I'd dreamt of. *I'm wearing a freaking tutu!*

I took a deep breath and closed my eyes, telling myself to remember my flying dream. It relaxed me. My gown had been soft, my hair like gold silk draping over my skin, and my wings... The memory of flexing those unique muscles between my shoulder blades flared, the sensation of expanding and filling my lungs growing stronger with each breath.

Something tickled my arm. My eyes popped open to see blonde hair spilling down my shoulders and brushing against my arms. I shrieked and then slapped a hand across my mouth. *No way! No way! Holy crap! No way!*

There were feet running up the stairs. "Samantha! Are you OK?" my mom's voice called out.

This isn't possible! I gawked at the long, blue dress covering my body, clutching it just to see if it were real. Soft, silky material slipped between my fingers—it was tangible. *All too real. What in the world is happening?*

"Samantha, what's wrong? Open this door!" my mom commanded as she jiggled the handle.

When did I lock it? I hustled across the room, my hair bouncing against my lower back. *I'm awake... this isn't a dream!* As if answering me, the pair of wings on my back fluttered. Positive I was hallucinating, I threw my door open, hoping my mom would set me straight.

"Oh, Samantha!" she gasped, the worry melting from her expression. "You look stunning!"

Holy crap! This is real? My wings flickered, but luckily for me, my mom didn't notice.

"Why'd you scream like that?" my mom demanded.

My mouth opened, ready to blurt out the truth. *Freaking out because I'm a fairy, Mom!* But instead, I stammered, "Oh... uh... a spider landed on me."

"Don't you ever scream like that unless someone's coming through your window, do you understand? I about had a heart attack!"

Poor Mom. My head bobbed up and down. She stayed a few minutes, fussing over my dress, hair, and makeup. She kept asking me how I brought the honey color out in my brown eyes, and where did I get such a real-looking wig. It took all my willpower not to breakdown laughing at the absurdity of it all. *Should be asking me how I grew a pair of wings!*

The moment she left the room, I rushed to my mirror. I hardly recognized my own reflection—thick, black lashes, a creamy complexion with rosy undertones in all the right places, which accentuated my cheekbones, my lips pink and fuller than I'd ever remembered them being before, and my neck so long and lean.

This isn't me! I wrung my hands together. *What should I do?* The answer was obvious. I should march downstairs and tell my family everything. Instantly, I saw my mom's reaction. The hysteria, the phone calls to doctors and specialists. The rumors and strange glares would never end. I couldn't do it. I needed a minute to compose my thoughts. Maybe the wings would just go away, and no one would ever have to know about it. It was a shot in the dark, but I clung to it like it was my lifeline. One thing for sure, there was no way I was going to the dance now. *I have to figure this out. Maybe I can make them go away. I mean, I thought about them and they appeared. Wonder how much I can control them?*

I inhaled deeply while concentrating on the muscles nestled between my blades. Flexing and expanding, my wings fluttered to life, transforming into a blur. I exhaled, and my feet left the carpet.

"Okay, now stop." I remained levitated. "Great idea, now I'm stuck up here. Maybe something different will work." I glanced over my shoulder. "Time to calm down." I felt ridiculous speaking to the wings like they were some kind of dog, but they responded by slowing.

Encouraged, I continued, "Calm, calm, time to be calm." The blur was becoming more distinct. I grinned. "Calm," I whispered again. Then the silver hum became two iridescent wings, and my feet sunk into the carpet. *Yes!*

The doorbell rang, and I shot into the air again. *You've got to be kidding me! Is this going to happen every time I'm startled?* My mom was coming up the stairs. *Calm, calm, calm...*

I'd barely landed when my mom gave one knock and opened the door. "Wow, I can't get over how stunning you look! I wish your sisters were home to see you. Jeremy's here."

"Hey Mom, I don't think I'm going to go. I'm feeling kind of lousy all of sudden."

My mom's face fell. "Really? Oh Samantha, are you sure? You look so gorgeous in that."

"Yeah, I'm just fighting this sore throat."

"Well, let me help you take those wings off so you can lay down." She took a step forward. "It's a shame; I think you'd enjoy yourself tonight." I froze. My mom's fingers reached out, touching my wings. "How did you even get these on in the first place? I don't see any fasteners."

"You know what? You're right, Mom. I think I'll go," I blurted, sidestepping out of her reach and bolting from the room. *I either go to the dance or be discovered for the freak show I am right now.* I decided to risk it. *Halloween dance, here I come.*

"Oh good," I heard my mom exclaim from behind me. "I think you'll have so much fun."

Descending the steps, I saw Jeremy's jaw drop.

"Holy cow!" he blurted out from the base of the stairs.

"Jeremy, I don't know where you got that, but it's the most incredible costume. She glows in it!" my mom gushed, following me.

"I didn't—"

I shook my head at him. "He doesn't remember what website he ordered it off, right?"

He must have gotten my hint because he closed his mouth and nodded. Wanting to get this night over with as quickly as possible, I grabbed my jacket out of the coat closet.

"You may want to take your wings off first," my mom commented.

My stomach dropped. "They were tough to get on. I'll just wear it like this till we get there." I held it in front of me and shoved both my arms through it backwards.

Just as Jeremy reached for the door handle, it turned, and my sisters walked in. Whatever they were discussing before, they stopped.

Jocelyn's eyes widened, and Krista whooped, "Holy he...ck," she finished for my mom's benefit. My mom hated curse words, no matter how mild they were.

I cringed inside, fearing that any moment I'd be found out. All it would take was one loud, unexpected noise and I'd be bumping into the ceiling. *I have to get out of here. At least at the dance, it'll be dark.*

Jocelyn fingered the dress. "Wow, Samantha. Where did you get this? It's like silky cashmere."

Not one for wearing either of those materials, I shrugged my shoulders. "Some store online. I don't remember the name."

Krista's eyes zeroed in on Jeremy. "Mm... you can't go like that. I need to fix you."

I had to admit, his black wizard cape and hat looked like a fifteen-dollar drugstore costume now. Krista grabbed his arm, yanking him upstairs as Jocelyn fingered my hair. I did my best not to shudder. What if she realized everything wasn't just a costume? What then?

"Where did you get this wig? It looks so real. I would love one of these. Maybe a red one so I can dress as Red Riding Hood." Her brown eyes studied me over.

Blood rushed to my face. Jocelyn wasn't the type to let details slide. *Darn her for so many questions!* "I, uh, same store too."

Jocelyn peered at the wings, her hand skimming along the edge of one. My mouth felt like cotton, and I swallowed hard. Her fingers were cold and dry. *I can feel with my wings!*

"What in the world?" she murmured. "I've never seen anything like these before."

I ducked away, unsure what to say. Luckily, I was saved by Jeremy and Krista coming back down.

"Doesn't he look better, Sammy?" Krista asked with a smug smile.

"Yeah, it's creepy," I said, meaning it. Jeremy's face was painted gray with black shadowing his eyes and mouth. He looked mean and I didn't like it, but I was glad he was ready to go. My mom pushed us together and took several pictures.

"Mom, its Halloween, not prom." I needed to escape the brightly lit living room. If my wings even shivered, I knew I'd really be known as the circus sideshow.

"I know, I know. But you'll thank me later," she huffed. "Be safe, have fun," she called as we finally left.

"We will. Thank you, Mrs. Campbell," Jeremy replied.

CHAPTER
Eleven

Ten minutes later, we pulled into the high school parking lot. Jeremy had tried to converse with me, but I was too distracted by my new form to respond much. Leaving home was a mistake. *I have wings! I can fly!* I had no idea how it was possible, but one thing I knew for sure... what I'd thought was a dream had actually happened. My wings quivered. *I know, I know. Trust me; I want to get away from here more than you do.*

Jeremy opened my car door and I followed him to the gym, careful not to walk too close. I didn't want him to accidentally touch me. The gym doors were opened, and music blared out at us. I was glad to see only blackness in the opening. No lights on would make hiding so much easier. As my eyes adjusted to the dimness, I made out paper Halloween decorations—orange pumpkins, white ghosts, and something black, which I assumed were cats or maybe bats. Fake cobwebs hung from the ceiling, and an obnoxious strobe light lit up one corner of the gym. I slowed my pace, trying to sink back into the shadow of the wall. Jeremy went a few more steps, glanced around, and then spied me. He gave me a strange look, which with his makeup was more like a glare.

He moved closer. "What's wrong?"

"Nothing."

He grabbed my hand, and I wished the gesture brought me comfort, but it didn't. There was a DJ at one end of the gym, and a long refreshment table at the other. I knew which side I wanted, but Jeremy made his way towards the music. *Jeremy always thought himself the dancer.* I glanced around; everyone was in costume. No one seemed to notice mine. I tried to relax a little. It was going to be fine. Then a slow song began, and Jeremy led me to the dance floor.

I stiffened as his hand landed on my lower back. His hand brushed the bottom of my wings; they recoiled. He pulled me close, but I was too distracted by the hand still touching my wings to protest our tight proximity. I arched my back, trying to put some distance between his hand and me, but it just brought my chest nearer. He grinned, obviously misinterpreting my movement.

Great.

Feeling dizzy, I gazed over his shoulder, trying to concentrate on a set point to clear my head. I chose the clock, staring at the second hand ticking away at its circumference.

Wait, that's on the other side of the gym. I blinked a few times, and then scanned the room; details I shouldn't be able to make out so clearly glared back at me. *That girl's bag of chips has 'only 150 calories' written on it, that guy's shirt tag says medium, and the tall kid in the back is going to lose all his makeup with how many cracks and flakes he has on his face.*

Nausea enveloped me, reminding me of the weeks following the cabin when I could hardly keep a piece of bread down. *What's happening to me?* I pinched my eyes shut, focusing on my breathing, and trying to ignore the bile rising at the back of my throat.

I must be imagining things. No one can see like this. I peeked out, hoping my superman vision was gone. First thing I honed in on was a small tear in an orange paper pumpkin hanging on the fall wall. *Crap, crap, crap!*

My gaze dropped, landing on a sparkling tiara, followed by blonde hair pulled up in a high chignon, dark red material draped across shoulders, and finally a long, white, high-waisted dress, which touched the floor. *Jen.* At her side, I met aquamarine eyes gaping back at me. My pulse quickened, blood pounding in my ears.

It didn't matter we stood a gym floor apart and in the shadows of a darkened room. I had no doubt Blake saw me; the shock in his expression was almost comical. While Jen jabbered at his side, Blake had come to a halt. It felt like forever we stared at each other and then he arched an eyebrow at me, a crooked grin spreading over his face.

Surprised I look good for once, huh, Blake? I hated to admit I'd been wrong about the costume. *Guess I don't know my Jane Austin.* Blake wasn't in tights or knickers. Instead, he was in a sleek, form-fitting, black suit complete with tails and tall, black boots. *Got to give it to Jen, he does look pretty hot right now.* Jeremy whisked me around, and my friends were gone. Had all that happened in one turn of a dance? When we'd completed our nauseating rotation, I searched for Blake again. My heart squeezed when I saw them approaching; his aqua eyes were still glued to me.

"Wow," he mouthed silently when our eyes locked. The song thankfully ended, and Jeremy somewhat reluctantly let go of my waist and then hand. I scooted apart farther, hoping he wouldn't notice. I wanted to give my wings plenty of girth.

"Is that *really* you, Samantha?" Jen asked. Her tone was strange.

I gave a nervous laugh. "Yeah, it's *really* me."

I swear I caught confusion in her eyes before she was grinning and saying, "Oh… well… for hating getting dolled up, you sure did it right."

Though her words were kind, I couldn't help but notice the oddness in her tone. Was it *that* unusual for me to get 'dolled up' as she put it? Jen seemed truly puzzled by my appearance. *Oh my gosh, she can tell! I should leave now before I'm once again six o'clock news!*

I cleared my throat. *Just act normal.* "Jen, you look amazing! Just like Emma."

Jen did a small curtsy. "Why, thank you. What do you think of Blake? Isn't he the perfect Mr. Knightly?"

I glanced over; Blake's eyes met mine. I stammered, "Uh… you look sort of like him, I suppose."

"You mean, I look *better* than him," he quipped.

Terrified my head would bob like a buffoon agreeing with him, I tucked my hair behind my ear and forced a glance at Jeremy. I caught the tail end of his eye roll. My annoyance at my own stupid behavior gave way to Jeremy's. *Why does he have to showcase all his feelings so freely?*

"Want to get us some drinks, Jeremy?" Cliché or not, I needed a bit of space from him at the moment.

He glanced at me and sort of grumbled an agreement.

Blake's eyes followed Jeremy as he strode away. "Really, you picked *him?*"

Not wanting him to say more, I countered, "You just need to get to know him. Deep down, he's really a lot of fun." *Lies, lies, lies. . .*

"Yeah, I can tell," Blake muttered, and then glanced down at Jen tugging at his arm.

"It *is* really hot in here." She flashed him a huge smile.

"Would you like me to get you a drink too?" he asked.

"Oh, would you?" Jen said, acting like the idea hadn't occurred to her.

I did my best not to stare at his backside as Blake walked away. His broad shoulders and tapered waistline were making it difficult though. *What's wrong with me? Blake's not my date—he's Jen's.*

"Oh, Samantha, Blake's the best date ever!" Jen blurted, reconfirming my own thoughts. "Oh yeah?"

"You should've seen him at my house earlier. He was so great with my little brother, Kenneth. I can tell Blake adores him. He spent the whole time talking just to him."

So in other words, he ignored you, Jen. Stop, I chided myself. *Be nice. I should be happy for her.* I sighed. *Who knows, maybe Blake does like her. . . It was so hard to tell with him.*

Jeremy returned too soon, handing me a drink. I sipped gingerly, wanting to put off more dancing as long as possible. Two people entering the gym caught my eye; a couple dressed as the Mad Hatter and Alice in Wonderland. Wearing a tall, green velvet hat, a crooked, polka-dot bow tie, and periwinkle dress coat, I had a suspicion I knew who it was.

"Mack?" I called out. The Mad Hatter turned my way. His expression was hard to read under all the white makeup, but I didn't miss his eyes sweeping up and down my body. I shifted my weight, hoping he didn't stare too hard at my wings. The Hatter let out a boisterous laugh and rushed to me. I knew I was right. It was Mack.

He was breathless, grabbing my arm. "Sammy? Is that you?" Mack's question sounded so serious.

I slugged his shoulder with my free hand. "Of course it's me. Who else would it be?"

His expression was hard to read with all the white chalk. I stared back at him. *Can he tell my wings are real? Oh my gosh! What do I do?* I inhaled deeply, waiting for his answer.

He squinted back at me, both of us caught in a weird moment. I swallowed.

"Samantha?" He said it slow enough that it came out a question.

"Yes?" I drawled back, trying to act casual. I was dreading the question bouncing in his head. *Surely, he won't blurt it out in front of everyone, right? Maybe he will pull me aside later and ask if I'm really a fairy.* I cringed at the absurdity of my own thoughts.

"You surprise me again." He stepped closer, his eyes meeting mine. "I hardly recognized you." He straightened up. Then with a goofy grin, he nudged my chin with his knuckle. "My little minx, you."

I tittered nervously, trying to recompose myself. I was happy Mack's attention turned to Jeremy. "Wow, check out your evil wizard hovering over you like a possessive—"

"You guys look awesome!" I cut in, as Jeremy stiffened.

Mack nodded, his snarly afro bobbing, and jumped back to Monica's side. Her Alice dress showed off her lean legs. A small, white, top hat donned the crown of her black hair.

Monica smoothed her white apron down. "Hey, Jeremy."

"What's up, Monica?" Jeremy's tone was surprisingly pleasant.

A loud song began, and Mack tugged on his date's arm. "Come on, Alice. Let's get you to Wonderland."

Monica smiled, but it was directed more at Jeremy than Mack I thought, and followed him.

"He's just too weird. I don't know what Monica sees in him," Jeremy muttered.

I opened my mouth to defend my friend but Blake was back, handing Jen her drink.

I forced myself to ignore Jen fawning over Blake's arm, saying to Jeremy, "Why do you care who Mack's with?"

"I don't," Jeremy said with a frown.

Blake's lips twitched as he stared at the floor.

Jen gulped down her drink and then pulled on Blake's hand. "Let's dance!"

I tried to see if he looked happy about it, but his face was a blank slate as he trudged after her. I felt Jeremy's hand on my arm and cringed. Apparently, he had the same idea. I groaned inwardly and let him pull me to the dance floor. At least we were with Blake and Jen. The four of us formed an awkward group. Being in the middle of a crowded dance floor, Blake bumped into me more than once. While I was terrified he might touch my wings, his closeness sent shivers of excitement through me. I couldn't understand why I wanted to be near him so bad. I hardly knew him. Shouldn't I be feeling that way about my boyfriend, or ex-boyfriend, or whatever Jeremy was?

My inner turmoil was pushed aside when Mack rushed past me, jumping into the middle of our group. He gave me a lopsided grin and then began performing the jerkiest break dance I'd ever seen. The best part was it was on beat, his body's rhythm matching the music. His enthusiasm was contagious, and I couldn't help but laugh. Then I found myself moving closer to him. Not one for attention—I wasn't sure what my plan was. There were already quite a few teens gathering to watch him dance.

"Sammy!" Mack crowed, pausing for a moment, long enough to throw all eyes on me.

Crud! What am I doing in the middle? Not only did I hate dancing, I knew it only took one person to realize my wings were real and any semblance of a normal life would be over for me. Time slowed, my heart beat matching the thumping music. I couldn't tear my gaze from Mack. His brown eyes lit up, and his face appeared delighted.

He gave me a wink and whispered, "Come on, Sammy girl. Just try."

I opened my mouth to protest, realizing my legs were moving and then my arms. I glanced down. My whole body felt taut; my muscles pulled tight like they were ready to spring into motion. Then I was moving again, my torso rolling like it was boneless and my limbs finishing each rippling wave. I gasped. *I'm dancing... break dancing!*

Mack beamed back at me, his smile wide. "There's my Sammy! Sweetness!"

I grinned back at him. It was exhilarating to picture something in my mind and have my body respond so fluidly. It reminded me of another time. My wings flickered, and I prayed no one noticed. Thankfully, all eyes were on Mack, who had dropped to the floor, spinning on the back of his neck and head.

No way I'm doing that, not with these wings... or ever. I glanced around the hooting crowd and met Jeremy's scowl. *Why does he have to be such a killjoy?* My moment in the spotlight was over, so I grinned at Mack, who was still going strong, and tried to melt back into the group. I was ignoring Jeremy's eyes boring a hole into the side of my head, when someone bumped my other hand. I glanced over. Blake stood close, his warm hand lingering near mine.

"I take back the whole two left feet thing," he said.

"Thanks." I waited for a sarcastic comeback, but his eyes held steady, gazing back at me, his hand still brushing against mine. I couldn't tell if it was an accident or not, but it made my pulse race. I could feel the adrenaline tingling up my spine. My senses felt heightened. The warmth radiated from him, his scent reminding me of the woods on an autumn morning, his skin so smooth that I knew it would feel silky against my face.

I don't know how it happened, but next thing I knew, I was in Blake's arms, my body moving with his. Only this time, neither one of us had left feet. This couldn't be real, could it? I wasn't really dancing with Blake, like this, in front of everyone. *Even in front of Jeremy… oh my word!*

I knew I should break away from him, but I couldn't, not even when the song ended. Blake's face was inches from mine. I'd never felt anything like this before. Every part of me wanted to feel his hands securing me against him. His eyes were darting between mine, his brow knitting as his lips turned down. *Is he upset with me?* I tried to back up, but I couldn't. *Does he feel it too? Like we are being pulled together?*

He ran his hand through his hair and exhaled. Reality hit me and, feeling ridiculous, I stepped back. I couldn't read Blake's face. I couldn't tell if he wanted me to stay by him or go away. What was I thinking dancing with him like that? *Jeremy must be livid.* I turned, expecting to see him storming up to me, but he wasn't. I peered around, surprised to find him next to Monica.

Jeremy caught eyes with me. I didn't know what to make of Monica's scowl directed at me. Jeremy moved away from her. I decided to walk over to meet him, reluctantly leaving Blake's side.

"Have fun with Monica?" I asked when we were close enough.

Jeremy hesitated, some of the determination leaving his face. "Uh, yeah. Sorry, she wanted to dance with me."

That explains why Blake doesn't have a broken nose right now. "I don't mind. You can dance with whomever you want. I danced with Blake."

Jeremy frowned, glancing over my shoulder. *Probably glaring at Blake.* Lucky for me, a friend came up to Jeremy, diverting his attention from Blake and me. I couldn't help myself; I shuffled away, completely dogging my date.

"Where's the fire?" Blake asked from behind me.

I turned around, happy to see who had followed me. "Is it that obvious?"

He chuckled. "Little bit. Not that I blame you."

Man, you look good tonight. I giggled. Trying not to straight up ogle him, I glanced around. To my surprise, I spied Jen and Mack dancing together.

Blake followed my gaze. "I told Jen it'd make Mack's night if she asked him to dance."

"Good idea." I was thrilled for Mack. He was spinning Jen in rapid circles as she laughed. "You must be so sad to share your date with someone else."

"Nope. It's going to be a lot more painful for Jeremy."

"Why do you say that?"

Blake didn't answer but grabbed my hand. Fire coursed through my veins, and I didn't pull away.

CHAPTER
Twelve

I hadn't noticed the slow song until Blake drew me closer. His hand barely brushed against my back, almost as if he were afraid I'd break.

"You're right; this is going to be very painful for Jeremy," I murmured.

He glanced down at me, his smile not the crooked, confident one I was used to. Though his hand was weightless against the crook of my back, the warmth from his fingers seeped through my gown. Our other hand was intertwined, resting against his chest. I found it difficult to breathe or think straight. Was I imagining the heat coming off us? It felt almost electric. We rotated and I spied Jeremy, hands on hips. I cringed. I lifted my free hand off his shoulder and pointed at the back of Blake's head, mouthing, "Sorry". I wanted to imply that this dance was Blake's idea.

Jeremy grimaced and stalked away. I hoped Blake didn't notice my silent message, but as we came close to Mack and Jen, Blake pointed not too subtly to my head and mouthed, "Sorry," to Jen. I stifled a grin. The truth was I was just glad he was okay with me throwing myself into his arms earlier. At least, that was what I decided had happened.

Blake gestured with his chin. "Good to see Jeremy moves on quickly."

I turned to see what he meant. Jeremy was dancing with Monica again.

"Oh. Guess we all got our dates wrong tonight," I said.

Blake glanced at me. "Wow, look at you."

"What?"

"Actually admitting you're wrong."

"Why do you say that—because I didn't go with *you* tonight?" Wishing I didn't notice how close our mouths were, I resisted the urge to take a step forward..

"Well, yeah, there's that. And of course, Jeremy's a total tool."

"You really like to call him that, don't you."

"I do have way more *colorful* names. Want to hear them?"

"Mm... think I'll pass, thanks."

His eyes met mine. "What do you see in him anyway?"

"Um... I really don't know anymore." I chuckled and shrugged. "I guess he was just the first boy to like me." Being a tomboy came with its drawbacks... Namely, no one asked you out. Jeremy was sort of my first real boyfriend.

Blake's mouth dropped open, looking as if he was about to disagree with me, but he must've changed his mind. He shut his lips and shifted his gaze away from me. I could easily tell where he was now staring—Jeremy and Monica.

"It's just weird right now with him because he's acting like he didn't break up with me," I admitted, watching Jeremy turn Monica in circles.

Blake stared at me. "Wait, *he* broke up with *you*? He's a bigger dink than I thought."

"Stop." I swatted his shoulder. "It's not his fault."

"Oh really?" He shot me an incredulous look.

"I accused him of being my kidnapper, and he wasn't happy about it."

Blake grunted. "Why'd you think it was him?"

"It was something he said. Jeremy used to call me *his special girl*."

"Why doesn't *that* surprise me?"

"What do you mean?"

"Haven't you noticed how possessive he is over you? He gets

crazy if anyone even looks at you."

I glanced over his shoulder at Jeremy; he glared back at me. I tried to smile, but it came out strangled. I looked away. "He's just the jealous type, I guess. If it makes you feel better, he's never liked Mack either."

"I know."

I glanced at him. *You do?*

Blake cleared his throat. "So since you told *him* yes, I'm guessing you don't think it's him anymore."

"He had alibis."

He was quiet and then glanced at me. "Sam, can I ask you something?" Seeing the way his eyebrows furrowed, I wasn't sure if I wanted him to, but I nodded anyway.

"Did the guy say anything else to you in the cabin?"

My stomach somersaulted. *Should I tell him?*

"Sam," he urged, "it could be important."

For some reason, the words rushed out. "He told me I'd fall in love with him." There, I said it! A whoosh of relief and terror rushed through me simultaneously.

"What?" Blake stopped dancing, his hand tightening on mine.

I met his brewing eyes, the aqua blues storming before me.

"I told him I'd never love him, that he was a monster." I swallowed. "But he said the best part for him was I wouldn't know who he really was until it was too late." My bottom lip trembled.

He pulled me closer, his hands holding me firmly against him. Somewhere in my mind, I realized we were dancing again.

"Did he say anything else?" he asked quietly in my ear.

I wanted it all off my chest. "Yes, that he'd made the blend special for me and… that he's always loved me." Blake's body jerked in my arms, like my words stung him. I plodded on. "That I was beautiful, smart, and… and… I knew him."

"*You* know *him?*"

I swallowed, trying to moisten my cottonmouth. I wasn't

prepared for Blake's reaction. His gaze looked a thousand miles away, staring into nothingness.

"Yeah, but I have no idea who he is."

His eyes came back into focus, piercing into mine. "Did you tell *anyone* else this?"

"No. I was too scared. I felt like if he knew I'd told someone, he'd get to me somehow. I know it sounds stupid."

I wondered why Blake stopped dancing and then realized the song was over. Panic seized me. Would he leave me? Now that I spilled my guts, would he walk away and leave me in the suffocating darkness?

"No, it's not stupid. I'm so sorry I brought this up. I know it's painful for you, Sam." Blake studied my face. His lips turned down.

I tried to shrug it off, but I was having a hard time getting air in. "It's okay. I'm fine, really." The words came out hoarse. "I know you care about me. As a friend, I mean."

"Yes, as a friend," he murmured, moving his hand from my back, leaving it feeling cold and exposed. Instinctively, I clutched at his other hand, not wanting him to let go of me altogether. He seemed to study my face and then steered us to the side.

"You're looking pale, Sam. Are you sure you're all right? I shouldn't have brought all that up."

"No, no, it's okay. I'm fine, really." But I wasn't. My head was spinning. *Is this what Cinderella felt before morphing back?* I hoped not. I wasn't sure what I'd be wearing or if I'd have anything on at all!

"Sam, I need to tell you something." He hesitated, his eyes flicking to my wings. It took all my willpower to keep them from fluttering back at him. "I'm going to California."

That was unexpected. "What? When?"

"Tomorrow."

I simply stared back at him.

"I'm going to visit my brother for a few days," he explained.

My voice wouldn't cooperate, my throat constricting.

"And I need to see some friends," he finished.

My heart squeezed. "When are you coming back?"

"Not sure, probably end of the week."

"Oh," I choked out. My air was completely blocked, and I could feel myself drowning again. The water was covering my face, filling my nostrils, my mouth, my eyes, my lungs. I sucked in, desperate to relieve the burn in my chest.

Blake's eyes darted between mine. "Sam, what's wrong?"

I could hardly tell him I was reliving a childhood nightmare that haunted me ever since the accident.

"Nothing, I'm fine," I managed, my ears ringing. *He doesn't need to know I'm no stranger to therapy. He already thinks I'm messed up enough. Besides, the drowning was a long time ago.* I thought the therapy had worked. At least, my parents stopped making me go. My mom said it was because I screamed at the therapist, telling her I was fine and not ever coming back. However, I had no memory of that, and why would they listen to a nine-year-old child anyway? *Why am I reliving this fear now? Of all times!* It was like my abduction had ripped open my old wounds, like a Band-Aid taken off a bit too soon. I felt raw and vulnerable again.

He opened his mouth, a question clearly forming with how far his eyebrows were bent, but someone stepped between us. Jeremy.

CHAPTER
Thirteen

J eremy made sure it was the last time I was near Blake, or Mack
or Jen for that matter. The rest of the dance was miserable. I was
relieved when the DJ announced it was the last song and to grab
that special someone now. *Well, I know one thing for sure now. I'm definitely over Jeremy. I don't care what he tells everyone. I'm done.*

We moved in slow circles, Jeremy quiet, and me feeling guilty.
If I had just been honest with him from the start, we wouldn't both
be in torture. I glanced up at him. His scowl made my stomach drop.

"What's wrong?" I asked.

"It makes me mad."

"What?" *Let me guess, me dancing with Blake?*

"Because of some freak show, you'll never be the same," he
muttered.

"Where did that come from?"

"It was so good before. He ruined what we had. I can see it on
your face. You didn't want to be with me the whole night."

I bit my lip. *Guess Jeremy read me like an open book.* "I tried to tell
you, Jeremy. I just need more time."

"Whatever, that's not it. You just don't feel it anymore. You
should've just told me, Samantha. I'm not dumb."

"Why don't we go talk in your car?" Not only did I want to
avoid a scene in front of everyone, I was anxious to go home. I'd
made it the entire night without shooting up in the air, and I wanted
to keep it that way.

He stared at me for a moment and then shrugged. "Yeah, sure, whatever," he muttered, striding away from me.

I stared after him. *Oh boy*. I had the feeling this wasn't going to be a fun ride home. Taking a deep breath, I squared my shoulders and forced my feet to plod after him. *Just get this over with*, I told myself, leaving the gym. The dance was over now, and the foyer rapidly filled with teens.

I was berating myself for being such a chicken in the first place when I heard it—a growl directly behind me.

I stopped midstride, my heart thumping. Planted to the floor, I couldn't turn around. Blood pounded in my ears, and my fingers turned to ice.

He's here. I'd know that mechanical purring anywhere. *He's here! He's behind me!*

This was it; the moment I knew would come, though I hadn't pictured it in such a public place. Even still, it was straight out of my nightmares. The monster voice said something, but it was too muffled to understand. My wings shuddered.

Oh crap! Luckily, in the pressing crowd, no one noticed. Someone touched my arm and I yelped, barely keeping my feet on the ground. I prayed no one saw the sudden movement of my wings.

"Jumpy little thing, aren't you?" Blake teased. His amused expression soon gave way to concern, his hand landing on my shoulder. "Sam, what's going on? What's wrong?"

I did my best to keep my voice steady, but my words choked out anyway. "It's him... that voice!"

His eyes turned to steel as he glanced over my shoulder. It was strange, but I could tell he was scanning the crowd, like he knew what he was searching for. One long, guttural laugh and Blake's eyes honed in on his target. He glanced at me. "Stay here."

"Blake, wait!" But he was gone. Trembling, I rotated slowly. My legs felt like jelly, and my throat was dry. I located where it came from—a guy wearing a long, black cape. He roared with that sickening, altered voice. He was surrounded by friends, his back to me.

Blake got in his face. "Who are you? Take off your mask."

The kid shifted to stare at Blake, and I saw his gory mask. They weren't allowed at the dance, but now that it was over, he must've put it on.

The growling voice barked back, "Whatever, man."

Blake didn't move. "Take it off."

"What are you—the school police or something?" he jeered. Blake's hand shot forward, grabbing the caped arm. The kid jerked back. "Get off me, man! What's wrong with you?"

"I'm going to ask you one more time to take off your mask." Blake's words came through clenched teeth.

The kid laughed; the monster-like growl I could never forget. "Whatever, loser."

"Wrong answer." He threw the guy against the wall.

Others noticed the scuffle, and a crowd gathered. I flushed and wrapped my arms around myself.

The kid yelled back, "What the devils wrong with you?"

Blake tore the mask off and yanked the hood down, ignoring the squirming teen. I was surprised Blake held him so easily with one arm. I recognized the kid immediately; a shock of thick, red hair poked out from the costume. Freckles smattered the pale kid's face. A small, black box was in his mouth, which he spat into his hand.

"What's your name?" Blake asked, still holding the guy against the wall.

"Let go of me, man." Blake didn't let go. "Ok, I'm Mike. Now get off me!" The kid pushed back at Blake, but he didn't budge.

"Where did you get that?" Blake gestured to the voice box.

"They're everywhere. I got it at the Halloween Superstore. It's like ten bucks. Everyone has them. Now let go of me, you freak!"

Blake stared at Mike's face for a moment, inhaled deeply, and then slowly released him. "Sorry, Mike, my mistake."

"It will be if you ever try that again," Mike muttered, shoving him away. Blake didn't look like he even noticed the hit.

Mike stomped away with his friends, probably humiliated, and I ducked my head. *This is all my fault. Tons of kids probably have those things. And now because of me, Blake attacked some random kid.*

"What was that all about?" Jen asked breathlessly.

I glanced over, seeing her for the first time. "Nothing."

"Why did Blake do that?"

I wondered how Blake dismissed Mike like it couldn't have been him. How would he know?

"It was just a misunderstanding," I said, catching sight of Jeremy in the outside door. His expression said it all. I knew what he was thinking. *There she goes again, accusing some poor guy of being 'the monster'.*

"I better go," I said to Jen. Blake walked over to us. I opened and shut my mouth, finally managing, "Blake, I'm sorry, I thought—"

He touched my arm. "Are you ok? Sorry he scared you."

The final tingles of adrenaline disappeared, and my knees buckled. Luckily, Blake was there to grab my arm, helping me stay upright.

"Let me take you home tonight," he demanded more than he asked. Jen gasped. That was not what she'd like, that was for sure, and I hated to admit it just wasn't an option for me either. I had an unpleasant conversation with Jeremy to look forward to. *Ugh...*

"Thanks, but I'm fine. Jeremy's waiting for me."

Blake slowly released my arm. "Okay," a smile twitched on his lips, "but if that weasel tries anything, you know where to find me."

I was about to respond, but Mack and Monica waltzed over.

"Well, well that was a lot of drama." Mack glanced at Blake. I could've sworn something passed between them, not really tension, more like communication. Then Mack's brow creased as he gazed back at me. "Are you okay, Sammy?"

"Yeah, what can I say? I attract drama." I tried to grin back at him, but it felt forced and unnatural.

"Well, looking like that, you better watch out." He cocked his head at me, as if debating, and then shot a look at Blake. "You taking her home?"

"Nope, Jeremy."

Mack nodded slowly, and I just stared at both of them. It dawned on me what it was passing between them. They were friends. When did that happen? Well, whenever it was, I was glad.

Since Jeremy was quiet, I decided to dive into the uncomfortable silence and explain how I wasn't ready for a relationship right now. I knew it was an excuse. Truth was, I didn't want anything to do with Jeremy anymore, but I didn't have the heart to say it.

He didn't buy it. "Explain Blake then," he retorted.

"What do you mean? Blake's my friend."

"Oh yes, *friend*. You like that one, don't you? First Mack, now Blake."

I wanted to roll my eyes at him. "What are you talking about?"

"I've put up with your *thing* with Mack, but I won't with Blake," he spat back.

"Okay, this is ridiculous!" I said, losing patience. "First of all, it's really none of your business anymore who I'm friends with. You ended us, remember? And as for Mack, we've been friends since we were kids. Besides, we hardly ever do anything together anymore!"

He sputtered. "You're kidding, right? You take off with him all the time. Or used to, before... well, you know... this summer. You'd be gone all day and not answer your phone. Then I'd see you together at the mall or at some store."

I racked my brain. For some reason, I had no memory of what he was talking about. All I did know was that he was sounding very much like a stalker right now.

I decided to change the subject. "Well, Blake and Mack *are* my friends. I don't know why you are giving me such a hard time anyway. I didn't mind you dancing with Monica tonight."

Jeremy glanced over and sighed. "Well, I guess I might as well tell you. Monica and I dated after I broke up with you. I kept it quiet, mainly because I wasn't sure that I really wanted to end us. After I saw you back at school, I knew it'd been a mistake. I told Monica I was taking you back. She was pretty mad about it all."

I glared at him. *Of course you assumed you could just take me back. Ugh. And no wonder Monica gave me dirty looks all night! She probably asked Mack out just so she could be near you.*

"You never *even* asked me if I wanted to be with you again. You just assumed I did, and you told everyone I was *still* your girlfriend."

"I thought you were the same; I didn't know you changed so much."

What an arrogant... I thought of a host of dirty names, all of which Blake would've loved. Why couldn't he get it through his thick skull? I didn't want to be with him because he was a jerk—not because the cabin experience changed me.

I fumed inside, debating if I should say anything else. Thankfully, we pulled into my driveway, and I undid my seatbelt. He shoved the car into park and reached for his door.

"Don't bother. You don't need to walk me to the door." I jumped out.

Jeremy's eyes widened and then to my surprise, his shoulders slumped. "So this is goodbye then?"

Uh, yeah! "Afraid so. Night, Jeremy. Sorry I changed too much for you."

He shook his head. "Hope you're happier with Blake. Maybe he can handle your crazy."

I slammed the car door shut, trying to ignore his last jab. Poking my head into my parents' bedroom, I informed them I had fun but was tired and going to bed. Leaning my forehead against my door, I exhaled slowly. With the tense ride home, I'd temporarily forgotten about my much larger problem. I had wings. As if sensing my attention, they fluttered back at me.

What was I going to do? Who knew when *and if* they'd ever

go away? I'd made it through the dance, but what about tomorrow? What then? I'd have to tell my parents the truth. They wouldn't exactly believe I loved my Halloween costume enough to never take if off again. I braced myself for what would follow the discovery. It would be more than national news; it'd be world news. I shuddered. My wings wiggled back at me.

I glanced over my shoulder at them. My heart felt heavy. "What am I supposed to do with you?" I whispered.

I sensed their answer. It screamed inside my soul. *Fly.*

"All right, I give. Let's see what you got."

My wings needed no more urging. I was airborne instantly, my wings a blur of silver. Within seconds, I realized my room was too cramped; I knocked my lamp over and slammed into my mirror. I hovered by my window, debating. The desire overwhelmed me, my fingers itching to unlatch the lock.

What if someone sees me? I forced myself to land, taking deep, slow breaths to calm my rapid heartbeat. I crawled on my bed, laying my head on my pillow. *Wonder what Blake would think if I showed up at his window like this?* I giggled and then sobered. Tomorrow loomed before me like a chasm. My life had been anything but normal up until now, but somehow, I knew all of that would pale in comparison to what awaited me at dawn

CHAPTER
Fourteen

A whistling whine woke me. Confused, I bolted up, catapulting a pillow that must've been on my face.

Seeing my bedding strewn across my bedroom floor, I moaned, "What a night."

I glanced over my shoulder, bracing myself for the inevitable. I gasped. My wings were gone! I exhaled, relieved and confused at the same time. The whole experience felt very much like another crazy dream. I ran my fingers through my now-short, brown hair. I wasn't sure what I was more scared of; the fact I had no idea why I'd even had wings, or that they could sprout out whenever they wanted. What if they came in the middle of family dinner or worse, walking down the halls at school?

No point in stressing over it now. I stood and reached toward the ceiling, stretching my stiff joints. My chest felt heavy. Was it only the wings making me feel sad or could it be because Blake was leaving today?

My phone whistled again. *Speaking of Blake.* I snatched it off my nightstand, seeing I had missed four text messages. I opened them and scanned. They were all from Blake.

Hey, you up?

"No Blake, at seven AM, I was not awake," I said, opening the next one.

Want to come over? I'm not leaving until tonight.

I grinned.

Wake up already!

That text woke me up. I looked at the clock, seeing it was almost ten already.

Please don't tell me you stayed up all night with Jeremy.

That was his last text.

Don't worry, I texted back. *Jeremy's climbing out my window now.*

My phone buzzed back.

Haha...Want to come over?

I bit my lower lip, realizing I wanted to see him more than anything.

I'll be over soon. Need to talk to parents first.

That's good.You should tell them everything.

Forty minutes later, I was sitting across from my parents at the kitchen table, waiting for their response or for them to at least breathe again.

My mom was the first to sputter, "Sammy, how could you keep this from us? This was important information!" The chair scraped noisily against the floor as she popped up, snatching the dishes as she went. I stared at her, surprised by the outburst.

"Lydia," my dad said evenly.

"Well Darrin, *she* should've told us sooner." Dishes crashed into the sink. "It means the guy's still here, someone she, *we*, probably know!" My mom turned, hands on hips.

For some reason, her words hurt. Anger flowed through me, and I rose from the table to face her. *How dare she be mad at me?*

"What's wrong, Mom, afraid of what people will think of you? Your crazy daughter is at it again."

My mom gasped. "Sammy, how dare you say that to *me*? That's not fair, and you know it! How could you do this to...? We've only wanted to protect—"

I was breathing hard, jaw clenched. My bottom lip trembled.

"Lydia, wait, stop," my dad cut in, his tone firm. Then to me, his voice turned gentle, "Samantha?"

HIDDEN *Monster*

The knots in my stomach disappeared, and I was surprised to find my hands had been balled into fists. My shoulders slumped. *What's wrong with me? Of course my parents are upset! I lied to them. I'm hurting them all over again.*

"I'm sorry," I mumbled, the subsiding anger left me feeling somehow alone.

"Oh my goodness, Samantha," my mom gasped. "I'm so sorry."

My eyes widened as my mom practically bowled me over hugging me. I was at a loss for words. I patted her back awkwardly.

"It's okay, Mom. I shouldn't have said that stuff."

She just sobbed into my shoulder. *What just happened?* My dad stepped closer and placed a hand on her shoulder.

"Lydia, hon, we're all in uncharted territory, come here." My parents embraced, and my mom cast one more look over her shoulder at me.

"I'm so sorry, Samantha. I thought... I mean, I didn't realize..." Her words faded, and I wondered what she was trying to say.

She glanced at my dad. "I'm the worst mom ever," she whispered.

"No, hon, that's not true. Why don't you take a hot bath? Try to relax."

My mom sniffed and nodded. She quietly left the room, and it was only my dad and me. He glanced at me and then ran his hands through his hair.

"Well, that was interesting," he said.

I tried to give him a small smile, but it was forced.

"Samantha, I want you to know that none of this is your fault. We *all* just want to keep you safe." His gaze held steady. I nodded back at him, ready to end the conversation.

One thing's for sure, there's no way I'm telling them about the wings now. I could only imagine the reaction I'd get then. *Mom would be hospitalized.*

An hour later, I trudged along the road, hands shoved into my cotton, hooded jacket. It had taken some convincing for my dad to be okay with me walking over to Blake's. My mom was tucked in her bathroom, and I was happy he didn't consult with her on the decision. He had hesitated, told me to be safe, and I bolted out the front door. I needed air.

Plodding through the leaves, I hopped up on the sidewalk when there was one. Worn grass was more common than cement in my neighborhood. The wind picked up, and I zipped my jacket as the leaves scurried across my feet. The chilly air tickled the back of my exposed neck, and goose bumps shot across my arms. I quickened my pace. It was a lot colder than I thought when setting off. Blake's house wasn't far and I knew I'd be there soon, but I couldn't shake an eerie sensation nagging at me. I glanced around, scanning the bushes and trees, but nothing but autumn colors stared back at me. A twig snapped. I whirled, my heart thudding. *Nothing, probably just a squirrel.* I scurried forward, my pace brisk. I knew something was off. There were no birds chirping.

It was too quiet. I felt it. I knew someone was watching me.

I did one last three-sixty, my eyes scouring my surroundings. My skin prickled, my ears straining to hear. Deathly silence greeted me. I sensed it, somewhere in my body, a tingling dread flooding me. Someone's eyes were following me. Next thing I knew, I was in a full-blown sprint, my legs pumping, my lungs burning as I pummeled through the undergrowth. Dashing up the Knightley's porch steps, I gulped in air and banged on the door. While I waited for someone to answer, I turned around and surveyed the trees.

"Samantha?" Anna said from behind me.

I spun back around. "Hey, Anna," I puffed. She opened the door further. I happily left the woods and whatever was out there behind.

"Did you run here?" she asked.

"Uh, yeah. Is Blake around?"

"Yep, he's out in the barn, working on his motorcycle."

"He has a motorcycle?" I asked, glad we were moving farther

into the house. My hands were still shaking, my knees feeling wobbly from adrenaline.

Anna didn't seem to notice my frayed nerves. "He got it before we moved. My mom wasn't happy. She kept telling him he was going to wreck all the time."

"Did he? Wreck, I mean?"

Anna pushed her naturally highlighted hair behind her shoulder. Her face became animated as she leaned into me. "You know how they say the biker's the one who always loses in a wreck? Well, not with Blake. The bike lost, sure, but Blake was fine."

"Really? Well, that's good."

"Not to my mom. Now Blake's fixing the bike instead of junking it like she wanted him to. My dad stays out of it. And when Jaxon sided with Blake, well, my mom lost it."

We passed through the living room, heading to the back of the house. I felt like I could finally breathe properly. "So Jaxon thought Blake should keep it?"

Anna grinned. "I think he thought it'd give Blake a project since we were leaving California. Probably afraid Blake would get bored here," she glanced at me, "but he didn't know he'd meet you."

I felt my face flush as I wondered if by 'he' she meant Blake or Jaxon. I steered the conversation to what was weighing on my mind.

"I'm sure Blake will like seeing Jaxon again and maybe some friends while he's there."

"Yeah, he'll probably see Kate too," Anna said easily, while my heart squeezed. *Who's Kate?* "That's Blake for you, though. He takes off all the time. I wish our parents gave me half as much freedom."

Dying to ask who Kate was, I forced out another question. "Where does he go?"

"Mostly camping and hunting with Jaxon. It's so unfair because they never let me go with them."

"Maybe it's a brother thing," I said as Anna's forehead wrinkled up.

"Yeah, well, it's not like he doesn't still have school like me. Did I tell you he got to go camping for like three weeks before we moved here? Three weeks! My mom freaks when I miss like two days of school. It's so unfair."

"That is a long time," I said, realizing this was striking a nerve with the poor girl. It took all my willpower not to squeeze information out of her about Kate. "Well, tell you what, while Blake's gone *again*, why don't you and I go mountain biking?"

She beamed back at me. "Really? You mean it? That'd be awesome. Want to see my bike? It's in the barn too. Come on."

Anna pushed the back door open, and howling wind slapped our faces.

"Geez, why's it always so windy here? And cold," she complained as she shoved her hands into her jeans pocket.

"Don't worry. You'll get used to it." I wanted to add, *Just wait until the snow comes*, but I didn't want to scare the California girl too bad.

I knew the barn Anna was talking about. It was known as the Peterson's red barn, named after the family who had originally owned the homestead. Set back about thirty yards and surrounded by wood-planked fence, it was often the backdrop to local family photos. I wondered if Mrs. Knightley knew she could end up with strangers in her backyard, as the previous owners, the Kelly's, gave photographers a green light to help themselves. We hustled the remaining few feet, both of us ducking our chins to escape the brisk air. Anna pulled the door open, and we both slipped in.

The barn smelled musty, yet clean. It took a second for my eyes to adjust to the dimness. I spied a cherry-red hot rod and whistled as we passed it. Everything from the paint to the chrome hubcaps sparkled back at me. Most of the barn was full of boxes and bins. Knowing the Knightley's had moved in not too long ago, it made sense. The back wall had the makings of a workshop with saws, sanders, and power tools on it. My eyes scanned the area and then discovered Blake lying on his back beneath his motorbike. Without looking up, his hand reached over and grabbed a ratchet.

"Blake, Samantha's here," Anna announced. She grinned at me. "I'm going to go grab my bike to show you. Be right back."

I nodded and glanced over to see Blake was sitting up now. "Hey, looks like fun."

"More than you know." He ran the palm of his hand across his forehead, leaving a long, black streak behind.

I giggled. "Nice."

"What?" He glanced at his blackened hands. "Oh."

"It looks like the bike's winning to me." I hated the fact I found him attractive even with his jeans and T-shirt covered in oil.

He tossed the ratchet aside. Standing up, he rubbed his hands on a rag. I wasn't sure why. It wasn't like it helped.

"I like to let her think she's winning." He winked, patting the seat.

"Anna said you wrecked it." The bike appeared fine to me, but what did I know?

"Yep. Mangled her pretty good."

"Does it run?"

"Not yet, but close. I want to make sure she's all better before I take her out again."

"You talk like she's your girlfriend. Better be careful, Jen might get jealous."

"Jen and I have an *understanding* now."

I glanced at him. "Oh really. So what is that *understanding?*"

"Well, after an unfortunate mishap last night," he began, and I cringed. Did he mean throwing that kid against the wall? But instead, he said, "I let Jen know that although I was flattered she kissed me, it wasn't going to fly between us."

I gaped at him. "Wait, Jen kissed you? When?" *Why didn't she call me? Oh yeah,* I realized, *because he said he ended it. Poor Jen.* I did feel sorry for her, while slightly elated at the same time.

"Last night, when I drove her home, so now that it's over, it's just you and me, babe." I would've been thrilled if his words were directed at me, but he was stroking his bike's handlebars. *Clearly not meaning me.*

"You do make a cute couple. Should I leave you alone?" I asked.

"Naw, she's not the jealous type."

I wanted to come up with a witty comeback, but Anna was rolling her bike towards us. "What do you think?"

I recognized the brand, taking in the size of the rims and the suspension. "Nice." I squatted down by the gears.

Anna dropped down next to me. "You think it'll work? I want to get really good at it."

"It will more than work. I know just the trail, not too hard, pretty level, nothing too technical, but it has awesome views." I stood up, catching Blake's eye. His expression was hard to read.

"How about Monday, after school?" I asked her.

"Yes! Perfect!"

"You guys going riding?" Blake asked.

Anna practically bounced off the ground. "Yes. Samantha's going to show me how to mountain bike. I'm so excited!"

"I figured she should get to do something fun while you're gone. She told me how you always camp without her." I meant it in jest, but Blake's face flushed. He glanced at his sister and for a split second, I could've sworn he looked nervous.

He cleared his throat. "You would've attracted the bears."

"What? No, I wouldn't," Anna retorted.

"Anna, what's in your pocket right now?"

"I…" She stopped.

"Yes?" he asked.

Anna turned to me and said sheepishly, "I have a sweet tooth."

Blake's eyebrows rose.

"Okay fine, Blake. Licorice bites, but bears don't like candy."

Blake chuckled, and I stifled a giggle. Anna rolled her eyes at her brother, and he tossed a clean rag at her. It was fun to watch them banter. Under it all, it wasn't mean spirited. As Blake cleaned up his tools, Anna filled me in with all the freshman gossip she could think of. I tried to be polite, putting in the occasional, *Yeah, really*, and *Oh my gosh*. Blake's lips twitched into a grin, clearly amused by his sister or that I had to listen to her.

"Hey," he interrupted, and I turned my undivided attention to him. "I'm almost done out here. Why don't you go inside?"

Well, that's not exactly what I hoped for.

Anna whooped. "Okay, come on, Samantha. Let's go in my room."

I shot a glance at Blake. "There's nothing I'd like more, Anna."

He snorted back at me.

CHAPTER
Fifteen

"**Y**ou have to hear this next one. It's totally the sweetest song ever," Anna exclaimed. I rolled onto my side, trying to dodge the pile of CDs Anna had sprawled across her bed, and sat up. I found it endearing that she preferred CDs. With all the new phones, gadgets, and music players, the little, round discs were all but obsolete.

I had to admit that after spending twenty minutes in her bedroom, I enjoyed Anna's excitement. *Sort of nice to be silly and girly for a change.*

Anna flitted over to the stereo and cranked the volume up. I tried to figure out its appeal. *Must not be my type of music.*

"What are you trying to do, kill Sam with your crappy boy bands?" Blake cut in.

My neck snapped to the side to see Blake standing in the doorway. Greasy clothes were replaced by clean jeans and a baby-blue T-shirt. Wet curls hung at his neck. However, I noted that his hands were still stained a muddy gray. As if sensing my gaze, he tucked his hands into his pockets and leaned against the doorframe. *If I only I had a camera. Darn him for looking like a J.Crew model right now.*

"These guys are not a boy band. How many times do I have to tell you? They're unique. A little emo mixed with pop," Anna explained. Blake's eyes met mine.

"Want to go for a drive?" he asked.

My heart thumped, and I had to fight to keep my voice even. "Sure." I glanced at Anna, wondering if she'd want to join us. It wasn't that I would *mind* her company, but I hoped for some alone time with her brother.

She wagged a finger at Blake. "You better drive careful. I don't think she wants to go a hundred miles per hour."

"Yes, Mom."

I glanced at him. "Should I be worried?"

"Naw," he drawled back at me.

"Whatever, Blake." Anna's hand flew to her hips. I grinned. *Got to give the girl an A for being so passionate about everything.*

Blake's eyes danced back at me. "Come on." His crooked grin coaxed me to my feet. Five minutes later, I snapped my seatbelt in, double-checking that it was secure. Blake turned the heater on low, but the air coming out was still cold.

My stomach flipped within me as he slid the key in and hit the clutch.

"Don't worry. I won't go that fast, okay?"

I gave him a nervous laugh. *It's not the speedometer I'm worried about. More like what could happen on this drive.* I pressed my palms on my jeans, trying to push all the possibilities from my mind.

He shot a glance my way and chuckled. "What's wrong? You've ridden with me thousands of times."

Exactly, to and from school. But where are we going now? I hoped he attributed my odd behavior to Anna's warning.

"Yes, well, that was before I knew about your lead foot," I managed.

He gave me a wink and shifted into gear, the car lurching to life. Within seconds, we were on a county road heading north, the hunk of metal we rode in purring as it hugged the gentle turns in the road. I tucked my hands under my thighs, staring out my window. Autumn colors swirled by, broken up by the occasional house, wooden fence, or barn.

Blake flicked his stereo on. "Now, this is real music."

I instantly liked the unfamiliar song; the slow beat matched the singer's smooth tone. I wanted to tease him, say how he'd been wrong, but everything about the moment was too perfect. *Yep, this isn't like riding to school.* I glanced over, and our eyes met. *He's different somehow...*

My face flushed and I stared ahead, recognizing our location. "Heading to Baker's Bridge?" I asked. A local hot spot in the summer, the bridge was usually packed with teenagers sunbathing on the rocks and jumping off the cliffs into the rushing Animas River.

"Yeah, is that okay?"

"Sure." I shifted in my seat and then almost gasped when I felt a strange sensation spread across my shoulder blades. *Oh, please no! Not now!* My heart's thumping was no longer over Blake maybe kissing me. I was terrified of transforming again, wings and all. *Maybe Blake won't freak out too bad...*

I wrapped my arms around myself, bracing for the change.

Blake glanced over. "Are you warm enough?"

"Uh, yeah, I'm good." *Just about to pop wings, no biggie.*

The car slowed down, and he peeked over at me again. "Sorry, I didn't realize how fast I was going."

Guess I look pretty nervous. I forced a grin. I might as well act normal until my wings made their grand appearance. "No worries, I've had a good life. But seriously, you're going to kill yourself driving so fast."

"Not likely."

"Why do all boys think they can't get hurt?" I wasn't sure why I was turning all motherly on him. *So not sexy.* Not that I was an expert in *that* department.

"Oh, I can get hurt, but it's been a long, long time. Trust me. We're fine." He glanced at me. "Just relax."

"I am," I lied.

His hand reached over and secured mine, tugging it off my lap and pulling it closer to him, where he rested our intertwined fingers on his thigh. I swallowed hard, his hand warming mine. The strange feeling in my back ebbed as adrenaline trickled through my veins, my skin tingling where we touched. I inhaled deeply, relieved I might live another day as a normal teenage girl, taking a car ride with a boy.

I tried to allow myself to enjoy the moment. The stereo's music rolling with the bends in the road, the scent of the clean leather seats, and the warm heater vents blowing on my face. *If this isn't a date, I'm stumped.* I'd never felt anything like this before, definitely not with Jeremy. Every sense in my body felt awakened and on edge.

Should I tell him the truth? I needed to talk to someone about it. My heart stirred. *And I like him... a lot.* I chewed on my lower lip and glanced over at him. His eyes were on the road, one hand hooked on the top of the steering wheel.

I opened my mouth, ready to let the words fly, when he asked, "Want to get out and walk around?"

I peered out my window. I'd been so wrapped up in my thoughts that I hadn't realized we'd arrived. "Sure."

He parked and turned the key. I knew he had to let my hand go to get out of the car, but I still didn't want him to. He gave my fingers a quick squeeze and released my hand. We climbed out, and I realized how close I'd been to divulging everything.

"You going to be warm enough?" he asked.

"I'm fine. I didn't grow up on the beach like you, this is nothing." As soon as his eyes were diverted, I zipped up my jacket. *Cold is still cold.*

He came around the car to me, and I hoped he'd reach for my hand again. He seemed to hesitate and then shoved them into his pockets. Disappointed, I slid mine deep into my jacket as well.

"Have you ever jumped off the bridge?" he asked as we meandered closer to the cement bridge wall.

"No, and I never will."

"Really? Why not? Looks fun to me."

We stayed close to the side of the bridge, avoiding the passing cars. The shoulder offered a small space to walk along. I peered over the wall at the water rushing below.

"Dare you to do it now then," I joked.

"Okay." I wanted to roll my eyes at his crooked grin, but he actually lifted his foot to the wall's edge, hoisting himself up.

The thought of him entering the icy water below made my stomach sink to my knees. Panicked he'd follow through with it, I grabbed his waist from behind and tugged back on him.

"Wait! What are you doing? I was kidding!" I yelled at his backside.

I could hear him chuckling, but I didn't let go. *Stupid boy!* My arms formed an awkward cocoon around his middle.

He stepped back down and turned around fast, leaving me still embracing him. "If you wanted to hold me, you could have just said."

I released him, my face feeling hot. "No, you just scared me to death acting like you'd jump, that's all."

"I wasn't acting. I would've done it. This is nothing. You should've seen the cliffs—"

"But its freezing! You'd get pneumonia!" I protested, cringing that my hands had landed on my hips.

"Naw, I'd be fine, but I'm glad you're worried about my safety." He winked, still dishing out that cocky grin of his.

"I'm not worried," I countered, feeling unhinged. *Probably because he's toying with my worst nightmare.* Logically, I knew he didn't know, but it still irritated me. "I don't care if you do jump, just not while I'm around, okay?"

To my surprise, his grin vanished, his eyes turning contrite. "Are you afraid of heights, Sam?"

"I'm not a fan of them, no." I could feel his eyes still on me, but I didn't know if I wanted to divulge more. *Oh, might as well. He already thinks I'm nuts.* "It's not just that though. I'm afraid of water."

I braced myself for his snarky comment. *I mean, what seventeen-year-old admits to being afraid of water?*

His tone was soft. "Don't you know how to swim?"

I kept my gaze locked on the rippling water below. "Yes, my

parents forced me to take lessons. I almost drowned when I was nine. I just don't like to be under the water long. It freaks me out."

When it remained quiet, I peered over at him, meeting his gaze. "Well, that'd scare anyone. What happened?"

"It was the one time I went to California." I laughed mirthlessly. "We were at a beach in San Diego. My sister, Jocelyn, was with me when a wave hit us. I just remember tumbling under it, sucking in water and sand, and then being pulled further out. I'd come up, hear my parents screaming, and then be thrown under again."

I tried to suppress a shudder, but it rippled through me anyway. "I couldn't see anything in the blackness, and my eyes kept burning. I just remember swallowing what felt like gallons of salt water."

I inhaled reflexively, trying to relieve the pressure settling on my chest. I didn't want to meet Blake's eyes. I knew he'd see terror written all over my face. For whatever reason, my near drowning had marked the beginning of therapy, confusion, and periodic blackouts. It gave way to me being known as the poor crazy Campbell girl, the one who wasn't a model or volleyball player, the one who never quite fit in.

His hand touched my arm, his fingers sliding down until he secured my hand in his. "That sounds horrible. How did you survive?"

With his warm hand wrapped around mine, the crushing heaviness on my chest began to dissipate. I felt like I could breathe again. *I can do this.* I faced him.

"That's the weird part. I thought I'd died. Everything stopped. I was in this strange, black void... I couldn't feel pain or fear... just peace. And then next thing I know, I'm coughing out salt water on the beach. I just remember seeing my dad sobbing over me. My family said it looked like I'd swam to the surface somehow, and then my dad had grabbed me and swam me to shore. So I don't know. One minute I'm dead, the next I'm okay."

"You don't remember swimming up though," he asked, his brow furrowed.

"No, but I could've sworn…"

"What?"

"Nothing."

"Come on, Sam, tell me. You can trust me." His tone was eager. His warmth radiated up my arm, tempting me to move closer.

"K, don't laugh though. It felt like someone was with me. I didn't feel alone."

He grinned. "Maybe it was your guardian angel." I slugged his shoulder, and his eyes flew open wide. "What did you do that for?"

"You're making fun of me." At least, I thought he was. I didn't know how to take this suddenly serious Blake.

He pulled me close to him, his free hand sweeping the hair from my face. His fingers lingered near my jaw, sending goose bumps shooting across my skin. "No, Sam. I'm not."

His gaze darted between my eyes and then down at my lips. The uncertainty in them left me reeling. *Is he going to kiss me?* My heart squeezed, and my breath caught in my throat. I felt my body gravitate toward him. *Oh gosh, I'm the one leaning in…* I couldn't stop the pull I felt toward him. My neck turned up, my lips parting. His breath tickled my face.

"Sammy, baby!" a voice boomed out in the distance.

Blake's head snapped back and I rocked unevenly forward, realizing how close we had been to kissing. Embarrassed yet disappointed, I searched the bridge, spying the source of the call, although I already knew who it was. Mack.

"Impeccable timing, Mack," Blake muttered. I peeked over at him. *Wonder if he wants to kill Mack right now too.*

Mack jogged over. I could've sworn his grin faltered a second when he saw Blake's hand on mine, but then he laughed loudly. "Wow. Fancy meeting you two here, of all places."

"Yeah, fancy that," Blake said dryly, but I didn't miss the smile spreading on Blake's face and I relaxed. It was such a relief; Jeremy would be spitting bullets right now if Mack had appeared.

"Hey Mack, what's up?" I asked, wondering what he was doing wandering up here by himself anyway.

"Oh you know, off saving the world, same old same old. How about you two?"

I grinned at him. "We were just debating if we should jump." *Or kiss.*

"Brrr," Mack replied, shaking his shoulders. "No thanks, there are parts of me that don't like turning blue."

Blake chuckled, and I rolled my eyes at both of them.

Mack turned to Blake, his lips twitching. "An *old* friend's back."

Blake visibly started, but then his face went blank. "Oh really?"

Mack nodded. "Saw him today."

I looked to Mack and then Blake for answers.

"Who are you talking about?" I asked. I didn't miss the boys' swift glance to each other. Suddenly irritated that *my* childhood friend, Mack, kept secrets with Blake, I turned on him.

"Come on, you have to tell me, now that you brought it up," I complained, fearing I sounded like a whiny baby.

Mack squinted. "Kory. You probably don't remember him."

I racked my brain. *Kory? Oh yeah...* "The guy Jen had a crush on?" I asked.

Mack flinched, and I felt bad because I knew he liked her. "Yeah, that guy."

What's Kory have to do with this? I racked my brain to remember what I knew of him. We went to the same elementary school until they discovered he had cancer. Our school had done a huge fundraiser to help pay for some new cancer treatment he was going to get, and then his family moved away. Years later, he'd showed up in middle school. I probably wouldn't have even realized who he was except for the fact that Jen was obsessed with him from eighth grade on.

"Didn't he move away when we were sophomores?" I asked.

"Yeah," Blake answered, instead of Mack. *How would he know? He didn't live here.*

I turned to ask when I noticed Blake's jaw clench as his eyes narrowed. He stared out over the bridge.

Swallowing back my question, I glanced at Mack. "So what? He's moved back *again?*"

Mack cocked his head to the side. "Yep. Maybe it's time to get reacquainted. Huh, Blake?"

"Yes." The word came out flat, lifeless. Blake glanced at me, his face softening. "Sam, I'm sorry, but I think we better head back. I have... a few things to do before I leave."

The drive back was quiet; I slumped in my seat, the pain of disappointment smarting. I had hoped this outing would have a very different outcome. But since Mack's announcement, Blake had turned quiet, almost moody. He seemed a thousand miles away, not right next to me.

I cleared my throat. "So, are you going to tell me what you're thinking about?"

His eyes widened, as if remembering I was there. "Oh, sorry, zoned out there."

I hiked my shoulders up. "So... how do you know Kory and why do I get the feeling you don't like him much?"

He sighed heavily. "Kory used to live in California. Let's just say the last time we saw each other, it didn't end well."

I wanted more, but I had a hunch Blake wouldn't expand. Instead, he said, "Sam, can you promise me something while I'm gone?"

I folded my arms across my chest, tempted to say 'no' to whatever he was about to ask. *Why's he keeping secrets from me?* Then realization seeped in; wasn't I doing the same thing by not telling him about my wings?

"Okay, sure," I muttered.

"I know you love to go biking and running but while I'm gone, can you be *extra* cautious? In fact, I don't think you and Anna should go on that ride anymore."

"Wait, what? Why not? I promised her we'd go. What's going on, Blake?"

"Nothing, nothing's going on."

"Yeah, right…" I glanced at him, and my words faded. He reminded me of a first time snow driver; shoulders stiff, hands white knuckling the steering wheel, and eyes flickering to the rearview mirror repeatedly. Apprehension replaced my frustration. *Are we being followed?*

I stared at him. "What's wrong, Blake?"

His eyes met mine briefly, and then flashed back to the road. "Nothing, just promise me, okay?"

I had a horrible, sinking sensation in my gut. "Okay, fine. I promise I'll be careful, but I'm not backing out on Anna."

He glanced my way and then sighed. "Always the stubborn one… I see why you two get along so well." He grinned. "I'd never hear the end of it from Anna if you don't go, so on second thought, keep that date."

"Haha."

"But stay away from Jeremy," he added. His light tone let me know it wasn't my safety he was worried about—he just couldn't stand the guy.

"No worries there. Let's just say Jeremy and I have an *understanding* too."

"Oh really?" Blake's eyes danced back at me. "Best news I've heard all day. Spill it, and don't spare the details, especially the parts where you told him what a moron he is."

Relieved to see Blake's playful side, I told him everything, poor Jeremy becoming the brunt of all our jokes.

After Blake had dropped me off and I climbed the steps to my bedroom, the weight of the afternoon hung on me like a noose. It started with the nagging suspicion that someone had been watching me outside Blake's house, and that maybe he wasn't that far off telling me to be careful.

CHAPTER
Sixteen

"Samantha, your hair looks so dang cute!" Anna said for like the fifth time that afternoon.

I grinned back at her. "Thanks, Anna." Taking a swig from my water bottle, I scanned the area. We'd stopped riding for a minute, both of us sitting next to our bikes. I felt bad postponing Anna's ride until Tuesday, but I'd decided after Blake left that I needed to fix my roots. They were quite the eyesore. My mom had been beside herself with joy, and Monday became Campbell girls' pampering day. Even my sisters joined us. By the end of hair appointments, shopping, and pedicures, riding was out of the question. *No wonder my dad hates clothes shopping—it's exhausting!* Still, I had to admit I enjoyed my hair being back to its natural sandy blonde and my clothes fitting my shape again.

"Check out that view," I gasped, the valley below us bursting with the last of autumn's colors. In a few more days, this would all turn a muted brown.

"Wow! That's gorgeous," Anna agreed. "So much better than anything we had in Anaheim."

The mention of California got me thinking about Blake, which wasn't too hard to do anyway. My heart squeezed painfully. I missed him more than I wanted to admit to myself. "I bet you miss the beach though, right?"

Anna nodded. "Yeah, I do. One day I'm swimming with my friends and the next, we are packing up to move here."

"Sounds pretty sudden."

"Yeah. My dad's been with the same company for years and out of the blue, he gets this huge promotion. Within days, our house is up for sale and I'm telling my friends goodbye."

"That's got to be tough. Bet Blake didn't want to go. Being the football player and all, he probably left a lot of girlfriends behind." *Like maybe Kate?* I prayed Anna would take my bait. Anna cocked her head to the side. "Blake didn't really have a girlfriend, actually, but there were lots of girls who kept trying to be."

Not exactly a comforting thought. "Was Kate one of those girls? Sorry, you mentioned her before. I'm just curious." I hated pumping information out of Blake's little sister, but I had to know. *I'm so pathetic.*

"Yeah, she used to come over all the time, so we sort of became friends. Kate told me they'd kissed once, but then nothing else happened. Pretty sure she wanted to be more than friends. I just assumed Blake told her he wasn't interested because she stopped coming around."

Did Blake change his mind about Kate? Was that why he hurried home? I glanced over at Anna. *Wonder what she thinks of Blake and me? That we're just friends too?*

"I can tell Blake likes you way better, Samantha," Anna said, as if she'd read my mind.

I couldn't help but grin. "Oh really? And how do you know that?"

"He talks about you."

I was unconvinced. "So, he talks about me more than Kate?"

"No, he *talks* about you. He never talked about anyone to me, especially girls. I only knew about Kate because she hung out with me, but Blake told me all about you before I'd even met you."

"Oh." I wasn't entirely sure what Blake had told her and decided to play it safe. "Well, that's good."

Anna's eyebrows shot up and down. "Why? Do you *like him* like him?"

Oh boy, this is what I get for unleashing a fourteen-year-old girl's inner gossip! I tried to backpedal quickly.

"I do like your brother. I'm not exactly sure what we are, but that's our little secret, okay?" I didn't really wait for her response. I could tell she wanted to know more, so I asked, "Hey Anna, you knew a lot of Blake's friends, right? Did you ever meet Kory?"

That sidetracked her. "Huh, no, I don't think so... but Blake did have a lot of friends. Why?"

I decided to be truthful. "No reason, really. I just knew Kory from school, and Blake said they went way back. He didn't seem to like him much."

Now Anna appeared puzzled. "It takes a lot for Blake not to like someone. Kory must be a weasel."

I chuckled. "I guess. I only ever felt bad for him. He had leukemia when he was a kid, but he got better. He seemed nice enough though."

"Oh, well, maybe that's how Blake knows him. I bet they went to the same place."

I stared at Anna. "What do you mean?"

Anna hesitated, clearly debating something in her mind. Then she leaned closer. "If I tell you, promise you won't say anything to Blake, kay? For some reason, he gets all weird about it. Doesn't want anyone to know or something, but you'd think if you were cured of cancer, you'd tell everybody, right? I mean, what's the shame in that?"

"Cancer?" I cut in, "Blake had cancer?"

"Yep, leukemia. They did radiation and chemo. It went into remission for a while, but it came back. I think he was six or seven. He almost died. I don't really remember it all because I was three, but I guess during it all, Jaxon wouldn't leave his side. The only memory I have of it all was Jaxon's girlfriend playing with me while he tried to help Blake. I just remember thinking she was the most beautiful girl I'd ever seen... but Jaxon stopped dating her about the time Blake got better."

Not interested in Jaxon's love life, my mind mulled over what she'd told me. Blake had almost died when he was little too? "How did he get better?"

"My parents took him to this really expensive cancer clinic in Santa Barbara, a couple of hours away from our home. Jaxon drove him for all his treatments. That's probably why Jaxon wanted to be a doctor, come to think of it. Anyway, after Blake got better, they'd take off camping a lot. So I guess," Anna conceded, "I can understand why my parents let him do whatever he wants. He beat out death."

We decided to head back a few minutes later, the ride back to the truck quiet. Anna concentrated hard on the downhill scaling, trying to keep up with me. I made sure I slowed frequently, calling out commands to help her. It wasn't too steep. At least, I *hoped*. I couldn't shake the image of an imaginary Kate kissing Blake. I knew Anna thought Blake liked me more, but how much did Anna really know? I could only assume Blake and Kory had met at that cancer treatment place in Santa Barbara. Why had things ended badly for them? They had both obviously been cured. What could be worse than having cancer?

CHAPTER
Seventeen

hy am I so uncomfortable? I tried to turn over in my bed but something hard pushed back, coming between my mattress and me. I grunted, rubbing my eyes. Seeing my dark room, I wondered what time it was when I felt an undeniable shuddering on my back. I bolted up, gasping. *No, no, no! Oh, please no!*

Even in my dimly lit room, I could make out my reflection in my mirror. Long, blonde hair, a silky, blue dress, and yes, two iridescent wings. I groaned. I'd hoped beyond hope my wings would never reappear. It would make my life so simple and easy.

Okay... moment of truth; I need to show my parents.

I stood up with that objective, but wandered to my window instead. Pressing my palms against it, my breath fogged up the glass. The desire to tug it open and take flight made me lightheaded. *This makes no sense.* Then, like living a dream, my fingers unlatched the lock and pulled the window up. There was no screen. I'd pushed that out long ago when I was seven and determined to climb down the oak tree banging against my window. The long branches reached out to me, almost asking me to climb aboard. I stepped up onto the windowsill, my toes gripping at its narrow surface. Crouching, I peered down. I no longer needed those branches.

Somewhere in my mind, Blake's promise tugged at me, but I'd never felt such a need in my life. Something urged me to jump off. Pinching my eyes shut, I inhaled and flexed the muscles between my shoulder blades. My wings sung back at me, a blur of motion. They were excited. I stretched my arms out. *Will anyone see me? It is dark...*

but still?

Then I didn't care if they did. I needed this, as bad as I needed the air in my lungs. I plunged forward, confident my wings would carry me. I allowed a free dive until I was feet from the ground, and then I doubled back, shooting straight up into the sky. My house disappeared in the dark trees surrounding it, as I soared higher and higher.

Something nagged at me. I focused on the sensation. *It's like a strange yearning... to what though? East, I need to go east.*

The speed at which I shot across the sky made me feel giddy; all my senses in overdrive. The smells from the woods below greeted me, welcoming and familiar. The whistle of the air, as I effortlessly sliced through it, hummed in my ears. I was crossing over a small mountain range; I'd be there soon. Passing the last, green knoll, I saw it. Lemon Reservoir, the closest body of water by my house. Suddenly, I felt anxious, like I couldn't get to the water fast enough.

The reservoir was long and skinny, perhaps four miles long and only a half a mile wide. Slowing my speed, I skimmed over the beach. The water line was lower, being late fall. Though the water was dark, almost black, with small ripples from the breeze, I found it beautiful.

Intrigued, I plummeted closer to the reservoir's surface. Then realizing what I'd been craving, I dropped both arms down, letting them cut through the water as I flew across. An assault of cold droplets splashed my face and chest, but it only made me want more. Reaching the beach on the other side, I doubled back. This time, I didn't stop with my arms. I plunged my entire body into the water. Submerged, I opened my eyes. Where was the paralyzing terror? I felt only exhilaration. Somehow, I was still moving, gliding under the water. My lungs didn't burn as I held my breath. Nothing made sense. None of this should be possible! I burst through the surface and shot back into the air, gulping in oxygen.

I glanced over, worried my wings might be damaged now that they were drenched. Didn't butterflies die when theirs got wet? All four iridescent wings buzzed back at me, their movement fluid. I hovered a moment, staring at them in wonder, and then I shot up, twirling in tight circles. *I'm so in trouble.* The adrenaline, the rush, coursed through my veins like a wicked drug, and I knew I was addicted.

I stopped and glanced down at the reservoir. *Again!*

I nosedived, my childhood nightmare forgotten. I didn't fear the water—I *needed* it. My face hit first, the shock of icy water on my skin thrilling. I dipped in and out of the water, soaring like a bug skimming the top to drink. My long, wet hair clung to my naked skin and drenched dress. Logically, I knew I should be shaking with chill. It was autumn and in the middle of the night. The forest surrounding the water's edge was on its last weeks of life, leaves fluttering to the ground in lifeless clumps.

I should be freezing, but I'm not. And I've never felt happier.

I zigzagged across the water's surface and each time I reached the shore, I'd double back to be near the dark water. I wished I could do this all night, but I knew at some point I needed to fly home. *Who knows how long my wings will last?* I skidded to halt, hovering, and stared at the blackened shoreline. The trees cast deep shadows from the half of a moon in the sky.

That was when I felt it—an overwhelming sensation that I wasn't alone. I heard an inhale at the same time I caught a new scent in the air. With all my reckless diving, I'd overlooked it. It assaulted me now, demanding my attention. *Musky with a mix of something… mint?*

I strained my ears, trying to pick out the new sounds I was noticing. Insects, lots of them, in a chorus of thrumming night sounds, and then an exhale, like someone had been holding their breath. I cocked my head to the side; there it was again. Someone was breathing, slowly, deliberately. I scanned the trees. Somewhere in its vastness, someone or something was hiding. I squinted, willing my superhuman vision to return, but it seemed my hearing and sense of smell were the only things going crazy now. I sniffed at the cold air, reminding myself of Blake's dog. What did it mean? *Do I smell someone's scent?*

As my skin crawled with goose bumps, I remained frozen, the water inches below my toes. I should fly, get out of here... what was I waiting for?

When a branch bounced and the leaves shuddered, something took over me. Instead of fleeing, I shot straight forward, determined to know who or what was out there. At first, I saw nothing and then for one split second, a silhouette formed before me. I was right! *Someone is there!*

The figure shot up the side of a tree, snapping the branches as it went. As soon as the person cleared the top of the foliage, I saw wings. *Someone like me!* There was no time to second-guess myself. I pushed hard after the shadowed person, too dark to tell if it was male or female. The speed he or she flew at made it obvious they didn't want to be caught.

"Wait! Please!" I screamed, but they only flew faster.

I dug deep, giving my wings everything I had. The gap began to close between us. I plodded on, finally making out details. *Jeans, T-shirt, broad shoulders, and short, dark hair. It's a guy.*

Then he shot forward with a sudden burst that left me painfully behind. I struggled for a few more seconds, gulping at the air like a fish out of water, but his figure rapidly shrunk away. Suddenly, he was completely gone. I stared at the space where he had been.

Crap! He got away.

I sucked in air and redirected myself to head home.

Who was he? *What* was he? *One thing I know for sure now, I'm not alone. There are others like me.* Plagued with questions, I tried to ignore the exhaustion settling into my bones, managing to get myself back in through my bedroom window. I practically crawled across my floor. Still sopping wet, I tugged my blankets down off my bed and rolled up into them.

Okay. If the wings are here when I wake up, I'll have to tell my family. But if they aren't... well... I'm finding out what the heck I am first.

There was no reason for me to hit national news if there were other winged people out there, right? Besides, part of me wondered if the shots in the cabin had more to do with this than I'd thought before. There had to be a reasonable explanation for all of this, and I was going to find it.

CHAPTER
Eighteen

"**S**amantha, are you asleep?" Jen asked.

My head jerked up, my eyes popping open. Apparently, I had been. Jen sat across from me at the lunch table.

"What? Oh sorry, yeah... I didn't get much sleep last night." It'd been a long week already. With missing Blake more than I cared to admit and then last night's activities, I felt completely drained. To my delight, I'd awoken in the morning to a bare, wingless back. *Gives me at least one more day to figure this out.*

Jen's eyes sized me up. "Are you feeling okay? You look awful."

"Gee thanks." *If you only knew, Jen.*

"Sammy, you know I don't mean it that way," Jen protested.

"Yeah, I know," I assured her. "I'm fine, just tired. That's all."

"Well, talking about my pathetic love life probably put you to sleep," Jen said balefully.

She was taking Blake's rejection hard. I felt bad, but psychoanalyzing why he didn't like her was torture for me. Usually, I would reassure her that the guy was a jerk anyway and she was better off, but I couldn't bring myself to do it this time.

"Are you feeling bad about Blake?" I asked, cringing over my own words.

"Blake? No, I was telling you about Kory."

All sleepiness was forgotten. "Kory?"

"Yeah, you remember him, right? He'd moved away and then all of sudden, he's back again. And he looks so good, Samantha!"

"Wait, you've seen him?"

9

"Yes! That's what I was about to tell you about when you dozed off on me."

"I'm awake now, tell me." I hoped I didn't sound too eager. I just knew Kory's arrival had to do with Blake's abrupt departure. I wasn't sure how though.

"Well… yesterday after school, I went over to Mack's house."

I stared at Jen. To my knowledge, she didn't usually do that. *I'm sure that made Mack's day.*

Jen flushed. "I wanted to ask him about Blake. I know they're friends now."

Oh, that's why. I nodded for her to continue.

"Anyway, I got there and didn't know Mack had some guys over. So I walk in the living room and there's Kory! I about had a heart attack. I'm sure my face went red."

Kory was at Mack's house? "Really? Who else was there?"

Jen waved her hand impatiently. "I didn't recognize the other two guys, I only knew Kory. Oh Samantha, he's always been cute, but now… he's freaking hot! It was a complete nightmare! He hardly even acknowledged me!"

"Jen, I'm so sorry. That totally sucks."

"It's fine. He was all worked up about something. Honestly, I don't think he even remembered me anyway. He's changed so much." She paused. "One thing's for sure… he doesn't like Blake at all."

I swallowed hard. "How do you know that?"

"That's what I wanted to tell you about because it was all so weird! So as soon as I got there, it was obvious Mack wanted them to all leave. He sort of hinted that he wanted to be with me alone."

I tried not to smile. Of course Mack wanted to have Jen all to himself.

Jen continued. "So Kory was like sure, whatever, and then walks up to Mack saying, 'Blake better stop being so naïve and stupid. I've warned him, this threat's real.'"

Jen paused, and I asked, "What did he mean?"

"I have no idea but one of the other guys starts laughing, saying something about Blake thinking he owns Tonbo Island, but things are changing."

"Tonbo?" was all I could think to ask.

"Yeah, weird right? Kory told Mack, Blake can run to Tonbo for answers, but he'll only get more lies. That's when Mack got all serious, which is so odd for him, you know. He just said, 'Got it, Kory. You better go.' Then they all stared at me. That was when Kory all of sudden smiled at me and said he'd see me around. Then to Mack, he said something like, 'Consider it a warning. We've got a bug problem.'"

She sighed heavily and then scrunched up her eyebrows. "Why are boys so confusing? Do you think Kory really wants to see me again?"

I stammered, "Oh… uh… yeah, probably. Maybe you will." Wondering if Kory actually liked Jen was definitely the least of my quandaries. *What in the world did all that mean? Threats? Bug problem?* I was sure Kory had everything to do with Blake taking off. Now I just had to unravel the rest of the puzzle. *Starting with—what is Tonbo Island?*

⁂

"Argh…" I growled at my laptop. What I'd hoped would be an easy Google search turned into a frustrating half hour of wading through useless information.

Finding nothing under 'Tonbo,' I tried Tombo. According to Wikipedia, it was a small island off the tip of Guinea. Not great at geography, I'd typed that in next: a country in West Africa. *What does Blake have to do with West Africa?* My hunch said nothing.

I'd even tried the word Tonbo by itself. The way Kory's friend had talked about it, it sounded like Tonbo might be a person. That had led to Japanese cartoon characters. Sitting on my bed, I stared at my keyboard. Nothing was fitting together. I continued to scroll through the Tonbo choices. A website popped at me.

"Tonbo-Dragonfly-Japanese Art," I read aloud. Curious, I clicked on it. The first thing I learned was the word *tonbo* meant dragonfly in Japanese. *Well, that's interesting. Not very helpful, though.*

I scanned through the Japanese writings anyway, desperate to make some kind of connection. The calligraphy was foreign but beautiful. Realizing I didn't know what any of it meant, I decided on a new tactic.

I typed in *dragonflies*. Page after page depicted the winged insect in all its variations, colors, and forms. Studying the iridescent wings, I felt a tingle in the middle of my back. They were similar to what my wings had looked like. *Could it be possible?*

I closed my eyes, willing those muscles to work, longing to feel the freedom it brought. Nothing. I opened my eyes. Still just me—painfully human. Just as well. What would I have done if I had transformed? We'd just had dinner and my parents thought I was doing homework. *Not a good idea to be flying around my room when my mom comes to check on me.*

I glanced back down at the screen; one line caught my eye. '*Symbolism of the dragonfly.*' I opened the page and read. Five minutes later, I sat back, eyes wide. The article spoke of the agility of the dragonfly's wings, the power in its stroke, the strength in its form, the incredible speed in flight, its affinity for water and ability to be one with it, and the incredible eyesight…

Hadn't I felt all those things flying? I thought of my four wings; they appeared to be wispy, yet I knew them to be firm and tenacious in flight. I stared at the images of dragonfly wings. Deciding to try one more search, I typed in five letters: fairy. *Maybe there was some kind of mythical dragonfly fairy.*

Magical winged creatures, mostly female, filled my screen. From dark and sinister to cute and cartoon; there was a wide range of fairy classifications and art. After searching through the different wings—short and pointy, draping and long, birdlike with feathers, butterfly-esque, I finally found one that resembled mine.

Red locks flowed down her back and four insect-like wings emerged from her back. The caption under the photo said, 'Long Lady, Dragonfly Fairy.'

So what am I? Some sort of dragonfly fairy? What does that even mean... that fairies are real?

I spent another twenty minutes or so reading about Fairy, or Fae, folklore and legends. They were often mischievous, causing mayhem for humans, and had mystical abilities and magic. As for humans suddenly becoming a fairy, the only thing I could find was the lore of fairies switching their babies out for human ones. The person grew up thinking they were normal until one day they realized they were different. Then they discovered they were really a fairy and their parents weren't really their mom and dad.

Thinking how my sisters and I all had the same brown eyes, I sort of doubted that was what happened to me. *Unless we're all fairies.* I laughed aloud. *This is ridiculous! I need answers.* Only problem was, I had no idea where to get them.

CHAPTER
Nineteen

ightmares plagued my sleep that night and finally, after what felt like hours of restless stirring, I opened my eyes. I peeked at the clock on my dresser. Three fifteen. Rubbing my fingers across my face, I froze. I sniffed at the air; it was cold with a hint of mint... a musky mint.

I'm not alone.

Lying on my back, I debated my options. I could scream. I could try to make a run for it. Something nagged at me and then it hit; I should be terrified right now. If someone was in my room, shouldn't I be scared? Instead, I felt nothing but curiosity. I knew that scent. *It's the same person who watched me the night before.*

He could have chased me then instead of fleeing, or even attacked me now in my sleep. *He's not malicious*, at least I hoped. So that left another option— maybe he could tell me what I was. After all, he was one too, right?

Even though I'd reasoned away my fears, my hands shook as I pushed the covers back and sat up. In that split second, I could've sworn something shifted in one corner of my bedroom. Staring at that space, I saw nothing but my dresser.

Great, now what? I inhaled slowly. *Yep, he's totally here... So, what, he's invisible?*

I tossed my covers aside and this time, I saw something jump, almost like someone wore my bedroom as camouflage and when they moved, it shifted to disguise my visitor, but not fast enough. That split second was long enough for me to make out a form, crouched down in the corner. I wasn't feeling so confident anymore.

I swallowed hard and cleared my throat. "I know you're here, so you might as well stop trying to hide." I wished my voice hadn't quivered, but it had.

I heard a gasp across the room. Apparently, he didn't know he'd been discovered. He chuckled as I deciphered the figure standing up and then just like that, my visitor appeared.

Now, I gasped. "Kory?" I instinctively grabbed my blanket back to cover myself.

Dressed in jeans and a dark green T-shirt, he was taller and broader than the last time I'd seen him, but that was over two years ago. He gazed back at me, his black hair slicked back, looking wet. Then I noticed what fell down at his sides—long wings. As if feeling my prying eyes, his wings flickered.

"I knew you were special, but I had no idea how sharp your senses were," he said.

I gaped at him, trying to formulate my first question. He remained planted in front of me, his hands clasped together. Then he cocked an eyebrow at me.

"So, now what? Are you going to scream for Mommy and Daddy?"

My back went rigid. Even if I wanted to, I wasn't about to let him know that. How dare he act all cocky when he was the one who broke into my bedroom? *I have every right to be freaked out right now! What's he doing in here anyway? Watching me sleep?* I shuddered.

"No," I spat, "now you tell me what the heck you're doing in my room!"

Kory grinned. "I'm sorry; do you want me to leave?"

I bit my lip, debating, I really wanted him gone, but I wanted answers more.

He took my hesitation as an answer and flew toward my window. *Crap!* "Wait!" I called out, decision made. "Don't go."

He chuckled and faced me. "This so much fun, Samantha. Or do you prefer Sammy?"

"I don't care what you call me; I just want to know what's happening to me. What are we? Some kind of fairy?"

Kory cringed. "I hate that freaking word."

"What... fairy?"

"*Yes!* Do I look like Tinker Bell to you?"

I bit my tongue, the temptation to say yes overwhelming. *But this isn't Blake or Mack.* I didn't know how Kory would react.

"Okay, so if we aren't fairies, what are we then?" I asked.

"All right, Sammy. I'll make you a deal. I answer your questions and then you answer mine."

I couldn't imagine what he could want to ask me, since I knew nothing of this strange new world, but said, "Fine."

"We are Dragon Fae."

"Fae? Isn't that just another word for fairy?" I asked, remembering what I'd read on the computer.

"Oh, aren't you the little expert?" Kory said sarcastically. "No dragon wants to be called a fairy, except maybe Blake."

Blake? What does he have to do with this? I didn't ask, worried Kory might clam up since he didn't seem to care for Blake.

"What do you mean dragon?" I asked, hoping to keep Kory talking.

"Mm... I was sure you at least made *that* connection. Man, maybe you need more help than I thought." Kory sighed and then proceeded to sit at the end of my bed. I eyed him warily.

"Haven't you noticed our wings look like dragonflies?" he asked.

Maybe I wasn't so far off after all. "Okay, so what does that mean, that we're some kind of dragonfly mutants or something?"

He grinned. "In a nutshell, pretty much." He pointed at his chest. "I'm a dragon," he pointed at me, "you're a damsel."

I stared at him. It sounded so absurd. "So when you say dragon, you don't mean big, old, flying reptile, right?" I just had to make sure.

"What? No. That's just the name for male Dragon Fae. It's easier to just say dragon. And since damsel is the name of a female dragonfly, that's what Tonbo decided to call the girls."

"So you're saying we're *literally* part bug now?" As much as I hated to admit it, part of what he said made sense. "How's any of this even possible?"

He brown eyes grew dark as he scowled. "I'll let your *boyfriend* explain *that* to you. He should've been the one telling you all this in the first place, not me."

"What are you talking about? I don't have a boyfriend." My mouth tasted sour from the acid creeping up my throat. I wasn't sure I wanted to hear his answer.

Kory crossed his arms. "Damn Blake for being such a coward. He's a stupid fool for believing Tonbo in the first place."

He glared at me. "Then he has the gall to do *this*."

My tongue felt sluggish as I formed the words, my ears ringing. "I don't know what you're talking about."

His voice was low, his eyes like steel. "Put the pieces together, Samantha. You were given shots in the cabin, and now you're a damsel. Don't you see it?"

My fingers and toes felt numb.

"That's why I'm like this... all those injections... that person changed me," I murmured. I'd been right, it *had* all stemmed from my abduction, but my mind refused to see how Blake was connected to it all.

He snorted. "Blake and I got our shots at the cancer clinic; that's what cured us of cancer. We didn't know then we were different. We sort of figured that out later. Blake's like us, Samantha. He's a dragon."

I could only gape back at him. *It can't be true! Can it?*

"Don't you think it's odd that Blake shows up right after you'd been changed?" he asked.

I shook my head, refusing to believe Kory's words. "No, it couldn't have been him. He was in California while I was in..." My words faded as Anna's words filled my mind. 'Did I tell you he got to go camping for like three weeks before we moved here? Three weeks? My mom freaks when I miss like two days of school, so unfair.'

Camping? Blake could have been anywhere during that time, including here. My stomach sickened. *No... I don't believe it. It doesn't feel right.* Then it hit me. *Because I love him. I don't want it be real. I yearn for the monster who created me. Just like he promised I would.*

My hand flew to my mouth as I gasped.

Kory nodded. "Finally seeing it, aren't you?"

"Why?" I whispered. "Why would he do this to me?"

"Ah, now that's my question for you. Blake despises who we are. That's why we don't *exactly* get along. He thinks we should be ashamed of what we've become, hide it from the world. I, on the other hand, see only our limitless potential. It cured me of cancer. The blend of dragonfly DNA with humans has revolutionized life as we know it. We are invincible. We can't get sick, and we live for a very long time. Why stifle that?"

I stared at him, hardly comprehending his words. All I could see was Blake's crooked smile and aqua eyes, all I could feel were his arms around me while we'd danced. My fingers touched my lips, remembering how close we'd come to kissing on the bridge. *And all along, he knew what I was, what he'd made me become. It's all been lies. I'm just some kind of freaky game to him!* My eyes welled, and I steeled myself inwardly. *No tears, not now. Get answers from Kory and then get him out of here.*

"What's Tonbo Island?" I asked firmly, trying to keep my voice steady, the lump in my throat making it difficult.

Kory cocked his head to the side, considering me for a moment, than with a long sigh, he ran his hands down his thighs. To my surprise, he offered me a smile, his eyes softening.

"You know, Samantha, I feel sort of bad for you. You didn't deserve any of this. This isn't your war. Sorry you got caught in the middle of it."

For some reason, his words stung and the threat of tears overwhelmed me. "What war? Who's Tonbo?"

"Okay. You deserve the truth. Tonbo's our creator, the mad scientist behind it all, if you will. Tonbo Island is his. That's where most of the Dragon Fae live, those who can't morph back. You see, some of his earlier creations weren't as advanced as we are. They're stuck as dragons or damsels. As you can imagine, they make quite the spectacle."

"Why don't they just become invisible like you were?"

"The camo? Yeah, that came much later too. Speaking of which, stop flying around without it."

I thought of the lake and him watching me. "So that was you at the reservoir."

"Yeah. I decided to let you see me for a bit, before I camo'ed out. I wanted you to know you weren't alone."

Oh, how sweet, I wanted to say sarcastically. Somehow, I didn't quite think that was his real motive. "I don't know how to do the camo. I don't know how to do any of this. I can't even control when I become a... damsel. It just happens sometimes."

Kory's gaze held steady as I watched his wings disappear. Then without shifting his position, they reappeared.

"It's not hard," he said.

"Sure, you make it look so easy," I muttered.

"Just relax. Think about how it feels to flex those muscles. You're fighting it. Give in to it. I know you feel the pull to change. It's who you are now. You need to let yourself transform."

I wasn't sure why I was going along with what he was suggesting. I didn't trust him. Sighing, I closed my eyes. With an inhale, I focused on the muscles between my shoulder blades. I felt the tingle, and then a strange craving filled my stomach. I'd felt it before, when I wanted to get to water. I let myself fall into it, letting it wash over me. I exhaled and opened my eyes.

Kory grinned back at me. My wings draped down my back, touching my bed, and my cotton nightgown remained. "I don't understand," I whispered, touching the side of my head. "My hair's short."

Kory arched an eyebrow at me. "That's what scissors do."

"No, it's usually long and I'm wearing this blue gown."

"Oh yeah, I sort of wondered about that the other night. You must have gotten a new blend. Usually, you can't alter your appearance, like clothes and hair and stuff."

Another conversation played into my mind, the words of the monster. *'Trust me, this is for your own good. And this one is a special blend. I made it myself.'*

"He did this," I mumbled.

"Who, Blake? Yeah, I told you he did."

I flinched and then redirected to Kory. I couldn't think about Blake. I just couldn't.

"If you're really looking out for me, why didn't you just talk to me the other night?"

"I wasn't sure how much was true or not. I had to see for myself. Sorry, I should have then."

"What do you mean?"

"I haven't seen Blake for a long time, but it's no secret you're his pet. He's been checking on you for years, ever since the clinic."

"But he lived in California—" My ears were ringing, my stomach feeling ill.

"Ha! Do you know how long it takes to fly here? Like two hours. Coming here was no big deal. He watched you, Samantha— everything you did. Everyone knew about it at the island. Blake wouldn't be with any damsel, not even Kate. Poor thing. He changed her and then wanted nothing to do with her."

I felt nauseous, swallowing the bile at the back of my throat. *This can't all be true!* And yet, pieces to a puzzle were fitting together a little too easily. Anna's words about Blake camping almost every weekend were all just covers to come see me. And Kate, a girl who wanted more from Blake than just friendship.

"Then one day, there are rumors all over the island that the *one* girl Blake coveted was missing and then weeks later, dragons report seeing her flying in the woods."

I racked my brains. *When did I do that? Oh, that first night. I'd thought I'd been dreaming… I met Blake the next morning.*

"I had to come see if it was all true," Kory said. "Blake conveniently forgot he despised changing people long enough to change you, the one thing he wanted. *Bloody hypocrite.*"

I hadn't realized I'd moved until I shoved Kory to the floor. Something inside me had snapped; I wanted him off my bed, far away from me.

"Shut up! Just shut up!" I commanded in a hiss, flying into his chest.

He shot up into the air and grabbed my arms.

"Listen Samantha, I'm not the bad guy here. I'm sorry you fell for Blake, I really am. But you need to know the truth. If Blake won't tell you, then I will."

"Why do me any favors? You hate Blake. You probably hate me too," I said through clenched teeth. I tried to wrestle my hands out from his, but it was no use.

"Because whether any of us like it, we have a lot bigger problem then why Blake changed his puppet—"

"Don't call me that! I'm not his pet or puppet, and he doesn't own me!" I breathed out, wanting to yell, but not wanting to wake my parents. I shoved my weight against him, trying to push him toward my window.

He held his ground, pulling me closer to him. His breath tickled my face, his brown eyes bearing down on me. "Okay fine. All that matters to me is understanding why he did it."

I shook my head at him. "What? Why do you care? This whole thing is a little too X-Men-ish for me."

Kory's grip relaxed, and his grin reached his eyes. "Exactly. And even Magneto and Professor Xavier have to work together sometimes."

I wanted to remind him that Magneto was the psychotic bad guy but instead asked, "What do you mean?"

Kory grunted. "As much as it pains me to admit, I need Blake's help."

I squinted back at him, pulling my arms back. "Let go of me."

"Are you done trying to fight?"

"I don't know, I'm thinking about screaming."

"And let your parents see the real you? Good idea, better yet, let's scream together."

"What happened to the nice Kory I remember?" I asked, realizing with all the noise we'd been making in my room, I was surprised my dad wasn't banging the door in already.

"That kid's long gone. And whether you like it or not, the old you is gone too. Quit fighting who you really are."

"Are you done, Dr. Phil?" I hated his face so close to mine.

He let my arms go and shoved me back. "Quite. I've been here long enough anyway."

He stepped up to the window, his wings expanding out.

Shoot! I think he is leaving this time!

"Wait, Kory," I begged. "I still have more questions!"

He shot me a sly grin. "If you want me to stay, just say the word, Sammy." He opened his arms to me. "I can stay all night if you'd like."

I rolled my eyes at him, ignoring his innuendo. "You never told me why you need Blake's help."

I didn't like how his eyes suddenly swept up and down my body. He cocked his head to the side. "You know, I think I'm finally seeing why Blake likes you so much. You're a confusing hot mess."

I glared at him. "Pretty sure you're the confusing one out of the two of us."

Kory chuckled and then took a step closer to my window. He pressed his hand against the windowpane. "We've got a serious bug problem, Samantha." The playfulness in his voice was gone.

He faced me. "Blake doesn't believe me, but he will. I've

tracked *it* here."

My skin crawled. "*It?* What do you mean, like a dragon, like one of us?"
Kory grunted. "Sort of. Let's just say not all of us are *nice*. We're
hunters by nature."

"What do we hunt? Wait, don't tell me I'm going to start sucking
people's blood!" I was only halfway joking.

"No, we only do that during full moons."

"*What?*"

Kory chuckled. "You *so* need help. We're not vampires. They
don't exist."

I threw my hands up at him. "Thanks for clearing that up. Last I
checked, dragonfly people didn't either."

He leaned closer. "Like I said, we're hunters. We live for the
thrill of the chase. You can't tell me you haven't felt it yet, the need
for speed, to search, catch a scent in the air, and be in the water." His
eyes danced back at me. "Most of us spend our time stalking our prey."

I swallowed. "Scents," I mumbled. The way his eyes raked my
face, I desperately wanted to step back. *Stay strong—don't show fear.*

"We emit a smell, I guess you could say, our own unique
marker. Yours, my dear, is," he inhaled deeply, his face drawing closer,
"intoxicating. You're attracting a lot of attention. So be careful."

"You smell like mint and cologne," I blurted.

His eyes met mine and then he stepped back, laughing. "Could
be worse."

I was relieved he was no longer close. "So if you don't suck
blood, what's all the hunting for? What do you do with your prey
when you catch it?"

"That depends on who caught you. Most of the *civilized* ones just
catch and release, sort of like fishing. Actually, a lot of us fish, gives
the thrill with no harm. Since dragonflies are born and live in the
water for a long time before taking flight, we are drawn to it too."

"I know, I've felt it," I admitted. "So what happens if a bad one
gets you?"

He grunted. "Whatever they want. There are a lot of murders and rapes never explained that are unsolved. Probably our kinds' fault."

"Maybe Blake's right. We shouldn't exist."

"It's because of Blake that we're like this. If we weren't hiding in shame of who we are, we wouldn't have suppressed anger. We could teach and guide those who are different. Look at you. No one's showed you anything, no one's teaching you, and you're stumbling along about to get yourself killed."

I hated that I agreed with Kory. *I did need help. Why didn't Blake say anything? He knew what I am. Why didn't he help me?* Then I remembered the rest of it. *Because it's all a game to him. It's the one big hunting thrill, and I'm just his prey.*

This time I couldn't stop the tears that filled my eyes. They fell freely down my cheeks. Kory broke eye contact and shook his head.

"Listen, Samantha, like I said, you didn't deserve any of this. It's not your fault Blake picked you. I shouldn't have vented my frustrations out on you. But you need to know that there's a hunter here—a *bug*. He's ancient, as old as Tonbo, and he's vicious."

I sniffed. Embarrassed by my tears, I swiped them away. What Kory said scared me. The idea of someone who could fly, track smells, and hunt while invisible to the naked eye was terrifying!

"Why's he here?"

Kory opened my window and peered into the night. "I think he's tracking someone. I'm not sure who yet," he turned to me, "so be careful."

Without another word, he vanished and I barely made out his camouflaged form shoot through the window. I inhaled. The mint was gone; he was gone. *Crud, he didn't show me how to do the camo.*

I walked back to my bed, my wings twitching on my back. The weight of everything crushed down on me. *Blake? It's Blake?* I couldn't seem to get enough air in; the room wouldn't stop spinning. I'd trusted Blake. I'd told him everything. He'd been my hope, what'd pulled me out of my depression, and what made me want to get up in the morning. How could that all be a lie?

How am I going to live without him? My heart squeezed, the crushing pain unbearable. I clambered onto my bed and curled up, hugging my knees tightly. My wings fought the sheets. *Crap, I don't even know how to get rid of these things.*

I tried to relax, to wish them away, but then racking sobs took over. I bit into my pillow as I screamed. *Tonight, I will cry*, I decided, as I gave in to the pain, *but tomorrow, I'm getting answers.*

CHAPTER

Twenty

"Samantha, are you up, hon?"

I rolled over, but my eyes didn't want to open. They felt sealed shut with dried-up tears. I rubbed them gingerly; the lids still felt puffy. My nose refused to breathe.

"Yeah, I'm up," I muttered. My mom walked into my room at the same time I realized I might have wings. When she didn't scream or ask why I was wearing a Halloween costume, I figured I was okay. *Lucky for me, the wings seem to disappear when I fall asleep.*

"Are you just getting up? I thought you'd gotten up hours ago," she said, her eyes summing up my appearance.

I cast a glance at my vanity mirror. The night had not been kind to me at all; my face was splotchy, my eyes puffballs, and my hair a tangled bird's nest.

Mack would love this, I thought, running my fingers through the knots. At the thought of my friend, something dawned on me. Why was Kory at Mack's house in the first place? What did he have to do with all this? Was it just because he and Blake were good friends?

Realizing my mom was waiting for an answer, I said, "Uh... yeah, I sort of slept in, I guess. I didn't feel too good last night." *Thank heavens it's Saturday. Can't imagine going to school today.*

"Well, that explains all the noises in your room. I almost checked on you, sounded like you had a fitful sleep."

I bit my lip and continued running my fingers through my hair.

"Well, are you feeling up to company?" my mom asked.

"Um, I guess."

"Okay, why don't you hop in the shower? I'm sure Blake won't mind waiting ten minutes. He got home last night."

My stomach dropped. *Blake.* I frowned. I should feel terror but instead, a surge of excitement coursed through me. I'd missed him so desperately for days it was like my body had conveniently forgotten about last night's reveal.

Blake's a dragon… a creepy, lying, jerk! And I don't mean anything to him.

I must have nodded because my mom said, "Okay, I'll let him know," and left the room, shutting the door behind her.

My heart squeezed as I tried to embrace the truth. *I've only been a game for him. Like Kory said, I'm his puppet.* Something he wanted to manipulate, chase, hunt… and then catch.

As much as it killed me inside, there was a small corner of my heart that refused to believe it. I'd felt his concern over my welfare, I'd swear it was sincere. *I'm a fool.* Since when was I a good judge in guys? *Look at Jeremy, my one real boyfriend—a total jerk.*

I didn't know how long I sat on my bed, frozen with indecision, when I finally glared at my reflection in the mirror. *Blake thinks he caught me. Well, he doesn't know that I know. And I'm not his prize.* I squared my shoulders as the tears cascaded my cheeks.

I wasn't giving him the satisfaction of knowing I'd fallen for him, that I'd fulfilled his prophecy. What was he going to do then? I tried to ignore Kory's words about 'bad' dragons. I refused to believe Blake could be one of them. I couldn't imagine him hurting anyone… then the image of the squirming kid Blake had effortlessly lifted off the ground with one arm filled my mind. Still, that'd been for me… I groaned. That'd all been a show. Oh, how he must have been laughing inside, reveling in playing the hero!

I can't do this. The tears burst free again. *I can't face Blake. How could he do this to me?* I buried myself in my covers, sobbing into my pillow. So much for telling myself I'd only cry over him last night. A few minutes later, there was a soft knock on my door.

"Samantha?" my mom's voice called through the wood that separated us. "Are you getting in the shower?"

"No. Mom, can you tell Blake I'm too sick to see him today?" I managed to get out, choking back my tears long enough to talk.

There was a pause, and then my mom said softly, "Okay, honey. I will. Get some sleep."

I tried to ignore my phone for the rest of the day. The first few times it whistled at me, the melodic tones letting me know I had a text, I peeked. They were all from Blake. First teasing me for being sick because I'd stayed up all night with Jeremy, then being touched that I'd exhausted myself worrying about his safety while away, then finally wanting to know if everything was okay and asking if he could do anything for me. After that, I turned my phone to silent mode. I couldn't bear him pretending to care for me. Or could it be I couldn't stand that part of me still wanted to believe that he did, that somehow this was all a misunderstanding?

Around dinnertime, my dad popped by my room. I'd religiously stayed in bed, sickness a perfect mask for the depression settling over me. The truth hadn't liberated me from the fear like the therapist had promised; it had sucked the desire to smile, to eat, to laugh, to do anything that required any effort out of me. After I'd gotten the tears under control and my frumpy appearance could easily pass for illness, I'd opened my door up.

So when my dad entered, he came straight to my bed and sat at the end.

"So how you feeling, kiddo? Mom said you're sick today."

I sat up and leaned against my headboard. "Yeah."

He cocked his head to the side. "Stomach bugging you again?"

No, just my broken heart, I wanted to say. "Yeah and I'm achy all over."

"So I'm guessing you don't want dinner then? Maybe some soup?" he asked.

"No, I'm good."

"Mm," he hummed. I knew my dad loved me, but I had the sinking suspicion his concern was over more than my onset of sickness. "So Blake called," he said finally.

I'd been right. "Oh yeah?"

"He's really worried about you. Maybe you could call him," his eyes shot over to my cell phone sitting on my nightstand. The red light flashed back at us, letting everyone know I had messages waiting for me.

Darn, I shouldn't have left it sitting there. By the way my dad's eyebrows rose, I knew he was wondering now why I was ignoring my cell. Even with being sick, sending text messages took little effort.

"Okay I will," I said simply, hoping he wouldn't ask more.

He hesitated and then asked, "Everything going okay for you? You know, since you're back in school and all?"

"Yeah, it's great." My lie was obvious.

"You know you can still tell me *anything*, right?" my dad asked.

"I know. Don't worry, Dad. Everything's fine… really."

"Samantha…" Now his tone sent a shiver of worry through me. Maybe he hadn't come up just to discuss why I was ignoring Blake. "I want to tell you something, but I don't want to scare you or anything. Your mom thinks we shouldn't worry you with it—"

"What is it, Dad?"

"There's been another kidnapping. It happened last night. It's been all over the news today."

I couldn't control the gasp that flew from my lips. I shook my head, trying to regain composure.

"Who was it?" I asked.

"A girl from your school. I don't know if you know her. Cally Jenson?"

I stared back at my dad. I didn't know her *that* well, but a girl with sandy-blonde hair and hazel eyes filled my mind.

"Yeah, I had some classes with her. What happened?" I tried to keep my voice calm and steady. I needed to know every detail, and if my dad saw me go hysterical, he wouldn't say another word.

"They don't know a lot right now. Her parents said she'd left to go to a friend's house last night, but the friend said she never got there, and she never came home. They found her car just off the highway, in the ditch, driver's door open, her purse, money, cell phone, everything still in there, but she's gone." His eyes peered back at me, the pain in them evident, "Listen, I don't want this news to hurt you in anyway, but I feel you need to know… Samantha, your kidnapper might be back."

I was grateful for my dad's honesty. He was right; I needed to know this. The timing of it all wasn't lost on me either. *Blake got home last night… another coincidence?* Part of my heart shouted back at me, *Kory just got here too! It could have been him. Why do I believe Kory over Blake?* As much as I wanted to hope Blake had nothing to do with my abduction, I couldn't understand why he wouldn't have said something to me already. He'd seen me with my wings. *Why lie, why hide?* Too much of what Kory said made sense for me not to doubt Blake, no matter what my heart said.

No one bothered me the rest of the evening, leaving me trapped in my own personal prison. *I'm sure my parents are happy that I'm safely tucked away in my bedroom.* At least they didn't have to worry about me inside the home. My dad would lock every window and door tonight, and probably sleep with his 9mm ready. *Surprised he hasn't stuck one of his guns in my nightstand… just in case.* Though I wasn't proficient with all my dad's firearms, I'd gone shooting with him enough to know I could do a lot of damage.

The funny thing is, if he knew where the bad guy would actually enter the house, he'd make my bedroom firearms headquarters. My window stared back at me as I lay on my bed, almost mocking my situation. I hated that I longed to slide the glass open and take off for the reservoir. *Kory's right—I do crave water now. But it's not safe out there.*

One thing bothered me. Even if Blake was the one taking girls for his own whim and pleasure, Kory had come seeking Blake's help. Which meant one thing—the 'bug' Kory referred to was a bigger threat than what Blake had done to me. *Kory hates Blake, but he is willing to work with him to get rid of the real monster.* I thought of Cally and shuddered. *That poor girl. She must be terrified right now. Does Blake have her tied up to some bed, slurring scary words to her? Or,* my spine tingled, *does the bug have her?* Could it be possible Blake wasn't the kidnapper this time? Perhaps the real hunter had found its prey? *And,* my heart begged, *maybe the bug had something to do with my abduction too, not Blake.*

I turned over, not wanting to see my black windowpanes anymore. I knew it was too early for me to sleep. Having spent the entire day in bed when I wasn't actually ill, I felt restless. Maybe if it were darker in my room, I could relax better. I sat up, snapped my lamp off, and then settled down into my covers.

When I inhaled deeply, I caught the scent, faint, but there. My heart stopped. It wasn't Kory's... it was different, and familiar somehow. I commanded myself to breathe steadily, the scent difficult to pick up. *I don't think he or she is in my room this time.* With Kory, his smell overpowered me. This time, it was barely discernible. *They must be outside my window.* I remembered the small crack at the top of one of the panes and figured that was how it came through. *Someone's there. Breathe in... breathe out...*

I waited for the shattering of glass or, I realized with a start, for them to merely slide it open. I was pretty sure it remained unlocked, since I hadn't fastened the lock shut since my last visitor. *Dumb me, you'd think I'd learn my lesson!*

Nothing happened. No sounds, no movements, nothing. Just the faint, earthy smell of the woods mixed with something warm like amber or honey. The scent tugged at my memory. I bit my lip so I wouldn't make a sound when I realized who it was. Memories of warm skin, a neck so close to my lips, smelling of a sweet autumn morning… Blake.

I couldn't move. It felt like hours as I waited for the scent to be gone, but he remained there. The later it grew, the more rampant my emotions ran wild. My face twisted in anger and then spilled tears. All the while, I was so glad I wasn't facing the window. I didn't want him to see and hear anything. I tried to keep my breathing regular and even. Time droned on slowly. I kept waiting for the scent to disappear. Surely, he must be bored of watching me sleep, but it remained there, soft, faint, and constant. *What's he doing? Stalking me some more?*

When the clock read 4:07, my body grew heavy and my mind began wandering into strange places. When my own inner dialogue became nonsensical, I gave in. I didn't care what Blake did outside my window—I needed sleep.

CHAPTER
Twenty-one

The smell of waffles woke me. My stomach grumbled, and I realized I hadn't eaten anything since Friday. I slid out of bed, pulling a pair of jeans out of my dresser along with the nearest shirt. Depressed or not, I couldn't handle another day in my bed. Twenty minutes later, I was me, showered, dressed, and making my way downstairs.

Being Sunday, my entire family was home, including my sisters. Jocelyn was piling her plate with only blueberries and strawberries.

Krista rolled her eyes. "Just eating fruit isn't good, Joc. It's full of sugar, you know."

"What do you think those waffles are? Just more sugar. At least this is natural," Jocelyn answered. At the same time, she put a few strawberries back into the bowl.

"You two, will you both just eat some food?" my dad grumbled. He glanced my way. "Samantha, how are you feeling?"

"Good," I answered, making my way towards my mom.

She turned around from the waffle iron. Her eyes were rimmed in red. *Has she been crying?* "Are you hungry, honey?"

"Yes, starving. Thanks, Mom." I took the proffered plate and then proceeded to load my waffle with syrup, fruit, and whipped topping. Sitting down at the table, I met my sisters' gazes: Jocelyn's a mixture of envy and revulsion, and Krista's a smug look of satisfaction.

My dad grinned at me. "Glad to see you're feeling better."

I took three quick bites, hardly chewing what was in my mouth. My stomach felt like it was going to eat itself; I was desperate to appease it.

I swallowed and nodded. "Me too."

The house phone rang, but I didn't pay much attention to my mom answering it because my food had disappeared from my plate and I still felt ravenous. I glanced up to see Krista twirling her fork around in her syrup, waffle still there. I found it sad that even though Krista openly mocked Jocelyn for making her starvation obvious, she struggled to eat much herself. I stabbed another waffle off the stack, feeling slightly guilty my sisters' both struggled with something I didn't really understand.

"She *is* feeling better. Why don't you come on over? We're just having breakfast," my mom said into the receiver.

My hand froze in the air, the whipped topping forgotten. I whirled around to stare at my mom. *Who's she talking to?*

"Sounds good, Blake. I'll let her know," my mom answered.

My hand shook and fearing I'd drop it all, I set my food down. The plate's clang on the counter echoed in my ears. My vision tunneled in on my exit, and I strode from the room. *Just have to get to my bedroom,* I told myself. *And then what? Say I'm sick? I just said I felt better.*

"Samantha?" my mom called after me.

I paused at the base of the staircase, the steps calling to me, promising me a way out of this mess.

I glanced at her. "Yeah?"

She appeared relieved, though I'm not sure why. "Blake's coming over. Is that okay? He was so worried about you yesterday, poor kid. He called us like three times to make sure you didn't leave your room and stayed in bed all day."

I stared at her. *Why would he do that?* "Oh really? Yeah, that's fine. I'm just going upstairs to... put more makeup on." At least I'd come up with a believable lie this time.

She smiled brightly. "Good idea. I'm pretty sure with how much he worries about you, he really likes you."

I hoped my smile didn't look strangled and then I rotated, taking the stairs two at a time. I had to get away before my façade broke down. Once my door clicked shut, I glared at my vanity table. Ironically, the excuse I'd given my mom was the first thing I decided to follow through with. I dabbed lip gloss on, smeared on eyeliner, and brushed mascara through my lashes. I told myself the makeup gave me something to focus on other than my jumbled nerves and nauseous stomach.

When the doorbell rang, I cringed. I had yet to come up with a plan. I didn't know how to act. *Should I get him somewhere private and confront him?* My insides contracted. *Be alone with him? What am I thinking? That's absolutely out of the question! He's a psychopath! A lying monster who took pleasure in terrifying me!*

I heard footsteps coming down the hall. My eyes darted between the door and my window. I heard a knock at my door, and I wrung my hands together. *Maybe I could fly out of here...*

"I'm coming," I called, knowing suddenly disappearing from my room wasn't really an option.

I turned the handle and pulled the door open; a pair of bright aqua eyes met mine.

He stepped forward, making his way into my room before I could make a sound. I backed up, my eyes wide, my voice failing me.

Blake's eyes studied my face, and the amused smile died on his lips. "What's wrong? You look like you've seen a ghost."

This is it—do I yell at him or do I scream for help?

I panicked and clamped my mouth shut. I didn't know what to do. I felt conflicted on so many levels. I didn't even know Kory. I mean, should I really trust just his word anyway? So what if what he'd said made sense. There might be another explanation.

He frowned. "What's going on, Sam?"

I hadn't realized I'd continued backing up until my legs bumped into my bed. Losing my balance, I fell back, plopping down on my blankets. I righted myself and jumped to my feet. My face flushed. Of all the ways to act, this wasn't what I'd hoped for.

Blake stared at me, his eyes widening. His tone was firm. "Sam, tell me what's wrong."

I squared my shoulders. *I can do this. I can face my fears.*

"I know what you are and what you did," I said, finally finding my voice.

His face drained of color before me. Then he seemed to force a crooked smile. "What are you talking about?"

"Just stop." I shook my head. "I know you're the one who did it... who took me... and put me in the cabin."

His eyebrows furrowed. "*Wait... what?* Sam, what are you talking about? It wasn't me—"

"Don't lie to me! Don't you *dare* lie to me!" I shouted the words, and then slapped a hand across my mouth. For whatever reason, I didn't want my family bursting into the room. I knew than my anguish over what he had done to me beat out any fear I had of being alone with him. I needed to vent, to scream at him.

"You did this to me! You changed me. And then you've watched me like I was some kind of toy. You enjoyed playing with my fears!"

He stepped forward. "Sam, you have to listen to me. Let me explain things."

He got too close, and I shoved his chest with my hands. "Stay away from me! Don't ever touch me again," I growled. All my hurt was channeling into anger, and I found it extremely empowering. I needed to be mad, furious, and then I'd be safe. *Don't let him see my broken heart!*

"Sam, please." His voice caught and I couldn't help but stare at his eyes, the pain evident in his expression. *Darn it.* My resolve began slipping. I hated that I hesitated, that I wanted desperately to hear his explanation, to believe him again.

"Why?" I whispered. "Why did you do this to me?"

He moved fast, too fast for me to react, pulling me into his arms. The last place I wanted to be because as much as I hated him, despised everything he was, his touch still comforted and thrilled me at the same time.

His lips found my ear. "Sam, I swear to you, it wasn't me. I'd never hurt you. You have to believe me."

I rocked back, trying to detangle myself from him. He released me immediately.

"I know the truth, Blake."

"Why do you think it's *me* all of a sudden? What happened?"

"Kory told me everything."

His face hardened. "*Kory?* And you believed *him?* You don't know anything about him, Sam."

"It doesn't matter what I know of him. He told me the truth! You're a dragon, aren't you? I know you are, so stop trying to de—" Blake morphed in front of me, his wings spanning out, wickedly beautiful.

My eyes widened; my hand flew to my mouth. His wings were brilliant, larger and longer than mine or Kory's; my bedroom light made the faint, iridescent blue and green hues in them dance back at me. Until that moment, I'd had my doubts about what Kory had said. I had wanted everything to be a lie. But now, I had proof. Blake was a dragon.

"I won't deny it," he murmured.

"So it is all true," I whispered through my fingers.

His wings disappeared; his eyes bored down on me. "That's probably the *only* thing Kory told you that's true. I never took you, Sam."

"Then why didn't you tell me you're like me?"

His jaw muscle bulged, and his face seemed conflicted. "I wanted to. So many times I almost did. But I wanted you to know me first, trust me, so you wouldn't freak out."

"So you lied to me? How can I trust you now?"

"I never lied to you."

I sputtered to respond. "But you never told me anything! I

turned into a... a damsel right before the dance, show up terrified by what I am, and you don't say *anything?*"

"I tried to! I wanted to take you home that night, remember?"

"Okay, then why didn't you tell me the next day then? We drove all the way to the bridge. Why not then, huh?"

"I wanted to on the bridge." He gave me a sad-looking smile, more of a grimace. "I figured that way you could run away from me if you were freaked out and not be stuck in my car. But Mack showed up and— "

"No, no, you could've still done it," I cut in. I hated that his excuses were getting to me. "Stop lying to me. Kory said you've watched me for years, stalked me, and everyone knew it on that island. He told me all about Kate. He told me you were obsessed with me, and Anna said you'd gone camping the very same weeks I was in the cabin." My voice cracked.

"I was looking for you!" Blake blurted, taking a step forward. "Those weeks Anna talked about, I was scouring *everything* trying to find *you.*"

I stared at him. "I... I don't understand. If you hadn't been stalking me, how would you even know about me? We hadn't met yet. Why would you be looking for me?"

Blake's face fell. "I... you're right. I messed up. I should've told you everything."

I stared at him. Was he admitting to what I thought he was?

His eyes pled with me. "Sam, we need to talk. But we can't stay in your bedroom."

"Why not?" I folded my arms across my chest.

He glanced at the door. "Don't you think your dad will wonder what we're doing up here so long?"

Darn it, he's right. My dad is probably on his way up right now with the wrong idea. My parents weren't fond of boys in any of our rooms; it was a rule Krista detested since she felt nineteen made her an adult who could make her own decisions. That was usually when my dad would remind her it was all the more reason for her to get her own place and pay her own bills. Playing it smarter, Jocelyn just hung out at her boyfriend's place. Personally, I agreed with my dad. I never liked Jeremy, or any other boy, in my room anyway. Too much personal stuff for him to see, and I'd much rather be outside running or scaling some mountain on my bike anyway.

I knew all these thoughts racing through my head were my way of stalling. Of course, we needed to leave my room. I was sort of surprised they sent Blake up here anyway. *Guess my going back into hibernation mode really freaked my parents out.*

I didn't know what to do. Blake stood between the door and me, his eyes begging me to listen to him.

"Sam, I know you don't believe me right now, or trust me. Let me at least explain my side to you. We can sit in my car, right outside the house if you'd like. Please hear me out and then if you still think it's me and hate me, you have my word that you'll never see me again."

My heart squeezed. I should be relieved. He was the monster. *Right?* I shouldn't want him in my life. And yet, the thought of not seeing Blake made me ache.

I met his penetrating gaze. I wanted to remain stalwart. I didn't want him to know how badly my heart throbbed. *Maybe it wasn't him.* My gut told me not to trust Kory completely, but too much of what he said about Blake made sense. *And Blake's a dragon! He has been lying to me about that this whole time. He could've found the time to tell me...Why keep it a secret?*

The war waged on within me as the seconds ticked between us.

I inhaled deeply. With my exhale, I said, "Okay, fine. Let's talk."

He must've been holding his breath because it came whooshing out with my statement. He hesitated and then gave me a small, crooked smile, definitely not his regular, confident one.

"Thank you, Sam."

I nodded and strode from the room. I couldn't bear to look into his eyes anymore. They were swimming with way too much pain. It weakened my resolve.

Once I'd reached the landing in the living room, I knew I had a choice to make. To the left was the kitchen, with my family all safely eating breakfast. To the right was the front door, where an unknown fate awaited me. One scream, or even a few spoken words to my parents, and Blake would probably be kicked out of my home. Maybe they'd even call the police, but who knew if anyone would even believe me at this point. I'd been wrong before with Jeremy.

And all my proof is wrapped up in the fact that we are both half-bug, winged creatures now. Do I really want to open that can of worms up?

I could feel Blake's eyes on me from behind. *Wonder if he is nervous.*

I hated that a world without him in my life sounded like the real torture. *I need to be sure he really is the monster.* My heart needed to know it too, not just my mind. I squared my shoulders and stepped toward the kitchen. I poked my head in the door. *This is it...*

"Blake and I are going for a drive," I announced. "Be back in a bit."

I heard Blake sigh over my shoulder. *Guess he was a bit worried.*

My mom grinned and Krista winked at me, mouthing the words, 'Way to go'. I swallowed as I left my family, my security, behind. Blake followed me to the front door.

He grabbed the handle and opened it for me before I could. *Like being chivalrous would win him bonus points at a time like this*, I thought. Instead, I said, "Thanks."

Inwardly, I grumbled at myself, *I'm way too eager to believe him!* He practically dashed to the passenger side and again swept the door open for me. I snuck a glance at his face as I climbed in. The earlier pain I'd seen there was replaced with a look of resolution. I had a funny feeling in my stomach. *Maybe this is a mistake.*

CHAPTER
Twenty-Two

The car roared to life, and Blake fiddled with the heater and controls. He glanced at me.

"I heard you say drive. Are you sure you want to leave? We can stay right here if you'd like."

"No, my sisters are home and knowing my luck, they'll argue at the living room window over what we're doing in here so long."

He opened his mouth but then must have second-guessed himself. He kept his thoughts to himself, as he pushed the clutch in and shifted into gear.

I stared out my passenger window as we entered the main highway. Autumn was on its last leg. Clusters of orange-yellow leaves still clung to the cottonwoods, but many branches were naked, scratching at the sky. I rubbed my hands down my arms, and Blake turned the heater up.

The air in the car felt palpable, like it would take a sledgehammer to break through the tension between us. My emotions plummeted into anger and betrayal, only to climb hesitantly back up into the messed-up recesses of my heart, where I desperately longed for him to pull me into his arms and make it all right again. It was a dangerous, silent rollercoaster.

I felt his eyes on me. "So what did Kory tell you?"

I glanced at him. "So you can decide how to twist it? No, you talk first. You explain yourself."

Blake nodded. "Fair enough. I'll start with when I met you."

"In the woods?"

He grunted. "No, long before that. Well, maybe I should go further back. Did Kory tell you where he and I met?"

"Yeah, and Anna told me about you having cancer too."

"Okay, so what Anna didn't tell you, because she doesn't know, was Jaxon dated a damsel. He didn't even know at the time, but when she found out I had cancer and it didn't look like I'd make it, she told, well more like showed, Jaxon what she was. She explained to him how she'd been sick as a kid too and a Dr. Tonbo cured her. She told him the shots would change me forever, but the only thing he cared about was saving his kid brother." His voice caught, and he cleared his throat. "So Jaxon decided it was worth it and convinced my parents to let me try it."

"So your parents know what you are?"

"No, they don't. Jaxon feared they wouldn't let me do it, that they'd find it too risky. Plus, Jaxon's girlfriend refused to reveal herself to them, so they would've thought he'd gone crazy anyway. My parents just thought it was an experimental drug that had been approved by the FDA in critical trials but wasn't mainstreamed yet." He glanced at me. "Once you're a dragon or damsel, you're not supposed to go around showing yourself to people. At least, that's what Tonbo wants. He doesn't believe the world is ready for genetic mutations at this level. And I agree with him. We'd have dictators performing experiments on prisoners in concentration camps all over again."

"You mean like the Germans did to the Jews?"

"Exactly like that. In fact, that's a lot of the reason we are in this mess. Kory disagrees with me. He thinks we should proudly broadcast we exist. Anyway, we can talk about that later. It's not important right now."

I nodded. I had so much to learn about this Dragon Fae world I was now a part of, but that could wait. *I need to know if Blake's the monster. Everything else takes a backseat to that.*

"I didn't realize at first that I'd even changed. I just knew I'd live to play sports and eat Doritos." Blake chuckled. "Kory too. We were pretty much inseparable then. We had to go back to the clinic regularly for our treatments. Back then, you had to get the shots for like six months for the transformation to be complete. It's gotten faster over the years, usually taking a few months."

He glanced at me. "Yours was the fastest I've heard of. A matter of weeks."

I wondered if that was part of what made my blend 'special,' as the monster had called it.

"Did you blackout with the shots?" I asked.

His eyes met mine briefly. "No, our treatments, from what I can tell, were nothing alike. Yours was like a freak show, all set up to mess with your head. There was no reason to tie you up like that unless..."

"What?" I prompted when he stopped.

"Well, your shots were different. Maybe the faster treatment made you have to be secured. I don't know. Either way, there was no reason for the charade. Whoever did this to you wanted to terrorize you. I know you still think it was me, but I swear it wasn't. I'd *never* hurt you or try to scare you. And when I find the *dragon* who did this..." He stopped talking, his clenched jaw muscle bulging. "They will pray for mercy they won't get."

I stared at him. His forehead vein was pulsing, his chest heaving. No one could act out fury that well, could they? *Maybe he's telling the truth. Wait, Sam. He's still got a lot of explaining to do.*

Like he'd read my mind, Blake said, "After the six months, Jaxon insisted on taking me camping. Looking back now, I'm sure his girlfriend told him to do that. They knew I'd morph, and Jaxon figured it'd be better camping than at home. It was sort of like yours, actually. One night I just woke up out of the tent, in the middle of the woods. I didn't remember how I'd gotten there, so I just started running back to camp. Then all of a sudden, I was flying."

Blake stared out the windshield. "It was exhilarating and freaky at the same time," he mumbled. "I'm sure you felt the same way."

I nodded. "I thought I'd dreamt it all."

"Yeah, me too." He hesitated and then glanced at me. "I saw you take off that night... prettiest damsel I'd ever seen," he finally admitted, grinning. I shifted in my seat, my face flushing under his stare.

His eyes moved back to the road, and he continued. "I could tell you weren't going to make it home before passing out, so I stayed with you. In camo, of course. I had to keep you safe. You were emitting all sorts of scents. You attracted a lot worse things than bears that night."

I thought of Kory's words. "Did anyone try to get me?"

Blake nodded. "But don't worry, I took care of them."

Them? I shuddered. "I had no idea."

"Right before you woke up, I raced home and got Misty. I wanted to reassure you, let you know you were okay, but you would have bolted. We hadn't officially met yet then."

"Yeah, about that?" I asked.

He sighed. "I know, I know... I'm getting ahead of myself. Let me back up again. So after I'd morphed, Jaxon explained everything to me. He took me camping a lot, to help me learn who I was. Because once you're a dragon or damsel, you're not the same. I was lucky Jaxon's girlfriend told him what it would be like for me. She told him to keep me near water, teach me to fish to help channel my desires and appetites, or else I'd lose myself completely to the dragon."

"What do you mean?"

"You have to realize, Sam, that you are now no longer just human. You have dragonfly DNA in you now. Their ways come with it; they love to hunt and chase. They love a good thrill. They're agile, fast, equipped to fight, and live a long time. Well, when you combine that with the human parts of us, like hormones, an interesting thing happens. One thing Tonbo hadn't counted on. It's not just our strengths that were added to. Yes, we can fly, our five senses are off the charts, but our frailties and weaknesses are magnified too. We crave adrenaline rushes and power. And it's even worse for dragons then damsels."

"Why?"

"Well, let's just say dragonfly DNA really amps up our testosterone; a lot more than it does for girls. Many dragons turn violent quickly, want to have control, and want *certain* things more than they should."

"Like what? You mean you want to have…" I flushed when my mind filled in the blank.

"Yes, our sex drives are pretty much out of control," he finished for me.

I knew my cheeks were flaming red. I wasn't sure why his statement made me so embarrassed. Probably because I didn't like talking about sex. I felt like an awkward ten-year-old child with my parents staring down at me.

"It's hard for damsels too. Don't get me wrong. You feel invincible, like you can do anything and beat anyone that stands in your way."

I nodded. "I know what you're talking about," I murmured. I thought of flying, diving in and out of the water. I'd felt empowered. I could see where it could be extremely dangerous if you gave into every craving.

"Jaxon looked out for me, did his best, but he didn't understand what it was really like. The rush of being a dragon is addicting. I mean, don't get me wrong. Kory and I did plenty of stupid things together, sneaking into places we shouldn't, but soon, pranks weren't enough for Kory. He always wanted the next thrill, to push it a little further. All he cared about was the adrenaline rush; he didn't care who got in the way of that. And his attitude toward those who weren't Dragon Fae grew worse. He started thinking he was better than they were. I mean, we were technically faster, stronger, and smarter. So you can see where a kid can get some messed-up views of who he really is. The one person who kept me grounded was Jaxon. Being around him reminded me of who I really was."

Blake cleared his throat. "So when Tonbo told me I would outlive my family, including Jaxon, I sort of got depressed."

"What?" I interrupted. Kory had mentioned long life too, but I'd been too upset to really think it through. "What do you mean?"

Blake's eyes softened as he glanced over at me. "We live a very long time. Dragonfly lives are long for insects, so when their DNA combined with ours, it, well... extended our lives too. We still die, we aren't immortal, but..."

I gasped. "How long do we live?"

"Tonbo's the original dragon and he hasn't died yet, so I don't really know."

"How old is he?"

He hesitated and then glanced over. "He was born in the 1800s."

"*What?*" My head was spinning.

"He's an old man now. I don't know how much longer he will be here." There was another hitch in Blake's voice. "Most of us remain looking twenty or thirty for a long time. Around a hundred, we start aging again."

"*Are you serious?* How is any of this possible?" What had started out feeling like a dream was rapidly becoming a nightmare. I didn't want to live for hundreds of years—to outlive everyone I loved and cared about. Sadness filled me. I would watch my children, grandchildren, heck, great-grandchildren pass away. I gasped. *That's assuming we can even have kids! Maybe I'll never get married now... Maybe a family is out of the question anyway.* My stomach didn't feel so good. I didn't dare ask Blake about it. I wasn't sure I could handle the answer just then.

"I know it doesn't seem possible, but somehow it is. I'm sorry, Sam. I never wanted this for you. You didn't need to be changed. You deserved a healthy, normal life." He sighed heavily. "Kory loves the fact that we live so long. It's one of the many things we disagree about. He doesn't care about his future. Like I said, he is addicted to the rush of being a dragon. But I always felt like I needed more than that to be happy with what I was now. I needed to find a purpose." He glanced at me, his gaze intense. "I found it when I was ten."

"What was it?"

"More like who. I'd spent the night fishing in San Diego with some dragons, but that morning, I just sat on the beach, staring at the water, feeling restless. That's when I spotted a girl out too far, being pulled under the waves. I heard her dad yelling, saw her older sister trying to grab her, but she was gone under the water before anyone could help her."

I stared back at him, goose bumps crawling down my neck and arms. I knew the scene he was describing all too well.

His eyes studied my face, and then he stared at the road again. "I knew then what I needed to do. I hit the water at full speed and I found you, sinking like dead weight. When I grabbed your waist, you opened your eyes. You couldn't see me, I was in camo, but your hands felt my arms and then traveled to my face."

In all my horrible memories of being under the water, I couldn't recall feeling anything like that. *But why would Blake make that up? Maybe I've suppressed more than I'd thought.*

"I did?" I asked.

His brows gathered. "Yes, you don't remember?"

"No."

"I thought when you said at the bridge you felt like you weren't alone, you were talking about me. You were definitely conscious, at least for a few seconds. I knew you were confused because you couldn't see me, but you felt my face with your hands."

I shook my head. "I must have blocked all that out. I just remember this feeling I had, well, more like a voice that said I'd be okay, to relax. That's what I was talking about at the bridge."

He glanced at me. "Oh." He sounded disappointed.

"But you were the one who saved me?"

He gave me a half smile. "Yeah. You passed out right before we surfaced. I was terrified you'd died because you hadn't gotten any air in before going unconscious. I swam you to your dad and made sure he got you to the shore safe. I stayed right next to you while they tried to resuscitate you. It was the longest minute of my life. When you coughed out water, I started breathing again. I'd found my purpose, Sam." His eyes met mine. "It was you."

CHAPTER
Twenty-Three

My face flushed. "Me? What do you mean?"

"I felt peace with what I'd become. If it meant I could save others, than it was worth out living all my family."

Regardless whether or not I trusted him, I'd never seen Blake so open. For the first time, I began to understand him. He'd been only a kid, worried about the day he wouldn't have his older brother to look out for him. He'd been lonely, and then he'd saved me. What little boy didn't want to be a super-hero?

I met his gaze. "So you helped others too?"

"I did. Well, at least I tried, for a while. Most were little things, nothing too dramatic. But since you were the first one, I was sort of obsessed with you." He glanced at me and chuckled. "I'm being totally honest here. What do you expect? You were a pretty girl, and I...well, I had a crush on you."

I knew I shouldn't like hearing those words, but they made me happy. I wasn't sure what to say. To my relief, Blake kept talking. *Maybe he has been dying to tell me everything after all.*

"Kory teased me when I started flying here just to check on you. He told everyone on the island about my crush, made me sound like a stalker. By that point, I couldn't care less what Kory said or did. When I saw you were in counseling, not dealing with the near drowning well, I felt like I needed to watch out for you. There was just something about you; I couldn't leave you alone. I had to make sure you were safe."

Now I stared at him. "So you *have* been watching me for years."

He gave me a crooked grin. "Okay, I'll admit saying it all out loud it does sound sort of creepy, but Sam, I would never hurt you and I'd never change you. Like I said, I wanted you to be happy, have a normal life." His tone became firm.

"But what about Kate? Kory said you changed her."

He glanced at me, but he said nothing. The car slowed, and he signaled to pull off on a small county road. We came to a rolling stop in the middle of farm fields, nothing for miles. Nerves fluttered through my stomach, and my fingers turned to ice. Was all that talking just to get my guard down?

He left the engine purring. I wanted to hold my hands in front of the heater vents, to warm them, I but folded my arms across my chest instead.

Blake faced me. "Kate's a long story."

"I'm listening."

He let out a low whistle. "Kory thought I needed to accept my fate. He made fun of my hero escapades, thought they were ridiculous. When we hit the teenage years, it only got worse. He moved back to Durango in eighth grade, really to spite me, now that I think about it. He kept pressuring me to change you, but I wouldn't. I thought the discussion was over, that he'd let it go, but I was wrong."

His eyes turned sad. "Anyway, a couple years ago, Kory told me about this sick girl named Kate. He said there were other ways to be a hero ; I could help save someone who would die by changing her into a damsel. I'd promised myself that no matter how much I wanted to be with you, I wouldn't change you for my own selfish reasons. You were healthy. You didn't need saving again, at least not that way. But I was sixteen, and well... I am a guy."

I stared at him. "So in other words, your hormones took over?"

His eyes seemed sad. "I hate to admit it, but yeah. I decided I would help Kate become a damsel. And then, maybe, if it just happened to work out, I'd have someone in my life too. I went to Tonbo, and he agreed. He told me I could have anything I wanted to make me happy."

"That sounds sort of self-indulgent."

"Not if you know Tonbo. He's a good man. You'd need to meet him to understand."

"I'd love to."

Blake looked surprised. "You would?"

"Yes, why wouldn't I? I'm a damsel. I want to know everything about him and his island."

His smile reached his eyes. "I'll take you there whenever you want. We could go now even."

I bit my lip. I hated to admit I wanted to say yes. Somewhere along the line of Blake's explanation, I'd begun to believe him. Maybe even trust him again.

"Finish telling me what happened with Kate first, then we'll talk about the island."

The light in Blake's eyes immediately died. "Okay, but Sam, please know this isn't one of my finer moments. I should've known better. Sick or not, I shouldn't have thought I could change Kate so I'd have a girlfriend or even a friend. Kory did it all the time, but I found it repulsive the way he treated damsels." He sighed. "But I guess I'm no better. I did it too."

He stared out the windshield.

"I met Kate in the hospital. She didn't have much time left. She'd had a heart transplant, but her body rejected it and her antibodies attacked it. When I explained what I could do, what the shots would do, she begged me to change her. She said she didn't care what it meant, that she'd rather live. I tried to convince her parents to let her come to the facility in Santa Barbara, but they wouldn't listen to me. They just kept saying, 'she doesn't have cancer, there's no way it can help her like it helped you'. And they were right to think that. I didn't know what to do. Kate told me just to bring the shots to her. When you get them, you can't eat or drink much."

As he said this, I wondered if that was why I'd been given so little in the cabin.

"The shots make you sick. You throw up for days." Blake confirmed my suspicions.

"I know. I couldn't keep anything down either," I mumbled.

His face fell. "I worried about that when I saw how thin you'd gotten; I wondered if you still felt bad."

Our eyes met, his aqua blue ones filled with concern. My heart squeezed, and I longed for everything to be like it was again between us.

"I wish you would've just told me, Blake. Why all the secrecy? If it wasn't you, then you had nothing to hide," I said finally, breaking the tension.

"Sam, you were scared of your own shadow. When I moved here, I wanted nothing more than to talk to you. You can't honestly tell me you wouldn't have ran straight to your parents and told them you met a crazy guy in the woods if I had?"

"Well, yeah, I probably would've then. But you could've done it later."

"I know, and I'm sorry I didn't. You mean more to me than anything, and I've only wanted to protect you."

I swallowed. The way his eyes caressed my face, and the softness in his voice, melted the rigid walls within me.

I cleared my throat. "So what happened with Kate?"

He sighed. "I did what she wanted. I gave her the treatment. It was tough not getting caught by the nurses, but it worked. After weeks of visits, she improved. The doctors had no idea why. I was glad she got better and I did care for her as a friend, but it didn't take long after that to know she wanted more than that. But I couldn't feel that for any girl because I was… already in love with someone else."

Did he just say he loves me? I shook my head. "But you'd never even met me, Blake. How can you say that? You didn't even know me then."

"I did know you, Sam. In some ways, better than you know

yourself."

I stared back at him. The feeling in the car had changed; I wasn't sure when it had gone from strained friction to anticipation. My racing pulse and flushed face let me know my body refused to believe Blake was a monster. I tried to retrace his words, find some gap in his reasoning. *Surely, it can't all be true can it?* My eyes studied his face. He didn't flinch or look away. He waited for me to speak, to fire the next accusation at him. I tried to clear my jumbled thoughts. Had he covered everything? Something nagged at me, but I couldn't place it.

He just said he loves me. My heart lurched in my chest and my fingers turned to ice. Whether or not I wanted it, those words stirred something up in me. I broke eye contact; I had a hard time processing things with him firing up all my desires.

"So how did you find out I'd been taken?"

"I'd been camping with Jaxon, on my way to see Tonbo, when I heard about it. I freaked out and raced back, totally thinking he'd finally done what he'd taunted he would."

"Who are you talking about?"

"Kory."

"You thought it was Kory?"

"Like I said, he moved back to Durango just to bother me. After he'd convinced me to change Kate and saw I didn't like her that way, he started teasing me for not having the balls to change you myself. The day he said he'd do it if I wouldn't, things ended bad between us."

"What do you mean?"

"I beat the tar out of him, and he ran away with his tail tucked between his legs."

"That's why he moved away again? But his family?"

Blake laughed. "Yeah, well, being a dragon has its advantages. Your mind works pretty quickly, and you can arrange for a lot of things to happen. So moving away with his family wasn't hard for Kory to arrange."

I stared at him, realizing something. "Just like you made your family move here."

His smile faded. "Yeah, well, once I knew you were in trouble, I decided it was time to be closer. And if you'd become one of us, I wanted to be right here to protect you. I began searching for Kory, trying to catch his scent anywhere. I figured if I found him, I'd find you. But there was no trace of him. He hadn't been around here for a long time or I'd know. So I kept searching for you."

"I want to believe you, Blake, but you could've just as easily had me tied up and been arranging for your family to move here." I had to say it.

"You don't have to believe me, Sam. Just ask Mack."

I stared at him, a tingling sensation crawling down my spine. "Why would I ask him? What does he have to do with all this?" I had a hunch I knew, but I wasn't ready to accept it.

"Because he helped me search the whole time. Sam, Mack's a dragon too."

CHAPTER
Twenty-four

"No way!" I blurted, not wanting it to be true. I should have known. It was sort of staring me in the face with Kory showing up at Mack's to warn Blake about the bug, and Mack and Blake's friendship that seemed to come out of nowhere. It all made sense and yet, shock still left me speechless. *Why didn't Mack say something to me either? He saw me at the dance with my wings.*

Blake nodded. "Mack and I go way back. I met him not long after I'd saved you."

I held my hand up. "Wait, wait… I can't… I need… give me a second." I knew I was stuttering, but my brain felt overloaded. This was just too much information at once for me to process.

Blake cocked his head to the side and then pulled out his cell phone. He didn't say anything as he sent off a text. When he'd finished, he turned to face me.

"Want me to take you home?" he asked.

"What? No… I just can't believe all this, that's all. You just told me one of my best friends is like us. When did that happen? And I don't understand why he didn't say anything to me. He could have told me too, you know."

"Yeah, well, he wanted to. But we both agreed we would wait—"

"Wait?" I interrupted, "Wait for what? For me to get killed? To fly around like an idiot, not knowing how to do the camo even? What the heck, Blake!" It infuriated me that the two boys I trusted most in my life had both lied to me. My hands curled into balls, the sting from my nails piercing my palms empowering. I'd felt this feeling before, when my mom had been upset with me for keeping information from her. It felt like something had taken over. *Is it the damsel in me?* At the moment, I didn't care either way. I wanted to revel in the fury. I wanted to hurl myself against the boy who sat next to me. So calm. So sure of himself. Lying to me. Keeping things from me. Saying it was for my own good. Like I needed to be handled with kid gloves.

I glared at Blake, his eyes searching mine.

"Sammy?" he said slowly, it coming out like a question.

My rage was momentarily derailed by him not calling me Sam. Not that any of that mattered right now. Still, it was enough for me to take a deep breath.

"I'm just frustrated right now. I don't understand why you and Mack waited," I grumbled.

Blake reached over and gingerly touched my hand. When I didn't resist or move away, he took my hand in his, his warm fingers sending a shock through me, like an electric jolt. My breathing became deeper, faster, and my heart began throbbing. It was like the tide had come in and sucked my anger away from me, leaving me exposed, like a naked crab clawing at the wet sand for comfort and safety. Now the only thing swimming were my eyes.

Great. Guess having damsel-amped hormones means I'm going to feel like I have PMS for the rest of my life. Ugh.

"Sam, I can't tell you how sorry I am. Mack was nervous on how you'd handle knowing about us. We both were. It killed me, watching you fumble through it all. But we never left you unprotected. If I wasn't there watching you, then Mack was, like when I went to California. That night Kory came was one of the few times you were alone. And, just my luck, he used the opportunity to turn you against me. I guess I still can't trust him." Blake muttered the last words.

I glanced down at his hand holding mine. Our fingers were blurry through the unshed tears. I sniffed and blinked hard, letting them spill down my cheeks. I needed them gone.

"I'm fine. Or will be. I'm stronger than you give me credit for."
I hoped I sounded a lot more confident than I felt.

He looked me over and then gave me a crooked grin. "I always
knew you were a strong girl. Never once doubted it. If I could go
back and do this whole thing over, trust me, I would, Sam. I still can't
believe someone *actually* did this to you. I mean, like Kory told you,
everyone knew I watched over you. It took gall to even go near you."

It felt strangely comforting to see Blake's cocky confidence
returning. Even if it still irritated me to no end, this was familiar
territory. This was us again.

I snickered. "Oh really? You're *that* tough, huh?"

His eyes widened, and his grin spread. "Well yeah. I'm sure
Kory at least alluded to my physical prowess."

His words triggered the question that had been nagging at me.
"He did actually."

Blake grinned. "You know, Kory isn't half bad after all."

As glad as I was to see his playful side, I needed to know what
this 'bug' Kory had mentioned was.

"He said he needed your help destroying an ancient dragon bug."

Blake's smile turned into a grimace. "Yeah, he fed me the same
lies too. Sam, that's what got me to leave for Tonbo Island and Mack
to be out searching, so Kory could get you alone. Don't you see?"

"No, I don't. You were going to the island before you knew
Kory was even back."

"Well yeah, I was. When you told me everything at the dance,
saying you got a special blend, I knew I needed to get to the island
right away. Not everyone has access to Tonbo's latest serums. I wanted
to find out who could've gotten it and truthfully, I wanted to make
sure it wasn't Tonbo himself who had orchestrated it all."

"What? Why would he have? He's never even met me."

Blake sighed. "Because he wanted me to be happy."

I stared at him, lost for words.

"Tonbo's dying; he won't be here much longer," Blake explained.

"He needs an heir, someone to take over the island and manage the Dragon Fae when he's gone."

"I still don't understand. What does that have to do with changing me?"

"Because for whatever reason, Tonbo took Kory and me under his wings, treating us like the sons he'd never had. When we got older and he saw how reckless Kory was, Tonbo decided I'd be the one who inherited the island. He felt I understood what it meant, the responsibilities that came with it."

"Wow, that's incredible, Blake."

"I told Tonbo no."

"Why? I thought you'd want to be in charge."

"Kory wants to be in charge. He threw a holy tantrum when Tonbo told him he wouldn't be the next leader. He left the island and caused a lot of trouble on his way out. I tried my best to clean up Kory's mess, but a lot of dragons and damsels followed him. Kory's charismatic; he knows how to talk and make people listen. His group feels they shouldn't have to be governed by Tonbo's rules anymore. They feel that Dragon Fae are the superior race now, and we shouldn't have to hide it from the world."

"It *is* so X-men," I said, remembering how I'd thought the same thing with Kory.

"I'm down with being Wolverine." Blake chuckled, and then glanced at me. "I'm not a leader, Sam. I don't want to tell people how to live. And the last thing I want to be doing is overseeing scientists making up new concoctions, blending DNAs to see what new monster we can come up with. I'm grateful to Tonbo for saving my life and that will never change, but I don't want to lead the island. It's too much—"

I offered, "Responsibility?"

"Power," he finished.

I nodded, hoping I understood it all. "So why would changing me help you want to lead the island?"

HIDDEN *Monster*

"Well, Tonbo knew how I felt about you. I went to see if he changed you so that I would have you there, you know, by my side while I took over. So I wouldn't be alone anymore."

"I guess that makes sense. But you don't think it was Tonbo, do you?"

"No, I trust Tonbo. He told me there had been break-ins lately. Serums had gone missing. And to his knowledge, there hadn't been any major changes done to the latest treatments. He thought someone had snuck it off and made their own modifications."

"Do you think it was Kory then?"

Blake grunted. "Not sure. When Mack met us at the bridge, telling me Kory was back in town, I knew I had to get to him fast before he took off. I felt bad driving you home not explaining myself, but I decided once I knew more and got back from the island, I would tell you everything. Plus, at the moment, all I could think about was beating Kory's smug face in."

"So did you?"

"Oh I confronted him. And he swore up and down he'd been hunting for a bug's scent he'd picked up on. He went into so much disgusting detail about where he'd been for the last few months and all the proof that this bug actually exists, it got me... well, believing him. When I'd searched for you while you were in the cabin, I'd never once caught a trace of Kory's scent. I figured he'd told me the truth. Kory's ruse worked and I left for the island, convinced that there were bugs still alive, even though Tonbo swore they'd all been destroyed years ago. Mack stayed here to search for the bug and to keep you safe. He left you for a bit right before I got home. That's probably when Kory came. I thought I smelled him when I got to your window that night, but I hoped I imagined it."

"So you were there that night?" I asked, remembering Blake's scent I'd picked up on after Kory had left. At the time, I'd been freaked out because Kory had painted Blake as a stalker. Now, I knew the truth.

"Yeah, I stayed all night. If Kory spoke even a half truth and there is a chance there's a bug in Durango, I'm not leaving your side."

Our eyes met, my heart thumping audible. His words made so much sense. All the missing holes in Kory's story were filling in, and this time, Blake wasn't the bad guy. I felt my face warming, realizing we still held hands, and I was no longer afraid of Blake. I'd been so engrossed in his explanations, so ready with the next question, that this pause caught me unaware and left me gazing into his eyes.

His voice turned soft. "I couldn't figure out why you cried all night... and when you wouldn't see me yesterday... I got scared."

In that moment, all I could see was a ten-year-old boy leaning over me, terrified I wouldn't wake from my near drowning. *He's still just as terrified of losing me.*

The lump lodged in my throat made it impossible to speak. Instead, I squeezed his hand, hoping he'd understand my feelings for him. His eyes darted between mine. He moved fast, his hand cradling my neck, bringing my face closer to him. There were no secrets between us now. He loved me. *And I believe him. He's not the monster.*

My moment of elation was shattered by a resounding thump on the roof. I yelped in surprise. Something had landed on top of the car, but Blake didn't remove his hand or even jump.

Instead, he growled, "Perfect timing again, Mack."

"Mack?" I gasped, aware that our mouths were still inches apart. I was half tempted to plant one on Blake right then and there, even if Mack was on the roof.

Blake let me go, slowly sitting back, grinning.

"Yep, and so help me, Mack, if you dented my car with your grand entrance, there will be hell to pay," he hollered up at the ceiling.

I heard muffled laughing from above, and then Mack plopped down on the ground beside Blake's window.

"How did Mack know we were here?" I asked quietly. "Did you send some sort of secret dragon signal to him, or did you track us with our scents?"

Blake grinned and held up his phone. "Nope. Sent him a text."

"Oh." I'd forgotten about the text Blake had shot off earlier. *He must've told him to come because I'd been so upset about Mack being a dragon too. Speaking of which. . .*

I jumped out of the car and marched around to Mack. He grinned back at me, his wings spanning out on either side. Where Blake's had flecks of greens and blues in their iridescence, Mack's had reds and oranges laced through them.

"So glad you finally know!" He beamed.

"Mack," I said firmly, my tone making his smile falter. The accusations I'd been so ready to fire at him were already dying on my lips. Hadn't Blake told me enough? Both of these guys, my friends, had only been trying to keep me safe. If I believed Blake, which I did, it meant that I had to forgive Mack too.

"Sammy?" Mack asked, his face turning curious, one eyebrow arching.

I took in his tousled, black-brown hair and sparkling green eyes, noticing he wasn't wearing his thick-framed glasses. He waited for me to say it was okay. I glanced at Blake; he had the same anxious expression on his face.

I took a deep breath and with the exhale, I concentrated on my back muscles. I willed myself to morph. It happened easier than I'd expected. I was surprised the locks of hair were back, not waist-long this time, but hitting me about mid-back. At least I still wore my jeans and T-shirt. *Which now that I think about it, did I just rip holes in it for my wings?* I'd never paid attention to that before because the gown had an open back.

There was no time to wonder because Blake transformed before my eyes, too. His wings spread out, the sun's rays illuminating his brilliant array of cool colors. He turned, and I saw the holes that had ripped in his T-shirt. *We must go through a lot of clothes.*

I glanced at my wings, curious for the first time whose mine resembled more. I was transfixed by them. In the sunlight, mine had no real color at all, more like liquid silver had been drizzled over them, leaving them sparkling back at me. Though mine were not as long as either of the boys—I wondered if that was a damsel vs. dragon thing—I felt proud of their beauty. They were something to behold. *Maybe Blake's right; I do make a pretty damsel.*

I glanced at the guys. They were both still waiting for me to make the first move.

"Okay. I forgive you both. But," I added when they both grinned, "don't lie to me again. And don't think you're done explaining yourself. Especially you, Mack."

They both agreed with me quickly, assuring me I could know about anything I wanted to.

"Honestly, I need a break from all this heavy talk," I admitted. It'd been too long since my last flight, and my wings itched to soar. Besides, I'd never flown with friends before. "Want to take off for a bit?" I asked.

Mack glanced at Blake, and he shrugged. "Why not? There's nobody out here. We can ditch the camo for a bit."

Oh yeah, that's the other thing I wanted to ask him about! I still had no idea how to do that. However, Blake grabbed my hand, and we were airborne. Questions could wait. The damsel in me took over, and I wasn't about to fight her.

CHAPTER
Twenty-five

Flying with Blake and Mack was incredible. I had half hoped being the most recently changed and having the newest formula would give me an edge, but I was wrong. Both of them could not only leave me in their dust, but their accuracy in maneuvering amazed me. It soon became clear Blake's ability far outdid ours. *Guess it's like anything in life—it takes lots of practice.* Seeing Blake's skill, I wondered if that was why Kory needed him. I glanced over at him flanking my right side, Mack ahead of us a few paces. Blake was purposely going slower to stay near me. He was a natural, his muscular body gliding along as his wings sliced through the air. *He makes a tough dragon.* His eyes met mine; the irises more brilliant than I'd ever remembered them being. Everything about him seemed to be illuminated. He grinned and flew closer to me.

"Do you like it?" he asked breathing hard.

I closed my eyes and grinned, shooting straight up into the air doing pirouettes. I shouted, "*Yes!*" the whole way up.

I could hear Blake laughing below me and then felt him surge up next to my body, mimicking my spins. I didn't know how he kept our wings from becoming a tangled as we spun together, his body pressed close to mine. I gasped at the new sensation filling me, Blake's scent overwhelmingly appealing. Our eyes met, his dancing with the rush we both felt. He cradled my face in his hands. Somewhere in my head, I knew we had to stop spinning, or at least be aware of where we were going. *There are tall trees and mountains, right? And Mack is probably watching . . .*

I had a hard time breathing. I felt lightheaded, disoriented. And I knew it wasn't from the flying. Blake lit a fire within me. Our wings slowed down; it felt like we were dancing in the air, with Blake taking the lead.

His eyes probed mine. "Sam? Do you still think I did it all?"

In that moment, I didn't care what I believed—my heart and body had taken over. I wanted Blake more than I'd ever wanted anything in my life. *Just like the school dance.* I hadn't realized then, my damsel side had taken charge, throwing me into Blake's arms to dance.

"No, I believe you, Blake," I said, my hands covering his.

His grin turned boyish, like a kid at Christmas. He pulled me into his arms, embracing me as we slowed enough to be hovering in the air.

"Thank you, Sam," he whispered into my ear, his lips brushing the skin, leaving goose bumps in their trail.

"You're welcome. Blake… I want to tell you something." My heart felt like it was going to burst from my chest. I had to tell him how I felt. I had to relieve the pressure building up within me. "I—"

"Hate to interrupt," Mack blurted, suddenly too close. "But we have company."

One second I was about to confess my crazy love for Blake, the next, both boys are disappearing right before my eyes. I fumbled to feel Blake's body still. He held onto me. I felt his forehead press against mine.

"Sam, listen to me. You need to camo out now!" His words were laced with urgency.

"I don't know how!"

"It's easy, all you have to do—" His words were cut off when something slammed into the both of us. The impact pushed me back, knocking the air out of me. I gasped and then scrambled to feel Blake again, but he was gone. I could hear him though; the sound of punches, groans, bones popping, and yelling assaulted my ears. Someone invisible must have attacked him, or maybe it was the other way around. I couldn't tell.

Off in the distance, I heard Mack yell out, "How do you like them apples, sucker!" Then his words were muffled by his gasping groan, like he'd been punched in the gut. Scanning the sky, I could decipher silhouettes shifting, changing their camo to match their surroundings. I wondered who they were and how many were here. By the sounds I heard, I knew there were at least three or four of them. Seemed like Mack and Blake were fighting off multiple assailants.

"Sam, get out of here!" Blake growled from above me.

His words snapped me into action. *What am I doing?* I didn't know how to camo, but I knew how to fly. As much as I wanted to help them, I knew I'd be no match physically. I jetted downward, pushing my wings to their limit. In my haste, I made the decision to head for the trees, spotting a place where the pine trees were thick. I needed to somewhere to hide. I prayed no one had followed me, but I felt like a huge target for the taking. *Curses! Why didn't I learn to camo first thing?*

I hit the trees hard, breaking branches as I tried to slow down. If my escape hadn't drawn attention, my crash landing would. I swore under my breath as I clutched at one tree's trunk, ignoring the sting of the thousands of scrapes and bruises I was receiving. My wings finally stopped and I clambered up on a branch, pressing my back against the bark. I didn't want to be on the ground. I gulped in air and slowly exhaled, straining to hear anything above my panting. Sweat rolled down my forehead and dripped into my eyes. I'd never flown that hard before.

Nothing. Not even the sound of the fight high above me.

I exhaled and swiped the sweat off my face.

Then I heard it. A hiss of air and a creak of a branch right above me.

I froze. *Crap, crap, crap!*

I inhaled sharply, paying attention to the scent. *No musky mint...
not Kory. Not woodsy, not Blake.* I realize then I had no idea how Mack
smelled. *Better give him a sniff next time.* When Dragon Fae were
camo'ed, you relied heavily on your other senses, that much I was
learning. I held perfectly still. There was definitely a smell to my
visitor.

It reminded me of a cellar. Cold, dank, and smelling of rotting
potatoes. *Ugh...*

I shrunk against the bark. I knew he or she could see me. I sensed
they were watching, waiting. I willed myself to become invisible. But
nothing happened. *How is camo so dang easy to Blake?*

I felt like I'd been frozen in place forever. I didn't know why he/
she hadn't done anything yet when it was apparent his/her friends
had no problem attacking my friends. *What is he waiting for?*

My spine tingled. I'd felt this feeling before. He was stalking me.
Like a mountain lion biding his time, getting to know its prey's habits,
patiently waiting for the importune time. *Why not now? I'm defenseless!*

I tried to still my breathing, to stop hyperventilating. I felt the
tree tremble ever so slightly. Maybe my fear caused him to move;
maybe he liked me being afraid. Maybe this was what he was waiting
for. To see the terror on my face when he attacked. I commanded
myself to calm down. *Focus on what you know. That smell, have I smelled
it before?* For some reason, the memory of walking to Blake's that day
came to mind. *Is this who I'd sensed watching me? That followed me to his
house?*

My gut said yes. *Well, that's something, I guess.* I honed in on the
details surrounding me. The faint sounds of the battle carried on
somewhere above me. I heard Blake growl, and then there was a
yelp. I prayed it wasn't Mack. As worried as I was for them, I knew
my situation had proven to be much more precarious. I focused on
my visitor. I tucked its stench away, determined to never forget it. Its
mustiness made me wonder. *It smells old. Blake doesn't believe bugs exist
anymore, but can he be wrong? Maybe it's what Kory's been tracking. I don't*

even know what a bug really is? Is it just a really old dragon? What makes it a 'bug' anyway?

If I survived this, I'd get my answers. Time seemed irrelevant. I had no idea how long I'd been on that branch. My breathing had steadied, the sweat on my face and chest dried, leaving my skin feeling cool. Its stench grew stronger. *Is it getting closer?*

I had to know. I forced my chin up and scrutinized the branch above me, straining to make out the minutest details. Amid crisscrossing branches and leaves bouncing in the breeze, that was when the silhouette of a hulking frame became visible. I gasped. *He's a monster!*

He crouched down only a few feet above me. How he didn't crash through the flimsy branch he perched on was beyond me. Bugs were definitely not the same as dragons. *I'm so dead...*

The outline of its head was double the size of mine. It tilted it to the side, as if considering me. I swallowed, but my eyes remained fixated on it. I couldn't look away as I steeled myself for it to lunge at me. I knew it wanted to... I sensed it wanted to.

Should I say something? Beg for mercy? But my lips felt sealed shut.

Then it exhaled slowly, deliberately loud. *I think he knows I can see him now.* There was a low rumble, raspy, yet wet sounding. Like an old man who needs to cough. *Is it laughing at me?*

Ask him what he wants! my mind screamed, but I couldn't. What if he said the words I hated? What if he said I'd love him one day? *Then I'd know he's my monster... Although, he's twice the size of the guy in the cabin...*

I opened my mouth just as its head snapped upward. It took me a second minute to refocus on him. He searched the skies. That was when I realized the battle overhead had grown quiet. I heard nothing, no groans or grunts from punches received.

"Sam!" Blake called down.

The branch above me snapped up violently. A blast of wind hit my face, the impact from the wake his massive wings had left behind.

The thing had taken off, the smell of it fading away.

"Blake!" I screamed. "Watch out!"

I thought for sure it would attack him. Blake became visible, soaring down into the trees. His T-shirt was all but threads, his chest bare and glistening in sweat. Cuts and scrapes covered his arms, and blood trailed from the corner of his mouth. As his wings carried him to me, he ripped what was left of his shirt off and wiped his face clean.

I searched for the musty smell, but the bug was gone. It hadn't wanted Blake; it wanted me.

He landed beside me, grabbing my arms. His eyes searched me up and down. "Are you hurt?"

I didn't miss the panic in his voice. "No, he left me alone. You're the one who's hurt."

"Wait, he? You weren't alone?" Then he released me, sniffing at the air. If it weren't a serious time, I probably would have laughed. Images of Blake's dog came to mind. But now wasn't the time.

I heard him gasp and breathe out, "No way," then his eyes bore down on me. "Stay here." Before I could say another word, he had disappeared, bursting through the trees.

I wanted to plead with him not follow the thing that had hovered over me, but I knew it wouldn't matter. If Blake had caught its scent, he wasn't coming back without putting up a fight. That much I was sure of.

I felt something stir on the other side of me at the same time the scent of orange citrus and spices wafted at me. It reminded me of the potpourri my mom used to burn, but more subtle. He ditched the camo fast enough that I didn't have time to be afraid.

"Did you know you smell like potpourri, Mack?" I exclaimed.

At the same time, he asked, "Sammy, you okay?"

Then I noticed Mack's appearance. I gasped, "I'm fine, but you're not." A deep gash above his right eye left a river of blood flowing down his cheek and dripping off his jaw.

"It's all good," Mack said, shrugging. "That's nothing. You

should've seen the other guy." He lifted his arm to wipe it away with his sleeve.

I grabbed his arm, stopping him. "No, wait, you'll make it worse. Let me do it." I searched for an adequate bandage, and then settled on ripping the bottom half of my T-shirt off. It was pretty clean, better than Mack's filthy one. Cool air hit my naked stomach as I dabbed up the blood running down his face and then pressed the clean side of the cloth against his injury.

His hand covered mine as he took over. "Thanks, Sammy, I got it."

Our eyes met, and since I stood a bit lower on the branch, we were exactly eye level. For a moment, we stayed like that, saying nothing, his hand holding mine. It felt familiar and comforting on some level. *Well duh, Samantha, he's only been your best friend since fourth grade,* I reminded myself. Honestly, it felt like more than that though. I had a weird feeling we'd stared at each like this before.

I pulled my hand free and nodded. "Glad you're okay, Mack."

His eyes searched mine and then he grinned. "Like I said, you should have seen the other guy."

CHAPTER
Twenty-six

"It's not hard. You are overthinking it," Blake said, standing in front of me, his legs shoulder-width apart and his arms clasped behind his back.

"Easy for you to say, you've been doing it for years," I muttered, getting frustrated with Blake's impatience with me. "I'm trying," I said, holding my hands up. My skinny fingers remained flesh colored and painfully visible.

"Let me have a go at it, Blake. Sammy listens to me," Mack said with a crooked grin.

I made a face at Mack. "You are no help either. Listen, I just can't do it, okay! Maybe my special formula's missing the camo bit and that's what made it *special*."

Blake seemed to consider me for a moment. Since he'd returned from his fruitless search, which had ended in a dead end, he'd been nothing but agitated, pacing back and forth, wringing his hands together, cursing in some language I didn't understand, and demanding I learn camo. It had started out with him gently taking my arms and explaining how easy it was, but after thirty minutes of unsuccessful attempts, he'd turned all drill sergeant on me. I knew deep down, it was because he wanted to protect me.

But now we'd been at it for over an hour, and I'd turned tired, cranky, and hungry.

Mack shook his head. "Tonbo wouldn't allow that to be taken out of any of his formulas, no matter what the beast might have done to it. The chameleon DNA has been in there forever. That can't be it."

"Mack's right, Sam. You can do it. It's a part of who you are. All you have to do is——"

"Think of my surroundings, think about what I'm touching, feelings, smelling, I know, Blake, I know. You've told me a thousand times. It's not working, okay? I've been trying! Don't you think I want it to work just as much as you?" My voice hitched up an octave with every second. *Uh oh… female hormones are taking over, and not in a good way!* My eyes were stinging, and my throat closing up. *I'm going to cry. Great, just great.*

Blake's eyes widened, and his stance relaxed. "Sorry, Sam. I'm pushing you too hard. How can you do anything starving to death?"

"How did you…?" I began asking

"Know? Because you just flew harder and longer than you probably ever have," Blake answered.

"And flying does stir up quite the appetite," Mack confirmed, rubbing his stomach. "How about some fishing?"

"Another time, Mack. Until she can camo, it's just too dangerous. Let's head back. Your family is probably wondering where you're at, Sam."

"What time is it?" I asked, realizing the daylight was fading for the first time.

"It's about five," Blake answered. He glanced around and said, "Okay, I think we probably made a statement in the skies earlier. We should be fine flying back to my car at least. But keep alert," he added to Mack.

Mack nodded and was airborne. He flew fast in several directions, and then returned.

"Coast is clear," he announced.

"Mack has an uncanny sense of smell," Blake said. "If he says we're good, we're good."

"Okay," I said, smelling the air for myself. No rotten potatoes; just warm honey and the woods after the rain, Blake. And if I focused, I picked up on the hint of ginger, or perhaps cloves, Mack.

Blake levitated but didn't take off. He was clearly waiting for me to lift off, but I felt completely drained. Still, I pushed my wings into action and rose next to him.

"I still can't believe you guys had to fight off dragons in the first place. What did they want, anyway?" I asked, ignoring the fatigue settling into every ounce of me.

Blake looked surprised. "Don't you know? They wanted you, Sam. Your scent's enough to drive any dragon crazy."

I gaped at him. "Are you being serious?"

"Yeah." His eyes danced back at me.

"So four dragons showed up just to *smell* me?" I asked, giggling. Maybe it was the effect of my adrenaline fading, leaving me exhausted that brought on the laughter. Either way, what they were saying just sounded ridiculous. I knew I could pick up others' scents too, but that didn't mean I actively hunted them down for that.

"Four? More like thirty," Mack snickered, staying just ahead of us as we flew.

I gasped. "Thirty?"

"I don't know, I think Mack's being modest. Thirty wouldn't have gotten close enough to give me these." Blake gestured to the scrapes on his arms. "I'd bet it was at least fifty."

I wanted to snicker at his exaggeration, but I wasn't sure he was joking. I'd seen enough of the guys now to know that they were formidable opponents.

"For shizzer," Mack sang, flying on his back so he could face us. "Got to get you indoors Sammy. You're too delish for the taking."

I snorted at Mack. "Whatever." He flipped back around and flew ahead, chuckling.

Still, what they said worried me. *How can there be so many dragons in Durango? It's not a huge city. Just how many Dragon Fae are out there anyway?* I hadn't realized I'd lagged behind Blake until I felt his arms wrap around me, pulling me close to him.

I cocked an eyebrow. "Can't resist my scent either, huh?"

Blake wasn't grinning, though. If anything, his face appeared concerned. "You are irresistible, but it's not that. You're exhausted; let me fly you back."

I wanted to protest, but he was right. My joints ached, my limbs felt like dead weight hanging from my body, and my wings protested every flap.

"Okay, just this once," I said, semi-hoping he wouldn't hold me to that agreement. I let him secure me against him, one arm tucked under my knees, and the other holding me firmly to his chest. *His bare chest. So tempting… oh, why not?* I caved and leaned my face against his skin. Almost instantly, my eyes fell shut. I was sort of surprised his hard muscles could be so comfortable. The air slapping against my body soothed me, lulling me to sleep like a cradled baby. I felt safe in his arms. *Blake will do whatever it takes to keep me safe. He's been doing it since he saved me from drowning. He loves me.*

Something within me stirred—an exuberance I hadn't ever felt before. A part of me felt thrilled I trusted him again. *Must be the damsel in me. Well, that makes two of us!* I wanted to say to her. I grinned, realizing how silly that sounded, and nestled my face into Blake's chest. He responded by tightening his grip on my body. I couldn't stop myself from falling deeper into the grogginess. *Guess Blake knew I was about to pass out.*

As the dream world tugged at my consciousness, my own breathing deep and even, I felt Blake's lips brush the top of my forehead, his kiss leaving a fire behind. I yearned to tilt my head up and let his lips make their way to my mouth.

But Mack's words sliced through the air. "So? Was it one?"

Blake's body stiffened, and a moment passed. *He must be deciding whether to answer. Hopefully, he thinks I'm asleep.* Then I felt his voice rumbled against my cheek. "Tonbo lied. It's definitely a bug and damn it all, it's hunting Sam."

CHAPTER
Twenty-seven

You'd think after Blake acknowledged the fact that a bug not only existed but was actively hunting me, I would have had no problem staying awake, but the next thing I knew, there was a hand shaking my shoulder.

"Sam, wake up. You're home," Blake said softly.

I didn't want to open my eyes yet. Then I realized who spoke and that I no longer felt his arms holding me. My eyes popped opened. I sat in Blake's car, seat belt on, parked in front of my house. I glanced over at him. He wore a clean shirt, hair brushed, and his mouth no longer bleeding. Mack was gone.

"What happened?" I asked, running my hand across my face and smoothing down my hair. Felt like I'd been asleep for days.

"You fell asleep, and I drove you home. Oh and I stopped by my house and grabbed some new clothes. Wouldn't do for your parents to see me shirtless, now would it? Your dad might get the wrong idea about what we've been doing all day." He held up a hoodie sweatshirt. "This is Anna's. It's the best I could do for you since your window was locked."

I stared back at him, not understanding, and then glanced down at my naked midriff. *Oh yeah.*

He grinned. "Not that it's a bad look for you."

I took the proffered hoodie and unsnapped my seatbelt so I could slip it on. "Haha. I was trying to help Mack."

"He's fine. We heal fast." He cocked an eyebrow at me. "But while you're playing nurse, I might have a few scrapes that could use bandaging."

I zipped up my hoodie. "I bet you do." He chuckled, and I made a rash decision. "You think the bug's after me?"

The light in his eyes faded as his smile fell. "Oh. So you weren't asleep after all."

A yawn pushed its way through my words. "No, I was, but I heard you tell Mack there's a bug."

Blake seemed relieved, and I'd wished I had stayed awake longer. *Darn it. Perfect time to eavesdrop and I conked out!*

"Yeah, well, by the scent I caught by the tree, I'm pretty sure we have another one."

"You mean there are more of those things? It was a humongous!"

"Wait, you saw it?"

"Well, no, but I could make out its silhouette. That was scary enough for me."

Blake seemed to consider my words for a moment. "Your eyes are better than mine."

I stared at him. "What do you mean?"

"I can't see a dragon once it's in camo."

"Then how did you fight today?" I asked.

"All sense of smell and sound."

"Oh. I think I can smell pretty good too. I caught the bug's scent. It smelled like a musty cellar with mildew and rotten food in it."

"That's a pretty good summation. What do I smell like to you?"

I smiled. "Better than that."

Blake grinned and leaned in toward me. My pulse became rampant. He brushed his face against my neck, his lips trailing along slowly, leaving a fire behind.

"You're like Hawaiian flower, sweet and fresh," he whispered, kissing my collarbone, sending goose bumps crawling across my skin, "and like a coconut cream pie."

I couldn't help myself and ruined the moment by saying, "I smell like a pie?"

Blake sat back and grinned. "What? It's the best I've got. I'm no poet."

"So you're telling me all those dragons wanted to get at me because I smell like a pastry?"

At the mention of dragons wanting me, Blake's expression sobered.

"Sam." His tone hushed my giggling. "I'm not worried about dragons, I can handle them and so can Mack. Besides, once they know you're my damsel, they'll leave you alone. But a bug is a whole other problem. They're ruthless and strong. It's one of the few things Kory and I agree on. Bugs have to be destroyed and fast."

"Do you know how to kill it?" I asked, trying to swallow back the fear rising in my throat, while liking he referred to me as his damsel. Was that the same as saying I was his girlfriend in the Dragon Fae world?

Blake sighed and nodded. "Tonbo promised me that the one Kory and I killed was the last one. But apparently, that's not the case. I don't know, maybe Tonbo just doesn't know. I need to talk to him, find out who this one might have been."

"What do you mean, might have been?" I asked.

"Tonbo knew them before they became monsters. He created them. They were to be super soldiers in WWII. The Nazis forced Tonbo to use the serum before it was ready. He knew the risks but the lives of his family were at stake, so he injected ten of the strongest, fastest, most cunning soldiers the Germans had with it. Well, needless to say, it backfired. The dragons were not only huge, but they were completely out of control. They didn't like to be told what to do or to work as a team for that matter. They began a killing spree among the Nazis, and even killed a few of each other, which wasn't a bad thing. Tonbo barely escaped and rushed home to Czech to save his family, but he was too late. One of the bugs beat him and slaughtered his wife and kids. Tonbo went into hiding, desperate to perfect the serum. He wanted to make himself a super soldier to avenge his family's deaths. To right his wrong."

I could only stare. It sounded like a sci-fi movie gone wrong. I couldn't believe this could all be real.

"By the time Kory and I heard the rumors of Tonbo's monsters, all but one had been killed by Tonbo's dragons. We were young and joked we would slaughter the last bugger." He chuckled. "Guess we fancied ourselves Ender and Bean. Kory being Bean, of course. I suppose that's where the nickname bug came from, come to think of it. Anyways, we became obsessed with killing it."

"Did you? Kill it, I mean?"

"Yeah. Just as we turned fifteen, almost like a birthday present, word spread that the bug was found hiding in Montana. We gathered a team, and we destroyed it. Lost a few other dragons in the process though." Blake paused. "After the kill, Kory got crazy cocky, saying we were invincible and that the world should basically bow down to us. I just saw dead dragons at my feet. I don't want that responsibility, Sam. I still don't. But I will join with Kory to kill this thing."

I reached over and took his hand in mine. How could I have ever doubted him? To think that this morning I had been trying to run away from him, scared to death of his touch. Now, I wanted nothing more than to be near him.

Blake stared at our fingers and then to my surprise, frowned. "I need to talk to Tonbo."

My heart squeezed painfully. I understood why he had to go, but I didn't want him to. "Okay. Going back to California then, to the island?"

Blake pressed my hand against his lips. "Yes, but I want you to come with me this time."

It took some convincing for my parents to be okay with it, but my dad must have seen the wisdom in letting me get away, because he finally said to my mom, "Lydia, Samantha needs some fun. It will be good for her. Besides, Mack's going with them and they will be staying with Blake's brother's family. I think Samantha will enjoy it."

He hadn't said what we'd all been thinking—California would be far from whoever was abducting teenage girls here. Earlier today, while we'd been out flying, and fighting dragons, another girl had gone missing in Cortez, Colorado. That was only an hour away. *And poor Cally is still missing.* I hated that I knew that neither girl probably had a chance of being found. *The bug got them, and if I'm not careful, I'm next.*

I threw my clothes into a small suitcase. There was something bothering me about the bug, though. *Why didn't it take me instead of the other girl? It had the perfect opportunity. Blake and Mack were off fighting other dragons, who just happened to have showed up at the same time. Coincidence?* Blake had alluded earlier to the fact that bugs don't work well with others. They liked to fly alone, so to speak. A tap on the window interrupted my thoughts.

I would have been startled if Blake hadn't told me that he and Mack would be keeping watch tonight. *Good thing he at least knows how to be invisible.* I'd hate to think what my dad would do if he discovered him in my room right now.

I went to the window and unlocked it. It immediately slid open, and I felt the warmth of his skin brushing against my arm.

"Coast clear?" he whispered.

"Yes, everyone's gone to bed. And my door's locked. You should be fine."

Blake appeared before me, wearing a black T-shirt and jeans, his hair hanging in wet curls on his neck. *Looks like he went home and showered.* I was glad for the time alone I'd had before he'd showed up. I had jumped in the shower too, quickly shaving my legs and washing my hair. I'd left my short mane wet and spent the rest of the time debating on what to wear or whether to put makeup on or not. Part of me wanted to get dressed up for when Blake got here; the other part was exhausted and needed sleep. If I were honest, I wasn't entirely sure what his intentions were when he had told me he'd come to my room later. I knew logically he wanted to protect me, but my room? At night? My nerves were a jumbled mess for the past hour, wondering what would happen now that there was no Mack to interrupt.

I had finally settled on a pair of flannel pants and a white T-shirt, with no makeup. *Tomorrow's a big day, and I'm not as strong a flyer as Blake or Mack. Today showed me that. I need some sleep if I'm going to keep up getting to the island.* But seeing Blake in front of me, I wished I'd put on at least some mascara. I felt plain and underdressed compared to him.

He closed the distance between us, reaching out to brush my hair away from my face, tucking what he could behind my ears. His fingers lingered, his thumbs gently pushing my chin up to face him. My stomach felt like I was free falling as a rush of heat flooded my body. I'd wanted to kiss him for so long.

In that split second, he wasn't the self-assured Blake I'd grown accustomed to. I saw the hesitation, the uncertainty in his eyes. He was the little boy who rescued me, who watched over me, protected me, grown to love me, and had thought he'd lost me forever this morning. *He's wanted this longer than I have.* I wanted to savor this tender moment forever, freeze time if it were possible.

My heart ached for him. Instinctively, I cupped his face with my hands. It must have been the prompting he needed. He pulled me closer, his hands moving around to the base of my neck. The electric pull between us was palpable; I needed to be in his arms, almost as badly as I needed air, or my wings craved flying.

His mouth landed on mine, his lips warm. He didn't push hard, not rushing. He caressed me gently with his lips, working my mouth open, tickling every nerve in my body with his tender kiss. I gasped and he pulled back, his eyes darting back and forth between mine. Was he worried I didn't like it?

My head was swimming, my legs felt numb. I'd never felt like this before. I more than liked it. I inhaled deeply, trying to regain my bearings.

He must have liked my response, because he grinned and the assertive Blake I knew took over. This time when his lips landed on mine, there was force behind them. I staggered but he held me upright, one arm leaving my neck and wrapping firmly around my waistline. I returned his affection, kissing him harder than I'd ever kissed before, only semi-aware that my fingers were tangled in his hair, tugging at his roots. I felt frantic to get more of him. *This is crazy!*

His lips traveled across my jawline, down my throat, across my collarbone, and back up behind my ear. It was like he knew every button to push; I became mush in his arms. I was positive I'd have fallen to the ground if he hadn't been holding me upright. When his lips found mine again, I felt the itch in my back, realizing for the first time that the damsel in me was about to come out. I couldn't pay attention to that; Blake's incessant kissing captivated all my senses at once.

I'd always wondered why kissing was such a big deal. With Jeremy, I'd found it sort of messy, sometimes bordering on gross if he just ate something, but this was nothing like that. I'd never felt so alive and dizzy at the same time; I couldn't get enough of his mouth. I wanted to taste everything in it. When my tongue left my mouth and gingerly entered his, I shocked myself. His hands clutched at the back of my T-shirt, crushing my body into his, as his tongue met mine. No trace of old Pepsi, definitely not like Jeremy. Only the lingering tastes of mint, wet and warm. *I'm going to pass out if I don't get some air in.*

He stopped abruptly, breathing hard as he stared back at me.

"Wow! That was better then I'd ever hoped for," he said, grinning.

There was my little boy again. I flushed, embarrassed for some reason. "Really?"

"I've been fantasizing about kissing you since I was ten, so yeah, this is better." He planted a few pecks on my lips. I giggled and he scooped me up in his arms, giving me a tight bear hug. His mouth found my neck and bit me playfully.

"I thought you said we *aren't* vampires!" I squealed in a whisper. In all our passionate kisses, I forgot we did *not* want to wake my family.

He chuckled and set me back down. "Just one last nibble. You really need to get some rest, Sam."

"Oh, easier said than done, with you in here," I said, my heart still galloping. I tugged my shirt down, discovering it had hiked up a bit during our kissing.

"Why? Do I *tempt* you?" He raised one eyebrow.

I slapped his arm. "Stop it," I growled. "You know you do."

He grabbed both my wrists and next thing I knew, his arms had trapped me, his mouth on mine. I supposed I should have felt some measure of panic. I mean, there was no way I was getting away from him unless he let me, but he didn't force his kisses. They were gentle and inviting. *And I trust him.*

Then Blake moved me to my bed, setting me down, his lips still pressing against my mouth. I was about to protest, worried we might go too far, when I realized his body wasn't following mine. We'd stopped kissing, and he remained standing on the floor next to the bed. He ran his hands through his hair and left them resting on the top of his head.

"I need to focus on *other* things. You're totally distracting me." He let his hands drop, and his hair fell in a mess of curls.

"Oh, don't act like this is *my* fault," I protested.

"It is your fault. No dragon can resist coconut cream pie. You know *that*."

"You're such a dork. You know *that*, right?"

He flopped down next to me and pressed his finger to my lips. "No more kissing for you tonight. You've had enough."

"You think you're intoxicating me, huh?"

"You tell me." He leaned in and kissed my throat, working his way to my mouth.

My own breathing embarrassed me. *Darn him!*

He withdrew his mouth. "Guess that answers that." He scooted off my bed.

"Wait, where are you going?"

"I have to keep watch," he stated, peering around my room. "Don't you have a chair or something?"

"Oh, come on; just sit on the bed next to me." I hopped up, pulled the covers down, and climbed back in, covering myself up. "See, I'll be a good girl and go to sleep." I patted the top of the covers next to me.

He considered me for a moment and then sat at the foot of the bed. "This is probably better. Won't do to be making out if the bug comes."

"Or my dad," I mumbled.

"Yeah and there's *that*. Not sure who I'm more scared of."

"Ha! Like my dad intimidates you."

"If he doesn't let me see you then yes, I am terrified!"

CHAPTER
Twenty-eight

"**I**s she awake?" a male voice asked in a hushed tone.

I tried to place who it was, wanting to say, 'yes,' but my lips wouldn't move and my eyelids felt like they'd been dipped in lead.

"I don't know," Blake murmured.

I became aware of his hand brushing my hair back. The warm thing I was laying on wasn't my pillow, but Blake's thigh.

He carefully removed me from his lap, my head landing on my cold pillow. *Okay, enough of this.* I had to know what was going on. I forced my eyes open. Blake climbed off my bed, and Mack stood at the foot of it.

"Good morning, sunshine." Mack beamed.

"Hey, Mack." I sounded so groggy. I cleared my throat.

"Well, I guess it's not technically morning yet," Mack continued.

"What time is it?" I asked, my gaze fixated on Blake stretching out. Last thing I remembered, we were talking, with him insisting on staying at the bottom of my bed, acting like I had the flu. *I must've fallen asleep, and he decided to sit by me after all.*

"Three o'clock," Blake answered, yawning. He glanced around the floor. Spotting his shoes, he stooped down to put them on.

"Are you leaving?" I asked.

"Yep, Mack's turn for watch."

"Oh." I heard my own disappointment and hoped Mack wouldn't take it personally. I wished Blake would return to my bed so I could lay my head on his lap again and he could play with my hair. *Just my luck he waited until I was asleep to snuggle.*

Blake finished with his shoes and walked over to me. I sat up as he leaned down to me. To my surprise, his lips met mine for a soft, quick kiss. *Guess he doesn't mind PDA.* I wrapped my arms around his neck and hugged him, then he straightened up and gave me a crooked grin.

"Like you said, we aren't vampires. I have to get a few hours of shuteye before our big day. You're in good hands with Mack, so go back to sleep, okay?"

"Okay," I agreed, surprised to see Blake pull his T-shirt off. His pecks and abs were enough to make me swoon. *How's a girl to sleep with that in the room?* I wanted to shout. *What's he playing at?*

I realized why, though, when he morphed into a dragon, holding his shirt in his hand. *Suppose we can't rip through all of our clothes, all the time.* I only had a second to admire his magnificent wings span, the iridescent blues and greens reminding me of his eyes, and then he was gone. Since the window lay open, probably from Mack coming in, the warm, woodsy scent was gone within seconds. *Guess he wasn't kidding about getting some sleep.*

Being preoccupied with Blake's departure, I'd sort of forgot about my new visitor. I glanced at Mack.

"Hey you." I grinned. "I feel like such a baby, with you two having to watch over me."

Mack plopped down at the end of my bed. "Sammy, it's not babying. That bug wants you. This is no different than police protection for someone a serial killer's after."

"Thanks, Mack. I feel a whole lot better." I leaned against my headrest.

"Oh. Guess that didn't sound so good, did it? Sorry." He raised an eyebrow at me. "So... you and Blake, huh?"

"Yeah, sorry about the kissing." I felt embarrassed, though I wasn't sure why. Mack and I had been telling one another about our love lives since puberty. *Though we never locked lips in front of each another.*

"No worries, I'm happy you two finally hooked up. I'm telling you, that boy has been whipped for years. I thought he'd end up blowing it all and move here when you started dating Jeremy to tell you the truth. He got pretty jealous."

"Really?" I asked, realizing Mack knew so many things I did not. *I think it's time Mack and I have a heart to heart.*

"Yep. Blake couldn't stand the guy. Jeremy's shallow, but he's harmless. I told Blake that, but when you disappeared, he went unglued. He sort of *helped* the cops dig into Jeremy's life, turned *everything* inside out. We had to make sure it wasn't him. Sorry it ruined your thing with Jeremy. Although, he tried to get back with you anyway."

"Yeah, well, *that* is definitely over now. Last time we spoke, he basically wished Blake good luck with handling my craziness."

Mack looked appalled. "What a wiener."

"I know, right?" I muttered. "Hey Mack, mind if I ask how you became a dragon? I mean, we've known each other forever. I had no idea."

He cocked his head to the side. "I don't mind at all, Sammy. I've been like this my whole life. It's all I've ever known."

Does that mean Dragon Fae can have children? I wanted to ask.

He added, "I remember showing my parents my wings for the first time, screaming my head off, and them trying to act all calm. Really, they were totally freaked out too."

Guess that rules out his parents being Dragon Fae. "How old were you? Who changed you then?"

"I think I was about three or four when I first morphed, but I was changed right after I was born."

"I don't understand. How did that happen without your parents knowing?"

"My parents did know. You see, I was born premature and my lungs weren't developed enough to live without support, and even that wasn't going very well. I weakened every day. I'd been in the ICU for about four months, hooked up to machines, when my great uncle showed up and told my parents about Tonbo's treatment. Turns out I had a dragon for an uncle." He grinned. "Anyway, at that time, changing infants was all but banned in Tonbo's book. He had no idea how the baby would react to it. But when my uncle took my parents to his island, Tonbo had no choice but to hear them out. They showed him pictures of me, told him it was their last hope. I'd die if they didn't try something."

"So Tonbo did it? He changed you?"

"Yup. I didn't know about any of this until the day I sprouted wings. My parents tried to explain it all to me. I took it as well as could be expected, and then they took me to the island. Being so young, I needed to learn how to control my wings. Tonbo had warned my parents the day might come that they'd have to be separated from me at least for a little while. My parents took me to Tonbo, and I lived with him for a few years."

"Really? How old were you? Your parents just let you go?"

"Well, not exactly. They moved to Santa Barbara where they could work. Tonbo had a private jet bring them over to the island as often as they'd like to be with me. So I wasn't totally abandoned. It sort of felt like I was in a boarding school really. They came to see me at night and on the weekends. I studied under Tonbo during the day."

"Wow. You must be pretty close to Tonbo then?"

"Yeah, I love that old man." Mack's voice grew soft. "When I was about eight, Tonbo decided I was ready to be back in society. He trusted I could control my morphing. My parents moved us back to Durango. We still had our old house; they'd just rented it out while we were gone. That was the year before I met you."

"Oh. When did you meet Blake?"

"I'd met him and Kory while living with Tonbo, but I didn't know them that well. It was after I'd moved back, somewhere in the middle of fourth grade, that Blake showed up at my house and asked me for a favor."

Mack scratched his temple and chuckled. "Should've known the favor would have brought me nothing but trouble," he mumbled, grinning.

"What was it?" I asked.

"You." He winked. "Blake had just saved your life and wanted to keep an eye on you, make sure you'd be okay. Tonbo told him I lived close, even went to the same elementary school as you."

"Oh. So that's why you became my friend?" For some reason, it made me feel weird, like our friendship wasn't genuine.

"I could've easily kept on eye on you without even knowing you, let alone becoming your best friend. It was the excuse I needed to meet you. I only helped Blake because that meant I got to be near you."

His grin set my fears at ease. I felt something stir with in me, a warm, comfortable feeling. *It's nice being around Mack again.* I wasn't sure why we'd had such a gap lately. *Probably because my thoughts have been on a million other things... the cabin... my wings... and Blake.*

"I had no idea how much you really did for me, Mack. You never made fun of me because I feared water, even though you missed out on a lot of lake trips and river runs."

He shrugged. "They're overrated."

"And when everyone thought I was a little crazy for blacking out all the time, you never cared what they said. You kept coming to see me after the cabin, even though I just stared at you like a broken doll." He flinched at the mention of the cabin, but I pressed on. "Honestly, I don't know what I would've done without you."

He shifted his gaze away from me and down at the floor.

Not sure why he seemed uncomfortable with my words, I added, "So I'm glad Blake asked the favor, even if I've brought you nothing but trouble." I grinned, relieved to hear him chuckle softly.

"Hey, about that? Are you still afraid of water... and blackout and everything?"

"Nope." I beamed, "Mack, it's the best thing ever. I feel like this heavy weight has been lifted."

"One of the nice things about being Dragon Fae is it heals your broken pieces," he murmured, almost more to himself.

"I love *that* part. The living forever bit, not so much." I rubbed my arms.

"Well, at least you will always have Blake... and me."

"True." I felt like there was something unspoken and weird between us. I couldn't put my finger what it was though. "Hey, Mack?"

He glanced up at me.

"I'm sorry I've been such a cruddy friend lately," I blurted.

Mack gaped at me. "Are you serious? Sammy, I'm the cruddy friend here. You should have never been taken. It's my fault it happened. I should've watched over you better."

Oh... maybe that's why he seems upset. He blames himself. "Mack, don't be ridiculous. None of this is your fault."

He shook his head slowly. "I'm just glad the bug didn't torture you too badly when he changed you."

"You think it was the bug?" I asked.

"You don't?" He sounded surprised.

"I'm not sure. I mean, why would he let me go? Sounds like they just catch and kill. I'm pretty sure they won't find those other girls. Why would I be any different?"

"Good point. That's one of things Blake's hoping Tonbo might have answers for. Maybe the bug's treating you different because, like the guy said, yours was a special blend."

"So do you think that's why I can't do the camo, because of my blend? I keep trying, but it doesn't work," I grumbled.

He shook his head. "Mm... I don't think so, but who knows? Want to try one more time with me?"

I considered him for a moment. "Sure. Let's give it a go."

Mack grinned and moved over to sit next to me, taking my hands in his.

"Okay, Sammy, go ahead and change."

I stared at him. "You mean into a damsel?"

"Yeah, unless you had something *else* in mind." He lifted his eyebrows up and down.

I punched his arm. "No." I knew him well enough to know he was teasing. For as long as I could remember, he'd crushed on Jen.

I focused on my back muscles and heard my shirt rip at the same time my wings banged into my headboard. I moved forward a bit, to give them more space. I immediately checked my hair, curious to what I looked like. Short, blonde hair, white, plain T-shirt. *Nothing fancy this time.*

Mack grinned and then leaned in closer. "Okay, listen to me carefully. You are a lot stronger and smarter than you give yourself credit for. I know you can do this." Mack's gaze burned into mine. "You've overcome so much already. Think of this as one more step in your evolution. Just relax, let your mind wander. Don't think about anything right now. Let yourself go. Find the dark corners of your mind. Don't fight them, crawl into them."

At some point, I closed my eyes. Something about his words and tone were hypnotic. I felt so desperate to get the camo working that I was willing to give his mantra a try.

"Are you there, Sammy?" he asked.

My eyes fluttered open. "Yes, I'm here." But I wasn't there. I was gone! Where my knees had been, I only saw my blankets. I could see Mack, feel his hands still holding mine, only mine were gone.

I gasped. "Mack! It worked! I can't believe I can do it now!"

He grinned at me, his eyes not quite making eye contact since he couldn't tell where mine were.

"I had no doubt you could do it. Like I said, you're a strong girl, Sammy."

"I don't understand how I did it though. I didn't picture anything like my bed or blankets. I just relaxed and 'crawled into my dark spaces' like you told me to," I said, still reeling at how odd this was.

I stared at where my legs should be. With my keen eyesight, I could make out my own outline.

Mack squeezed my hands and then let them go. "You're a unique creature. I realized when normal methods didn't work, maybe your mind plays a bigger part than the rest of us. You need to relax, let go of all your fears. They've been such a part of you for so long that I think you've built some mighty walls in that pretty head of yours. I just wanted you to find your true self in there."

"Thank you, Mack." I instinctively reached out and touched his face. Not being able to see my movement, I caught the surprise in his expression when I made contact, my fingers brushing against his cheek.

"No problem-o. I'll do anything for you, you know that." His tone was chipper, almost too chipper.

"Thanks," I repeated, withdrawing my hand quickly, not sure why I'd done it in the first place. *Glad I'm invisible, so he can't see how red my face is about now.*

"So how do I get back to normal?" I asked.

"Crawl out of the dark places," Mack said, throwing up his hands and chuckling. "Honestly, I'm not really sure with you. With me, I just think of my flesh, picture what my hands look like, and there they are."

"Humph," I grunted. "This might be a disaster. Maybe I'll spend the rest of my life invisible, nobody knowing I'm even there." I'd said it as a joke, but the words sent a ripple of fear through me. My body jolted, my insides screaming at me to do something to keep that from happening. I hoped Mack hadn't heard the gasp that had escaped me.

His hands fumbled to find me, and I slipped my invisible hands into his.

"Sammy, now listen to me, girl. I'll never let that happen. I know you're scared, but you're going to be fine. Look at our hands." He held up his own, taking mine with his. "Picture what this feels like. My hands are warm; yours are cold. What would your fingers look like in mine? Skinny, white, bony, maybe gnarly and freckled."

I smirked at him, and then realized he couldn't see me. "Very funny." But his words worked again. Maybe his teasing was enough to get me to relax, who knows. Either way, my hands instantly appeared, covered by his.

"Ah, there you are." Mack grinned.

I lunched forward, hugging my friend. "Thank you, Mack."

He patted my back. "I will always help you find yourself, Sammy. You don't have to be scared, okay? Now you better get to sleep or Blake is going to kick me in the head."

"What?" I sat back, not sure if he was being serious or not. You never knew with Mack.

He winked and scooted off the bed. "I'll be right over here." He positioned himself in the corner. "Now sleep, you must."

"Yes, master," I mumbled, grinning. I settled down into my covers and was surprised how quickly his words worked on me.

CHAPTER
Twenty-nine

"Look what I can do," I boasted to Blake, but he kept lifting my bag up and down, staring at it. We were at our rendezvous spot, some place in the middle of nowhere, waiting for Mack to show. At some point while I slept, Mack must have returned home, because I woke up to an empty bedroom. Blake had shown up an hour later to pick me up.

Now he was hefting my bag around. I had no idea what his interest in it was, but I decided this was a good time to show him what I'd finally learned to do.

"Blake?" I said, hoping to draw his attention back to me, but instead he flopped my bag on his hood and unzipped it.

"Sam, you're going to have to leave some of this stuff behind. I mean, we're only going to be gone for two days. What do you have in here anyway?"

I stepped forward, not thrilled with the idea of him going through my personal things. He turned to me and held up the one thing I hoped he wouldn't find. It had been an impulsive thing to add. I'd stolen them from Krista's closet.

"Really?" he asked, a grin spreading across his face. "Not sure how well black stilettos will hold up in the sand, but I'm so game for these."

I snatched the shoes from his hands. "Well, I didn't know what it'd be like there. Sue me for thinking it might have a restaurant or two." I prayed my irritation would hide how mortified I felt.

In the movies, the girl always has a little black dress and heels...

"Why are you going through my bag, anyway? Its private property, you know," I snapped, trying to grab it from him. He swung it out of reach.

"You *are* right. There are a few restaurants. Good thinking." He grabbed the shoes from my hands and shoved them back in, "Okay, those are coming. And so is *this*." His eyes widened, his fingers holding up silky, black material.

Darn it, he found the dress I'd stolen too.

"Look at you packing for our romantic getaway," he cooed, his eyes dancing.

I slugged his arm. "You just changed my mind about what I want to bring. Now give me back my bag."

His smile only deepened. "Oh, don't get all huffy. I didn't mean to hurt your feelings. It's just, we're going to be flying for a while, and with you being the stubborn girl you are, insisting on carrying your things, this is going to get to heavy. I'm only trying to help, honest."

"Oh." I suppose I hadn't thought about the weight of it all. And I *had* just told Blake in the car that I would be the one toting my bag. "I'll be fine. I'll take stuff out."

Blake zipped up the bag and threw it over his shoulder. "Nope, I'm carrying this now. There's no way I'm letting you take that swanky, black dress out. Or those heels." He winked at me. "Now, what were you about to show me?"

I tucked my hair behind me ears, still feeling flustered by Blake going through my bag and insisting on being chivalrous.

"Okay, fine, I give," I said. "But I get to carry it for a bit, okay? Even if it's only twenty minutes."

"My little mule." He gave my chin a nudge with his knuckle.

Argh… sometimes he nettles me to no end. Half of the time, I wasn't sure if I wanted to slap his face or kiss it. I took a deep breath, trying to clear my mind.

"Okay, hold on. I have to find my center." I giggled a little at how silly that sounded.

"Take your time," he said, no longer smirking. His eyes watched me intently.

I morphed into a damsel, glad I'd pilfered a few of Jocelyn shirts, since she liked the more open-back style, anything to show off her shoulder blades. I'd found them too revealing and cold, but now, they were very convenient since stripping my shirt wasn't exactly an option for me, like it was for the boys. And after last night, I'd realized I couldn't rip through every T-shirt I own.

Something tickled my arms and back. I glanced down and saw long, blonde hair. *There seems to be no rhyme or reason to my damsel side.* I closed my eyes and focused on what Mack had said. *Find my dark, quiet place and crawl in.*

It took a second, and I wasn't sure if I'd done it, until I heard Blake exclaim, "Sweet!"

I opened my eyes, expecting to see him, but he must have camo'ed out, because I was left with nothing but his scent. Then his hands landed on my face. At first softly, feeling for my contours, and then slipping down to my shoulders and then behind my waist. His lips landed expertly on mine, as his hands pressed on my lower back, bringing my body closer to him. It was a strange sensation, kissing someone you couldn't see, only feel. It awakened all my other senses, heightening the taste, the sounds, the feel of Blake's mouth pressing down on mine.

Kissing as a damsel magnified everything; my stomach plummeted to my toes, my knees threatened to buckle, and the instinct to wrap myself up in his arms overwhelmed me.

"Hey you guys, I may not be able to see you what you two lovebirds are up to, but I can hear all too well, remember," Mack said, appearing close to us.

I jerked back so fast, embarrassed and terrified by my own actions. Blake ditched the camo before I did. I took a minute to recompose myself, smoothing down my hair—since it had decided to be waist long again, it needed some taming—and letting the heat fade from my face. *Thank heavens for Mack. I'm going to have to learn how to control my damsel self.*

When I finally reappeared, both boys ogled me.

"What?" I asked, instinctively glancing down. I saw why their eyes were like saucers; I no longer was in jeans or my sister's shirt. The long, blue gown was back, shimmering, and hugging my hips.

"What the heck!" I groaned.

"Must be that special blend," Mack said with a whistle.

Blake shrugged his shoulders. "Just one more thing to ask Tonbo about." He stepped closer to me. "But in the meantime, you do look breathtaking, my dear."

"Ugh," I grumbled. "How the heck am I supposed to fly in this getup?"

Blake wrapped his arm around my shoulders and gave me a squeeze. "You did it before, remember. Only this time, you know you're not dreaming."

Since I wasn't as a strong a flyer as the boys, the flight took closer to three hours. It blew my mind that a dragon or damsel at top speed could reach four hundred miles per hour. Mack had tried to explain the math behind it at one of our rest stops. Something about how a dragonfly, which is only a couple of inches long, can fly up to fifty or sixty miles per hour. He then had gone into the metaphysics of it all, completely losing me. All I took away from it was since we are between five and six feet tall on average, we can go that much faster.

We made our last pit stop in Santa Barbara and since I wasn't exactly sure what I'd be left wearing if I morphed back—the blue dress had come out of nowhere—Blake bought us some sandwiches at a deli, and we ate in a park back in the trees, out of sight. Being anxious to get to the island, I gobbled my food and then was left to watch the boys finish theirs. They seemed relaxed, chatting about island stuff, but I couldn't focus.

"Ready for this?" Blake asked, his hand wrapping around mine.

My stomach clenched. "Yup, no turning back now." I hoped I sounded better than I felt. *Why am I so nervous? It's not like I know anyone there.* I knew the answer. *Because everyone knows Blake. And knows I'm the girl he obsessed over for so long. What if I do something to embarrass him?*

Blake and Mack both slung their bags around their shoulders, and I realized why they both preferred to carry satchels. It hung at their sides, the strap resting above their wings. Seeing Blake tug my bag up over his other shoulder, I felt sort of guilty. It looked so cumbersome. I'd carried the dang thing for at least forty minutes before I practically begged Blake to take it.

We all camo'ed out and soon the beach of Santa Barbara fell behind us. The salty sea air clung to my skin while the swelling beast of water rolled below us. The further out we got, the stiller the waters became with fewer breaking waves. As we flew mile after mile, I sensed Blake's mood change. He shifted to be nearer to me, and then his hand clutched mine.

"Remember, Sam, some of the islanders have different *opinions*. Just ignore them if they aren't uh… *nice* to you okay?" he said, his lips finding my ear.

Great. Just great. I'm already nervous enough. I wanted to see Blake's face, to know how serious he was, but all I got was his sky-blue outline.

The last thing I wanted to do when we arrived at the island was to make a scene. I wanted to slip in as inconspicuously as possible, but before we even saw land, Mack called out, "Let's ditch the camo; we're almost at the main channel."

"Main channel?" I asked. "I thought it was an island?" I concentrated on reappearing, hoping I'd be back in my jeans. The guys were already visible. Blake drew nearer, and his eyes met mine.

I figured I must have gotten it right, but then he whistled.

I glanced down at myself. "Darn it," I grumbled. "Why do I morph into this stupid dress all the time?"

Blake shrugged. "I don't know, but I sure don't mind it." He pointed off to the horizon. "The islands are over there. Over the years, Tonbo bought a whole channel of them. We will land in City, that's where Tonbo is. It's sort of like our capital."

"And it's named City?" It seemed like an over-simple title to me.

"No, the island's really called Akitsushima. Means Dragonfly Island in Japanese. There's a legend about a Japanese founder who was bitten by a mosquito and then eaten by a dragonfly. Not sure how it all ties into the islands, but it gave Tonbo the idea to call it that. Most of us find that a mouthful. I don't even know who started calling it City, but it stuck."

I gazed in the direction he pointed. "So why do you guys all call it Tonbo Island?"

"That's like our country's name. And the islands each have their own individual name, for the most part. Does that make sense?" Blake gazed back at me.

"Yeah, I guess so. So Dragon Fae don't really see themselves as like Americans or Japanese anymore? They are their own nation?"

"Pretty much. But that mentality sometimes causes problems."

I wanted to ask more, but Mack hollered, "Land ho!"

I searched the horizon and caught sight of something off in the distance. Looked like a bump of dirt on top of smooth, liquid glass.

"Is that City?" I asked, my stomach twisting within me.

"Nope," Mack answered. "It's one of the outskirts."

"Huh?" I asked.

"The small islands where the ancients live are the outskirts. Better to steer clear of those, Sammy," Mack yelled back to me. He was taking the lead, flying ahead.

"Yeah, we won't be visiting them today." Blake took my hand, staying by my side. "Don't worry, Sam. We'll be in City soon."

I didn't have the heart to tell him I dreaded landing on City most of all.

They were right. Once we'd passed over a few lush islands, which looked like nothing but rock formations and greenery from my vantage point, one very large piece of land came in view. *City.*

I swallowed hard and pinched my eyes shut. *Here goes nothing.*

CHAPTER Thirty

T he name fit. The first thing I noticed when we landed, and my feet sunk into the warm, white sand, was the skyscrapers right in front of me. Sure, City had all the trappings of what I'd expect an island to have—a beautiful beach, palm trees, lush foliage, humid-sticky air, and the sweet scent of tropical flowers in the air, but it also appeared to be an actual bustling city. *I think I know why the name stuck.*

"This is the largest island, about fifty miles long. So we have a little bit of everything here. Mountains, waterfalls, and private pools a few miles to the east, more secluded beaches on the north shore, and of course, the downtown life is here," Blake said just as three young dragons buzzed past us with boisterous laughter. They seemed oblivious to our presence until the wings of the last one clipped my shoulder hard, almost knocking me into the sand.

I gasped, and Blake shouted, "Hey, watch it!"

Immediately, the dragon halted, while his friends kept going. His lanky body seemed rigid as he turned around, stuttering, "Oh, I'm so sorry, Blake. No harm, no foul, right?" Then the dragon noticed me, and his green eyes widened. "Is that...?"

Blake cut him off. "You're good, Serif, just be more careful. She's never been here before."

Serif's eyes opened even further, the green in them reminding me of two big apples. He nodded rapidly and took off to catch up with his comrades, further up the beach.

I stared at Blake. "Is everyone afraid of you here?" I asked.

Blake's eyebrows rose a bit. "What? No. Why?"

"He practically flew away with his tail between his legs!"

"In case you haven't noticed, Sam, we don't have tails." Blake glanced over at me. "Unless you're hiding one under that dress of yours."

I shook my head at him, and Mack leaned over, mumbling, "He doesn't fear Blake, Sammy. More like respect. Everyone hopes Blake will be the next to take over."

"Okay, okay, enough of *that*, Mack. I'm not taking over," Blake cut in.

Mack shrugged. "It doesn't matter. They all want you—*not* Kory."

At the mention of Kory, a conversation I'd had with Jen came to mind. Hadn't she said she'd overheard him and his friend discussing how when Blake showed up at Tonbo Island, he acted like he owned the place? *Seems to me they got it wrong. It's the island that acts like he already owns it.*

Finally, the beach ended and we stepped on to a boardwalk made of well-worn wooden planks. *Thank heavens.* Wading through the sand in a tight dress wasn't easy. I knew I should be sweating but, instead, my skin felt like it was covered in a sticky layer of slime. The humidity was a far cry from the dry Colorado air I'd grown up in.

I wanted to ask why we'd stopped flying anyway, since walking proved hot and slow, but the boardwalk led to a busy street, not paved with asphalt but cobblestones. Instead of engines roaring past, I heard only the buzz of winged dragons and damsels flying by.

Beyond the 'street' was an open plaza. It appeared to be the center of City. So far, the dragons I'd met were guys my age, so it stunned me to see dragons and damsels in all walks of life. I stopped and tried to drink it all.

Young ones played games, painting on the sidewalk with large paintbrushes or flying past chasing Frisbees. Teenagers clustered around what appeared to be open cafés. Strange, loud music blared from that vicinity and, at closer inspection, I decided that a rainbow must have bled out all over the teens' hair. There was every hue imaginable. Middle-aged ones darted around like they had a purpose and places to go. And then the elderly, who weren't moving quite as fast, all gathered around the small tables, where some sort of board game was being played. *Kids doing sidewalk art, teens with dyed hair, and elderly playing chess... maybe we aren't so different after all.*

Then I took another look. Something definitely registered different. I found myself searching for one ugly damsel or out-of-shape dragon. Not one. *Everyone's gorgeous.* The dragons were all shirtless, regardless of age, and even the elderly ones had nicely shaped, tight abs. *This is bizarre.*

The damsels' dress varied from jeans to skirts to dresses, although none wore a gown like mine, and I couldn't wait until I got a chance to change. They all seemed to share the style of their shirts—open backed with a tie behind the neck, leaving the shoulders bare. Some dipped low in the front, most of the teens, while others covered up to their necks. Still, I had to grin. *Sort of odd seeing grandmas wearing halter-tops. They should film a promo for plastic surgery here.* Although, faces weren't necessarily fake looking or uniform. The Dragon Fae just radiated beauty, no matter what their nose shape and size was, or how large their eyes were. It mesmerized me.

A damsel's face popped into my line of vision, disrupting my view of paradise. I jumped back a bit, surprised by her sudden proximity. I gaped at her; her eye color matched her lavender hair.

Her gaze swept up and down my frame, and I couldn't tell if it was malice or curiosity in the squint she gave me. She took a step closer to me, bringing her face inches from mine. She tilted her head to the side, as if considering me.

Sweat rolled down my back. I glanced to my sides, hoping one of the guys would say something. Then I noticed the purple-eyed girl wasn't the only one gawking me. Everyone around us had stopped their normal rhythm of motion I had just been admiring. Now all eyes were riveted on me.

Oh boy. So not what I wanted.

Mack waved his hands, like he was shooing flies away. "Nothing to see here, folks." His tone was casual.

The girl with purple eyes sighed and gave me a fleeting smile before she took off.

Mack touched my arm and murmured, "Since Blake's sort of a celebrity here, it's big news to finally see his girlfriend. Just think of the paparazzi back home."

"Oh," I said, peeking to see if I was still under surveillance. No one directly stared, but I caught several whispering and pointing in my direction. Blake's face didn't look too happy at the moment.

"Do they all know about me?" I asked.

Blake cleared his throat. "Yeah, that's probably my fault. When I was here last time, it caused quite a scene, I'm afraid. I accused Tonbo even of doing it, much to my shame. It's a small island, and gossip spreads fast. Everyone knows you were abducted, that someone changed you, but no one knows much more than that."

To my relief, Blake's wings shifted into action and his feet lifted off the ground. "Feel up to flying again?" he asked. Mack rose too, and they both stared at me. Then it dawned on me, they were walking for my benefit, to give me a break.

I let my wings sing to me, flapping until they blurred. "Definitely." *I am more than ready to get out of here and away from all the prying eyes.*

A cold blast hit me, sending goose bumps down my back and arms. Flying over to Tonbo's main office building had cooled me down considerably. Now stepping into the air-conditioned skyscraper was downright bone chilling.

The first thing I noticed, once my eyes adjusted to the dim lighting, was the tile floor below me. Made up of thousands of mosaic tiles, the hues ranged between jade and sky blue, the swirling patterns within reminding me of ocean waves. It was beautiful... and vaguely familiar somehow.

I shrugged and plodded after Blake, who approached a large, square receptionist desk, in the center of the vaulted lobby. Glancing up, I counted ten levels before hitting the marble ceiling. Several enormous chandeliers filled the lobby with candescent lighting. *That's why it seemed so dim when we first came in.* Flying over, Mack had told me this was twenty stories high. *Wonder what's above this? Tonbo's secret lab where he concocts his serums?*

Each level up had hallways wrapping around with doors leading to heaven knew what. I'd assume offices, but being so far out of my element, I had no idea. This could be a hotel for all I knew. Since there were no railings or side walls, the floor levels up looked like balconies or flat roofs from my point of view. Dragons and damsels shot to and from levels, and once they landed, they proceeded to shuffle all businesslike to the door they needed. *Wonder what the hurry is?* Even though I knew they couldn't fall, seeing them hustle along a walkway with no rails was creepy. *Guess there's no elevator here, or emergency stairs.*

The sound of water gurgling caught my attention next. I glanced over to gape at a tall fountain shooting water straight up, its dancing offshoots performing a water show. All that was missing was the music. There were so many large planters filled with vegetation and towering palm trees that I wasn't sure if the lobby was more of a Grecian palace or a tropical forest. The only thing that seemed slightly out of character was the humongous, bush-like tree filling the entire left side of the lobby. It shot up perhaps fifty or sixty feet. Dark green, tropical leaves fanned out and cantaloupe-looking fruit dotted the entire thing.

"What's that? I thought melons only grew on the ground, not in trees," I asked, pointing.

"That's a breadfruit tree. Tonbo loves the stuff. Personally, I think it's rather tasteless," Blake answered.

Four damsels in a business suits, albeit, button-up, backless tops and short skirts, sat at each side of the receptionist area, all facing different directions of the lobby. If I hadn't been with the guys, I wouldn't have known which one to approach. They all had a sleek piece of metal over one ear, which was not attached to anything I could see. *Are those their phones? Wonder what kind of cell reception they get here?*

We drew near, and their attention turned to us. I could feel four sets of eyes bearing down on me. I shifted my weight and bit my lip.

"Tonbo heard you were coming; he's expecting you. He's in his study like usual, Blake," the damsel with long, brunette hair said with a tone of familiarity. She too wore a white blouse that left her back and shoulders bare and a short, black skirt and tall heels to match. Gorgeous and sexy all wrapped up in a petite package. I couldn't get used to all the perfect people here.

When she turned to the side, her bronze tinted wings shimmered back at me and for a split second, I could've sworn I'd seen them before. I studied her face. Did I know her? Who was she?

"Thank you," Blake said, lifting off. I followed his lead.

"Thanks, Kate," Mack announced, and I almost choked on my tongue.

Kate? Like the Kate that's in love with Blake? The one Blake changed? My mind buzzed with questions, and I glanced to Blake for answers. The cringe he tried to hide told me everything.

I didn't have time to react or even say hello to the damsel, the guys were already soaring up the levels. *Is it just my imagination, or is Blake suddenly in a hurry to get away?*

CHAPTER
Thirty-one

This was it—the moment I'd anticipated and dreaded since Blake had told me he wanted me to join him on this trip. Had that only been yesterday? Time seemed irrelevant at the moment. This was the one person who might have answers. *Don't get your hopes up, Samantha*, I told myself.

I wasn't sure what I'd expected but when the double walnut doors swung in and a short, long-nosed, bushy-browed, little old man stood in front of us, I was taken aback. Had I expected someone taller or perhaps with a bit more of a commanding presence? I didn't have time to wonder because he grinned from ear to ear and embraced Blake, Mack, and then me.

His arms felt small around my waist, and his thick, gray hair tickled my chin. I had the resist the urge to call him a little munchkin, because he felt so impish during our brief hug.

Then he stepped back and I gaped at his eyes—onyx with wisps of silver in them. I could only stare.

"We meet at last, my infamous friend," Tonbo pronounced, his voice rich and deep like the ocean itself.

I stuttered to respond as he stroked his surprisingly tidy goatee. His black eyes widened, and his lips twitched into a goofy grin.

"Ah, but where on my manners, come in, come in," he exclaimed, releasing me from his gripping gaze. I felt like I was waking from a dream. *What just happened?*

Tonbo gestured to me. "Damsels *always* before dragons."

Blake chuckled. "Yes sir." And Mack nodded. "You got it, boss."

I had no choice but to go first. *Nothing to be afraid of, it's just his office...*

But the room I entered did not resemble your standard office. There was no desk that I could see but instead a round table off to one side, with a water fountain babbling behind it. Rocks formed a mock mountain with a mini waterfall cascading down it. I was tempted to run over and stick my feet in the crystal pool; the water splashing down sounded so refreshing.

The heavy-looking, round table had elaborate carvings etched into its worn wood. High-back wooden chairs, upholstered in dark blue velvet, were tucked all around it. *Feels so Knights of the Round Table. Doesn't really fit an island... more like a castle.*

I glanced around; there wasn't a bare wall to be seen. Bookshelves spanned the entirety, crammed with everything from magazines, the last few decades of New York Times Best Seller's list, to ancient-looking, leather-bound volumes. On the opposite end of the room, away from the fountain, three long tables sat with probably a dozen chairs behind them. From here, there appeared to be maps strewn across them. *Looks like some sort of classroom.* It even had a whiteboard on the wall. *Strange. Nothing screams mad scientists, more like eccentric History or English teacher.*

I wanted to ask so many questions, but Tonbo pointed us toward the round table saying, "Please excuse my untidiness, I'm afraid I have been enjoying my trainees' company lately. We can cause catastrophes sometimes." He chuckled at his own joke.

I glanced to Blake, who shrugged his shoulders.

Tonbo pressed his ear with two fingers, saying, "Dara, have some tea brought up and," he glanced at us, "have you eaten yet?"

We all shook our head. "And a proper lunch. Fetch us something fresh," Tonbo continued. He glanced at me. "You care for seafood? Fresh crab legs, perhaps?"

I nodded, still struggling to find my voice in his presence. *I take back my earlier assessment. Tonbo does command attention and respect; he practically hypnotizes people. Must be those eyes.*

Then I heard Tonbo say, "Yes Dara, lots of legs, shrimp, and clams. They're my favorite this time of year. And oh my, almost forgot, I am completely out of gummy worms."

Say what? I gaped at the man, while both Blake and Mack chuckled.

I wasn't sure if Blake just waited to be polite, or he didn't want to spoil his own meal, but the moment the dishes had been cleared and the dragon and damsels doing the work had left, shutting the wooden doors behind them, Blake blurted, "There's a bug in Durango."

Tonbo didn't seem surprised or ruffled. "Are you sure?"

"I'll never forget a bug's stench."

Tonbo shook his head. "So Kory's claims are true then? How can this be?"

"I don't know, but it hovered over Sam, didn't touch her," Blake said through clenched jaw.

Mack proceeded to fill Tonbo in with the rest of story, informing him of the other assailants while all the while, Tonbo locked eyes on me.

When he stroked his chin and mumbled, "Strange indeed," I knew he thought the same thing I did. Why didn't the bug follow 'bug M.O.'? Why didn't he grab me when he had the chance?

"I wanted to go over your list of soldiers, your research at that time, the procedures, everything, just see if there is some small detail we missed," Blake said.

"Of course, anything I can do, but I know of only the ten, which have each been properly disposed of. You and Kory took care of the last one, Arno Clemens."

Blake grimaced. "I don't like to think of who that thing was before. By the time we got to it, there was nothing left to spare or pity."

"No, no, you're quite right, Blake. What those early injections had in them, no man could fight. It was a Jekyll and Hyde mess. Now, there are many safety measures put into the serum. I never want to repeat that mistake again." Tonbo's brows seemed to grow heavier with each word he spoke.

For some weird reason, I wanted to tell Blake to stop pestering the old man. He obviously didn't know anything about this bug. Why make him feel bad for what happened hundreds of years ago?

I glanced at Blake; his eyes met mine. *Why indeed?* It didn't take long for me to realize that Blake wasn't firing question after question. *What did we hope to gain from this trip?*

Still, we lingered in Tonbo's office for several hours, using the long 'student' tables. Tonbo had everything Blake had requested brought up. I didn't want to pour over it. Honestly, the details from World War Two were just too horrifying for me to read. I hated what happened to the Jews in the concentration camps. It disgusted me to see what the German soldiers had forced men to do in the name of science.

I hadn't realized Tonbo had moved near me until I heard him say, "The Japanese feel the dragonfly symbolizes courage, strength, and happiness."

I jumped a little. Seeing his wrinkled face before me, I forced my mouth to work. "Is that why you chose that name, Tonbo, because it's Japanese for dragonfly?"

He arched one bushy eyebrow at me and grinned. "Yes indeed. Most of Europe saw the dragonfly as evil. I liked the Japanese take on it. And after so many years of wishing I could've done it all over again, I decided to embrace the positive."

"Blake had told me you're really from Czech," I said, desperately trying to recall any details I'd learned.

"Ah, again right you are. I was born in the Lands of the Bohemian Crown, or as you would know it, Czech. The year was 1824, our country, I guess you could say, got caught up in the spirit of revival.

Science had exploded. I was fascinated by it, drawn to it. Studied under Johann Mendel at the gymnasium in Opava. Had so much fun working with his bees." Tonbo's voice grew quiet. "That's when the scientific exploration of genetics was innocent."

"Mendel? That name's familiar. Wasn't he known as the father of genetics or something like that?" School had never been my strong suit, but the name rang a bell for some reason.

"I think your science books referred to him as the father of modern genetics. And as he should be. Started his work on pea plants, then the bees, those proved to be nasty at times. Can't always control the mating habits of the queen, you know."

"Oh," I said, not sure how else to respond. It was like having a conversation with someone from your school textbook.

"Poor fellow died before the beauty of his findings were ever appreciated. Such as it is with the brilliant among us, right?"

"So what happened after you studied with Mendel?" I asked.

At this, the old man sighed. "I became obsessed with genetic mutations."

I waited, hoping for more, but he grew quiet. I felt bad he was ashamed of his discovery. Speaking of which, I asked, "It that how you figured out you could mix DNAs?"

"Well, I didn't exactly fine tune it then. You have to realize, Friedrich Miescher just discovered the gooey stuff on bandages had microscopic nucliens, as he called them then. That was in ah... the 1860s, I believe. So yes, once he'd finished stuffing rotten, old Band-Aids under a microscope, I really went crazy with the idea of DNA, as we all call it. I injected myself with the first serum then."

"I thought the first time was with the soldiers, when it went all wrong."

"I would have been long gone by then. The Germans found me in 1920. By then, I was almost one hundred years old. I should've been dead. It would have saved us all a lot of grief."

"No," I said, reaching out and patting his shoulder. "That's not true. Your discoveries have saved so many lives." My eyes instinctively sought Blake across the room, but he was bent over an old parchment, oblivious to our conversation.

Tonbo followed my gaze. "Yes, I suppose you're right. Positive only from here out, I promise." He gave me a fleeting smile. "What I'd given myself was a simple mixture at that point. What the Germans wanted was super aggressive, immortal soldiers. When they saw what it had done to me, they forced me to change it, and try to add on to it. I lost everything after that."

CHAPTER
Thirty-Two

We spent the rest of the day with Tonbo, leaving his office, wandering through his elaborate gardens. His personal estate lay just beyond his sanctuary, as he referred to the lush acreage we meandered through. Having never remained a damsel for this long, I felt like I was finally growing accustomed to my super senses. Walking down the paths, I heard the crunch of pebbles under foot, while drinking in the scent of the intoxicating blooms surrounding us. Moisture kissed my bare skin as I let my hand brush the plants we passed. They felt rubbery, like the leaves were waterlogged. I tried not to giggle when Tonbo began rattling on about how horticulture was an underappreciated science, his manic hand waving both endearing and funny to watch. When he pointed to a large, bushy tree, the sensation of déjà vu hit me again. It rolled through me; suddenly, the garden felt hauntingly familiar.

I swept my eyes around, trying to place what could possibly be triggering such a feeling. I'd never been anywhere this tropical before. *And this looks nothing like Colorado.* Still, it nagged at me. Blake, who'd been walking next to me, slid his hand into mine. It broke the feeling of familiarity and snapped me back to the present.

"What do you think of the place?" he asked.

"Complete paradise." I grinned back at him.

He tugged at my hand. "Let's stop for a bit."

I watched Mack and Tonbo continue without us. I had to admit, I'd never been to a more romantic place. I didn't mind being alone for a minute. His eyes eager, he cleared his throat, and then ran his free hand across his mouth.

He took both of my hands in his. "Sam, would you like to live here?"

My heart stopped. I hadn't had time to think this all through. Being a damsel, I knew I wouldn't always be able to stay in Durango with my family. I knew they'd find out soon enough I was different. Blake had never wanted to take over for Tonbo. I could see now what a huge responsibility it would be. It would be like being told you were suddenly the mayor or maybe even the president at the age of eighteen. Even though the population was much smaller, they were a bit unruly, thanks to the unrest Kory's group of dissenters had caused. Did he hope I'd move here with him?

I gazed back into his eyes. *Does he mean now? Permanently? Is this a marriage proposal?* I gasped at my own thoughts and then realized Blake had only asked if I would like living here. *Slow down*, I told myself, *no wedding bells yet.* The scary realization for me was what my answer would probably be if he had asked me.

"Yes, I think so," I managed, and Blake exhaled. *Poor guy, I made him wait a bit.*

He leaned in and kissed my lips. I never wanted it to end, but he pulled back and glanced around. Then I caught the scent too, musky cologne with a hint of mint. We had a visitor, and I knew who it was before he appeared.

"Kory," Blake muttered, his hand tightening around mine.

Dark hair, broad shoulders, and a white smile. Kory strolled forward, his eyes sweeping up and down my body. I turned inward to Blake, trying to shield myself from his view, feeling like he had x-ray vision. For whatever reason, Kory gave me the creeps.

"Hello Blake, Samantha," he said, bowing his head to me. "Off for an evening stroll? All happily ever after for the two of you, I suppose." Sarcasm laced his words, "Funny that it did *all* work for you, Blake. How convenient. The girl of your dreams just *happens* to be changed and now look at you, walking Tonbo's personal, private gardens together."

"Let's keep our personal differences out of this, Kory," Blake said evenly. "I'm coming with you. Let me get Sam home first."

Kory's mouth had opened but apparently, Blake's words had changed his mind. "Finally something we can agree on." He grinned, did a mock bow, and vanished.

I wanted to ask Blake how the heck Kory knew we were here in the first place, but Mack and Tonbo had returned. Tonbo peered around, his brows knit, and his lips pinched together.

"Kory just left," Blake said. "I let him know we're joining him. We're going to find this bug, whoever it is, and destroy it."

Tonbo nodded and then sighed. "I'm sad I missed the boy. Would've enjoyed his company for a bit. It's been too long since his last visit."

I stared at Tonbo. *Doesn't he know Kory despises him?*

"Perhaps next time," Blake answered, his tone strained, as he draped an arm around Tonbo's shoulders and began walking back with him. Blake showing Tonbo affection made me happy. Behind the smiles and odd sense of humor, there was something desperate about the old man, as though he thought his soul was forever damned for his past mistakes. Perhaps showing compassion on others, like Kory, was Tonbo's way of trying to redeem himself.

I caught eyes with Mack, who shuffled to my side. He leaned in and murmured, "Tonbo chooses to love Kory. Like the Prodigal son, he hopes Kory will return one day."

I stretched and stifled a yawn. Hard to believe we'd flown here today. It felt like a week ago when I stepped onto the island. After the gardens, we had entered Tonbo's estate. One glance at Blake and me had informed Tonbo the grand tour would probably have to wait for tomorrow. Always gracious, Tonbo had fed us a delicious meal and showed us to our own private guest chambers. Each of us had our own room off the same hall. Blake had planted a kiss on my lips and told me to rest for a minute. He had a few things to discuss with Tonbo.

I glanced around the room. A canopy bed with privacy curtains pulled back, a lounging area with its own sectional couch and flat-screen TV, a fountain occupying a wall with a pool of water at least four-feet deep and six-foot long at its base.

I leaned over and ran my hand through it, surprised to discover the water was warm. Tempted to just jump in, I wondered when Blake would return. Did I have time for a quick bath? Watching the water drip from my fingers, I made a rash decision and locked my bedroom door. *He said to rest and I can think of no better way than this.*

I shimmied out of my dress. Having never actually put it on before, it proved a bit tricky to take off, since it was skintight. Once it cleared my hips and fell to the floor, I kicked it away with my foot. *Done looking like I'm heading to the prom or the Grammy's. Wonder if I throw it away, if it can appear again?*

I grinned as I tossed it in the nearest trashcan. "Take that. I'd rather wear a Mumu. Now, this is a bath," I murmured as I got in and lay down. Bubbles blew out from my nose as I pushed myself in all the way, the water covering me completely. It felt wonderful to wash all the stickiness from my skin. Feeling my body's buoyancy, I figured it was salt water and opened my eyes under water. I dug my toes into the side, forcing my body to go down deeper. My thoughts begin to wander, all sounds muffled out by the steady roar of water cascading down the rocks. I closed my eyes, totally relaxed. I supposed warning bells should have gone off in my head. *I am resting under water… perhaps not the best plan.* This would have terrorized me six months ago.

I didn't know how long I'd been under, it felt like it had only been seconds, but the next thing I knew, hands grabbed my waist, pulling me out of my 'tub' with a whoosh, water splashing everywhere. I tried to get my bearings as I sucked air in. I hadn't realized how bad my lungs were burning.

"Sam! Sam! Are you okay?" Blake's voice belted out. Then I

discovered I was cradled in his arms—naked. My wings poked out haphazardly as his arm held me up.

"Blake!" I screamed, desperate to cover myself with my arms, pulling my legs in higher with his other hand still under my knees. "What *are* you doing?" I scrambled around, not sure if I should lean into his chest or away.

He shoved a towel in my direction, averting his eyes. It felt like both of his hands were all too painfully on me. I wondered if he grabbed it with his teeth. The towel hit me in the nose.

He sputtered. "What am *I* doing? You looked like you'd *drowned!*"

I snatched it from my face, trying to cover myself. He seemed frantic, but I was even more so. "Put me down!" I commanded.

He did and I finished wrapping the towel around myself, a bit tricky with wings.

"I was just taking a bath! Why were you in *here?*" I asked, swiping the wet hair from my eyes. My hands shook, the whole situation mortifying.

Blake wasn't smirking or acting like a regular teenage boy might upon seeing a naked girl. He seemed agitated, worried. His breathing was hard, his brow still creased together.

"Just taking a bath?" he repeated, like he hadn't heard me.

"Yeah, don't you go under sometimes too?" I spat. I knew my anger was all a front, my face flaming red. I'd never been more embarrassed in my life. I didn't do naked. I was the girl who hid in the corner while dressing for gym class, praying no one noticed me. I'd always been shy in that department. My sisters had no trouble flaunting their skin, but I did. *Well, this just took the cake. I'll never live this down.*

"You didn't answer the door for a long time. I thought the bug had gotten you. I broke in," Blake answered.

I peeked at the door; sure enough, it lay wide open, with one of the bottom hinges busted out.

"Wow, I…" I began.

He cut me off. "I'm just glad you're fine. Sorry I freaked you out."

He took a step towards me, and I held out my hand. "Wait," I warned. I felt way too exposed still, and dripping wet in a towel didn't help.

"Permission to hug you, I swear, *only* hug," He lifted an eyebrow. "Unless, of course, *you* want more than that."

"Let me get dressed first. I don't trust you," I said, giving him a weak smile. *Or myself*, I should have added.

I went into the bathroom, locked the door, and pulled pajamas out of my bag. I stared at the tank top I'd brought to wear so my wings would have room. I glanced at my reflection. *Do I really need my wings now?* They felt cumbersome. *And I don't want to try to sleep with them.* I morphed back to normal and threw a T-shirt on instead. *Blake's seen enough of my skin tonight.* I ran a brush through my now shoulder-length hair. *One minute it's long, the next it's short. So weird.*

I came out of the bathroom to see Blake had changed too. "Oh good," he said. "Now we can snuggle." He made no mention of my hair length. Honestly, I wondered if he even noticed the difference.

"Sure," I said. *Like he just wants to hold each other.*

Turns out, he sort of did. We curled up on the couch, under a light blanket he'd found. We kissed some, but most of the time, I laid my head on his chest and listened to the thrumming of his heart. The later the evening grew, the more I realized Blake had no intentions of returning to his room. I peered up at him, and he immediately kissed my lips.

"I'll have you know I am doing my best to restrain myself. I know you're feeling a little weird about earlier."

I was impressed he'd somehow known the reassuring I craved right now, I got more from his arms than his lips.

"Yeah, I'd rather not talk about *that*," I grumbled.

"Just know, Sam, you are, and forever will be, the only girl for me."

His words caught me off guard. There was no teasing or sarcasm behind them, just straight honesty. I pressed my lips to his while my mind screamed, *Tell him you love him*! I knew I did. I'd never felt like this before about anyone. For some reason, those words terrified me still; as if I'd wake from a dream and relive the nightmare in the cabin the moment I professed my love. I knew it wasn't Blake and yet I hesitated. Somewhere between talking, kissing, and holding one another, I fell asleep.

CHAPTER
Thirty-Three

Beep. Beep. Beep.

I groaned. What was that confounded sound? Not my cell... I bolted upright. *I'm most definitely not at home.* I was curled up in the corner of the couch, covered in blankets, with no Blake. When had he left?

Beep. Beep. Beep.

Argh. I don't even know where that is coming from. Then I noticed my bedroom door was shut. When was the hinge fixed? *And is that a doorbell?*

I snorted. *Leave it to Blake.* He must've told Tonbo to put it in because I hadn't heard his knocking while underwater. I shuffled over to the door, my joints feeling stiff. I wasn't sure if the soreness came from the day of flying or the night on the couch. Bright light streamed in from my windows, and I could only assume it was still early morning.

"Blake, where'd you go?" I asked, opening the door.

My 'go' turned into 'go-o-o,' because it was most definitely not Blake.

I wrapped myself up in my arms. "Kate?" I blurted, and then I added, "I mean, you're Kate, right?"

I guess since I happened to be with the boy she was in love with, I didn't expect her smile to light up her hazel eyes.

"Yes! I'm so happy we finally get to meet, Sammy." Her voice was so pleasant. "I've heard such wonderful things about you for so long."

I swallowed hard, totally taken aback. "You have? Oh, same! Blake has spoken highly of you too."

I realized my mistake when she cringed, and she asked, "He has?" Then she tried to recover by adding quickly, "Oh, that's great. *Mack* has told me *all* about you."

Oh. Mack. Not Blake. I felt so stupid. *Explains why she called me Sammy, I guess.* I held the door open wider. "Want to come in?" I had no idea what she was doing here, but might as well bury myself in more shame. I knew I looked terrible. My knotted hair stuck up on one side, guess the side Blake hadn't been smoothing down with his hand. While she, on the other hand, was immaculately dressed, her face fresh and radiant, and her hair cascaded in loose curls down her back.

Her bare back. *No wings. Interesting.*

To my surprise, she nodded and entered my bedroom. We stared at each other for a minute, and I pointed to the couch. "Want to sit down?"

"Oh, no, I really shouldn't stay. Mack asked me to come and check on you after a bit."

"Mack?" I asked, while wondering why not Blake. And why Kate, of all people? This morning was just getting weirder and weirder.

"We're pretty good friends, Mack and I," Kate explained. "I know he's one of your best friends too. Seems we have a lot in common." Her words held no malice behind them.

You mean we're both in love with the same boy. I smiled, while feeling completely cruddy inside. From what I could see, Kate was nothing but beautiful and kind.

"Oh, that's good. Mack's the best kind of friend to have. He's gotten me through some tough times," I said, genuinely glad she had him in her life too.

"He is one of kind. I guess you could say we understand each other, know how it feels."

I thought nothing of her statement until she flushed and began fussing with her hair. *Oh. Maybe she means both of them know how it feels to have unrequited love. She loves Blake and Mack loves Jen.* I felt even worse inside. Time to change the subject.

"Speaking of Mack, is he gorging himself on breakfast right now? That guy's always hungry," I said with a forced laugh. I really wanted to know why she was here, and not the guys. Something felt off.

Kate pressed her hands on her stomach and ran them down, like she was trying to straighten out her blouse. *She's avoiding eye contact. This can't be good.*

"No, Blake and Mack left hours ago," she said slowly. "They want me to look after you while they're gone."

"Gone? Like fishing or something?" I asked, not liking how she kept tugging at the ends of her hair. *Silly girl's going to pull out all her hair if she doesn't stop.* I knew I wasn't really worried about Kate's locks. Everything about this conversation filled me with dread.

"No." Her eyes finally met mine. "They left with Kory. They've gone to kill the bug."

<hr />

"They did *what?*" I couldn't believe my ears. I tried to maintain face in front of this complete stranger, who I happened to want to make a favorable impression on. The last thing I needed was for Blake's rejected girlfriend to have the pleasure of seeing the one he'd chosen having a meltdown. And then it'd be all over the island.

Blake left me! Here! On an island, where I have no hope of leaving on my own! Of course, I kept all that to myself.

"I don't understand. He and Mack were leaving with Kory after they flew me home today," I managed to say with a somewhat even voice.

She frowned. "They wanted to, honest Sammy. But someone caught the trace of the bug's scent. Blake found Kory, and they took off. Mack came and told me to watch out for you and explain things. Then he left to catch up with them."

Something about her story didn't make sense. *Only problem is, I don't know which part.* Why hadn't Blake just told me? I glanced up to see Kate eyeing me. There was something in her gaze that unsettled me. *Feels like she's waiting for me to react. Like she almost expects a meltdown.* I shook my head. *I'm imagining things.*

"Oh crap." Reality hit. "What will my parents think? I'm supposed to come home tonight."

Kate shook her head. "Don't worry about that. It's all been taken care of."

"What do you mean?"

"Oh, well, Blake called your mom and told her you'd come down with the flu, but that you're in good hands with Blake's brother Jaxon being a doctor and all. Told her you'll be home as soon as you're up to traveling and not to worry." She seemed satisfied with her answer, but I couldn't help but wonder how Blake managed to do all that planning when he was in such a rush to get out of here.

I finally pegged what didn't add up. What was the point of this whole trip anyway? We didn't learn anything about the bug, about who'd taken me, or what'd done to make me different from everyone else. Kory showed up last night, almost like he was waiting for Blake to take off with him. Which would explain how Kory knew where to find us in the first place. And then to top it off, Blake had already planned my excuse for not returning home.

"If I didn't know better, I'd say this was all a ruse to stick me here while they kill the bug." I'd muttered my words, not really expecting an answer.

Kate sighed. "Oh, Sammy, you *are* too smart for your own good. Mack warned me about you, said you could figure things out. And I told him I'm a horrible actress."

I wanted to say, *what the heck are you talking about*, but I wanted to keep her gushing.

"Yes, well, you have too many nervous tells. Sorry, lying's not your thing, Kate." I offered her a smile, hoping to bait her.

"No! It's so not. Well, I guess you'd know sooner or later. You're right. Blake never planned to take you home today. He wants you far from the bug, safe, until it's destroyed."

I fumed inside, but I held my tongue.

"But I guess you already figured that all out. And then after what happened last night with the water, he knew you really needed to stay."

I bit my tongue hard enough to draw blood, but no gasp escaped my lips. *Say what?*

Kate seemed totally relaxed now, smiling and happy. "I'm so glad I don't have to pretend around you anymore, Sammy. I really would like to be friends. I feel like I already know you so well."

I stared at her and had to concede that none of my wrath should be directed at her. She seemed like an innocent, sweet girl, who got nervous when doing something she felt wrong, and yet, would bend over backwards to help anyone. Even the girl who'd unwittingly stolen the love of her life from her. *Why Blake isn't madly in love with her, I have no idea.* Thinking of Blake, my rage boiled. *So he planned all along to get me here, and leave me!*

I forced myself to smile. "I'd really like that too, Kate."

"Oh good! Well, let's get you off to Tonbo's office. I know he's waiting to get started."

There was no amount of tongue biting I could do to hide my surprise. "Started?"

"Oh. I'd thought you knew about that bit." Kate morphed into a damsel, her bronze wings captivating my attention again. It felt like more than déjà vu this time. *I swear I've seen them before.*

Her hazel eyes squinted back at me. "Everything okay?"

"Uh, yeah. I'm fine." I knew it'd sound crazy if I asked if we'd met each other before. There was no way.

"Hey, if it makes you feel better, I'd be mad too," she said, twisting her lips to the side and winking.

My gaze snapped up. "I'm not mad."

"Really? Not even a little bit? You're a better person than me, I guess." She hiked her shoulders up. "I mean, he left you here, and probably didn't even tell you about the tests he asked Tonbo to run today." She frowned. "I swear, Blake acts like everything and everyone should bow down to his plans."

I wanted to argue with her, but I found it difficult.

"Personally, I still don't see why Tonbo didn't choose Mack to run things. He practically raised him. And Mack is so kind, thoughtful." Her tone softened, and I bristled slightly.

"Well, Mack isn't exactly innocent in all this either," I muttered.

Kate's eyes widened. "What do you mean?"

"He knew about Blake's plans and didn't say anything either." I folded my arms.

She seemed to consider my words. When her staring became uncomfortable, I added, "Doesn't matter now, what's done is done. I should probably get changed."

She jumped a little, as if remembering herself, and nodded. "Yes, sorry you're right. Take your time. I'll wait outside for you, okay?" She exited the room, pausing at the door. She turned to face me. "I guess you're right about Mack and even though I may not agree with Blake's methods, I do agree with him about the tests. I think it's time you find out what makes you special, Sammy."

CHAPTER Thirty-four

I hate them both! *Okay, I don't hate them, but what the heck!* I fumed, ranted, and all but punched the wall. I had followed Kate obediently to Tonbo's office, let her leave me sitting at the round table, and then sat for a good hour waiting for him to show up. What happened to him dying to get started?

Maybe it's just as well. I needed time to simmer down. Tonbo was under the impression I came here to be tested. The only ones who had been playing the deceit cards were my friends. Even if this whole plan was to keep me out of harm's way and get answers, Blake hadn't been up front about it. He'd thought he had to scheme and plot to it. *He promised me no more lying.* I didn't like what that reminded me of. Was I fool to trust him? I dug my nails into my jeans, thinking of not only Blake, but Mack too.

Argh, what is it with those two? Why didn't they just tell me in the first place? *Because, I never would have agreed to this.*

"I don't care if they did it to protect me, I'm still mad," I mumbled, just to break the silence.

"Well, hopefully not with me too," I heard from behind.

I spun around in my chair and saw Tonbo walking into the room. "Oh no, I'm just..."

"I know you're upset, Samantha. Blake debated whether to tell you last night. He came to see me before the *incident*."

My face flamed—did everyone on the island know about my humiliating moment?

"I told him not to tell you. That it'd be best if he just left."

I stared at Tonbo. "Why?"

"Because, Samantha, you are a very complicated damsel. You have anger within you, and you are stubborn. You wouldn't have agreed, and Blake can't stand to upset you. After what happened in the water, it gave Blake the strength to go. He wants to know why you are the way you are. And that's why he didn't say goodbye."

"What do you mean, what happened in the water?"

"Blake knocked at your door for a good while and even after he'd broken the door in, it took him a few more minutes to find you under the pond. We can hold our breath for a very long time, my dear, but no one to this day has held it that long. You should've died."

"Oh. So is that why everyone knows about it?" I asked. Kate had referred to it too, and I began wondering who else knew.

Tonbo nodded. "Why else would they? It's unheard of, unprecedented."

"I didn't realize; I didn't know." *So it's not because I was naked and all that.* That probably never crossed anyone's mind but mine. Then his words hit me. *I should be dead?*

"But Tonbo, it didn't feel like I'd been under that long. I don't understand. One minute I'm under and the next, Blake's freaking out, trying to save me. It doesn't make sense."

"I worried about this." Tonbo sat on the chair next to me. "Samantha, you used to have blackout spells before, right?"

I nodded, slowly realizing what had happened. I'd passed out under water, and somehow managed to hold my breath. *Scary thought.* It was my first blackout since becoming a damsel.

"I'd hoped that was over now that I am what I am."

Tonbo squeezed my hand and sighed. "Not every serum's foolproof and whoever messed with yours added quite a bit of extras. One of which just might be sperm whale DNA."

"Really?"

"It's something we'd played with in the past, but hadn't put into practice just yet. We have to run clinical tests to see if the benefits outweigh the risks. We do that with any alterations that are made. Anyway, whoever mixed your own unique blend probably stumbled upon our research and decided to implement it regardless. Sperm whales can hold their breath for over an hour, though typical dives last more like a half hour. So…" He rubbed his hands together, his eyes lighting up with energy. "Shall we proceed to my water tank?"

"Um…"

Tonbo cackled. "Oh, I'm just teasing you, my dear. I'd never dunk you for that long. In fact, no dunking necessary. We have a very nice lab upstairs. Want to see it? Much can be discovered by even a simple collection of blood."

I agreed. "Okay, sounds good."

Tonbo practically jumped to feet. "Excellent, off we go then!"

Even though he'd joked about the water tank, my legs still wobbled as we exited his office. *Just how mad of a scientist is he?* We flew to the tenth floor and stopped in front of two metal, double doors, with a bright blue, flat monitor screen hanging next to them. Tonbo reached up and placed his palm against it; it buzzed, a white line tracing his handprint, like a child drawing with chalk, and then dinged.

"Welcome, Tonbo," a singsong voice said from the box.

"Why, thank you," he sang back.

The doors slid open, revealing an elevator. We climbed in, and Tonbo said, "My lab takes up the top ten floors and as you see, not just anyone can enter. Very few actually."

"So why can't we trace who got into the serum? Wouldn't it have to be one of your scientists, someone who had access?" I asked, pressing my back against the wall. Elevators always made me dizzy.

"Yes, you'd think it'd be that simple. But unfortunately, about a month before your abduction, there was a computer glitch. Someone hacked their way in and overrode the system. It shut down video surveillance cameras and the door scanner. Since it happened at night, we didn't catch it until morning. And by then, it was too late. Serum had gone missing. When Blake found out you were gone, he searched for you, yes, but he raided here for anything and everything. Trust me when I say we raked over every detail. Whoever took you, Samantha, was smart and covered their tracks well."

I considered his words as the elevator stopped and the doors opened. My eyes widened. Now this did look just like a scene of a CSI crime lab, white lab coats everywhere, glassed-in rooms, and tables with odd-looking equipment and machinery on it. Right smack dab in the middle was a breadfruit tree.

He caught my gaze and shrugged. "In case my trainees get hungry."

True to his word, I had a few needles poked into me, blood drawn, and one CAT scan... At least, I thought that was what it was. I held perfectly still in the cylinder, my thin hospital gown doing nothing to protect me from its cold, ceramic surface.

We took a break after the body scan, and Tonbo had food brought up to the lab. We ate in a private room, one without glass walls. I was glad to escape the eyes that had followed my every move today. I'd overheard a few whispered conversations, rolling my eyes at a few of the muttered phrases I caught.

"She's the one that held her breath."

"She got a new batch, so who knows what she can do."

"That's Blake's damsel, better steer clear."

Tonbo busied himself with tying a bulky bib around his neck. I wondered why until I saw what was on his platter—a whole heap of sticky, barbeque ribs.

I told Tonbo to surprise me and choose my meal. When I hefted the silver lid off mine, I was indeed surprised. No ribs, instead, a piece of grilled salmon, sautéed vegetables, and a slab of carrot cake.

"How did you know these are all my favorites, Tonbo?" I asked, impressed.

"I know many things about you, Samantha. Now, the damsel side, not as much, I'm afraid. I hope we can at least determine what exact strains of DNA were used."

"Will it explain how I can alter my appearance too, like my hair and that dress?"

Tonbo frowned. "That one perplexes me to no end. To change hair length is one thing, but to appear in different clothes is another matter."

"It's not just any clothes either, Tonbo. It's always that blue dress." *The one I threw away*, I thought with relish.

"Your first time morphing, you wore the dress, but not always?"

"Yeah."

Tonbo ran his thumb along his other hand's knuckles. "That I will delve deeper into. The sharper vision, sense of smell, even holding your breath, I can find logical explanations for. We've already found that your myoglobin, that's the stuff that stores oxygen in your muscles, is through the roof. Your red blood cell count is extremely dense too, which helps keep your brain," he tapped his temple, "oxygenated."

He held up a rib. "And the body scan showed some interesting workings within your metabolism. The way you break down sugar is quite fascinating. I believe you can slow it down to conserve oxygen, just like the sperm whale does."

"So that's what the person did to change it, added whale DNA?"

"I'd like run some more tests tomorrow. I might have some ideas about the blue dress. But yes, I'm fairly confident you have *some* strains of whale DNA. Not all, or you'd need some bigger clothing." He winked and took a bite of his dripping rib.

"That's a scary thought," I mumbled as I put a bite of salmon in my mouth, enjoying the lemon-butter drizzle it was covered in.

Tonbo agreed. "Yes, especially since you have the gene that slows down your metabolism!"

I found it hard to swallow my food down.

CHAPTER
Thirty-five

Tonbo had proven himself to be an excellent host the entire day, and when the evening came, he invited guests to his estate, including Kate, for some live entertainment. I had no idea what to expect as we were ushered into Tonbo's private theater. Being one of the few faces I knew, I was glad Kate sat next to me. Her presence helped buffer me from the prying eyes.

Apparently, rumors had already spread across the island that Tonbo himself had run tests on me all day to see what I was made of. I knew they were just curious, but their gawking gave me the creeps. *At least I found excuse to wear my black dress and heels. Too bad Blake's not here to see me in it.* I felt a wicked satisfaction that it was his own dang fault, and then I immediately felt guilty. *Blake's off killing a bug.* I bit my lip. I didn't know what I'd do if either Blake or Mack got seriously injured. *Just how hurt can dragons get before they don't heal?* I tried to force those thoughts away.

The stage lit up with performers, elaborately made up in costumes and makeup. The music shook the floor as damsels soared across the stage, flying in an intricate dance. The lighting turned pink, bathing everyone, including the audience, in its luminescence. Then dragons entered the stage and the music shifted to darker tones, a dark blue light chasing the pink away. That was when a fog formed on the stage, curling and inching its way towards the performers. They moved in it, gliding out their parts. When it dipped off the edge of the stage and began creeping its way up to us, I glanced at Kate, who smiled. She seemed delighted by it.

I, on the other hand, wasn't. It filled me with a sense of suffocation, which I knew logically made no sense because I could still breathe. *And even if I couldn't, I can hold my breath longer than anyone else here can. Just relax; it's just effects, supposed to make me fear the dragons on stage doing that weird dance.* I settled into my seat and took a deep breath. *See, not poisonous fumes.*

Still, when it temporarily blocked my vision as it wrapped me up in its tendrils, I shuddered and rubbed my arms. *Hope this ends soon.* The temptation to hold my breath kept nagging at me. *I should do it just to see how long I can. Plus, this fog reeks.*

I should've known the stench wasn't a good sign, but my senses felt off kilter. I glanced around; no one else seemed dopey. *Maybe I'm just tired.*

I cleared my throat and stopped breathing. *Just in case.* I didn't like the way the fog was making me feel, sort of dazed and sluggish. I glanced at Kate; she was apparently enthralled with whatever was happening on the stage, because her eyes were wide and her hands set ready to clap in her lap. Her mouth cooed and then gasped, one hand flying to her pink lips.

She turned to me. "Did you see that, Sammy?"

Guess I missed something good. I must've managed to nod because her eyes riveted back to the stage. The fog had cleared now, and yet I didn't feel right. I lifted my hand to Tonbo's arm.

He glanced over at me. "Enjoying the show, Samantha?"

I never heard my own answer. Next thing I knew, I was facing the cabin, grass tickling my bare feet. *Am I dreaming?*

The cabin loomed on the horizon, a dilapidated, wooden box sticking out of a meadow like a sore thumb. *That's not right.* I fixed it in my dream. Tall grass changed to broken branches, leaves, and pine needles. Trees shot up and crowded my old prison.

I don't want to be here, I cried over and over, but my body kept flying towards it. *Wait, I'm flying. I can get away,* I reassured myself.

Suddenly, the cabin was gone, but so was the light of day.

Blackness enveloped me. I felt something pull at me, fighting me, trying to take control. *No! Go away!*

The blackness won, and I passed out.

My eyes refused to open and yet, I felt awake. Or was I? I felt lucid enough to realize I'd blacked out in the middle of the performance. *Of all the times!* What had I done? Slumped on Tonbo's shoulder or worse, fallen to the floor? My hip and shoulder throbbed against the unyielding surface I lay on. *Yes, I'm on the floor. Good grief.* A small groan escaped my lips. I didn't recognize my own voice; it sounded like a muffled croak. *Like I have cotton balls stuffed in my mouth.* I moved my tongue around; my mouth was dry and caked in something metallic. *Is that blood?*

I forced my eyes open; a dim light flickered from somewhere behind me, streaking the wall I was smashed up against with shadows. Inhaling sharply, I smelled dank air reeking of wet wood and rotten garbage. I lay in a fetal position, my arms hugging my knees. From what I could tell, I still wore the black dress. I unlocked my grip on my legs and tried to lift my arm up; hot pain seared across my shoulder blades. I gasped, panting, until it finally ebbed and became bearable. *My wings are hurt! Where am I?*

I had to know; I took several steadying breaths and then forced myself to ignore the pain. Pressing my hand against the wall, I tried to propel myself around. Paint crackled under my fingertips, peppering my face with flakes. I pushed harder, fire coursing through my back and down my wings.

I screamed and then clamped my mouth shut, trying to control my breathing. I didn't want anyone to hear me. I'd learned my lesson in the cabin. No *good* thing came when I'd cried for help.

I'd managed to flip over and faced my new prison.

Right in front of me sat my only light source, a squat candle. Wax spilled down its sides and pooled on the ground, forming lumpy clumps. *Wonder how long it's been burning... how long I've been here.* The candle wasn't tall to start with, only a few inches high, and almost the entire center was hot liquid now. I could only gape at it; it felt like I was clinging to my last hope. The dancing flame seemed to mock me, as it buried itself further in the candle, shortening the wick. *Shortening my time with light.* I shuddered to think of the blackness I'd be left in when that happened. *No time to waste.*

My throbbing body protested, but I forced myself to sit up. I glanced over my shoulder, my wings appeared whole, but I wasn't ready to try them yet. I needed to know more. *Starting with, where am I!* Last thing I remembered was sitting in that theater, hating that fog.

I sniffed at the air. Definitely musty, old… like that fog had been. *Like the bug.* I sucked in air. *Oh my gosh! He has me! But how?* Tonbo had been right next to me the whole time.

"Stop," I hissed. *It didn't help to get hysterical in the cabin, and it won't help now! Need to think, Sam. How did you get here?*

My eyes took in what little surrounded me, hoping for a clue cement floor, rundown walls, and a pile of trash in the corner. *Well, that explains the smell.* I lay in perhaps an eight-by-eight room with no closet. *Maybe a forgotten cubby or hidden compartment.* Nothing on the walls but large, ragged holes. The image of a raging lunatic smashing his fists through the peeling paint filled my mind.

There has to be a way out, a door. I scanned the room and found a pitch-black opening directly behind me. My head had been near it the entire time I lay there. *Creepy.* The yawning, dark doorway terrified me. What waited for me in there? *Freedom or torture?*

Either way, I had to find out. My gaze fixed on the light in front of me, the wax dripping down. I didn't have much time left. I needed to act. My life depended on it. If the bug had me, he would come back. Taking in my battered state, I didn't think he planned on playing nice.

At least this time, I'm not tied down. I gritted my teeth and attempted to stand up. My vision became soupy, as I fought the torture shooting through my joints. I couldn't make it up further than my hands and knees.

I may be broken, but I'm not dead yet! And I'm not giving up. I shuffled forward, one knee, one hand, one knee... Then I stopped. I hauled back and gripped the hem of my dress. To my delight, it was already in shreds. I pulled at it with my hands, but discovered they were already bleeding from cuts and scrapes. I tore a large piece off with my teeth instead, reopening wounds and filling my mouth with blood. Spitting it out, I wiped my mouth clean with the back of my hand.

Using the scrap of material, I scooped the small puddle of hot wax up, cradling the light in my hand. Shaking with adrenaline, pain, and fear, I pressed my free hand against the wall and used it as leverage to pull myself to standing. *Got to get out of here.*

One step, two steps, three steps...

I thrust my flickering flame forward and entered the black void. The floor was no longer smooth. Felt more like dirt. The air smelled earthy. *Am I outside?* With the candle, I could make out the wall next to me, smooth rock, well worn.

I strained to see ahead but the blackness was velvet, thick and impenetrable.

I had the sinking suspicion I was in some sort of cave. Carefully running one hand along the wall, I shuffled forward. After several steps, the space I was in narrowed considerably. *Think I just entered a hallway or tunnel.* The walls were on both sides of me. I forced my feet on. *Eventually, this has to lead to somewhere, right? I just pray I get there before my candle gives out.*

CHAPTER
Thirty-six

I had no idea how long I followed the twisting, turning tunnel. At some point, I realized my pain was all but numb, either from healing or exertion. My breathing became stronger, and my legs weren't so wobbly. *Didn't Blake say we heal fast?*

I decided to test it and gingerly stretched my wings out. They bumped into the ceiling, letting me know that it was indeed lower than I hoped. I'd been deluding myself, trying to keep the claustrophobia at bay. I focused on my back muscles, flexing each one carefully... waiting for the stabbing pain. It never came.

I swallowed hard and flapped them, slowly at first. Again, nothing. *I'm healed!* I soared up, bumping right into the ceiling. In my moment of clumsy elation, I snuffed out my precious flame.

I swore at my own stupidity, and then cringed when I heard it echo down the chamber. *Stupid, stupid, girl,* I berated myself, *what are you doing? Shut up and get out of here!* Nothing I could do now but fly as fast as I could and pray for the best. I dropped the hot wax from my hand and took off, my wings smacking cold walls along the way.

With my sight limited, I opened up my other senses. I hoped my sense of smell would help lead me. I didn't want to imagine how bad it'd hurt if I flew straight into a wall.

When the air shifted cold and smelled of iron, I halted. I felt for the walls; there were none close enough to feel. *Must be some sort of large cavern.* I flew slower, terrified now to have a decision to make. *Which way do I go?* Becoming disoriented, I decided my safest bet would be to land. My bare feet pressed down on sharp, broken fragments. I gasped and lifted back up. *Crap. Can't walk through that.* Felt like broken glass. I flew a bit further and decided to test it again. Same result. I cursed under my breath, terrified I'd make the wrong decision and never leave this forsaken cave. Then I heard it.

A wailing sob.

I froze, my ears calculating the distance and direction it came from. *Sounds like it's on my right. Do I head to the left then?*

The moaning began again, and this time, I could tell it was definitely masculine. It was hard to tell from the crying if it was someone I knew. Could it be Blake or Mack? The racking cry began again, and I decided definitely not.

Whoever he was, he sounded miserable. And even if he was the one who threw me in here, he was probably my only hope of getting out. *Maybe I can sneak up on him… if only I had a weapon.*

I almost gasped when I thought of it, but bit my lip instead. Lowering myself down, I tried to be as silent as possible. I couldn't tell by the way the cavern echoed how close my sobbing friend was.

My fingers fumbled to find a lose shard, amongst the dagger-like surface I encountered. Finally, one chunk gave way and I hefted it up. I ran my hand along it. Felt like stone, maybe six-inches long and a few inches thick. To my delight, and pain, I discovered one end was extremely sharp. I wrapped my hand in my dress for a moment, trying to stop the bleeding from the injury I'd just given myself. I knew I didn't have time to make a bandage. My hand could wait. I needed to move now, before my captor knew I was coming.

The wailing continued, and I focused to hone in on my target. It took me a second to be sure; the sound bounced off the walls so much that it confused me at first. Feeling confident, I flew toward his crying. My wings hit walls, and I was comforted to be back in a passageway. *Especially if this leads out. Just have to get past whoever's making those horrible sounds.*

From the racking torment, the person sounded remorseful, which didn't exactly fit what I'd learned about bugs so far. Didn't they delight in killing? Have no conscience?

I slowed when I spied a splinter of light up ahead. As much as I wanted to beeline for it, like a moth to a porch light, I needed to be cautious. I slackened my pace. When I got close enough, I saw that the light seeped out from around a closed door. I inched forward, and the door opened just a crack.

I hesitated, weapon drawn, and then I stared ahead, the dark tunnel leading on. Maybe I could just keep going. I felt a surge of hope at the prospect of not having to face the beast within that room.

Then the crying became more distinct, words erupting out painfully clear. "How can I do this to *him*? He trusted me! I was all he had! For so long!" He sobbed; it sounded pathetic. "*I am a monster!* I should be destroyed!"

His words cemented me to the floor. I stared at the light before me. *Who's in there?* I didn't know if it was curiosity, horror, or just plain stupidity that kept me there listening.

His words were growled, like the anguish of someone damned to eternal torment. Still, I sat there, captivated by his sobbing.

"If I do this, I won't go on. I *will* find a way to end myself," he muttered between cries. I heard a scuffle from within, things falling to the ground. Was he with someone?

Time to go! No way am I facing two monsters! I rose up, ready to bolt, when he roared, "Blake will never know! Now shut up and let's enjoy her!"

The voice was the same, though the timbre had changed. It was like listening to Gollum arguing with himself. *Or,* I realized, *the man detesting the dragon within him.* Maybe there was some good left in this bug. The human part. The part that wailed at its own actions, that knew it was going to hurt Blake if it killed me.

That human part pleaded, "No! It'll destroy him! He needs her!"

I knew I should go. I was a complete idiot to stay, but I gravitated toward the door. It was open at least an inch—large enough for spying. I leaned in, desperate to glimpse within. The light blinded me a moment. Then my eyes adjusted, making out a figure standing, its back to me. No wings. Human.

Brown hair, tall, decent build from what I could tell. I didn't recognize him, and disappointment shot through me. I wanted answers. Who was this person who'd caused so much pain? Is this who swore I'd love him in the cabin? I didn't even know him. Nothing made sense.

The man clutched at his stomach, hunched over, and sobbed. "I refuse! I won't do it. Not this time." He gasped and doubled over, his words barely audible. "Anyone but her!"

Instantly, the man straightened and growled in a deep tone, "Already played that card! All those other girls can't compare to her! We've never hunted such a prize. Why deny us the satisfaction now? Nothing will quench this thirst but her, and you know it. Quit stalling. I'll kill a thousand others and still want her. Think of it as *mercy*. You're sparing them. Let *me* have *her!*"

It horrified and fascinated me. He *was* having an argument with his dragon side. *And it's over whether or not to kill me!*

And then, before my eyes, the man began morphing, a shriek tearing from his lips. His height shot up, his body tripling in size. His wings ripped out, tearing the flesh anew, blood splattering down his back. I saw then all the red, ragged scars marking him. Morphing tortured him.

I'd seen enough. Channeling the horror and adrenaline, I bolted, my eyes watering from either the speed or the terror I felt. Blind and in unfamiliar territory, I scraped against rough surfaces, dragged my legs through what felt like razors at times, hit my head, and slammed my body into hard rock more than once. I kept doubling back and pushing on. I had to get out even if I broke every limb doing it.

I heard the door crash open. It echoed down the chamber, ricocheting into a perverse surround sound. I wasn't sure if he followed after me. Did he go back to my room, hoping I was still unconscious there? How long did I have until he realized I was gone?

I pushed harder, faster.

Then I heard it. The roar of vicious anger coming from behind. He flew without light. *He knows these tunnels.* I didn't know why I hadn't thought of camo before. Digging within myself, while flying scared to death, I found my center. I had no real way of knowing if it had worked. Even if I held my hand directly in front of my face, I saw nothing either way.

But on the off chance my camo had worked, maybe it would help me hide. It was all I had… and the hard shard I'd hung onto.

I heard him approaching. The whoosh from his wings reverberated off the walls behind me. The air pressure changed with his flight pattern. Strange, but I could almost sense his movements from behind. When he turned to the side or angled down or up, I felt it within me. Like a sixth sense, I opened myself to it completely. *Feel him. Follow his movements. Track him.*

I only wished it worked as well with me. I couldn't sense the tunnel at all and, concentrating so much on the bug, I'd left myself too open to error. The impact of my skull smacking rock dazed me. My wings kept going, but I suddenly couldn't tell which way was up or down. My wings dragged my body haphazardly across a wall that felt like sandpaper before I could refocus on his movements. Once I felt his location behind me, I pressed forward.

"This is better than I'd hoped for, Samantha!" he yelled out to me. "Makes it so enjoyable." A wicked laughter flooded the tunnels.

He's so close! I darted to the left as my body grazed solid rock, trying to navigate the underground maze.

"Do you like it here?" he asked, his voice right behind me now.

I shrieked and he continued, each word sounding closer than the last. "I've always wondered what lay under abandoned mines. The outposts look so foreboding. Like rundown shacks with ghosts and goblins. Imagine my delight to discover the underground labyrinth. Home sweet…" Sharp claws grabbed at me, slipping off my arms, leaving gouges in their wake. "Home."

It happened fast, his body overtaking mine, wrapping me in his clutches from behind. His legs snaked around me, and my arms were instantly pinned, my wings crushed by his chest. I thrust my arm down, trying to spear him with my small dagger.

I hoped to hear a wail, but instead, the rumble of his laughter shook my frame. My weapon clattered to the ground, apparently bouncing right off his tough hide.

"Nice," he purred into my ear. "Now, let's get you back to my room for some fun."

CHAPTER
Thirty-seven

I fought him the whole way, but he was easily four times my size. By the time I saw the light from his opened door, I'd stopped struggling, trying to conserve some energy. Once I could see better, maybe I could figure a way out of this.

We went through the opening, and I was blinded by the light. I squinted, and then pinched my eyes shut when his enormous head rotated down to peer at me. Those black eyes would haunt me for the rest of my life. *That's if I live long enough to even have a nightmare.*

Then to my surprise, he let me go, shoving me to the ground. My eyes opened in time to catch my fall, bloody hands smacking the ground. I braced myself for the attack. Surely, he would do all that he'd promised to do, right? Have his fun... eat me for all I knew.

I waited, staring at my hands. I'd rather watch my blood pool on the ground than face him.

He breathed hard, his panting loud.

What's he waiting for? Maybe he wants to talk to me first...

I forced my neck to turn and absorbed all his horrid details. He had a barrel chest with scars decorating his skin, as if something used his body to sharpen its claws. His face was mostly human, albeit his features were out of proportion, eyes bug-like and positioned too far to the sides, small nose, enormous mouth, and brown hair spattering his skull in patches, not quite enough to cover it. His wings were horrifying and captivating. They started at his shoulders and dusted the floor with their ends. Instead of translucent with brilliant colors, they were mud brown, thick, with corded veins running through them. He stood over me, his chest heaving up and down.

Looking behind him, I took in my surroundings. It appeared to be a bedroom, if that nasty pile of cloth, springs, and feathers counted as a bed. Looked like a mattress after a tiger had gotten to it. There were a few metal, folding chairs, but nothing else.

I didn't know if it was stroke of genius or insanity, but I blurted, "You promised I'd fall in love with you, but I've *never* even *met* you."

His head cocked to the side, his eyes ogling me. "You may not know me, but I know you. You're all I heard about for so long," he growled. "Guess that's why I had to come see you myself. So you see—it's really *his* fault, not mine. He should've known better."

The monster roared and glanced away from me. "Just shut up! I don't want to talk! I want to *enjoy* her!" Still facing away, he sputtered, "But she should know why this is all happening. It's only fair."

I stared in a stupor, as he clenched his fists and faced me again, "She needs to know why we hunted her. Let her understand that at least. *Please.*"

We stared at each other, me too terrified to move. I wasn't sure which part of him had won the argument, and I wasn't sure if it even mattered either way. I was dead. I could see no way out of this.

He grumbled under his breath and then spat, "Fine." Reaching down, he hauled me to my feet. I didn't have time to react because he was throwing me at a chair. "Sit down. Guess I have to tell you *some things.*" He let out a stream of profanities.

Then, after he'd made sure I stayed in my chair, he grabbed my arm and, to my horror, ran his long, skinny tongue along my wrist. I tried to recoil, but his grip was iron. "Then, my dear, you'll be all mine. How I will savor finding out what makes you tick."

Think, Sam, he wants to talk... I tried to focus on what I could control instead of his repulsive actions. *Get him talking.*

"Why don't you change back—show me who you are? I will understand things then," I said, straightening my back, trying to be brave.

"You trying to trick me?" he growled.

"No, it's just I didn't think bugs... err... the ones Tonbo changed so long ago could morph. That means you are extra special, strong." I had no idea if these things ran on ego, but it was worth a try.

"*Tonbo* changed? Tonbo didn't do this to me."

"He didn't? Weren't you a super soldier?"

"Soldier?" he roared, laughing. "I'm no soldier. He gave it to me, and I took it. Played me like a fool, but nothing's going to change that now. Besides," he purred, "I like what I am."

"*Who* gave it to you?" I asked, hoping to keep him on topic.

He moved toward me, his arms reaching out. Maybe I'd run out of time. Maybe that was all I was getting. Then, to my surprise, he began morphing back. The creature collapsed down into the man I'd seen before. Only this time, I saw his face.

Brown eyes. *Kind*, brown eyes. Memories tugged at me. I tried desperately to place them. I'd seen them before. At the time, I'd been feeling terror and his eyes brought me comfort. This time, I could only gawk at them. My mouth dropped open.

"*You're the EMT!*" I finally croaked, remembering all too clearly that day. I passed out after running too long, and woke up to see those eyes.

The man's shoulders slumped. "I only get a minute with you. Then it'll take over. I've lost the battle. Don't talk. Let me."

I nodded, realizing that this might be my only time to escape too. I saw the open door in my peripheral.

"You were all he ever talked about. I knew how much he loved you, watched over you, and I assumed he'd never change you. He swore he wouldn't. So I decided I would change, become like him, so he wouldn't have to be alone," he gasped. Then he growled, "Oh, get on with it! Don't give her your whole damn story!"

I bit my lip. Should I bolt? How much longer would this man be here?

"Fine," he muttered to himself. "We were together when he heard you'd been taken. I'd been trying to get the courage to tell him what I'd done, but I was too ashamed. I realized the *thing* within me had taken control already. Something was wrong... my transformation wasn't the same as it was for others. But I couldn't tell him all that then; he said he had to find you. I wasn't sure why he kept up the pretenses, but I was hiding things too, so I didn't push. I told him to go, and I decided to find you myself." He sighed heavily, like he was resigned in his defeat. "Trust me, Samantha, I never meant to hurt you! To hurt anyone! I did all this," he struck out his chest, "for Blake!"

A thousand questions ran through my head. *He changed into a dragon for Blake—why?*

Who is he?

"So you changed me and then let me go? You were only doing it to help Blake. You knew he wouldn't do it, so you did, right? I'm sure Blake will understand—"

"No! He won't! I've done *horrible* things! I'm a monster! I tracked you down; your smell was so strong. Please believe me, I really only wanted to help. I found you tied up in the cabin. You were sleeping. I didn't want to scare you. I was worried if I woke you up that you'd think I had done it. I didn't want Blake to think that. So I untied you, got rid of the ropes, and waited outside the cabin for you to come to. About an hour later, you stumbled out. I stayed in camo and followed you for a few hours. Then I made an anonymous call to 911, saying I thought I'd found you. After that, it was easy. I joined the search team and led them to you. You see, I did it all for Blake. I want... wanted you both to be happy."

"You can still give that to us! Just let me go! Blake and I are very happy—"

He groaned and held his stomach. "No... I can't. You don't understand. I let *it* see you, smell you. It won't leave you alone. It's made me follow you, watch you."

Goose bumps covered my arms. My instincts were right. He had been hunting me.

"And then when that wasn't enough, I gave it... *others* to keep it satisfied." His face fell before me.

"Like Cally? You *were* in that tree with me," I said, realizing I'd been right.

"Yes. It wanted to grab you then. I was lucky some dragons were in the area and wanted to show off. They hadn't realized they'd picked a fight with Blake until it was too late. I fought the beast in me, made it take off. But I had to give it something in return." He swallowed hard.

"Where is she?" I asked, scared of the answer.

"She didn't last long," he whispered, his face contorted in pain. He held one shaking hand out toward me. "Samantha, I'm sorry. *It's obsessed with you.* I can't go on like this. I've tried everything I know of to rid myself of this thing, but it just gets stronger! I've tried to kill myself a thousand times, but I keep on living!"

The scars on his chest made more sense now. He groaned and then cackled. He was losing his inner battle.

I began thinking about the other girls' fate. *He can't die? And he won't stop killing until he gets what he wants. This needs to end.* I gazed back at him, knowing there was only one way for that to happen.

"I understand. Can I ask you a question before?" I couldn't say the words.

He nodded and licked his lips. I could see energy stirring behind his brown eyes.

"Did you tie me up in that cabin? Was it all you?" I had to know, even if that was the last thing I heard before I left this world.

The brown widened and then he winced, doubling over. "No, I'd only injected myself weeks before. Like I said, I kept trying to find the right time to tell Blake, to let him know he wouldn't be alone anymore. That his big brother would always be there for him." He groaned, his eyes turning black, his shoulders and back growing right before my eyes. He was morphing.

But I could only gape at him. *Big brother?* "Jaxon?" I gasped.

The man nodded. "I never would have injected myself, if I'd known…" His hands shot out as he groaned. His wings emerged, sounding like a cracked whip.

"Known what, Jaxon? *Known what?*" I shouted, jumping to my feet. The monster was here. I'd wasted my time, but I had to know.

"That *he* was going to change you after all!" he roared, the transformation complete. He grinned and lunged forward. "And I'm so glad he did!"

CHAPTER
Thirty-eight

I didn't have time to think about Jaxon's confession, that Blake was my monster, because the *real monster* was on top of me, knocking me to the ground with his claws.

"Stop! Jaxon! You can fight this!" I screamed out, my hands pushing back against the dead weight climbing on top of me, squashing my body with his. I didn't know what his intentions were—he didn't touch my dress or my body. *Maybe he's not going to rape me first; maybe I just get to die!* I hoped beyond hope. *Let it be quick.*

The weight of him on me was enough to end me; I had a hard time getting air in. Then his tongue began licking my face, and I convulsed. Maybe I'd been wrong about what he would do. If only I could get some leverage, do something! But my arms were pinned to the ground underneath him. He was literally smashing me to death, smothering me.

That's it! I stopped thrashing. I held perfectly still, letting my eyes roll back, just in case he watched my face. I stopped breathing, willing myself to think of my own metabolism slowing down.

He didn't seem to notice. His tongue was on my neck, his claws sinking into my arms as he held them down. Then he stopped abruptly. His weight lifted. A sharp pain seared my face. He'd slapped me, and I did my best not to flinch, letting my head fall to the side.

His hand fumbled with my wrist, and then his enormous head landed on my chest.

"No!" he barked. "You don't get to die yet!"

Don't breathe... don't breathe....

HIDDEN *Monster*

His fists pounded my chest. And then, to my horror, he tore my mouth open and his nasty lips landed on mine. It took all my willpower not to scream. He blew his foul air into my mouth. I wanted to puke. When he followed that with pounding on my chest, it dawned on me. *He's trying to resuscitate me!*

Was it Jaxon, the doctor within him, trying to save me? Did I come back to life?

Holding my breath was painful now. He was filling my lungs with air and then pounding them free. I had no choice; he was forcing me to stay alive. Yet, I kept my lungs still as I could, letting him do all the work and forcing my mind to drift away. *Picture you're under that tub again... picture you are lying in Blake's arms...* I cringed and prayed he hadn't noticed. But he was too busy bruising my sternum with his clumsy attempt at CPR.

Blake changed me? Could that really be true? At the moment, the terror over that paled in comparison to the fact that a deranged monster was trying to save me or kill me, I wasn't quite sure at the moment which. Either way, it was painful.

What do I do? Just wait until he gives up? Then the lips landing on mine felt softer. I almost opened my eyes to see who it was out of surprise, but I heard, "Let me save her! Just leave me alone while I do this!"

Jaxon morphed back to save me! Maybe he could be reasoned with. His hands were now on my chest, applying rhythmic compressions. *This is it. Take it or leave it.*

I took it and began coughing. At first, it was for show, but it felt so good to clear my full lungs that it quickly turned genuine. I tried to roll to my side as I coughed. His hands remained on me.

I opened my eyes, hoping to see kindness in his brown gaze. He was kneeling over me.

"Samantha! You're alive!" He sounded thrilled, but his eyes were already clouding over. "I shouldn't have saved you... it would have been better—"

"Jaxon, I know you don't want to hurt your brother, and I know you *don't* want to do this. Let me go! Let me go *now!*"

I didn't wait for an answer, shoving him back with my arms and forcing my wings into action. Surprised by my sudden movement, he fell on his back. I didn't wait to see if he was following, I shot out the door, flying hard.

This time, the tunnels were familiar, even in the blackness. It was like my body remembered its flight pattern from before. I didn't hit anything, all I felt was cold air slapping my skin. I dipped and zigzagged with its twists and turns. I didn't hear anything from behind. Maybe Jaxon was fighting himself, not allowing the bug in him to follow me.

I could only hope.

I didn't slow when the terrain felt new. I was getting farther than before! I pushed my wings harder, feeling the occasional graze as the tunnels narrowed. Then the scent in the air shifted, becoming fresher and cleaner. That was when I saw the hazy light above me. *A way out!* I changed directions and shot straight up. The light grew brighter, and my surroundings took shape. I was definitely in some kind of old mine shaft. The old timbers supporting the solid rock around me creaked and groaned. I spied a small staircase winding along the wall, up and up. A large, wooden door was at the top.

I made it! I zoomed toward it, my hands outreaching, desperately wanting to grab the handle. I was mere feet away from it when I heard the whoosh of wings from behind.

My instincts took over, and I swerved to my right. I felt his body graze me as he shot past, not expecting my sudden turn. I rotated around and aimed for the door again. I heard him growling out swear words as he reoriented his wings and doubled back at me.

He grabbed my ankles; I thrust my foot forward, kicking him hard in the head. I heard him grunt as his hands grappled for me again. The door got closer; I pushed my wings to their limit. My hands reached the handle and, to my horror, I discovered it was locked. It was the extra second he needed.

He wrapped me up in his clutches and chortled, "Think I'd leave my front door unlocked? Now, stop fighting this! No one's saving you. *You are all mine!*"

He shoved me down on the torn mattress. I sobbed uncontrollably, trying to fight him as he fastened my wrists and ankles together with duct tape. Then he retrieved ropes from the corner of the room and wrapped them around my torso, shoving my wings down. It was painful.

When he'd finished, and I was completely bound, something inside me shattered. My hope had been broken like a bone snapping in half. I'd given it everything, but he'd won. No one knew about this place. I knew of abandoned mines between Silverton and Ouray, Colorado, but this was Jaxon. He lived in California. I might be in Nevada or the Dakotas for all I knew.

Blake! My heart ached. *Please find me!* At this point, I didn't care what he'd done to me in the cabin or why. I wanted out of this place. I wanted to live.

He stood up straight, threw the tape aside, and began pacing the floor.

"Please, Jaxon," I begged.

"Shut up!" he roared back at me. "I'm done with your bewitching voice!" He picked the tape back up. "I never let the other girls speak. I was a fool to let you." He slapped the tape across my mouth. "So stop pleading. Jaxon can't hear you. It's time to get started. I'm dying to *taste* you!"

I screamed, even though it was muffled, and thrashed, trying to wiggle free. It didn't help. He reached out and pulled my arms forward. With one finger, he ran his sharp claw down my forearm, leaving a trail of blood and pain in its path. I gasped at the searing fire shooting up my arm and shoulder. My stomach clenched up.

"Don't worry, my dear. I've done this to enough damsels. It

won't kill you. You heal fast. You see, your blood lets me see how you work. I guess my inner doctor needs to be satisfied." He chuckled. "I've been so anxious to test you. I knew you were different. Your scent was enough to tell me that."

I convulsed with sobs. *Too bad I'm not special enough to save myself!*

Then, to my horror, he bent down and ran his tongue down my arm, licking the blood. I felt like I was going to be sick, but there was no option to throw up with my mouth taped shut.

I shook my head at him, my eyes spilling tears.

He sat back, my blood on his lips. "Yes, very different. You got a different serum, didn't you? So what's it do, I wonder? You see, I've developed a way to add to myself. Guess I have Jaxon to thank for that. I realized after I'd changed that I wasn't the same as Blake. And that I'd been tricked. I needed the camo DNA. So I hunted a few dragons and damsels, finally perfected the way to extract their DNA, and now look at me." He grimaced and disappeared before me. "I can do it too!"

What does he want me do, clap for him?

He reappeared and leaned in. "Your blood's so sweet."

I grunted against my tape. He considered me for a moment, and then mumbled, "Still, I wonder…"

To my relief, he stepped away and moved to the other side of the room. I hadn't noticed the closet in the corner before now. He opened the door and disappeared. I shoved my hands up and down, trying to free them from the tape.

I gave it all I had. This was my last few seconds. That was when I felt a tugging inside of me. Like a piece of me wanting to come out. I tried to focus, but it was incessant. My vision became hazy. *Can't pass out now!* I forced my eyes to stay open. Then, to my horror, I felt like I was fighting against myself. Like invisible hands were trying to pull me to the ground, force my eyes to close. *NO!* I shouted back at the feeling. *I'm not blacking out now! Last time I did, I ended up here!*

I gritted my teeth, letting anger wash over me, bathing me in a new strength and resolve. *I'm facing this head on! I can do this!*

The inner struggle ebbed, and I felt my body shift. I glanced down at my legs, no longer bare and bloody, but wearing jeans. *I'm morphing!* There was no blue dress. There was no long, blonde hair. From what I could tell, I was a brunette.

My bindings felt looser. Then realizing my whole frame was smaller, I understood why. *I'm not me anymore!* I didn't have time to wonder, as I began working my hands free. I could already feel my wings shifting with the extra room.

The bug—I couldn't think of him as Jaxon—reemerged, grumbling about something, staring at a book in his hands. When he glanced up, it landed on the floor with a thud.

"*Who the hell are you?*" He flew at me.

My hands were free, but my wings weren't. He landed on top of me, and I had only my fingernails to defend myself. I shoved them into his bulging eyes.

He swatted them away like they were nothing, shouting down at me, "What's going on here? Where did you come from? *What'd you do with Samantha?*"

From the looks of his hysteria, he had no idea who I was. *That makes two of us!*

His hands wrapped around my neck, easily cradling it in his massive hands. "I wanted Samantha! *Not you!*" He began to squeeze harder and harder.

I took one last, deep gulp of air, and once again held my breath. *Don't think he'll try to give me CPR this time.* At least, I hoped not. It didn't take long until he was satisfied he'd ended me. I made a show of it, thrashing around, and then suddenly holding very still. I let my body go limp when he finally released me, the mattress buffering my fall. I lay perfectly still, hoping he'd leave the room so I could escape.

"All that work! For *nothing!* I had my one chance, and she's gone! I don't understand where *you* came from. Maybe you aren't alone. I—" He stopped abruptly.

Then I heard it, a creak from outside the door. The scent of the woods on an autumn morning filled the room. My heart leapt. *Blake!*

CHAPTER
Thirty-nine

Next thing I knew, the door crashed open and Blake was barking out orders, "Mack, get the girl out here! Kory, flank my right side!"

I wanted to scream that it was really me, but there was no time. The bug met Blake head on, and Mack snuck around them to the left to get to me. I tore the tape from my mouth and began unfastening the ropes. My eyes never left Blake as he and the bug tore free from each other's initial attack and began circling one another. I had to tell Blake the truth. He needed to know who he was really about to fight.

A movement in the doorway caught my eye. Kory's frame still slunk there, a wicked grin on his face. *What can he possibly find funny about all this?* Then it hit me. He wasn't following Blake's orders. He wasn't going to help Blake at all, probably never planned on it either. *This was all a trap! He wants the bug to kill Blake!*

Mack had made it to me. I opened my mouth, trying to explain, but his eyes were wide.

"*Sammy? Sammy is that really you?*" he asked quietly.

He must be able to tell it's me somehow. "Yeah, it's me. Mack-"

But he cut me off, "I can't believe you did it! Let's get you out of here!"

He scooped me up, although I protested, "No! Wait, you can't leave Blake! *Kory's* not helping *him!*"

It was when I uttered Kory's name that the bug stopped his pursuit of Blake. His eyes rotated to the doorway.

"*You!*" he growled, trying to shove Blake out of his way. Blake didn't move and they became tangled in each other's arms again, the bug leaving bloody streaks down Blake's arms.

Kory's grin deepened, and then he disappeared from sight. I doubted he was using camo to help Blake win the fight. Then it dawned on me. *Kory's the one who tricked Jaxon.* He probably talked him into changing for his brother. *But where did he get the bug DNA?* Then I remembered that they had killed the last bug. Maybe Kory had extracted some of the bug's DNA before they'd destroyed the body.

"Kory!" Blake shouted after him, while sending the bug's head snapping back with an uppercut. But Kory was gone. Blake swore under his breath. "Should've known."

The bug moved fast, hooking Blake across the jaw, sending him flying backwards. "Get out of my way! *I end Kory today!*" the bug yelled.

"Yeah, well, that makes two of us who want to kill him, but *you're* not leaving!" Blake's foot shot up, connecting with the bug's chin. The impact from the kick sent the bug soaring back.

Blake glanced in my direction. "Mack, get her out of here! *Now!*" he commanded.

"No way are you facing this alone! I'm not leaving. Sammy's fine," Mack shouted back.

Blake's jaw was clenched, ready to argue, but then he gaped at me. Mack calling me Sammy had him confused; I could see it all over his beautiful face.

Blake wasn't the only one gawking at me; the bug's eyes raked my body up and down.

"*Sammy?*" the bug repeated slowly.

Durn it, Mack, you gave me away! I wanted to shout, but it was too late.

"But you were dead... How's this possible?" The bug rose to his feet. The pace in the room came to a halt; he didn't seem to notice anyone or anything but me.

Blake used that to his advantage and came at the bug from behind, wrapping his legs around its wings, practically standing on its shoulders. He threw his arm around the bug's neck, putting him in a chokehold. *He drank my blood... Can he hold his breath now too?*

Blake was exerting everything he had into suffocating the monster. It was a strange moment. The bug and I just stared at each other, as if time had frozen. He touched Blake's arm, almost like he was putting the pieces together. Then he strode forward, Blake looking like he was merely along for the ride instead of posing a threat.

He must be able to hold his breath or he'd be passed out by now.

The bug grinned. "I was right! You *are* special, Samantha!"

Like Blake weighed nothing, the bug ran straight toward me. That was when Blake released his chokehold and produced two long knives from his back. He must've had them stashed back there. Instantly, they were crossed and tucked under the monster's throat.

One quick jerk upwards with the blades and he'd be decapitated. The bug stopped, his black eyes calculating his next move.

I saw Blake's wrists move, the knives coursing upward, the blood oozing out.

"*Stop! Wait!*" I screeched. "Blake, you can't kill him! He's your *brother!*"

Blake's hands froze, blood dripping down his weapons.

"*That's impossible!*" he gasped, as the bug gurgled on its own blood.

"*It is!* It's Jaxon! *Kory* did this to him! That's why the bug wants Kory! That's why Kory brought you here! This was all Kory's idea!" The words gushed out.

I rushed forward, and I saw the uncertainty flash in Blake's eyes. Maybe he didn't really believe it was me. *Maybe he thinks this is another trap.* I tried desperately to focus on changing back. I didn't know how I'd done it before. I tried to think of Mack's words, *Find that quiet place within yourself.* I willed myself to look like me again.

When Blake's hostile expression melted, I knew I'd done it.

"*Sam?* Is it really you? I thought I'd lost you!" Blake choked the words out and then his eyes hardened, the aqua turning to steel.

"*You* did *this* to *her?*" Blake roared at the bug, the knives once again angling into Jaxon's throat.

"Blake! He can't stop himself! It's the dragon in him doing it!" I pleaded.

But Blake didn't seem to hear me. He had taken one look at me, and his jaw was set in stone. I glanced down at myself. My dress was shredded, and I was covered in scrapes, bruises, and crusted blood. My one arm still oozed from its long gash.

Mack's eyes were saucers, taking my appearance in. "Come on, Sammy. Let's get you out of here."

Maybe it was seeing me hurt and bloodied that changed his mind, but Mack grabbed my arms and began shoving me from the room. I tried to fight him. I needed Blake to understand that Jaxon wasn't totally gone.

"He tried to save me, Blake!"

Blake's eyes widened, and the tension in the knives slipped only for a split second. I could feel Blake's inner turmoil. *He wants to believe me.*

It happened fast. The bug threw back his head and hit Blake's face with a thud. I heard a loud crack and wondered if it was Blake's nose. They became entangled in battle, the bug using his bare arms to defend Blake's blows.

Blake's face appeared conflicted while his body went into autopilot. He literally began slicing the bug down with his dual blades, his moves fluid, each strike hard and fast. Blake easily dodged the bug's counterattacks.

The bug slowed down, slipping in its own blood.

I clung to the doorframe, not letting Mack take me away. *This isn't right!* Blake shouldn't have to kill his own brother! My heart ached for Jaxon, knowing he couldn't stop the monster he'd become, no matter how hard he tried. Tonbo had said it was like being Jekyll and Hyde. *This isn't Jaxon's fault! It's Kory's! He's the real monster here! And he escaped!*

I couldn't bear to look at Blake's face, his determination to save me, no matter what the costs. I didn't know what overcame me, but I tore free of Mack's grip and flew straight at Blake. I threw my body in front of the bug and held my hands out to Blake.

"*Stop!* You can't kill him!"

Blake's rage was derailed at the sight of me. In that second, I knew he didn't want this either. He hated what he had to do.

"Get out of the way, Sam!" Blake yelled.

"Jaxon's in there, Blake! You have to believe me!" I begged.

The bug wasted no time, its claws grabbing at me from behind, but Mack interceded, plowing it down with his own body. I heard Mack's yelp as the two of them collided into a wall. The bug threw Mack's body off him, and Mack didn't get back up. Blood began pooling under Mack's belly, spreading on the floor.

"Mack!" I screamed. *What have I done?* I rushed towards him, Blake on my heels, blades raised ready for the final kill.

I knew I had only a second to fix this and in that moment, I knew what to do. I stood between Blake and the bug, their course set for a deadly collision. I closed my eyes and searched my soul. I'd only seen the picture once, and I prayed it'd be enough.

I held my breath and gave it everything I had. I felt my body shrink; it was surreal and dreamlike. I didn't dare open my eyes, but I heard Blake gasp and the bug let out an unearthly howl. It must have worked because no one touched me, and it went silent. After a second, I peeked out. The room felt bigger from where I stood. I faced the bug, who was now insanely tall and menacing.

No one moved. I heard Mack's groaning. I longed to get to him, to bind up his wounds. But this had to happen first.

The bug's breathing was ragged, its eyes not leaving my face.

"*NO!*" he wailed. "Not *my boy!* Anyone but him!" He withered in pain, twisting and falling to the ground. He clutched at his chest and then pounded it, screaming.

I felt a warm hand slip into mine and gazed up to see Blake.

He whispered, "I don't know how you're doing it, Sam, but smart move."

I nodded back at him and then reached my hand out to the bug, who was visibly crying on his knees.

"Daddy." My voice was not my own, but the voice of a child.

With one last gasp of pain and anguish, the bug was no more. Jaxon was on his hands and knees before us. I couldn't help myself. I rushed toward him. Jaxon opened his arms to me, and I let him crush me against his chest.

"It's okay, you're going to be okay now," I said, wondering if Jaxon really believed I was his little boy. Either way, I was going to play the part. I'd hoped that Jaxon's son would be the last person he'd let the bug harm. Glad I'd been right.

Jaxon rocked back and forth, sobbing into my small frame. Then I felt strong hands reach down and detach me. I looked up to see there was no vengeance in Blake's eyes, only anguish. I stepped away, hoping Blake would do the right thing with his brother. Someone else needed my help. *Mack!*

I wasn't sure what I could do, small as I was, but I raced toward him, landing on my knees next to him. At my touch, he rolled over on his back and grinned. He looked terrible.

"That's trippy," he mumbled, giving my chin a nudge.

I tried to cover his stomach, where I could only assume Jaxon's claws had dug into during their tumble. But my little hands did nothing. I searched the room for something to use as a bandage.

Mack shook his head at me, removing my hands. "Don't worry, half pint. I'm fine. See…" He held up his T-shirt, and I grimaced at the holes in his flesh. "It's not that bad."

"*That* doesn't make me feel better," I said, a little wigged out by my own small voice.

Mack tried to laugh, but he ended up coughing. "I'll heal," he mumbled.

Jaxon's weeping caught my attention, and I turned to see

what was happening. Jaxon was still on his knees before Blake's feet, sobbing uncontrollably.

Blake's hand was on his brother's shoulder, but Jaxon refused to be comforted. Finally, Blake reached down and forcibly pulled his brother up to his feet. Jaxon's eyes remained downcast.

"Jaxon," Blake's voice was deep, "listen to me."

He shook his head, still refusing to meet Blake's gaze. I'd never seen such a broken man before. My heart ached for him, even though moments before he'd been trying to kill me. But that hadn't been the real Jaxon.

"I can't... I've tried..." Jaxon cried.

"We'll fix this together. I'm not going to let you fail this time," Blake said firmly, clutching Jaxon's shoulders with his hands.

Jaxon slowly raised his head.

"You're not alone anymore. You saved my life, big brother." Blake's voice caught. "Now, it's time for me to save yours."

CHAPTER

Forty

B lake secured Jaxon's hands, just in case the monster decided to reemerge. Jaxon didn't refuse the binding but seemed to welcome it. I decided it would be best to remain looking like Jaxon's son. I had no idea what his name was, I realized, but it didn't really matter. *Ask later... don't want to disrupt the effect it's having on Jaxon.*

Blake walked over to Mack, who was still lying on the ground, and nudged him with his foot. "You healed yet? Don't have all day, you know."

I wanted to tell him not to be so insensitive, but I noticed his expression. He might not say it in words, but he was worried about him.

Mack grunted and rolled to sit up. His arm wrapped around his stomach. "Tell your brother to cut his nails, will you?"

Blake grunted and grabbed Mack's hand, pulling him to his feet.

Jaxon mumbled from behind, "Didn't mean to hurt you, Mack."

Mack shook his head with a grin. "No worries, Jax. Let's get you to Tonbo for a little makeover. Pretty sure you want to ditch the enormous noggin too, right?"

"Mack," I gasped, not sure how Jaxon would take the teasing. We were lucky Jaxon was here and not the bug. I didn't want to push it.

"What? It's true," Mack protested. "I'm sure it can't be easy to find shirts that fit over that thing."

"Stop!" I tried to slap Mack's arm, but not use to my short stature, my hand barely grazed his elbow. He laughed and I noticed that everyone, including Jaxon, smiled. *Well, at least everyone's in good humor. Hope it stays that way.*

Blake decided he would tow his brother once we made it out of the mine; no one wanted him transforming to use his wings. And Mack would tow me, at least until we parted ways, since looking like Jaxon's son left me wingless as well. I had so many questions to ask, but now wasn't the time. Jaxon had to get to the island fast; we didn't know how long he'd be able to fight the bug off. Blake wanted Mack to see me safely home. To my relief, I'd only been missing for a few days and Blake had assured my parents I'd return as soon as I was over the flu and up for the drive.

We hustled through the underground labyrinth, only this time using torches. I thought having lights would be better, but I was wrong. The tight places and tunnels totally freaked me out. *Can't believe I flew through all this before!* Everything felt damp and smelled rank and old. I couldn't wait to get out, to breathe fresh air again. Once the stairs appeared, I glanced up to see the wooden door was now scattered down the stairs in pieces. *Guess the guys kicked it in when they got here with Kory.*

Kory. That name enraged me. He'd caused quite a mess and left us all here to clean it up. Blake was right; he couldn't be trusted.

Like it or not, the problems didn't end with Kory. Jaxon had confirmed it was Kory who convinced him changing into a dragon would be the best thing for Blake. As we climbed the steps, I decided I had to ask Jaxon one last thing before we parted ways.

Bright sunlight hit my eyes, and we left the underground world behind. As I stepped on to the wooden platform, I peered around to see we were inside a rundown shed, made of wood. Many of the planks were broken, leaving gaping holes in the walls, through which the wind howled. Loose timber above us rattled and clanked together. It felt like the whole thing might come down on our heads at any moment.

When Blake stepped over to Mack to make sure he was up to

the flight, I moved to Jaxon's side.

"Ready for this?" I asked.

The tears he'd shed before left his face looking like a zebra whose stripes were made of dirt.

He nodded. "I need this."

"Jaxon." I lowered my voice, "Why did you say before you thought it was Blake?"

Jaxon stared at the floorboards for a moment, and then met my gaze. "While we were camping, he left for a while. I figured he'd gone to see you. Then when he came back, he seemed agitated. Mack showed up the next day to tell us you were gone."

Jaxon glanced over at Blake and shrugged. "I don't know. I guess I assumed he'd done it. But I don't know really. It went against everything he tried to protect you from. Little did he know that he really needed to protect you from his big brother."

"That's not your fault," I said, feeling bad I'd brought any of this up.

"That's right. It's Kory's," Blake cut in. I wondered how much of our conversation he'd overheard. His expression hardened. "And he will pay for this."

I just couldn't believe Blake was the bad guy and decided to let it go. Like Jaxon said, he'd just assumed. There were still so many things I didn't understand. Like how had I ended up in Jaxon's cavern anyway? Where had Jaxon found me? Last I knew, I was safe with Tonbo and Kate. The moment Blake took off flying with his brother, I regretted not asking him that question. Once they were out of sight, I decided it was time to be me again.

Mack waited at my side, his eyes wide. "This is so incredible, Sammy. No one else can do this. Wonder how you are doing it?"

"Beats me." I closed my eyes and concentrated on my own features. I felt my body grow and shoot up at the same time. I opened my eyes.

Mack was close now, suddenly not so tall. He reached over and touched my face. "Are you still hurt?"

I glanced down at myself. I was back in the ratty, black dress, and my scrapes and bruises had healed. "No, I'm good. Just need a hot shower and some clean clothes."

Mack removed his hand, the spot he'd touched remaining warm. "Well, it won't do for your folks to see you like that. Let's hit my house first. Then you can clean up a bit."

"Yeah, you could use a shower too," I said, poking him in the rib.

He grunted, pretending to double over in pain. Then he chuckled and stripped off his bloody T-shirt. I couldn't help myself; I reached over and touched the healing wounds.

"That's amazing. You're like Wolverine," I gasped.

His hand landed on mine, and he winked. "And I'd love to say you're my Gene Gray, but I'm pretty sure you take the cake as Mystique."

My eyes met his. I wasn't sure why the moment felt awkward. Maybe it was that he referred to me as his Gene Gray when we'd only ever been friends.

I decided to laugh, even if it was forced, and removed my hand. I was glad Mack chuckled and said, "Come on, Mystique. Let's get home."

I nodded, and we took off. My wings had healed completely and I felt a new strength within myself. I didn't know if it was the fact I was alive, not dead in some underground mine, or if it was just being with my best friend again. Either way, the adrenaline pumping through me felt good.

As soon as we left the ground and I surveyed our surroundings, we were just outside of Ouray, Colorado, where many old, abandoned mining outposts remained. Since we were only seventy miles from home, we got back within minutes. We remained in camo all the way up and into Mack's bedroom window. He assured me his parents were at work, not that they'd care either way if I were there. We shed the camo.

"Just in case," he said, locking the door. "I want you to have privacy."

I knew Mack's bedroom well, having been there countless time. He went inside the adjoining bathroom to turn the shower on for me.

"Want me to head over to your house and get you some clothes while you shower?" he asked when he came back into the room.

"Yeah, that'd be awesome, thanks. Just grab whatever's laying around. I don't care."

"Okay, be back in a sec," he said, and then disappeared from sight.

I smiled, climbing into the shower, realizing that Mack's scent comforted me. Reminded me of Christmastime in the kitchen. *Wonder if he knows he smells like pumpkin pie?*

CHAPTER
Forty-one

I let the hot water wash away everything. All the blood and dirt swirled down the drain. I purposely enjoyed a long shower, knowing Mack had to fly to my house, sneak in, and get my clothes. When the water started to turn cold, I shut it off with the guilty realization that Mack still needed one to.

I dried off, wrapped the towel around my body, and poked my head out the door.

"Mack?" I called quietly, just in case someone had come home.

I peered around the room. No one was there. I shut the bathroom door, deciding I'd wait in here. The minutes ticked by. *What's taking him so long? Oh, please don't tell me my parents caught him up in my room!*

Getting anxious and impatient, I decided to try something. I stared at my reflection, my blonde hair dripping on my shoulders. *Okay, here it goes…*

I shut my eyes and focused on brown hair. That was all I could remember from her. I felt my body shift, the towel loosening under my armpits. I peeked at the mirror and gasped.

I was no longer me! I had shoulder-length, brunette hair, bright green eyes, and a freckled nose. I smiled at my reflection, pretty, not movie star hot, but nice looking.

I took the towel off. I was wearing those same jeans and T-shirt from before, no wings. *This is so weird. So who am I?* I'd seen one picture of Blake's nephew when Blake had come over to my house. But I'd never seen her before.

I heard some noises in Mack's bedroom and decided he must be back. I opened the door to see Mack reappearing, holding my clothes.

"Hey," I said as he turned around to face me.

"Sammy?" His mouth went slack, and his eyes widened.

"Yeah, it's me," I reassured him. "I wanted to try this out again, only wish I knew who this was."

"You don't know?" he asked, his tone seeming surprised.

"No, I have no idea."

Mack set my clothes down on his bed and then moved to his dresser. He pulled open his top drawer, riffled through the socks, and then retrieved a small photo. He held it out to me.

"Maybe this will help you," he said, his voice soft.

I stared at the photo in my hands. I recognized the girl only because I currently was her. I raked my brain, trying to think if I'd seen her before. Nothing came to mind.

I shook my head. "I don't remember. Who is this?"

"You really don't know, do you?" His words seemed like they were more for himself. Was I imagining the pain I saw in his expression?

"What's going on, Mack? Tell me why I should know her."

He shook his head and then sat down on his bed, sighing. Something about his demeanor made me feel sad inside. Always the lighthearted of the two of us, I'd never seen my friend so distraught. I moved to sit next to him, reaching over to take his hand in mine.

I wasn't sure how it happened, but the next thing I knew, Mack's lips landed on mine. Shocked, I wanted to shout, *What on earth are you doing?* But there was a part of me that liked it. My hand slipped behind his neck and, dumbfounded by my own actions, I began kissing him back.

He wrapped me up in his arms, his kisses turning more intense. There was something so familiar about Mack's touch. *But this isn't right!* I stopped letting him cradle me, and began pushing against his chest.

I turned my neck, pulling my lips away. "No, wait."

He jerked away fast, jumping off the bed.

I stared at him, confused at what just happened. Had he wanted that? Or was it just one of those weird moments? He ran his hands through his hair, not making eye contact. When he began pacing the floor, I had the feeling that this wasn't a random act. *Maybe he likes me.* Something inside me stirred. My heart ached to see him upset.

"Mack, stop," I said, standing up.

To my surprise, he stepped further away, continuing his pacing. "No, no, no," he mumbled. "This wasn't how it was supposed to go."

"What are you talking about? Kissing me? Mack, it's okay. Don't feel bad," I said, reaching out to touch him.

Breathing hard, he glanced over at me, and I saw the torture in his eyes. "Samantha, I'm sorry. I shouldn't have done that."

I stared at him. "Oh come on, Mack, was it that bad?" I teased. "Hey, we've been best friends forever. Sometimes, these things just happen."

He shook his head. "I shouldn't have done that. It won't happen again."

"Mack, I had no idea how you really felt. Why didn't you tell me?"

He met my gaze. "I did, but you don't remember."

"What? When?" I asked, an uneasiness creeping into my stomach.

He pointed at the picture I held in my hand. "That girl was some random picture you found. You hated looking like your family. You told me you'd rather look like her."

"Mack, what are you talking about? I don't remember any of this!"

Instead of answering, he took one step closer to me. "Sammy." His voice was low. "Say something. I need to know. I can't go on like this. Is it really over?"

I bit my lip. I wanted to remain friends. I didn't want to lose him in my life. Everything was happening too fast. "It doesn't have to be over."

"But you don't love me? You love Blake?"

"I... I am in love with Blake," I answered, my voice catching in my throat. I didn't want to hurt my friend. Why did that stupid kiss have to happen? Then I realized Mack was in love with me. Kiss or not, this was bound to happen eventually. *That's why Kate and he understand one another.*

"I'm so confused. I always thought you wanted Jen. I had no idea. I'm so sorry, Mack."

Without thinking, I tried to hug him, but he recoiled from me, jumping away like he was made of springs.

"You shouldn't hug me, Samantha. You're with Blake."

"I can hug friends," I protested, annoyed he kept calling me Samantha. "Kissing, maybe not." I hoped he'd laugh, but he didn't. He resumed pacing the floor, his agitated manner unsettling.

"Can we at least talk about this?" I asked.

When he didn't say anything, I wondered when he had told me of his feelings. I had no memory of it at all. *Did I say I liked him back?*

About to ask him, something struck me odd about his behavior. He paced, hands clasped together, taking six step forward, and six steps back. The hairs on my neck rose. *No... it can't be...*

I gasped, and his eyes riveted on me.

"I can't believe it... I *won't* believe it!" I stammered. I backed away from him, as he was ironically moving closer to me now.

"Sammy?" he asked, his hand reaching out. "Do you remember now?"

I gaped at him. "Oh, I remember," I whispered. "I remember *that pacing.* It was *you,* wasn't it? *You* were in the cabin!"

I wanted to bolt, but I was so shocked that I remained planted where I stood.

Mack's expression turned contrite. "Sammy, wait, you don't understand."

"How could you do that to me? You were the one person I always trusted! You did all that so I'd fall in love with you?"

He closed the gap between us, grabbing my arms. "I could only hope and dream you would love me one day. You have to believe me; I never wanted to go through with it. It was all *her* idea."

"*Who*, Mack? Enough with the games. I need answers!" I shook his arms free of me. Then it occurred to me. "Was it Kate who put you up to it?"

"Yes, but it wasn't just Kate." Mack hesitated. "It was Sammy's idea."

I wanted to punch him. "This was *my* idea? Are you insane! I know you expect me to believe a lot of things that I don't remember, but I'm pretty sure I didn't abduct myself!"

"No, but it's time you know the truth. You aren't Sammy. She's," his voice cracked, "long gone."

CHAPTER
Forty-Two

I stared at him, my chest heaving up and down. "What on earth are you talking about? You *are* crazy. I'm leaving now."

"No, wait, let me explain. Please, Samantha. I need to get this off my chest. I can't do this anymore. You're right, I betrayed you, my own best friend. And I lied to Blake." His face visibly paled. "Pretty sure I'm a dead man when he finds out. But you have to let me tell you what's really going on."

As much as I wanted to scream and throw a holy tantrum, his last plea got to me. More than anything, I needed to know the truth. I was done being confused.

"Okay, spill it. And when you're done, I leave. Don't touch me, and don't follow me. Do you understand? Or I will make sure Blake's not kind." I regretted my last words as soon as they came out. Seeing Mack's flinch confirmed that I'd gone too far.

Like it or not, it was still Mack. *Freaky liar, probably psychopath, but still Mack.* For whatever reason, I couldn't stomach seeing him hurt. It tore at something inside me, like a throbbing hangnail.

"You might want to sit down for this," he said gently.

I sighed heavily, and then shrugged as I plopped down on his bed. "Okay. I'm sitting."

To my relief, he stood far from me. "Samantha, when you drowned as a kid, it did something to you. When you were underwater, someone *else* took over. You have another personality within you. It's *Sammy*."

That wasn't what I'd been expecting, and my mouth gaped open to protest. There was no way that was true? Was there?

"What do you mean—another *personality?*"

"Sometimes, when someone's traumatized or really afraid, multiple personalities emerge to protect or defend that person. That's what happened to you. You don't remember it because you blackout when she comes and wake up when she leaves you."

My eyes widened. "Blake told me I'd felt his face underwater when he saved me, but I only remember this feeling I'd be okay and the next minute I was above water…"

Mack nodded. "Yeah, that was probably Sammy. That's when she first came to be. In your moment of sheer terror, she came to save you. Honestly, when Blake asked me to look out for you at school, neither one of us knew about your other side yet. After you and I'd become good friends, I saw her. Maybe six months after the drowning incident, we were out in your yard playing when you fell down. When you didn't get up, I ran over to see if you were okay. I must've been saying your name because all of a sudden you sat up and glared at me. You shouted, 'I'm not Samantha!'"

Mack chuckled a little. "I said 'sure, whatever, *Samantha*' and you hulled back and socked me in the nose. So then I was like 'fine, tell me who are you then?' And then you freaked out, got all scared on me, saying you didn't know."

I could only stare at Mack. I didn't want to believe this could be true. And yet, I'd been experiencing blackouts, going to therapy, supposing it had to do with my fear of drowning, and never really understanding why for as long as I could remember.

"I'd said something like, 'fine whatever, you're Sammy,' and you calmed right down. You told me to call you Sammy from then on, not Samantha. I thought you were just joking around and I humored you. Then it kept happening. You'd be all nice and then just shift into this bossy prima donna. We'd be out riding and then you'd dump the bike and want to go to my house so you could rummage through my science books."

"That does not sound like me at all," I cut in.

"I know, you hate science. And school. But Sammy wanted to study all the time. It was like she couldn't get enough. I tried to shrug it off for a while. And I debated whether to tell Blake, and then Sammy begged me not to tell anyone. That's when I heard your mom and dad arguing one day in the kitchen. You were up in your room, and I was waiting for you downstairs. Your mom kept saying how she didn't understand why you were so different. Why you kept lying about where you'd been or what you'd done all day. I decided I had to tell them what I'd seen. Your parents put you into therapy after what I'd told them. During your first session, Sammy came out. She was ticked at me for telling your parents. She emerged to tell the therapist to mind her own business. By then, your parents knew what was really happening. Your dad took it pretty well, kept being patient and calling you Sammy when you seemed upset. But your mom had a harder time with it. For whatever reason, Sammy came out more for her, and the two of them didn't get along at all."

Mack grimaced.

I swallowed hard. "This sounds too crazy to be true, but it makes too much sense. That's probably why Jeremy told me he'd catch me with you all the time and get all annoyed. I never understood what he was talking about. He saw us together when I was Sammy."

"*Jeremy*." Mack spat the word out. "Blake's right, he's the mother of all douches. Samantha, it didn't take long for everyone to think you were a bit off at school. I tried to keep the rumors from flying, but you'd pass out in class and then act strange, different. No one knew what to expect. Your parents let the teachers know of your disorder, but they wanted to keep it discreet for you. But that didn't matter to everyone else."

Another piece to my puzzle. "So that's why no one ever wanted to date me? And why only Jen and you were my friends?"

Mack gave me a sad smile. "Yeah. By the time we'd hit high school, guys thought you were totally hot, but steered clear. Until

Jeremy. He pretty much told everyone he didn't care if you had an IQ of ten, you were good looking, and that's all that mattered to him."

"Ugh. He just wanted to make out with me?"

"Pretty much. Blake and I wanted to deck him on more than one occasion. You see, I had fallen for Sammy while Blake was in love with Samantha."

I gaped at him. Shocking as it was, another piece fell into place. "Did Blake know about Sammy and how you felt about me... or her?" I asked at last.

"No, he didn't. I couldn't admit to him that I'd fallen for the girl he loved most of all, even if it was just one side of her. When Sammy realized how I felt about her, she pressured me to find a way to free her." His face saddened. "What started out as her trying to save you, changed. She felt she was stronger then you, so she could take better care of you. Keep you safe. She said she loved you more than anything... and that was why she had to find a way to be the dominant personality."

"What do you mean? Seems like she just comes whenever the heck she wants. I'm always passing out, waking up somewhere new." I gasped, realizing what my words meant. "That's what happened in Tonbo's theater, isn't it?"

Mack nodded slowly. "Yeah, I think she took over, flew back home. To do what, I'm not sure really. We were hunting, well, Jaxon. Truth is, Sammy wasn't always honest with me." He grimaced. "But I'm getting ahead of myself. I need to tell you how it all happened."

I nodded, not really looking forward to the bit about the cabin. I just couldn't stomach that Mack had purposely tried to terrorize me.

"Sammy was smart, like I said, and determined to find a way to heal herself. She was convinced that if she could fix her broken pieces, she would be the one left in control. You see, she can only emerge from time to time. Most of the times are when you're nervous, afraid, and almost always when you're in danger. She'd get so mad at you for mountain biking. She'd curse at how she'd find herself suddenly plummeting precariously down some slick cliff. She'd get you out of the scrape and then march to my house to use my computer." Mack glanced at me. "Or to do other things."

I felt my face heat. Was that why Mack's lips felt familiar and welcoming to me?

"Other things?" I repeated.

"Yeah, well, we liked each other. Sammy told me she loved me. She wanted us to be together. I'd never had anyone like that before. It happened one time when we were kissing. I lost control and—" I almost gasped at what he might be implicating, but he finished with, "I transformed into a dragon right before her."

"Oh," I said, relieved beyond measure that that was it.

"I knew I'd messed up. And she wouldn't stop with the questions until I'd pretty much spilled the beans. Once I'd told her all about the Dragon Fae world, and Blake, she figured out that he was who had saved her that day in the water. She immediately wanted to know if the scrum would work for her. Make it so she'd be herself permanently, never to disappear again."

Now I was beginning to understand why Mack had said it was Sammy's plan.

"So in other words, Sammy wanted *me* to disappear forever," I said.

Mack frowned. "Yeah, and that's why I told her no. As much as I loved her and wanted to be with her, I cared for you as my friend. I never wanted to hurt you, Samantha. You have to believe me."

"So what happened then? Why'd you end up doing it anyway?"

"Love makes you foolish and blind, I'm ashamed to say. Sammy started researching more and more into the science behind it all. Reading all about Alois Oldrich."

"Who's that?" I asked.

"That's Tonbo's real name. His Czech name before he changed it to Tonbo."

"Oh. So she still wanted to change herself... err... me?"

"Yeah. She became obsessed with meeting Tonbo. She begged me to at least take her to the island so she could see it. I don't know why I caved. She could be so persuasive. As much as I loved her, looking back, I can see how stupid I was. So I agreed. Found a time that Blake would be with Jaxon hunting, and I brought her to the island."

"Where did my parents think I'd gone?"

"I told them I wanted to take you with my family on vacation. At that point, your mom needed a break from well... you. Sammy made sure of that. And your parents knew that I knew, and Sammy would listen to me most of the time. So they agreed and we went 'with my parents to California.'"

"We didn't really though, huh?" I said.

"No way, but your parents trusted me. And my folks, they don't care when I head over to the island. They've long accepted that's a part of who I am."

"When did we go?" I asked.

"About four months ago, during summer break. I took you there. Showed you the island, even went into Tonbo's office."

"Ah... the tiles in the foyer. They were so familiar!" I gasped. "And so were Tonbo's gardens." I glanced at Mack. "And so was Kate."

He nodded. "Yeah, I introduced you to Kate. All the while, you remained Sammy. I was scared to death any moment you'd change back to Samantha. It was risky, idiotic, and I can't believe it worked. We stayed only one day. We left that night."

"But I would have looked like myself... and if I met Tonbo, why didn't he say anything when I went with you guys again?"

"Kate told me which days Tonbo would be visiting the outskirts. He likes to make sure the ancients are okay. So we went on a day he was gone. Kate made sure of it. I just couldn't risk him seeing you. He would've told Blake. He loves Blake." There was no envy in his statement about Tonbo loving Blake. If anything, I almost felt like Mack felt the same way about him. "We did try to disguise you a bit.

You wore a brown wig and big sun glasses."

"Well that explains why I felt like I was having déjà vu the whole time I was there. So then what happened?"

"Well, Sammy and Kate started talking. At that point, all I just thought was that the visit went great and the two of you had hit it off as friends. We headed home with me sweating bullets the whole way. After a few weeks of being home, I finally breathed a sigh of relief. No harm, no foul. Sammy even backed off from begging me to change her."

I stared at him. "I have a hunch that Sammy and Kate weren't just discussing their favorite bands."

"No, they weren't," he said, running his hand through his hair.

CHAPTER
Forty-Three

He began pacing and then glanced at me, stopping abruptly. "Sorry," he said, I guess realizing what that reminded me of. He seemed to hesitate, like he didn't want to tell me the rest.

"So then what, Mack?" I probed.

He sighed. "Well, then Sammy showed me that picture."

I glanced down, realizing I was still holding the photo of the girl I still was. In all my shock over Mack being my monster in the cabin, I'd forgotten to change back.

"She told me that if she could ever find a way to be herself, she was going to look like her," he said. Then he pointed at me, "Like you."

"So that's how you knew it was me in the caves? And why you thought when you came in today that I was really Sammy? And you kissed me? Because I looked like her?"

"Yeah. I thought she'd done it. But let me explain the rest. As much as I don't want to tell you what I did, I have to. I tried to ignore the fact that Sammy seemed like she had plans. I wasn't going to give her the serum and I knew Blake would never... so I figured you were safe. Then a few days before you were abducted, Blake discovered Sammy's existence. We'd been so careful. I knew I should've told Blake from the start, but I loved Sammy. And she begged me not to tell him. Why, I'm not really sure. Well, Blake came when I wasn't expecting him. He'd been camping with Jaxon. Anyway, when he saw you as Sammy, he knew something wasn't right."

Mack clasped his hands together. "He always knew you struggled.

He knew about the therapy. He knew you didn't fit in socially, but he only ever saw Samantha. And he'd tell me how much it hurt him to see you that way. I suggested once he changed you, that maybe you'd be happier, and he went crazy on me. He said you deserved to have kids, a family."

There was that question again, the one I'd never dared to ask. "Can't damsels and dragons have kids?"

Mack shook his head slowly. "It hasn't turned out too pretty when they've tried. So Tonbo banned it."

I tried to swallow the sobering news down. No wonder Blake was adamant about not changing me.

"Oh, I see," I said simply, when, really, my heart had broken. *But what about the young dragons and damsels I'd seen at the island?* I guess they must've been changed just like Blake and Kory were. Or maybe as babies like Mack. *No kids?* I couldn't think about that right now. *Later, not now.*

"I tried to explain to Blake that Sammy was a part of Samantha. He was pretty upset I didn't tell him sooner. I sort of downplayed how long Sammy had been around. Anyway, he left and went back to Jaxon."

"Jaxon said he'd thought Blake had done it because right before I was discovered missing, Blake had left for a bit and came back upset. Guess I know why now."

"Yeah, well, let's just say when you disappeared, it shocked Blake and me both. I knew you'd gone jogging that morning, like you always did. I thought nothing of it until your mom called me around ten, asking me if you'd come over to my house. That's when I feared what had happened. I rushed to where Blake and Jaxon were, determined to tell him everything. But when I saw the rage he had for Kory, I chickened out. I couldn't tell him until I was sure it was Kate. Honestly, I was afraid of what he'd do to her. So we began searching. I did contact Kate, but she denied everything at the beginning."

"So Kate did it? But I know you were there… your pacing…"

"Let me explain. Blake and I searched nonstop for two weeks. I told him I had to keep up appearances in Durango, check in with your parents and stuff. So we parted ways. Blake kept looking for you. When I got back to my room that night, Kate was there."

Mack's face paled. "I almost killed her myself at that point, before I let her speak. She told me it how unfair it was that Sammy and I couldn't be together. We loved each other and deserved to be happy. Kate went on and on, asking why it was up to Blake anyway? Why was he the one who got to choose? He never planned to change Samantha so he could be with her, or even planned to meet her in person. She felt Sammy and I should have a chance at love. Kate told me Sammy begged her to help, and she felt for her. Honestly, I wonder how much of it was because Blake never wanted Kate. Either way, they were the ones to orchestrate the break-in. Sammy's mad computer skills made it easy for her to override the system. Kate got the serum, and they altered it together. In all her reading, Sammy had done a lot of research on genes. She'd found DNA that would make it so she could be Sammy, look like herself, not Samantha, and would never fear water again."

"So that's why I can hold my breath... the whale DNA. What makes me change like this? I didn't think it was possible?"

"Kate told me Sammy read about the Mimic Octopus. It can change its shape, form, and even mimic other sea creatures to protect itself. Think about what you've done. You changed into this girl to trick Jaxon. And then you used your instinct to change into Jaxon's son to protect us all."

Everything worked, except the part where Mack fit in. I met his eyes. "So is that when you agreed to help them?"

Mack groaned. "Samantha, I'm sorry. I didn't know what to do. Kate said that Sammy had come up with the idea of attacking Samantha, tying her up, and making her scared. She was convinced that Samantha had to experience terror the entire time she was injected. It was the only way Sammy felt sure she'd be the one there."

He grunted. "But Kate said it wasn't working exactly as planned. Every time Kate went to inject you, it was you, not Sammy. Kate kept waiting for Sammy to emerge so they could finish the process, ditch the theatrics."

I waited when his words faded.

"Kate told me she needed my help. She was scared if we didn't finish this that maybe neither Samantha nor Sammy would prevail. You never know how the dragonfly DNA will affect someone. Kate told me I needed to be the one to force Sammy to come out, since Sammy listened to me most of the time. Kate said Sammy told her she wanted me to be the one to give her, or you, the last injection."

"So you were the one, that last time? Now it makes sense. The way you jumped at me... you did it to scare me. But you were different. You gave me water when I asked for it and you didn't shove it into my teeth, like before. You were gentler."

Mack's expression twisted up. "*I'm such a monster!* I should've untied you right then and there! I wanted to! It horrified me to see you like that!" He collapsed to his knees and covered his face with his hands. Through his fingers, I heard a muffled, "I'm so sorry."

"Just tell me the rest," I said softly.

He lowered his fingers. "As much as I wanted to end your hell, I knew Kate was right. So I finished it, made horrible promises, and tried to make you think I was Jeremy. I gave you your last injection and told you it was special. I hoped my words would trigger Sammy to come out, but they didn't. I went home sick to my stomach at what I'd done. I decided I didn't care what happened; I was going back the next day to let you go and tell you everything. But when I returned, you were gone. I didn't know then that Jaxon had freed you; I didn't even know about Jaxon being a bug. So I searched for you and caught up with you about the same time the rescue party did."

His eyebrows bent low, he frowned. "I came to see you the first night you were home from the hospital. I snuck into your room in my camo. When I saw you... I knew we'd destroyed you. You were no longer Sammy or Samantha. It was so hard to come back and visit you. I could hardly bear to see what I'd done to you." His voice cracked, and tears welled in his eyes.

He remained on his knees; we gazed at each other in silence. I was sure he waited for me to say hateful words. As much as I wanted to be furious for what he'd done and especially what he'd kept from me for so long, I couldn't muster any words. Instead, I watched his tears fall silently from his face, taking with them pieces of my heart. Whether it was Sammy or just me, I didn't know or care. I had feelings for Mack and, on some level, I loved him.

I cleared my throat. "Don't feel bad anymore, okay? You should've told me about Sammy, but so should have my parents. I can't be mad at you for listening to Sammy. You were in love. I understand. If anyone's to blame for all this, it's me. I'm my own monster."

CHAPTER
Forty-four

Mack tried to disagree with me, but I methodically picked up the clothes he'd brought, entered the bathroom, transformed back into myself, and got dressed. Once my hair was brushed, I came back out. I felt wooden in my actions. I wasn't sure if it was calmness or numbness taking over.

"Can you take me home? I need to talk to my parents."

Mack hopped to his feet and nodded. He didn't say anything while we rode in his jeep. And, at the moment, I had no more words for him. He'd told me everything. I was left to sway between being completely livid for what he'd done to feeling sorry for him. I opted for staying numb, rather than opening myself up to feelings and emotions.

The one thing I could focus on was that my parents hadn't told me the truth either. As much as I wanted to refuse to believe I had an alternate personality, I needed to confront them. I needed to know if I'd really had Sammy in me. And I knew Mack seem to think she was gone for good. *But is she? Didn't she fly back to Colorado? Didn't she throw me into the arms of a crazy, psychotic killer?*

We entered the house to discover my dad at was at work, but my mom was home.

The moment she saw me, she gushed about how worried she'd been and how glad she was that I was okay now. I tried to mumble some sort of answer. Mack began backing out the door, and I turned.

"No, stay, Mack. Please," I said.

Mack stepped back to my side. "Anything you want," he said

quietly.

My mom glanced around. "Where's Blake? Thought you'd be coming back with him."

"Mom, I know about Sammy," I answered instead, too tired to make up a story. *No more lies. . . or being lied to.*

My mom gaped at me and then glanced at Mack, who nodded.

"But the therapist said not to tell her," she stuttered.

"Her therapist's an idiot. She needs to know," he replied, folding his arms. "She should've known all along."

My mom's eyes were wide and with obvious hesitation, she finally glanced my way again.

"So it's all true then? I really have been two people this whole time?" I asked.

"Samantha, we tried everything to help you let go of the drowning experience. Your doctor thought the best course would be to not tell you about her, not make you aware of her presence. She worried if you knew about Sammy, it'd only strengthen her hold on you. We all hoped that when the fear finally ended, you'd be fine. And then right when you were finally getting better, the cabin happened. We didn't know what to expect after that. We thought for sure it'd be Sammy coming home to us when they'd found you. Your therapist warned us that Sammy would be a stronger force now, since she probably protected you while you were abducted. But you came back totally different. Not really acting like Sammy or Samantha. Your eyes seemed hollow. I can't explain it. Like you were a shell of the girl we knew."

I knew what she was talking about. I remembered those days all too well. I glanced over to see Mack frowning.

"Then Blake came into your life, and the spark came back," my mom said.

Mack flinched.

After an hour of talking to my mom, she'd filled in enough

blanks, told me too many stories, for me to doubt the veracity of their words. *I was Sammy. Sammy was me.* What I had thought was a mere nickname throughout my life was actually my friends and family wondering who they were with, me or Sammy. My mom told me that they could always test who I was by simply calling me Samantha first. If it were Sammy, she'd get mad. It seemed so ridiculous. *Sammy seems pretty immature.*

My mom left the living room and Mack, who sat next to me on the couch, glanced over.

"You okay? Your face keeps getting paler and paler," he said.

I didn't know whether to laugh or cry. I tried to smile, but I could only gaze back at him.

"Samantha, I can't tell you how sorry I am. I wish I could go back. I'd do a thousand things differently. I never would have listened to Sammy," he said in a low voice.

"Mack, I know." I wished I could say something to make him feel better. He wasn't the only one to blame here. In some weird way, it was my fault too.

"Well, don't worry. You won't have to be around me much longer," he admitted.

"What are you talking about?" I asked, thinking he was joking, but his face said otherwise.

"I sent Blake a text. I told him that you know about Sammy… and that I did the cabin. Pretty sure he's on the next flight back to Durango," he said with a sad laugh at his own joke.

I gaped at him. "Oh. Wait, what do you mean you won't be around? You think Blake's going to throw you in one of Tonbo's prisons or something?"

"Oh no. I don't deserve prison," he mumbled.

"Well, you don't deserve a beating either." I didn't like this new turn, even though I'd wished it earlier. Now that I knew Blake was coming, I felt like I needed to defend Mack, crazy as it was.

"I'll talk to Blake. He'll understand. He's working with his brother, who did a lot worse things than you," I said firmly. "Give Blake some credit. You're his friend."

"Exactly. And I totally stabbed him in the back. Don't you see it, Samantha? Stop being nice to me! I'm not worthy of your mercy or Blake's. Jaxon's a slave to the bug in him. I'm not. I have no excuses."

"Except for the fact you were in love. I don't care if I should hate you, I don't. And I'm not letting Blake hurt you either."

Mack wanted to go home, face his fate head on, but I was stubborn and made him stay in my room that night. He did, sitting in the corner. As much as I knew he'd been part of everything, my anger channeled more towards Kate and less at Mack. He seemed so defeated that I could hardly stand it.

"Mack?" I asked. The lights were off and even though he chose to be in camo, his scent filled the room.

"Mm," he answered.

"Why do you think Sammy's finally gone?"

"You didn't black out after becoming a damsel. I kept waiting for Sammy to appear, but she didn't. I'd begun to believe you'd won the fight. Even as much as I cared for Sammy, I knew it would be the right thing. I had let Sammy go, so to speak. Then we got word from Tonbo that you'd disappeared from the island after we'd gone. Tonbo said you'd passed out during the performance and when they roused you, you seemed different. You were bossy, angry, and wanted to get back to your room. Tonbo felt bad, thought you were mad about us leaving you."

"But you thought it was Sammy?"

"Yeah, and so did Blake. He totally freaked out because we both knew that you would wake up anywhere and not know how you got there. So we convinced Kory to take a detour. We checked all over Durango for you, but came up with nothing. I'm still not sure where you went as Sammy or how Jaxon ended up with you. You'd have to ask Jaxon, I guess."

"So why do you think she's not coming back though?"

"Well, I'm not really certain, but you woke up in the bug's caverns. You faced him head on as yourself and never once did Sammy come out. Maybe you finally showed her you are strong enough and don't need her anymore."

"Actually Mack, you might be right. Right before I changed into that girl, I had this weird feeling come over me. It was like something within me wanted me to pass out. And I remember telling myself that I was strong enough to do it. Maybe I did tell Sammy to go away then, so to speak."

"Sounds like it."

"I'm sorry, Mack."

"What on earth are you sorry for?" he gasped.

"That you didn't get to be with Sammy. That you lost her."

I heard a flutter in the wind, and then I felt his hand on my face. He'd flown over to me, but in the dark and with his camo, I hadn't seen it.

"I can't tell you how glad I am that you, *Samantha*, are the one who's here right now. You're the one who deserves to be happy. Not *me* and not *Sammy*."

I wanted to respond, but the scent of woods and honey overwhelmed me.

Blake's here.

I sat up as Mack's hand slip from my face. There was whoosh of wind and then both guys became visible. Blake held Mack by his shirt, slammed up against a wall with one hand.

"Blake! Stop!" I cried out, jumping up from my bed, rushing over to them.

"What *the hell* were you thinking Mack?" Blake hissed through a clenched jaw. I saw his free hand balled up into a fist.

"I have no excuses. Just do it, man," Mack replied.

"Wait, Blake, you don't know everything!" I tugged on his arm, trying to keep him from punching Mack in the face.

"I know enough. I confronted Kate. Something about her behavior was off. And she told me what they'd done. And I know Mack went along with them when he could've stopped it all," Blake retorted.

He shoved Mack against the wall again, but Mack refused to speak. *He agrees with Blake.*

"If he hadn't finished my injections, who knows what I'd be now! He had to do it! He only did what he did because he's in love with Sammy!" I countered.

This must have caught Blake by surprise because his eyes widened. "Is that true?"

Mack wouldn't meet Blake's glare. Blake shook him, but not as hard. "Mack, you're in love with her?" he asked again.

"I never meant for it to happen," Mack said. "Blake, get on with it, do what you want. I deserve it. I'm done lying."

My hand still clutched Blake's arm. I could feel his chest heaving. I didn't know how I wanted this all to end, but I knew I'd go crazy if Blake hit Mack. Even if he had it coming.

Blake swore under his breath, and then his grip slackened. Mack's feet hit the carpet. Blake released him and walked away, turning his back on Mack. Only I saw the pain etched in his eyes.

"Get out of here, Mack, before I change my mind," he muttered.

Before I could stop him, Mack disappeared from view and the scent of cloves and ginger disappeared with him. *He's gone.* And with him went a sliver of my heart.

CHAPTER
Forty-five

We held each other that night. The past day had proven to be emotionally exhausting and devastating to both of us. I cried more than once, and Blake just held me tight. We'd been deceived, lied to, and hurt in so many ways. As it got later, he'd locked my door and wordlessly climbed in bed next to me. I hadn't fought him. I'd welcomed him. He felt like the only warm thing left in my life.

He kissed me and cradled me in his arms. We didn't say much. Neither one of us wanted to express in words what had happened. Any doubts I might have had over my feelings for Blake were gone. He was the only thing that kept me grounded—the only thing that lifted the dead weight settling in my heart.

Around midnight, I finally poked my head up off his chest and asked, "Are you asleep?"

"Nope," he answered, his eyes still closed. His hand fumbled to find my face, stroking my cheek.

"What's going to happen to Jaxon?" I whispered. I had to know.

Blake sighed and opened his eyes. "Tonbo is doing everything he can to heal him. I made sure of that."

"Oh really? How?"

"I made Tonbo a deal. If he heals Jaxon, I swore I'd take over the island like he wanted. And do what needs to be done."

I peered up at him. "What do you mean?" Something in his tone unsettled me.

"Tonbo's afraid Kory might inject more people with what he'd gotten from that bug, if he hasn't already. We fear he's trying to build his own army of bugs."

"Oh no." I gasped at the implications.

"Yeah, from what Jaxon described of Kory's little 'lab,' I'm pretty sure he is. I think Jaxon was his first test subject. It worked out perfect since he'd asked Kory how he could change... for me," Blake's voice faded. He cleared his throat. "But then Jaxon proved to be out of even Kory's control. I think that's when he came up with the idea of getting me in on the hunt. It's a win-win for him. Either I killed the bug so Kory didn't have to worry about it, or it killed me."

"You think he'd actually do it? Basically release a bunch of serial killers?"

"Yeah, I do. I'm sure he's working on the serum now, trying to find a way to subdue the monsters to obey his will." Blake stopped and stroked my face with his fingers. "Sam, I have to stop him. I'll be moving to the island soon to make sure Kory doesn't succeed."

I'd been nodding along to what he was saying until he said he would be moving.

"Wait, *what?* You're leaving?" I gasped, sitting up. I hadn't thought *that* part out. Of course he'd have to leave. *To be closer. But...*

He pulled me back into his arms. "I have to go. If Tonbo fixes Jaxon, I gave my word."

"You can't lead it from here? Just make trips?"

"No, Sam. Especially if there are bugs out there." His tone was heavy.

"Blake, you can't leave me. You can't! I'll have no one. Not even Mack..." My throat completely closed off on his name. Blake's arms held me tighter.

"Mack's not gone forever, Sam," he grunted. "I'll find the little bugger after a bit... just not yet. I'm still mad as hell at him."

I glanced up at Blake and, to my surprise, his eyes were dancing.

"Why do you look happy all of a sudden? You just told me you're moving!"

"When do you turn eighteen?" he asked instead, ignoring my distress.

"Blake, who cares when my birthday is?" I punched him in the chest.

"I do. When is it?" He grabbed my hands and flipped me down on my bed.

As much as I wanted to be upset, the playful Blake triggered something within. I pulled his face closer to mine. Our lips met and a fire burst through me, breaking the heaviness on my heart. I kissed him, hungry to end the hurt within. And in that moment, I felt he kissed me with the same need. We stopped after a minute, both breathless, leaving our foreheads resting on one another.

"I want to know when your birthday is because I love you, Sam Campbell, and I want to know how long it will be until you are my Mrs. Knightly."

I sat back and gazed into his eyes. "Are you serious?"

He gave me a crooked grin. "Well, that depends on your answer."

"January twenty-eighth," I said, automatically.

He chuckled and kissed my hand. "Not exactly the answer I was looking for."

I could only stare at him, my mouth gaping. I still grappled with his implications.

"But Mack said we can't have kids," I blurted, and then cringed. *Of all the times to ask about that!*

"Whoa, still not the answer I was hoping for." He chuckled, pulling me into his arms.

I felt safe, like this was the only place I could ever belong. I peered into his eyes, his face hopeful, waiting on me.

"I love you, Blake," I said, voicing the words to him for the first time. I felt no fear; the monsters were gone. At least for the time being.

He grinned and kissed my lips. "That's more like it. You know, I'm beginning to believe there might actually be a silver lining to this hellish storm. And it's you, Sam."

We fell asleep together, pushing the worry over Kory being out there roaming free, Jaxon being enslaved to an inner monster, and Mack left alone and desperate, for another day. We needed this time. We needed to heal each other's wounds.

Yet, when Blake stirred later in the night and woke me, I became listless. His breathing was deep and even. I lifted my head off his chest and rolled on my back, staring at the ceiling.

"Sammy?" I whispered. "I don't know if you can hear me or not. Or how this works even. I had no idea you even existed until today, but you've known about me for a long time. If you are still around and can hear me, I want to say thank you. You saved me once from drowning. And you saved me again when you gave me Blake. He never would have even entered into my life, but would've loved me from afar, because he's that selfless. But I need him in my life. And I'm pretty sure he needs me too. So maybe all that plotting with Mack was all for me after all. At least that's what I choose to believe."

Blake murmured something in his sleep, and I settled back down into his arms. A weight had been lifted off me. I could breathe again. We'd face the world tomorrow. Tonight, it was just Blake and me.

At least, I was pretty sure it was just me.

Acknowledgements

I have to start with a HUGE thank you to my husband, Josh! I have to give him credit for helping me find my Ah-ha moment with this book. It wouldn't be what it is without you hon! Thank you for believing in me, supporting me, and not minding when dinner is late and the dishes aren't done.

A tremendous thank you to my three beautiful children! Thank you for letting your mommy disappear at random times to type furiously. I love that my kids want to know all about my stories.

To all my wonderful friends and family who supported me while writing this. Gail Wagner, for always being my first set of eyes to catch all my many mistakes! You always make time for my writing even though you are busy being an author yourself! To my Wattpad fans and readers, who have patiently waited for each chapter update, now you don't have to wait anymore!

Music played a huge part in writing Hidden Monster. Entire scenes and sequences were inspired by songs! A thank you to Imagine Dragons, Avicii, Great Big World, The Killers, and Blue October. I consider all these artist a great source for inspiration!

To Clean Teen Publishing, you are my writing family! Rebecca Gober and Courtney Nuckels, for believing in my writing and the thousand things you do behind the scenes to get my works published, thank you! To Marya Heiman, for my gorgeous yet creepy cover, love it! Dyan Brown for organizing everything from beta readers to scheduling tours! To Cynthia Shepp for providing excellent editing and feedback!

And lastly, and most importantly, I thank my God, for all the good things in my life!

About The Author

Born in Dekalb, Illinois, Amanda Strong has called Utah, Arizona, Hawaii, Virginia and now New Mexico home. Amanda has been spinning tales since she was a child. Her family still remembers finding her with bright pink glasses, hiding in random corners of the house while scribbling away in one of her many spiral-bound notebooks. You could say some things have not changed.

Amanda began her writing career signing with Clean Teen Publishing in the fall of 2013. Her first novel, The Awakener, book one in a young adult paranormal romance series called: the Watchers of Men, came out in October of 2013. She is currently working on book two, The Watchers, expected to come out in the fall of 2014.

When Amanda isn't writing, you can find her chasing her three rambunctious children around the house and spending time with her wonderful and supportive husband. On some occasions you can still find Amanda with her not-so-pink glasses, hiding in a corner reading her favorite young adult fantasy novels or working out only to blow her diet by eating ice cream.

CPSIA information can be obtained
at www.ICGtesting.com
Printed in the USA
FSOW01n1618061114
3401FS